Forbidden Mentor

by
Laura Mills

Copyright © 2001, 2005, 2016 by Laura Mills

First Printing, October 2005

All rights reserved.

Published by Mills Vivid Image, PO Box 384 Apple Valley, California 92307

ISBN: 978-0-9722172-0-0

Edited by: Dawna Conner

Cover art by: Deb Hoeffner

Credit To: Gust e-foundry & TypeSETit

Without limiting the rights under copyright reserved above, no part of this publication may be reproduced, stored in or introduced into a retrieval system, or transmitted, in any form, or by any means (electronic, mechanical, photocopying, recording, or otherwise), without the prior written permission of both the copyright owner and the above publisher of this book.

This is a work of fiction. Names, characters, places, and incidents either are the product of the author's imagination or are used fictitiously, and any resemblance to actual persons, living or dead, business establishments, events, or locales is entirely coincidental.

Printed in the United States of America

Chapter One

Richmond, England 1820

This glorious spring day started out like any other for Lord John Blackburn, but little did he know it would end on quite an unusual note. As he eased into his frock coat, pulling his black ponytail from beneath the collar, Vanessa Walker requested he stay longer.

"It's never enough, you know?" she said, smiling and enticing him with bewitching blue eyes and a seductive swing of an exposed thigh.

Ah, Vanessa. She tempted him with her fiery lovemaking but put him off when she challenged their understanding. In his favor, she had a few select suitors to keep her occupied and in financial means and for that John was grateful, but today she was pushing him beyond his tolerance level.

"John, you know I would give all this up for you," she told him, gesturing toward her pampered possessions.

"Vanessa, please. Why are you doing this and now when I'm late?" he questioned while buttoning the front of his coat.

"I know we have a mutual understanding." Her head bowed while her eyes lifted and searched his neutral features. She'd lost interest in other men. John was the only man she wanted. To her misfortune, he didn't seem to reciprocate. She knew she wasn't his only lover, although she could bet he saw her more often than the others, it was the "understanding" that she longed to change. But, no matter how urgently she wanted that change, he reminded her every time of their circumstances.

"Vanessa, surely we're not going over this again?" His eyes narrowed as his voice grew more serious. "What we have between us is physical. We have a grand time of it, but that's all it is. You are well aware that I don't have time for a relationship. My business needs my full attention. My thoroughbreds require it."

Vanessa sighed in heavy despair. "I know your horses come before me."

His level of frustration elevated. "You need to be fair about this, Vanessa. Don't make me say something you don't want to hear." He whipped his collar down flat.

She forced herself to break into a smile. "Don't be cross with me, John. I can't help but enjoy your company and it doesn't seem to last long enough."

Frustration faded from his features. "I enjoy your company as well." He pulled out a timepiece from the inside pocket of his coat and glanced at it. "I must be off," he said, making his way out the door. He turned, giving her one last lingering kiss. When his lips came off hers he smiled at her sulky expression, skimming his fingers through her platinum blond hair. "Good day," he said, while turning to leave.

Her hands grabbed at his coat lapels. "John, wait," she cried, stealing another kiss.

The Lord pulled back, tearing away from her. "I must go, Vanessa." He'd already stayed longer than anticipated. Vanessa was testing him again, he was well aware of it. Forgetting to supply them with contraceptives was intentional on her part, but he'd learn to come prepared, which irritated her and bothered him.

She acted oblivious to his distress, smiling at him as she gave him another quick peck before releasing him.

John skimmed the porch steps to his carriage impatiently instructing his driver to head for Middleham racecourse.

Settling in carriage, the Lord leaned his head against the soft black leather. His eyes closed as he thought about Vanessa. She was without a doubt one of his favorites, but of late a possessive nature seemed to be evident. Feeling a permanent entrapment coming about, he intended to reduce his visits with her. He wasn't looking for a wife and if she had any ideas regarding that issue, she'd find out how wrong she was. Yes, better lay off with her for a while.

His gray eyes opened after catching the scent of lavender drifting through the open windows. His sight found the purplish-blue plants that extended in rows along both sides of the main road in Richmond. The long stemmed flowers were reaching for the rare sun, making an elegant statement to their surroundings. Springtime was upon them.

John's features turned peaceful at the thought. Springtime always reminded him of his mother and how she loved this time of year. Eighteen years after her death he still missed her. Having a father with all other interests except his son, John had accepted years ago that his similarity to his mother drove his father away from him, so after his mother's death, at the age of twelve, John discovered his very own safe haven, the racetrack.

Encountering a natural ease with his thoroughbred companions that he watered and fed John had discovered acceptance, and within weeks, he found a true friend in

My Forbidden Mentor

another boy his age. That same boy and now partner that, John could bet, was waiting with restless patience for him at the front entrance of Middleham Racecourse.

Arriving at Middleham, John stared outside the carriage window as his driver maneuvered into a tight spot near the front access. The crowd appeared fierce today, just as John had expected. With races being held only three days a year at this particular track, the local residents from nearby villages would swarm in droves to take part in the entertainment.

The track held appeal for many. Some bet for investments, some visited old acquaintances, and some even dallied with prostitutes. The majority went for the races themselves. Local landowners depended on these temptations, including the added bonus of free entry, to lure enough people in to ensure a profit. Although this providence was set most of the time for smaller courses, at these gatherings the less fortunate people of everyday living evolved into a world of their own. The racecourse atmosphere became a place where social hierarchy blended and knew no bounds.

For some, horse racing was a day of entertainment. For others, it was a business opportunity. For John Blackburn, it was his life.

John found Robert standing in the same pose he always did when he was delayed. His stiffened body leaned into a thick wooden post with arms crossing over a broad chest and long legs crossing at the ankles. His scowling expression matched his stance and seemed to distort his normally carefree appearance.

John climbed out of his carriage, preparing for harassment from Robert.

As John strode toward him, Robert asked with knowing intentions, "Let me guess, Vanessa?" He knew full well of John's habits. "She's the only one who makes you this late."

John's answer began with a wide grin. "The wench is pushing her luck with her forgetful mind," he told him, adding, "I had to resort to my coat of armor for protection this morning. I hate using that blasted thing."

"Obviously not enough to skip another tumble with Miss Vanessa," Robert commented. He could never stay upset with John for very long, so in a matter of minutes Robert's short-lived irritation turned into teasing.

"Damn it all, but I hadn't any choice." John replied before adding, "You know I don't take chances with anyone, especially Vanessa."

"I know that, John. Still, it didn't stop you from strapping on the reserve so you could toss up her skirts again," Robert replied.

John just glared at his best friend, all in friendliness, of course.

"Well, then, it sounds like you've had quite a rough morning." Robert offered.

"Indeed." John agreed.

They turned to enter the track.

Both gentlemen shared a strong bond of thoroughbred racing and training, so working together proved favorable and successful for them. John, a self-starter, acquired an interest in horses at a young age, learning everything he could and building from there. With acquired success, he now had his very own training stables and invested shares in Catterick Racecourse.

Robert, on the other hand, had the same fondness for the brilliant beasts but his interest was induced by his father, from whom he'd inherited top hand knowledge. When his father passed on Robert acquired his extensive bloodstock, allowing him to carry on tradition.

Needless to say, John had the clout and money to finance and Robert had extended experience. Their strong friendship enhanced their partnership, which resulted in good teamwork, but most of all their combined passion for thoroughbreds was the key foundation for their continued success.

Today was no exception and would bring an important race with their top stallion, Chief, making roaring progress. A young newcomer to the track, he had power, grace and extreme speed, not to mention beauty. The dark amber of his coat gleamed glossy over the sleek solid muscles his powerful body displayed. He always held his head high and proud when strutting around the track, the coppery strands of his mane bouncing along with his almost conceited prance. Chief's desire to race required little motivation on the rider's part. He had a natural tendency to push himself, giving his rider an effortless ride. Chief was John's rising star and he was making a statement to the racing world.

On the way to a choice viewing box both men waved to familiar acquaintances, at the same time discussing their competition. While John and Robert conversed about their competition, a new competitor was preparing to ride at Middleham.

Chapter Two

Since the tender age of eight Melissa Howard had wanted to race thoroughbreds. As a young girl she had often observed her mother taking occasional bets to race along stretching green fields, much of the time beating her opponents. Melissa's visions went beyond mere racing for amusement, frequent and professional were more her style. At the same time she was well aware of society's view on the outrageous notion of women and racing, but it didn't stop her from forging ahead. She couldn't sit by and wonder about how it would have been. She craved the experience.

Today, at the graceful age of twenty-one years, Melissa gazed into a brilliant April sky, hardly believing she stood within the confinements of Middleham Racecourse readying herself for a landmark race. Indeed she was taking a big risk today, but her confidence soared. Even if her appearance caused controversy, to experience a real race against professional riders was all that mattered. Today she would test her ability, proving to herself that she was good enough to race with the best of them.

Her gaze shifted forward when Kurt called to her and motioned for her to follow him. As he led her gelding Melissa trailed behind, thinking how perfect it had been getting to know Kurt Spencer. He worked at her father's carpentry business and also as a groomsman for Middleham Racecourse. He was her ticket into the track, not as a bystander, but as a rider.

They passed through mazes of people before reaching the backstretch of the course, where only a few men and women remained. Melissa stopped but Kurt kept going beyond the stables toward what looked like an abandoned shack.

Kurt motioned to her again, informing her that the "grooms room," as they called it, would be an ideal place for her to hide until she was ready, and that it was big enough to house her gelding as well.

"Kurt, are you quite sure I won't be disturbed?" she asked while slipping through a creaking wooden doorway.

Kurt scanned the immediate perimeter before leading her gelding inside and closing the door. "Yes, Mel, at present all the groomsmen are busy. I should be able to keep them away for at least two races."

"That should be long enough," she agreed, looking at the blond haired, blue-eyed young man that was taking risks for her. She smiled in appreciation. "This means more to me than you know, Kurt. I'll repay you as soon as I'm able."

He returned a smile. Any kind of attention he received from Melissa Howard he considered encouraging. He left to give her privacy and returned to his normal duties so he wouldn't go unnoticed.

The bell sounded for the next race when Melissa scurried from the old wooden structure, heading toward the stables. She was now transformed from head to toe in masculine gear. Although her father's clothing fit loosely around her feminine figure, the bagginess served to camouflage her even more. Once settled into her disguise she casually stepped between and around the frenzied groomsmen, outriders, and jockeys who monopolized the interior of the stables. She made swift glances here and there in the search for Kurt, who had planned to meet her with her gelding in tow.

When she finally spotted him he was chatting with a tall intimidating figure. She stopped to study the backside of the man talking to Kurt. He had height but he also had width, his shoulders representing a finely-tuned gathering of muscles that broadened his natural physique. A man who was comfortable giving orders by the way Kurt kept nodding his head. When her partner in crime glanced her way she signaled with her eyes, but the man with the long dark hair dominated Kurt's full attention.

While precious time passed Melissa began to pace. Her fingers intertwined in tight motions before she realized her nervous habits could get her noticed. To take her mind off waiting she started back for the shack to get her gelding. She'd finally discovered a way inside an organization dominated by men and their horses. She wouldn't lose this chance, she just couldn't. Kurt had helped conceal her identity but now it seemed she was on her own. As she gained confidence once again her scattering thoughts began to clear. She was in deep concentration, half way to the wooden structure, when a finger tapped her on the shoulder. Startled, she didn't have time to think about her appearance before turning around. Relief flooded her when she saw it was only Kurt.

Sitting astride her gelding at the starting line she faced forward and didn't dare look at any of the other jockeys lined along both sides of her, still the feeling of being studied and observed became strong. She took in a calming breath just as a jockey next to her tried getting her attention, but luck was with her as the bell sounded and they were off. She couldn't worry about her concealment at the moment. Instead, she focused on winning.

But she was noticed, and not in the way she had feared. Lord Blackburn had a good eye for promising, talented riders. While watching his own horse race down the wide stretch of dirt John smiled with pride. Chief was flying by straining thoroughbreds, kicking dirt into their faces. Training the stallion himself, he considered Chief his masterpiece. The stallion's name flowing out of prospectors' mouths held enough evidence of Chief's newfound popularity. John knew Chief would win by a long shot. He could feel it in his bones: the horse was fast.

John continued cheering in silence, watching the powerhouse pulling ahead, having one last gelding to pass. Chief was able to pull away, but not by much. The unknown gelding stayed close behind and would not be left to choke on Chief's dust, but it wasn't the gelding that necessarily impressed John, it was the rider. Without realizing it, he began comparing his own jockey with the newcomer. The unknown rider seemed to encourage the speed of the horse, cheering him on with supporting gestures. Chief flew through the finish line, the gelding a close second.

John kept his attention on the unknown jockey who rode past Chief, going toward the stables without waiting for an outrider's assistance.

Having a single purpose in mind John told Robert that he'd return shortly, leaving Robert to handle associates who approached their viewing box in congratulations.

John continued to make his way toward the stables when he spied Kurt leading the fast gelding, not in the stables but behind it and toward the backstretch. By the time John reached the backstretch, Kurt had finished circling the gelding to cool him off and was leading him into a small wooden structure. Putting the gelding in that small building and not in the stables struck John as odd. He knew the young men used the old shack as a hideaway for themselves but he'd never seen them bring horses along, especially when they had limited space to contend with.

Not a trainer who usually disturbed the groomsmen, John strode in the direction of the building, curious more than anything about what was going on, when Kurt stepped out before him.

"Lord Blackburn, I was currently on my way to Chief."

"What's going on, Kurt?"

"Sir?" Kurt responded, a little shaken.

"I saw you lead that gelding in there. What are you gentlemen up to?"

"Well, sir, the gelding belongs to a friend of mine and I was looking after the horse. I've put him in a separate place, that's all."

"I see. Where's your friend now?"

"My friend is tending to the horse, sir. They like their privacy," he revealed, motioning to the small building behind him.

John's patience began to wear. "Does your friend have a name, Kurt?"

"Mel. It's Mel, sir."

"Kurt, I'd like to talk to Mel. Can you arrange a meeting for us?" John's suspicions grew with Kurt's continuing agitation.

"Well, what is it about, sir, if I may ask?"

Yes, something strange was happening here. "I was quite impressed with his riding skills. I believe he has tremendous talent and I'd like to know his plans for the future."

"Sir, Mel is an amateur."

"Kurt, I'd like to talk with Mel myself, if I may."

"When, sir?"

"As soon as he's done tending his horse." When Kurt stood there staggered and unmoving, John pursued further. "Are you going to let him know then?"

"Yes, sir," he responded with shifting eyes. "What about James?"

"James is busy with congratulations so he can wait a moment longer," John told him.

Kurt sauntered through the groaning wooden door, making Melissa jump at his early arrival.

"I thought you were caring for another rider?" she inquired, taken back by Kurt's quick appearance.

"I will be, but we've got trouble," he responded in distress.

"Trouble? What kind of trouble?"

"Lord Blackburn is standing right outside this door, inquiring about you."

"What? Well get rid of him, Kurt." What in the world is he so worried about she wondered as she continued brushing down her gelding.

Kurt stepped to her side, whispering in harsh tones. "I can't get rid of him, Mel. He's the owner of a couple of horses I take care of. He's a highly respected man round here."

"Don't tell me you're afraid of his title Kurt?" Melissa still couldn't figure out what was so urgent.

"That is beyond the point."

"Are you absolutely sure?" she asked, reaching for the gelding's tail, taking long sweeps with the grooming comb.

In defense, Kurt answered her. "I do not fancy myself being in the same circles as those superior snobs, but Lord Blackburn is different. He's a real person, like you and me."

"So what does he want to talk about then?"

"About your plans for the future. You impressed him with your riding Mel, and now he wants to talk to you about it." Kurt sat on a splintered chair, raking his fingers through his hair. "Of all the luck, why did you have to ride so well?"

He looked distressed and exasperated. "Forgive me for disappointing you Kurt, but that's what I came here to do." Now she was feeling sorry that she had put him in this position. She went over to him and put her hand on his shoulder. "Tell Lord Blackburn that I'm not interested in meeting with him and that I have another engagement I must attend."

"It will not be that easy with him. He sees potential in you Mel. He'll want to train you to ride on his team. I've seen it happen before. That's how he got James."

The grooming comb slipped from her dangling hand to the hardened dirt floor. "Train me? He's a trainer?"

"Yes."

"You didn't tell me he was a trainer Kurt."

"Why would it matter?"

"This is brilliant! In a thousand lifetimes I wouldn't have dreamed of this kind of luck! A trainer!"

"I don't know what you're rambling about Mel. It cannot work," he informed her as he stood.

"And you say that even though he's "Lord Blackburn," he's like you and me?" After he nodded she spun around. "This is turning out splendidly."

"Mel, have you heard a word I've said?" He had to snap her out of this daydream.

"What is it Kurt?"

"He thinks you're a man!"

John waited with controlled patience, disappointed that they spoke so low he couldn't hear. He went to lean against the building when Kurt came out. "Well?" John asked as he turned to face him.

"Mel's got another engagement Lord Blackburn and cannot meet with you today."

"That's it?"

"Sir?"

"You were in there quite a long time. You must have discussed this in length?"

"Mel has quite a lot going on," Kurt responded, finishing with a hurried statement. "I really must be off. I need to tend James and Chief."

Kurt took off in a hasty stride while John stood there watching him. Then he shifted toward the door, examining it. Something mysterious was going on here. Unable to contain his curiosity John burst through the old door, intent on confronting the young man who rode in the last race. After colliding into the rump of the gelding he stepped to the side of the horse, catching the sight of a young lady in the process of disrobing.

Hearing her gasp, John stood dumbfounded, letting the stroll of his eyes confirm the least of what he had expected to encounter. Men's boots were drowned by over-sized trousers which were being held up by a double-looped material of sorts. She'd been in the process of lifting an oversized shirt above her head, he realized, when his gaze rested on the prettiest, daintiest belly button he'd ever seen. She must have followed his blatant stare because all of a sudden her hands were in his sight, covering her stomach while shirttails followed covering her hands, which made his eyes leap to the part of her body previously protected. It couldn't be helped. He stared some more because further investigation verified for a fact that she had ridden in that race and almost beaten him. A leathered belt flattening her bosom exposed itself from the opening of the gaping shirt. Even though he'd already witnessed the truth self-consciousness had her hands struggling to hide herself from him. With one hand gripping at her shirttails and the other clutching her collar in a tightened grasp she looked positively devastated.

Purposeful gray eyes trapped hers, demanding a confrontation, and hazel eyes beamed back, returning the challenge.

"Who are you?" she asked, adding a bold gesture by raising her chin a notch.

Brave too, John thought as the sound of her voice permeated his ears. There was an earthly attraction about her. She stood mid-height, her face free of powder and rouge, with eyes that sparkled with flashes of brown and green, and her hair, at least the few strands he could see, gleamed golden. Knowing that a female body was nestled in men's clothing, and that same female rode like the devil, tempted him to make her the original offer he had in mind, except training with her would present a few added conditions. He trailed on that thought as he answered her. "Lord Blackburn. And who may I ask are you?"

Upon clearing her throat, she replied, "Melissa Howard."

When his gaze dipped below her neck she sought to adjust the situation. "Can you turn your back, please?"

His eyes lifted to hers. "Pardon?"

She clutched her clothing even tighter, thinking it should be obvious what she meant. "I'd like to change my clothing."

"Of course." He turned to face the door and took the opportunity to question her. "Have you performed this kind of act before?"

"Do you mean riding in disguise?" she replied, taking her clothing off in haste.

"Yes."

"No, this is my first time," she answered while tugging her father's over-sized boots off, sparing a glance his way to ensure he faced away from her.

All stayed quiet for a short time until sequential grunts of frustration sounded from Melissa.

When a cuss word was mumbled in between grunts, John took a peek over his shoulder, then wished he hadn't. At first he saw a leather strap tightening along her backside and then loosening when she finally gained release of the leather apparatus, but the last jerking effort that lent her freedom also caused a luscious side-to-side sway of her bared breasts greeting him in teasing glimpses of rounding softness. John swallowed hard and faced the wooden door again. There wasn't any way he could train this woman.

"Well you should make it your last," he stated in a cool manner.

What John couldn't see was a female with a temper that flared at his bold statement, motivating her to whip a lavender dress over her head, buttons undone, just so she could face his back and scold him. "How utterly brazen of you to offer me such advice," she voiced with fisted hands on her hips.

"I'm not being brazen. It's common sense," he said with a shifting of his head.

"Perhaps it's common sense for the average woman being influenced by her male counterparts, but I'm not average."

No, indeed you're not, John thought. "This is quite unfair, don't you think?"

"What am I being unfair about, Lord Blackburn?"

"Chastising me behind my back."

"I'd be delighted to do it to your face my lord, but my buttons remain undone."

Why did she have to reveal that bit of information? He had to get out of this secluded shack with the half-dressed young woman and the horse. He shifted to check on the horse since he had nothing better to do and wished he could be half as content nibbling on scattered grain. "Can I turn around yet?" he asked, agitated.

"One moment."

He listened to more shuffling before she announced that she was decent. Once he turned he didn't waste any time giving his opinion. "If I may make a suggestion, don't get caught again. The next person may not be as nice about it." And with that he turned and went through the door. Was

My Forbidden Mentor

he making a mistake, not giving her a chance? Come on John, how far would you get with a female rider?

She tried, with all her might she did, but restraint gave way. Unable to hold back any longer and knowing the possibility of seeing this man again was slim, her thoughts about his type of man came spilling forth. Not thinking of the consequences while peeking her head out of the wooden doorway, she raised her voice so he'd be sure to hear. "You seemed to be different but now I see you're like all the other men in the world: arrogant, loathing and self centered." Her voice kept getting louder the further he trailed away. "Against women's rights for anything except spreading their legs and having babies, and even that is in question!"

She'd hit a nerve, stopping him in his tracks. When he shifted back toward her with narrowed eyes, nostrils flaring, and teeth gritting, she smelled victory.

He spoke while striding in her direction. Her head slipped back inside the wooden building the closer he got. "My advice to you was for good reason. You could get in a lot of trouble with this, and you know I'm right." Her eyes squinted as he approached. "And as far as women's rights, I mentioned nothing on how I feel about the subject." His brows creased even more when he stopped in front of her. "Also, I would hope I'm not like all other men in more ways than one." Feeling satisfied that he'd put her in her place he made to leave, but then added out of pure maleness, "And another thing: women spread willingly for me, on their own accord. There's no forcing in that department, and I've had no complaints."

Redness claimed her honeyed cheeks and her eyes opened wide in shock. "That was more than I wanted to know about your personal life."

"You brought up the subject," he tossed back.

Her hands went to her hips. "Yes, but did you have to answer so honestly?" she said, her eyes daring his, then her gaze faltered as she tried looking away when the reality of the subject hit her again. Melissa wasn't shy about a lot of things but when it came to sexual intimacy, her experience lacked unlike other areas of her life. Her embarrassment became overwhelming when she saw that she hadn't hidden her reaction from him.

It didn't take long for John to figure out that he had an innocent young lady on his hands or that her experience seemed limited. He tried covering up the words that had already done damage. "I don't know what came over me. I suppose I was trying to make a point," he told her, and he looked away as well.

"Your point was well taken," she said with a shaken voice. There was a brief, uncomfortable silence between them until Melissa offered, "Forgive me for assuming the worst about you. It gets tiresome dealing day in and day out with the ways of the world, at least where women are concerned. I'll try to be more careful."

"You know that although I haven't any interest in causing trouble for you Miss Howard, you should be aware that there are others who wouldn't think twice about it."

"I am aware of that Lord Blackburn and I appreciate your being agreeable, however, I have to be honest here and say that my main goal is recognition, whether positive or negative. I need to be noticed."

"I understand your reasoning but positive acknowledgment would be a much better route."

"And how do you propose that's possible with the obstacles I have to face?"

"Well, knowing someone on the inside would help. Of course, I don't have as much power here as I do at my own track."

Melissa sat on the splintered chair to contain her excitement. "What are you saying, Lord Blackburn? It sounded as if you were making me an offer?"

"I had planned on it in the beginning, when I thought you were a man."

"Is that all, because of my gender?"

"Truthfully, yes."

"But if you have an interest in me as a rider why should my gender matter?"

John rested against the timbered wall adjacent to the door. "Because there are certain circumstances we would have to contend with."

Her brows rose elegantly while she made her inquiry. "Not able to rise to the challenge, Lord Blackburn?"

"Now who's being brazen, Miss Howard?" he stated in interested fascination.

"You strike me as a very determined man my lord, as in always getting what you want?" she teased.

"You're not only determined yourself Miss Howard, but perceptive as well."

"I have a proposition for you then. Why not begin training me and in that time you can decide for sure whether to have me ride for you. I will work extra hard to prove to you that a woman can ride just as well as a man."

He gave a short nod. "I haven't got a doubt that you'll ride well, my doubts lie elsewhere." Then, with an arch of his brow, he pointed out, "Let's say I agree with this arrangement. I begin training you and for whatever reason it doesn't work out. What kind of reward do I get in return when you've just received free training?"

"I can't imagine that happening," she answered.

He chuckled, not because she was being humorous but in reaction to her persuasive argument. "Regardless I'm not giving my time away for free. I'm a busy man Miss Howard. My time is worth money."

"You will make your money back and then some when I win for you," she urged.

He inclined toward her, speaking each key word in slow deliberation. "You are the most stubborn, bold, risky woman I've ever met."

She stood and met him halfway, her face inches from his, mimicking his slow deliberation. "And you are the most cautious, logical, follow-the-rules man I've ever met."

His teeth ground together. "Follow-the-rules?" He straightened, shaking his head. "Listen, I'm not cautious." He paused with tightened lips, not wanting to get into a battle of words with a woman he had met less than an hour ago. His head shook again as he peered at a ceiling of distorted wood, cursing aloud. "Damn my curiosity."

"Pardon me?"

"I was chastising myself," he explained, tilting his head in her direction.

"I've got an idea."

He saw a fresh gleam in her eyes and his hands flew up in position, as if to stop her words from hitting him in the face. "Please, I don't believe I want to hear this."

"Yes, you do. You can breed your top stallion to my mother's mare. She has championship in her bloodlines."

"What are you talking about?" he asked with focused interest.

"Insurance of payment for my training. An offspring of your top stallion."

"And what will your mother have to say about this?" He became fascinated at the plans she made without the knowledge of all parties involved.

"My mother won't, my father will. My mother has passed on," she informed him in a low voice.

John sympathized quickly. "I see. I'm sorry about your mother."

She formed the beginnings of a smile. "It's fine. You didn't know. And don't worry about my father, I'll take care of him."

He studied her for a moment. This was becoming complicated. "I don't like the sound of that." he said in weary contemplation.

But his doubts only boosted her confidence. "My father will back me. He's behind me in all that I do."

It was his turn to smile. "Including being here at a racetrack by yourself, and now alone with a man in an abandoned shack?"

Her features sent a flash of defeat. "All right, I admit he might be unknowing about my little adventure today and being alone with you. That might raise some questions." He sent her a smile of delight. "But he will understand once I explain it to him," she added.

His face went serious again. "And what if you were caught today? You would've needed to be bailed out. You don't think your father would not have become aware of this?"

"Yes, but it didn't happen."

He stared at her in amazement. "First of all, your idea of breeding our horses will not work because it has to be approved, and it won't be approved in time because Chief isn't a champion yet, but besides that, there's a lot to think about here. I'm not making sudden decisions on something like this, and I don't particularly care for the fact that your father is unaware. There would already be enough sneaking around. I don't want to include your father in that."

"You're right, of course, but I feel this a great opportunity and I don't want to lose it."

In that moment he realized, while studying the pleading look she displayed, that she had him thinking about this preposterous idea. He was fighting an inner battle, which was unusual for him, but nevertheless he struggled between her ability as a rider and her gender. He decided to go with his initial feeling and be on his way. She appeared socially proper again, donned in her feminine attire. Once she was near the stables and away from this abandoned shack no one would question her appearance.

He seemed dazed. "What is it?" Melissa asked.

"I'm not able to help you."

"Why not?"

"Because horse racing is a man's sport." He cringed inside at the ludicrous excuse he gave her.

Flabbergasted by his response, she responded in fear of losing her chance. "You can't believe that Lord Blackburn. You're interested in me, I know you are."

"Being interested and acting upon it are completely different."

The loss of opportunity struck Melissa so hard she was speechless. He meant to leave and carry on as if they'd never met. She continued holding her head high as he

My Forbidden Mentor

turned to the door to make his escape. Shifting toward her gelding in an attempt to ready him to leave, she hadn't expected to hear anything more from Lord Blackburn, especially his next words.

"Come here," he called out.

She was confused so she hesitated.

"Come here," he repeated.

"What is it?" she asked as he jerked her by the arm and placed her adjacent to the door.

"Just follow my lead," he directed, having her face him as he reached for the buttons along the back of her dress, unbuttoning them with speedy intent. He held her face against the lapels of his coat and while dropping his head next to hers he slid a warm hand inside the opening of her dress.

It was his hand on the skin of her back that had her worried. What right did this man have taking such liberties? Trying to lift her head was made impossible by the intense grip he had on her. Through a tightened jaw she spoke. "What is the meaning of this?"

She found out immediately when hearing the door creak open. A double burst of laughter gained volume then abruptly stopped. Next Lord Blackburn's voice sounded.

"Hello gentlemen."

Both groomsmen turned flush, realizing in an instant what was about to take place. Both acknowledged his presence and left, making sure to shut the door.

After securing the buttons on her dress John released Melissa. He had been prepared to deal with an angry young lady and she hadn't let him down.

"Having a grand time at my expense, Lord Blackburn?" she announced, flustered and fixing her hair.

"Not at all. Did you want to be exposed?"

Angelic eyes flared before him. "I was exposed."

"Not in the sense that I meant. Did you want to be found out?"

"Of course not, but did you have to treat me like a common,"

"Don't say it when you know it's not true," he corrected her and noticed that she seemed to be contemplating. "What is it?" he asked.

"I've suddenly realized that I let you use me in the way only a man could use a woman and get away with it."

"What else could I have done?"

His expression showed helplessness, but she'd been unprotected. "Said I was your cousin or something?"

"How original. Somehow, I don't see those young men believing I would be caught in this hideaway contraption with my cousin."

"What will it take for me to convince you that it is in our best interest to work as trainer and student?" While the weight of his stare bore down on her she offered, "I will camouflage myself. Really I don't mind."

She may be camouflaged to others but not to him. Professionally it would be a risky, bold move on his part to take in a female student. On the other hand, she challenged him, and the desire to take on this challenging situation grew when he imagined her racing his best horse and winning. Her weight was an advantage and so was her strong-willed determination.

My Forbidden Mentor

His first obstacle would be her father before making a final decision. "First I would like to meet with your father."

"My father?"

"Yes. I would like to get his opinion."

She thought about it before agreeing. "Of course."

"Are you not pleased that I'm even considering this?"

"Yes."

The mention of her father created a shift in her mood. "Miss Howard, is there going to be a problem with your father?"

"No, not at all."

"Because I'm getting a notion that there will be."

"No, absolutely not. I'm just going to have to explain my whereabouts today and also my meeting you."

Virtue and courage came to mind when he thought about the position she represented, and even though his mind still teetered about the circumstances involved, her driving energy kept pulling at him. Her determination was contagious. "I'll explain to your father. Today, in fact, if that will suit you?"

Her shoulders fell in relief. "Yes, thank you. And thank you for considering this opportunity."

"I can foresee the possibilities. And now that we've made preliminary plans, I don't see a need to be so formal. You can call me John."

"Melissa, please."

"Are you sure it isn't Mel?" He teased with a grin.

"It's Melissa."

"Melissa it is. Let me escort you home."

"Yes. That would be nice."

Chapter Three

On the way to her home John asked Melissa about herself and she didn't leave out any details. John discovered she was born in Darlington and had lived there most of her life. Her father had a carpentry business and was an incredible talent to his field. He was a very proud Scottish man.

Her English mother came from a background of prestige, met Melissa's father, and fell in love. In happiness her parents ran the carpentry business together, Anna taking care of the books, Phillip creating works of art.

They had a live-in nanny turned housekeeper named Miss Beckett, known to Melissa as her auntie. Since Miss. Beckett had been a part of the family so long it had only seemed natural that she continue to remain with them after the passing of Anna. She'd been a comfort indeed.

After Anna's passing the family decided to start fresh and so they moved to Scotch Corner. While living in Scotch Corner Melissa came to love the rural countryside and the freedom of open land all around. She gloried at being able to ride her gelding by rows of long-stemmed wildflowers and smell their delectable scent along the way. She painted a very descriptive picture for John, and though he had passed by the outskirts of Scotch Corner a number of times before, he had never ventured about the quiet land. Now he had a reason to.

The extent of John's sharing about his personal life bordered on private boundaries. John limited his information, telling Melissa he was from Richmond and had lived there his whole life and that his father was Duke Albert Blackburn with whom he didn't readily associate. He also told her that his mother had been deceased for quite some time. After the mention of his mother their conversation dwindled until reaching Melissa's home.

Arriving before nightfall, they both emerged from the carriage. John gave his driver Jess a break while he himself tended to Melissa's gelding. Both proceeded toward Melissa's gelding to untie him when Melissa came to an abrupt stop, seeing her father stepping out the front door of their cabin.

Expecting to give an explanation of her whereabouts Melissa spoke first before her father could. "Father, hello." She was cut short by her father's angered state.

"Where have you been Melissa Louise?" He spoke through tightened lips and narrowed eyes.

Feeling like a young child again and conscious of being humiliated in front of Lord Blackburn, her words were hurried. "I've been at the races in Middleham and this kind gentleman escorted me home," she told her father, and immediately winced while waiting for the eruption.

John continued tending to Melissa's horse keeping his eyes averted on the gelding.

Mr. Howard focused on Melissa, not paying attention to John or John's fancy carriage yet. "Middleham? You didn't inform me that you were going to Middleham!" His voice grew in volume with the shaking of his head "I should have known you'd be intrigued with the races going on right now," he said as his eyes beamed into hers. "You worried me half to death Melissa! You best mention it next time."

Melissa stepped toward her father, reminding him, "Father, if I had told where I was going, you would have forbidden it," she said, continuing to argue her point.

My Forbidden Mentor

"Precisely," Mr. Howard agreed. "I can't believe you went by yourself. I tell you girl, you've got more gumption than your own mother had."

It was much more difficult defending herself to her father than anyone else and he did have a right to worry. "Forgive me father, but I've already received a verbal lashing today," she explained as her eyes shifted in John's direction.

John could feel her fixed look on him that he sensed was a cry for help. After loosening the saddle straps he glanced up, finding Melissa smile in relief as she continued with introductions.

"Father, this is Lord Blackburn. Lord Blackburn, this is my father, Phillip Howard."

He was aware of her quick introduction as a way of diverting her father. Both reached across to each other and shook hands. "Mr. Howard," John said, giving a courteous smile.

"Lord Blackburn," Phillip responded. Thankful to see his daughter had arrived home safe, he also had a nagging concern regarding the possible underlying reasons for the lord's assistance. Phillip Howard cherished his daughter, and now that his wife had been gone for three years his daughter's life had become his. She was the epitome of his wife: headstrong, independent, and with a strong affection for horses. He realized it was unusual for a woman to be racing horses but he knew Melissa would thrive if given the chance. His daughter was very unique in her personality, intelligent, and above all, beautiful. Yes, he was a doting father. Being twenty-one, in the eyes of society she should have married by now, but Phillip respected her wish to marry when she was ready to, believing marriage was for a man and woman who truly loved each other, not just for convenience. Regardless, he would keep a watchful eye on the lord. Eventually a kind smile appeared on Phillip's gentle face. "It's a pleasure to meet you. And I thank you for returning my daughter to me," he relayed before hearing Miss Beckett call to him. He turned to his daughter. "Melissa, I'd like to have a word with you," he ordered.

Without falter she obeyed. They stood close, averted from John's view. "Yes father?"

"Your auntie needs my help. Don't let him leave until I can talk to him." His look was stern and meaningful.

She let out a breath of frustration. "Why father? He's done nothing wrong."

Phillip's voice dropped to a harsh whisper. "That's not the point. I need to talk to him before he leaves."

"You mean warn him." She was about to argue further when she realized her father's eyes were hardening with fierce domination, meaning he'd reached his capacity of being civil. "Yes father, I'll tell him to wait."

Phillip didn't say another word. Once Melissa complied he went inside to help Miss Beckett.

John witnessed in amazement the way Phillip handled his daughter. He couldn't hear their words but he didn't miss Melissa's reluctance to back down, but in the end she did. He gave her father a lot of credit dealing with such a wild cat. How did Phillip keep from going insane with such bold women in his household? How did he deal with male suitors? At this last thought he looked in her direction again. Her father had just entered the house, closing the door behind him, and Melissa remained standing there. John lifted the saddle off Thunder and took it into the barn.

Meanwhile Melissa led Thunder into the corral, thinking about what to say next. How was she supposed to tell a lord, "By the way, my father would like to lecture you about

My Forbidden Mentor

his daughter?" She was twenty-one years of age, for heaven sakes.

John strode out of the barn, interrupting her thoughts. "You're smooth, I must say," he shot out while retrieving the extra rope used to tie her gelding.

Melissa stepped over to him. "What do you mean by that remark?" she inquired, observing his strong hands working with the rope.

Averting his gaze from his motion to her face, he spoke with absolute audacity. "You, trying to work your father," he told her. Whether she realized it or not, that's the way it had happened.

He started to place the wound up rope in its proper compartment amid the carriage when her hand clasped over his, getting his full attention. "I do not work my father. I speak in plain terms. I tell him the truth," she pointed out. Then after seeing his eyes shift to their touching hands, she lifted hers away as if an invisible flame had lit it.

Continuing with his action, his response was not what she wanted to hear. "And when you're wrong, you want to bypass the whipping."

Her eyes grew wide and her mouth opened in astonishment. Beyond any doubt, he had agreed with her father. "I cannot believe you said that," she told him as her narrowing glare peered into him.

But he saw through her casual way. "I'm telling the truth as I see it. You didn't even inform him of where you were today," he responded as he propped against the black carriage, his booted ankles crossing and his hands joining together.

She stepped in front of him, her hands bracing her shapely hips. "There were obvious reasons for that. I thought you were going to talk to him for me?"

"I plan to. But you should have at least mentioned the track this morning. You're his daughter and he wants to protect you. You're well aware of how insane the track can be, especially for a young lady alone."

Well it seems Mr. Knowledge would learn firsthand about her father's protective nature she thought as a twinge of a smile pierced her lips. "You and my father should get along famously then Lord Blackburn, since he has bid me to keep you here so he can "have a word with you," as he put it," she retorted.

Even John's driver was astonished at the tone the young lady used with him and he was curious at how the lord would handle it.

A very devilish grin emerged upon John's lips. "You can be serious now and stop this ridiculous joke."

His calmness was utterly unbearable and it made her seethe. She had never met a man so blunt and arrogant. "Oh, I'm not jesting. I tried to save you from this confrontation with my father but he insisted, much to my embarrassment. He expects to see you when you're finished here," she told him in delight as he looked taken aback.

He couldn't believe it. The joke was on him. Lord, he hadn't dealt with protective fathers since adolescent age. He pushed away from the carriage. "We shall see who laughs last," he told her when her burst of laughter could no longer be contained. He shook his head and headed for the front door.

My Forbidden Mentor

After Miss Beckett seated him in the sitting room John took the opportunity to explore his environment. Quaint and cozy was how he would describe it. Popping sounds and immense heat coming from a large stone fireplace caught his attention. As his eyes followed the structure of stones they drifted to unusual looking wooden furniture, unusual in the fact that the engraved designing along the edges of the light colored wood was unique. John examined the chair he sat in, finding in amazing detail galloping stallions racing along the edge. He presumed Mr. Howard had built these magnificent wooden furnishings and was impressed.

After admiring Mr. Howard's work John thought about why he sat in this comfortable room waiting for Melissa's father to chastise him. To continue a relationship with Melissa it would be better to be clear with Mr. Howard from the beginning, no secrets, everything out in the open. In John's mind, honesty was always best.

Phillip's voice interrupted John's thoughts. "Would you care for something to drink, Lord Blackburn?"

John looked up at Phillip, seeing him swirl a golden colored liquid around in his glass. "Yes, do you have brandy?"

Phillip strode over to the bar. "Ah, brandy. Yes I do, although it may not be the brandy you're used to," he mentioned while retrieving a fresh glass and pouring into it a generous amount of amber liquid.

"It will be fine." He took the glass from Phillip. "Thank you."

"You're welcome." Phillip responded while taking a seat across from John and stealing a significant swig of his drink. "You may be a brandy man Lord Blackburn, but there's nothing like a good glass of scotch." He smiled toward John, who was nodding in agreement.

They chatted a moment about the differences in their preferences of drink, each loyally sticking by their choice. Then Phillip's smile faded and John knew it had come to the crucial point of this meeting.

"Lord Blackburn, I wish to speak to you about my daughter. I'm sure you already figured that out." Phillip tipped more scotch into his mouth.

John sipped some brandy. "Yes sir."

"I'm not sure of your intentions toward Melissa, but I pray they are sincere?"

Phillip gave John a warning glance if ever he saw one. John cleared his throat. "Mr. Howard, I offered your daughter a ride home, being I live a short distance from you. I haven't any designs regarding your daughter."

Phillip stayed silent as if digesting John's words. "Lord Blackburn, something must have happened to lend offering her a ride home?"

John was feeling cornered. He needed to explain the truth. "Mr. Howard, the truth is…"

"The truth is, father, that Lord Blackburn is the victim here." Both men swung their view in Melissa's direction. John's mouth was on the verge of falling open and her father's eyes widened in surprise. She stepped in closer, standing before them. "Yes, you see, I was simply minding my own business, staying on the outskirts of the racetrack watching the races, when out of nowhere this man appeared behind me." John sat frozen, awaiting the remainder of the story, and her father listened with unwavering enthusiasm. "Well he startled me of course, then seemed sincere when he suggested I observe his rapid stallion." John's eyes enlarged at her description. Phillip's brows narrowed in concentration. "I thought nothing of it at first. You know I love horses, so I proceeded to follow him when I realized he was taking me behind a set of changing sheds." John swallowed hard. "I'm quite embarrassed to admit that it took me so long to figure out what type of stallion he wanted me to see." She chuckled in the awkward silence. John's eyes shut, flabbergasted by her choice of words.

Phillip became appalled. "Melissa, watch your tongue!"

"I'm sorry, but father I wasn't sure how else to explain, which leads me to Lord Blackburn. Naturally I ran away from the awful man but I wasn't sure if he would follow me. Well, I became disoriented by the time I reached the front gates so I hid in the nearest carriage, which happened to be Lord Blackburn's." By now Melissa received the evil eye from John and a stunned, unbelievable expression from her father. "To arrive at my point, I explained to Lord Blackburn what had happened and he was nice enough to find Thunder and escort me home." She finished with the most sincere smile on her face as she ignored John's scowl and waited with impatience for her father's response.

It took extreme effort for John not to intercede. Ironically he sat there absorbing every last detail of a story she concocted in a matter of minutes. Incredible, he thought. Here he wanted to be straight with her father and she came in telling a story of half-truths, for whatever reason making an effort to save his hide. Even though he hadn't done anything for Mr. Howard to be alarmed about, there still existed the business agreement he and Melissa dared to venture. How would that issue be brought up now that her father had this other to deal with? *Perhaps I should leave that up to Melissa, the great storyteller*, he thought.

John looked from Melissa, who appeared calm and collected, to her father, who without any doubt bought her story. He would have fallen for it himself if he hadn't been there to witness the truth.

Phillip caught John's glance upon him and softness conquered his troubled features. "I owe you an apology Lord Blackburn."

John's eyes flashed to Melissa before responding. "Not at all sir. It's quite unnecessary."

"Oh but of course. I was about to accuse you with the notion of philandering with my daughter. My sincere apologies." Phillip held his glass in the air to salute John. "And my deepest thanks for rescuing her." He smiled, unaware of the façade, and swallowed a mouthful of scotch.

John debated a minute whether to unveil the total truth to Mr. Howard, but after shifting his view to Melissa again and encountering the desperate, pleading expression upon her not so innocent face, the debating was over. He cursed himself in silence for following along with the deceit and gave Phillip a smile, saluting his own glass in agreement. "I'm grateful that my carriage was in the right place at the right time sir," he said, watching Phillip take another swig, emptying his glass. To say the least Mr. Howard had become inebriated.

Melissa must have noticed also for she was at her father's side in a second. Taking his empty glass from him, she set it on a nearby table and ordered him, "Father you've had more than usual to drink tonight. I think you need to lie down in bed."

He lifted from his chair, taking her hand for assistance. "I think you're right, love. Apologize to Lord Blackburn for me, will you?" he asked in a low voice as they stepped toward the doorway. "I've been rude to drink so much and leave so abruptly."

Melissa glanced over to John. "Of course father." Miss Beckett got her attention when she came over to them.

"I'll take him to bed, love." She gave John an approving glimpse and then took Phillip from Melissa. "You've got company to attend to."

"Thank you auntie." Melissa reached over and gave her father a kiss on the cheek. "Goodnight, father." Her father said goodnight as he and Miss Beckett trailed off toward his room.

Melissa stood there for a moment watching them, nervous about approaching her company who still sat on the couch waiting for her. She hadn't wanted to make up stories for her father. In fact, this was the first time she had ever had to, but she couldn't jeopardize her chances with Lord Blackburn. She thought by saving his bum from her father he would return the favor by teaching her. It was quite amazing how fast she had come up with all the details of the story she'd made up. Feeling proud of herself, she turned to face Lord Blackburn with a smile on her face, only when she did, she discovered a definite glare of contempt. "More brandy?" she offered, prancing toward the bar.

"No, that isn't necessary." John returned in a perturbed tone.

"Very well, then." She placed the bottle back in its place.

"Are you proud of yourself?" John asked, interested to hear her response.

She took her father's place in his chair across from John. "No, of course not. I've never, ever done that before."

"You mean lie?" John pointed out.

Her eyes found his. She hadn't lied. She couldn't think of it that way. "I would never intentionally hurt my father," she hissed. "How can you be so ungrateful? I was saving your bottom after all!"

"Yes, I suppose you did, except I didn't get a chance to explain about our situation." He sat up straight, setting his glass on the table next to him. "I have to congratulate you though on your creative choice of words." His grin was meant to embarrass her along with the emphasis on the word "creative."

It must have worked, for within seconds her cheeks flushed. Her eyes veered away from his continuing gaze.

He continued to harass her. "You were amazing, you know? I admit at first I was upset that you cut in like that, but the way your story evolved I started to believe it myself." He hesitated, knowing his taunting unnerved her for she was looking everywhere but at him. He carried on anyway because he couldn't help himself. "It was enough to shame yourself, but you about mortified your father. A rapid stallion?" he chuckled. "How did you come up with that one?" By now he expected her to burst.

She stood, stepped over to him, and bent down to retrieve his glass from the table. "If you're finished I believe it's time you took your leave, Lord Blackburn," she said and by now not caring if she blew her chances seemed tolerable compared to enduring his insulting words.

He stood also, standing with just a foot between them. "Don't I deserve a reply to my inquiry first?"

He wasn't smiling but she could tell he wanted to. His close presence became intense. Her head had to tip back a bit to look into his face. "You've had your jollies, Lord Blackburn. I prefer not to respond." Why all of a sudden her heart began racing and her palms began sweating she wasn't sure. She should be furious with him but instead she became warm and giddy and nervous, very nervous.

His arms crossed over his chest. "Really, I'm curious to know what made you think of a rapid stallion?"

She crossed her arms over her chest. "Really, I prefer not to share that with you."

His head tipped to one side. "What if I'm never to see you again? Then I'll never know?" John baited and her eyes widened, just like he knew they would.

"You cannot be serious. You were going to make a decision regarding our arrangement," she said as her voice held urgency.

"True. But after tonight's episode and the fact that you won't indulge me..."

Melissa sighed. "All right," she said, her gaze diverting to the glass of brandy she held. She began swirling the liquid like her father did.

"And make sure it's the truth," he warned as his lips curved up in triumph.

Her eyes shot to his, her tone hissing again. "I never lie. I've told you that, except for this one exception," she reminded him, and then her eyes fell away from his handsome face when she began her explanation. "I had to think of something drastic that a man would want to do to a woman out in the open. Since I've never seen two people...mating," she paused to catch her breath and swallow to moisten her dry throat, "I, I went by horses, which I have seen mating. It appeared to take place at a very fast pace, hence the word "rapid." She swallowed again, searching for anything to focus on except him. "And since my presence involved being at a race track, I used stallion...to describe..."

John knew she had been overwhelmed in explaining so he stopped her. His arms unfolded and he said, "I've got the picture. I don't require a further description." He hadn't expected to become aroused, but the more descriptive she got, the more his body formulated a mental image of what she referred to. He needed a distraction. "You're a quick thinker Melissa," he told her, sounding rough while trying to relay a compliment. He took the glass from her hand and downed one more gulp of the amber liquid before handing it back to her. His day had been long and unusually entertaining, and one minute more in the same room with Melissa and his own rapid stallion would make an evident appearance. "The hour is late. I should be leaving," he said and started to stride toward the doorway.

"Will I hear from you?" she asked in a panic.

He stopped in the doorway of the sitting room and rotated halfway. "Yes. Either way I will contact you about my decision," he assured her, but she continued to look concerned. "Give me one week's time, all right?"

"All right," she agreed.

Guilt and doubt plagued her as she followed his movements out the front door: the guilt she felt for not confessing the total truth to her father, and the doubt that John didn't believe her to be truthful, which could affect his decision. Had she made a mistake tonight?

Perhaps it had helped that he did indeed get the last laugh, even if it was at her humiliating expense. She hoped it was worth exposing herself like she did, although after she had, his mood appeared to change. His strange behavior left her confused and discouraged. One week, he said. In one week her dream would live or die. I'm counting on you, Lord Blackburn, to let it live.

Chapter Four

John pondered the entire week since he'd last seen Melissa. Now, as he sat beneath his "thinking" tree, as he called the giant Mulberry, his body flexed into a languid stretch.

Clasping his hands behind his head, his eyes closed and he drifted into a peaceful slumber. What to do about Melissa? Not every woman attracted John and the constant gossip that he bedded any and every woman that came into his path couldn't be further from the truth. Although he had lain with a number of women in his time, John was very particular.

And now came Melissa, sweet Melissa, who held definite attraction for him. He thought back to her desperate attempts and with a curve of his lips, laughter bellowed inside him. The look in her eyes when she got caught was invaluable. He had never laughed so hard when he told Robert about what had happened. Then it dawned on him that laughter had been a rarity among his female acquaintances and it seemed so easy with Melissa. He couldn't help having desiring thoughts about her, and combined with her interest in thoroughbreds, it fascinated him. He never imagined meeting a woman whose involvement with the gentle beasts would match his. A decision had to be made soon, before she gave up on him and went out on her own again.

One week had passed, Melissa thought as she hunched down in her garden. Under a cloudy gray sky she set about trimming perishing petals from the rose bushes she had planted earlier in the year from bare roots. Gaping at their brilliant displays of color, she took pride in her small rose garden. Her attention remained focused while collecting fallen rose petals and smoothing rich blackened dirt back around each individual plant when a towering figure appeared.

"Melissa?"

She jumped when hearing the deep, inquiring voice. Lord Blackburn's voice. Her eyes closed. At last her future would be decided. She opened her eyes to the noticeable body heat penetrating around her and realized that he had crouched down next to her, studying her actions.

"Lord Blackburn," she acknowledged, her hands turning shaky as she resumed smoothing dirt around the plants.

"The roses are lovely and they look well-tended," John told her, finding the compliment coming easy for him.

Melissa appreciated the compliment but couldn't help being eager to hear what he had to say. He was here for one reason. She looked him square in the face. Was he to become her mentor? "Thank you," she responded with a generous smile. Was he tormenting her on purpose?

John smiled back, being quite aware that she must be feeling turbulent inside. Perhaps he should ease her mind. If his instincts were correct she would prove to be a valuable asset to his company if all went as planned. "Do you think you can work as hard training to be my jockey?" John asked and wasn't sure if Melissa had heard him because she hadn't reacted yet.

But not a moment later, slender arms flew around his neck, her motion rocking him off balance, though he kept them both from falling by bracing his hands on the ground. Her voice held excitement after comprehending his decision. "Oh, Lord Blackburn, I could kiss you."

My Forbidden Mentor

As soon as she realized her words, she loosened her grip and backed away from him. "I meant that as a figure of speech, of course."

John understood her excitement, but to avoid further awkwardness he carried on with the matter at hand while he stood. "May I presume you're happy about my decision?" he asked, brushing loose soil from his trousers.

He was giving her a chance. How could she not be happy? In fact, she was grateful. "I'll be the best jockey you'll ever have. You have my commitment and full cooperation."

John chuckled at her enthusiasm. "Yes, well before we partake in this adventurous endeavor, there will be stipulations we need to discuss," he said, crossing his arms over his chest.

"All right, let's hear them."

John grinned at Melissa's eagerness as he scanned their perimeters. "Is your father around?"

"No, he's working," she replied with clear impatience.

"Very well. We will discuss this now and then make arrangements to include your father another time."

"My father will appreciate that."

He followed her to the covered entrance of the cabin. They sat on a wooden swing and began going over the initial plans. Melissa agreed to most, taking exception to the last. John wanted sole dealings in regards to negotiations.

"I will be the one riding, Lord Blackburn, therefore, I certainly shall be involved in bargaining," she stated.

"Melissa, who has more experience here?" John asked in return.

"Does your experience include women for riders?" she implored, knowing she was his first female student.

"That's quite unfair. You know what I mean."

"I beg to differ. You will need a different approach presenting a woman."

"We will deal with that when the time approaches. Meanwhile, we will need to decide whether to choose the route of public display as opposed to camouflaging you."

"Very well, but be aware that I would prefer to be involved with negotiations," she made clear, pausing for a moment before sharing her private thoughts. "Wouldn't it be absolutely wonderful though to be able to race against professionals as myself, as a woman?"

"Yes, it would be," he agreed, realizing how much all of this meant to her, at the same time realizing the extensive challenge he'd gotten himself into.

They both agreed the next step would be to present their intentions to her father and further agreed to do it together.

But later that evening, while Melissa and her father were in the sitting room reading, she wanted to share with her father her chance of a lifetime. From time to time she would look up at her father, not concentrating on reading at all. No longer able to repress herself Melissa closed her book, deciding to say something, anything, to ease the pressure. "Father, I've come across a superb opportunity. I know you'll be pleased."

Philip's eyes lifted from his book to capture his daughter's. "Then spit it out, lass."

Her smile widened while she explained. "Well, do you remember Lord Blackburn?"

"Of course. He's the fine gentleman who rescued you last week."

"Yes, and he's a trainer, father, one of the best, and he has agreed to a trial training session with me!"

"What!" His book shut loud enough to make Melissa flinch. "Why didn't he talk to me himself?"

She regained her confidence. "He had planned on it but I wanted to talk to you first. You see he's not aware that I'm doing this without him," she explained and started to feel guilty at what she'd just admitted, remembering her agreement with Lord Blackburn.

His narrowed gaze stayed on her. "When did you have time to discuss this with him?"

She stood to escape his scrutiny. "When he brought me home last week," she told him as her footsteps took her before a large window where she could see blooming roses in her garden.

Phillip stared into her backside. "Tell me the truth, lass, was that all you did was talk? Why would he be so willing, huh?"

With a low gasp, Melissa turned around to face him. "Father, he was a perfect gentleman. He's seen me ride and that's the truth."

Phillip shifted in his chair, his hand reaching over to retrieve his glass of scotch. "At Middleham, I suppose?" he said and swallowed a bit of his drink. "How did you manage that? You seemed to have left that part out of your story last week?"

By now the excitement that had built inside Melissa had changed to utter disappointment in herself. "I'm sorry, father, but the point is that he sees true potential in me and he can help me achieve my dream."

Phillip didn't ease up at all. "What's in it for him?"

Instead of being offended by her father's remark, she carried on as if they were having a casual conversation. "I would ride one of his top stallions and make him money."

"Now there's gambling involved. Oh lord, lass, what have you gotten yourself into?" he responded in a sarcastic but serious tone. He couldn't believe their conversation and the avenues it kept taking.

Melissa stepped in her father's direction. "Father you've gambled yourself."

"That doesn't matter, lass. You're my daughter. You sneak into a racetrack not thinking about the consequences if your caught, and you attracted the attention of a lord who thankfully was nice enough not to turn you in. He probably waived that part so he could get paid in another fashion." His drink swished in violence as he took another swig. As the scotch coated his throat he realized there was no more denying that his little girl was growing up and making crucial decisions of her own, but they were insane, ludicrous decisions.

Stunned by her father's conclusion, she explained again, "Father, please. It's not like that. His interest lies in his horses and making money. Mine lies in racing. You know it's all I've ever wanted to do."

She was making sense and perhaps he was jumping to conclusions, but she was at a ripe age. He didn't doubt that Lord Blackburn, like any other red-blooded male, would like to pluck at his precious fruit. He set his drink on the table. "Before any of this takes place I want to see him. I want to talk to him again, in private, no interference from you. Then we'll all talk, you got that?"

Relief coursed through Melissa. "Of course, father. Thank you for being cooperative."

My Forbidden Mentor

His features turned tender. "Only because I love you so much. And if he is true to his word then I agree it would be a fine opportunity for you, but you have me worried about you. You're so headstrong, like your mother, worse I'm afraid."

She stepped next to her father, leaning down to place a kiss on his cheek. "I know father and I can't help it, but it's the only way to get what you want out of life."

"I know you're right love, but you've got to give your father a chance to catch up with you. Don't make any more plans without me, settled?"

She smiled when agreeing, "Yes father," and watched him return to his book, his brows creased with leftover frustration.

Melissa turned to retrieve her own book. Grand, just grand. Now she would have to let Lord Blackburn know that she'd talked to her father and that he requested another visit with him. She understood her father's concern but he didn't seem to understand the awkwardness that flooded her every time she had to approach Lord Blackburn because of her father. It wasn't as if she were courting the lord.

Melissa grabbed her book and strolled off to bed. She still planned on meeting Lord Blackburn in the morning, where she'd be fighting another battle. She had brought this on herself again. Why, all of sudden, when her life seemed like it was changing for the better, did it seem so tangled up? Tomorrow's another day, she reassured herself.

Chapter Five

The next morning John and Melissa stood inside John's private viewing box at Catterick Racetrack. John became furious when she revealed the discussion she'd had with her father. She had ignored their agreement. After obtaining a level of composure, he responded. "Damn it all Melissa! We had an understanding about this, did we not? What happened to your part of it?" His voice remained low but severe. His arms crossed over his broad chest, his lips thinned, and his eyes narrowed in consideration.

She didn't like the tension in his jaw. It was tight, like his teeth were grinding together. Perhaps they were. She couldn't blame him for being angry with her. At the time when she indulged her father she was beyond exhilaration and at the same time her admission served to prepare him, however she had not anticipated her father requesting another private conversation with Lord Blackburn. If she had known that was going to happen she would have waited, but now it seems she had overcompensated, going from telling lies, which was out of character, to telling more truth than be known. She hadn't meant to break their agreement. "Forgive me I never expected him to react that way. In the end he seemed agreeable."

John glared some more before tipping his head back to peer into a ceiling of blue sky and white clouds. After a moment of silence his head shifted forward. "Melissa, we have got to trust each other. If I cannot trust you, I cannot teach you." He saw a forgiving reaction in her, which he appreciated.

My Forbidden Mentor

She stood with hands clasped in front of her, her eyes worried, the edge of her teeth biting into her bottom lip. "I promise it will not happen again. I've made a terrible mistake and I feel awful about it," she told him and fell silent, waiting for his response, but when he did not speak she became desperate. "I promise you can trust me," she pleaded.

His arms unfolded and his hands went to her shoulders in a light grasp. "No more chances after this. Are you sure you understand?" he questioned as his features softened while clarifying his point.

She couldn't blame him. He'd done nothing so far to cause her to question him, yet time after time she'd done just the opposite to him. She gave him a generous smile, "I understand, and I don't blame you for being upset with me."

He squeezed her shoulders tighter, smiling in response. "I'm not upset anymore, what's done is done. I will meet your father again, and without your intrusion this time?"

"You have another promise on that. I assure you," she told him with confidence.

"Good. Now let me show you around the track and we'll discuss a time to meet with your father."

As they toured the track John explained his start involving horses, how he had traveled to Catterick Village to observe the horses and study the trainers, deciding that one day he would train his own horses and have champion racers. As John told his childhood story the words seemed to flow out of him. It was rare that he talked about himself and now, with Melissa, he was feeling free to do so. He went on explaining his increasing involvement as he became older.

Laura Mills

By age nineteen he had helped finance a new racecourse to be built for Catterick and within the next few years he acquired his first stallion, Monarch. After Monarch became a champion John purchased a couple of high dollar mares for breeding. The breeding of Monarch and his favorite mare, Clara, resulted in his present upcoming champion, his stallion Chief. Chief was born with the chestnut coloring of his father but the balanced temperament of his mother. He was John's masterpiece and he had molded him from birth until the present.

Melissa seemed intrigued. She would ask question after endless question about every process he'd endured. Her solid interest in his livelihood struck him with an unusual sense of comfort and ease. Never before had a woman listened to him with such depth. Never had his attention been so set on a woman and her reactions, for with Melissa he was learning to expect the unexpected.

Side by side John and Melissa rode toward John's home. They continued their chat about John's race course experience until reaching his manor. While John checked his messages from his service man Charles, Melissa took in the magnificent surroundings of his thoroughbred heaven. Before Melissa had a chance to explore the many glorious beasts John resumed his task of escorting her home.

After arriving at her home a short time later, they stood leaning against the wooden posts of the corral sharing horse stories while waiting for Mr. Howard to arrive home. The sound of horse hooves got their attention.

Phillip came to a stop and slid off his mare. Leading her toward the barn, he nodded toward them. "Lord Blackburn, Melissa."

My Forbidden Mentor

Melissa walked quickly to reach her father and offered to take care of his mare, knowing he was tired from work and that he and Lord Blackburn had important matters to discuss. "Father let me tend to your horse," she said as she took the reins from him.

Phillip sighed. "Thank you, lass." He gave her a weary smile, then turned his attention to John. "Lord Blackburn would you like to go inside and have a drink?"

John pushed away from the wooden post to fall in step with Mr. Howard as they made their way to the front door. "Yes sir, sounds fine to me."

This time their situation appeared more at ease because before John realized it he had a glass of brandy in his hand. Mr. Howard hadn't wasted any time supplying refreshments. They sat across from each as they had before, both taking generous sips before venturing into stressed territory.

John began. "Mr. Howard, let me start by saying that I believe your daughter has tremendous talent in racing." He took another quick sip.

Mr. Howard could tell this was just as awkward for the lord as it had been for him. It might have been easier to handle had John wanted to court Melissa, but in this case the circumstances were different. "Lord Blackburn, I appreciate your professional judgment regarding Melissa and I agree with you." He used the back of his hand to wipe a generous bead of sweat off his forehead. "And to ease your mind, I feel you're genuine about teaching my daughter to race professionally, but what I have trouble understanding is how you can possibly think to manage it? I mean, and I would never say this in front of my daughter, but you've got to know the risk you're taking here, with her being a woman, you know?"

"You're right about that sir, but I must say that your daughter can be very convincing, and with her talent to back her, it was hard to resist. I'm sure it's apparent that I've seen her ride or I would never have been so eager to agree." He leaned forward to set his drink on the side table. "And before beginning any training at all I've made it clear to your daughter that I wanted to get your approval and have you be aware of every aspect of the situation." Phillip looked impressed, his features taking on an expression of consideration.

Phillip lifted a small wooden box off of the table next to him. Opening it, he scooped a generous amount of tobacco, placing it in a wooden pipe and packing it down. He positioned the pipe in his mouth and before lighting it he offered John some. "Care for a pipe, Lord Blackburn?"

"No thank you, sir I don't smoke."

Phillip set fire to the packed tobacco and began puffing at it, causing smoke to seep out between his lips. "I'm pleased by your respect for my position Lord Blackburn, but I have another question I'd like to ask." John nodded in response. "What do you truly have to gain by having my daughter ride for you?"

It was a fair question, John agreed. "Well sir, top champion racers, which in turn will make me money. But the thought of having champion thoroughbreds that cannot be beat, that is my ultimate goal, and your daughter will help me achieve that goal. Without her, I'm not sure if I could get as far."

More puffs of smoke blew out of Phillip's mouth. "That's quite a compliment regarding my daughter. Is this fondness for my daughter exclusive for racing purposes?"

My Forbidden Mentor

He watched Phillip take another swig of scotch, placing the pipe back into his mouth. "Yes sir. That was my initial intention for your daughter and it remains the same."

"No thoughts of romance, Lord Blackburn?" Phillip asked with an arch of a gray brow.

"Mr. Howard, I won't deny that your daughter is very attractive but the endeavors we will take together have to be strictly business or it will not work. I will remain professional."

Phillip smiled at John's tension. "Thank you for your honesty, Lord Blackburn. I do have a request, though." He puffed a couple of times on the pipe. Being a man, Phillip knew how men thought, and even with the best of intentions, spending a lot time around a woman, especially an attractive one, could drain your willpower in no time. He'd had a similar experience himself with Melissa's mother which had ended in marriage.

John waited with extreme patience. All kinds of ideas were tossing in his head. "Yes sir?"

Phillip admired John's calm and confident attitude. "I would like your training sessions to take place here. Miss Beckett will act as chaperone of a sort, at least by being here at the cabin. Also, if your personal status changes with my daughter, I would like to be made aware of it."

It only took a second to understand what he'd meant and in that second he swallowed hard. "Of course, sir." John recognized the meaningful look in Mr. Howard's eyes. Man to man, all it took was that brief look.

Phillip liked him, he liked him a lot. He had a good feeling about the lad and a gut notion told him that this young man would forever be involved in their lives in some way. In what way he couldn't be sure, but there was an everlasting presence about him. "Thank you." He moved back to the subject at hand with a smile. "Have you ever taught a young lady before?"

John returned his smile. "No sir, I have not. It will prove to be quite a challenge."

Phillip's smile widened. "Lord Blackburn, I have to inform you that my daughter in herself is quite a challenge, much less the situation you two will be in. Please indulge me I want to know how you two plan to conquer this quest of yours?"

John obliged, telling him of the kind of training Melissa would need to be at peak performance. Then they'd move onto the more difficult task of getting her on the track in public.

Phillip had ideas of his own and so they collaborated their ideas, drank their preference of liquor, and laughed together at quirky thoughts about this or that. Unthinking, they forgot to invite Melissa in to help with any opinions she had to share.

At least that's what she thought when she heard the bellowing of laughter coming from the sitting room behind the closed door, but at least they weren't arguing, she reasoned. She leaned closer to the doorway, trying to pick up any words they spoke. Before they could say anything of importance Melissa had been caught.

"Melissa Louise." Miss Beckett whispered in disbelief.

Startled, Melissa scrambled from the doorway. "Auntie, you gave me a start," she gasped, her hand clutching at her chest.

Miss Beckett gave her a look of knowing better than that. "I'm not surprised you were startled, being sneaky like you were."

The blush on Melissa's cheeks gave away the innocent face she tried demonstrating. "Sneaky? I was curious, that's all."

"Curious? You were eavesdropping on a personal conversation and you know it, lass. Now get your bum in the kitchen and help your auntie with supper." Miss Beckett made a sweeping motion with her hands toward the kitchen.

Melissa delayed. "Auntie, they were talking about me. Haven't I the right to defend myself?"

When her auntie's eyes began to narrow and her lips thinned Melissa knew it was time to quit and she stomped off toward the kitchen.

Chapter Six

Miss Beckett was grateful to get out into fresh air. She hadn't relaxed like this in years. When Lord Blackburn had suggested a picnic by the stream today she had figured it would be more hassle than it was worth having to prepare food and then transport it, but when he sweetened the offer by having lunch already made and a carriage for travel, she couldn't turn him down. Acting as chaperone could have some benefits, she thought, sitting next to Melissa upon a blanket provided by Lord Blackburn.

The women admired the stream flowing by while John placed a basket of food and drinks near them. He sat down as well, inviting Jess over as he was lifting contents of chicken, ham, small red potatoes, cold slaw, and plum pudding out of the basket. Sampling the contents of food, they all commented on how good everything tasted. They laughed and joked, enjoying the afternoon on this sunny April day. Soon after the meal, John got up to collect his journal from the carriage while Miss Beckett stood, stretched and then walked adjacent to the stream's edge. Catching sight of Jess further down the stream immersed in a book, Miss Beckett stepped toward him and inquired of what he was reading.

John strode back to Melissa, who still sat upon the blanket, only now her legs were extended out in front of her beneath a sheer summer dress while her upper body rested its weight on the palm of her hands. He sat down beside her with his journal in hand unnoticed, he realized, when observing the tilting of her face toward the sun. With her eyes closed and honeyed features taking in the sun's rays, John's concentration veered. His gaze turned steady upon her, becoming entranced by the tender curve of her slender neck and the modest outward thrust of her bosom.

Laughter came from Jess and Miss Beckett from down the stream, swaying John's attention. He took a deep breath, bracing himself to concentrate on business again, when he returned his focus back to Melissa. Now the short sleeves of her dress were clinging to her elbows, allowing the front of the dress to expose even more creamy, round, and firm flesh.

He forced himself to cough to get her attention and when he did, his next reaction was impulsive. "Would you like to go for a swim?"

Melissa looked him over as if he were mad. "I hadn't planned on swimming. I thought we were to talk about a schedule?"

He tried keeping his face as serious as possible even while comprehending how ridiculous he must have sounded. Cold water at this point didn't seem so far fetched to him as he needed to calm himself somehow before Miss Beckett returned. "We are here to talk of a schedule. Spontaneity doesn't intrigue you?"

"I wasn't expecting it, I suppose. Besides, I didn't bring suitable clothing." She wasn't ready to swim with her mentor, that involved too much personal contact. Their relationship was supposed to be teacher and student. What was he thinking? "Perhaps another time, when I'm prepared," she responded as she returned his smile.

John couldn't help teasing her some more. "By the way, wearing suitable clothing is just a preference, not a requirement," he told her as the corners of his mouth curved upward and he almost laughed when he noticed her cheeks blushing.

It was frustrating the way he belittled her and thought to get away with it. Not quite sure how to express herself, she spoke the first thoughts that came to her mind. "I thought you were to teach me of racing horses, Lord Blackburn, not the ways of nature."

His expression of surprise was apparent but he was quick, lifting the basket from the blanket. "Shall I fill this basket with water to put out the fire?" he asked in sarcasm, continuing to fuse her.

Oh, he's got a lot of nerve, she thought, especially when he started it. "No, there isn't any fire here," she said.

"I was only jesting. I apologize for taking it out of context."

There was a moment of silence between them before John offered something to drink. "Champagne?" he asked while holding the bottle in one hand and popping the cork with the other. He was trying to occupy himself with anything to distract him from her slipping sleeves.

"Oh," she exclaimed, jumping as the cork popped off. While he poured the champagne, Melissa casually slid both sleeves of her dress back into place, then glanced over at him under dark golden lashes. He was preparing two more glasses of champagne when she couldn't help wondering if the daring action she took to sun herself made him uncomfortable. When his eyes caught hers staring she turned away and commented on a bluebird fluttering through the branches of a tree.

Giving her a genuine smile he held out her glass. "Do you like champagne?" he asked.

"Yes, I suppose so. I've only had it one other time. It tasted sweet and had lots of bubbles, which made my nose tickle," she giggled while touching her nose.

My Forbidden Mentor

His white teeth showed between seductive lips as she took the fluted glass from him. His voice was enticing as he stretched out in the same position as she. "Try it and see," he said.

"Mm, yes, this is the same, better than I remember and just as bubbly," she giggled again.

Laughing with her, she was about to take another sip when he stopped her. "Wait. I think we should make a toast," he suggested, watching her eyes widened in surprise as she nod in agreement. They held their glasses high and John went on. "To...us and our future succeeding accomplishments."

Melissa smiled, feeling happy that her dreams were about to come true. "Hear, hear."

Their glasses clinked together. For a brief second their eyes met while both sipped some champagne. For a moment longer they held each other's gaze over the rim of their glasses when the sound of footsteps approached them.

"Are you two celebrating without us?" Miss Beckett asked playfully as she stood before the blanket they sat on.

John smiled up at Miss Beckett. "Of course not. Here you are." He handed Miss Beckett hers and motioned to Jess to join them.

They both said their thanks and then Miss Beckett requested a toast of her own. With all four glasses in the air, she began. "To...friendship. May it be everlasting." Four glasses of champagne clanged together.

After a short while both Jess and Miss Beckett excused themselves by clearing the disarray of dishes. They both headed for the carriage to look through and discuss more of Jess' books.

Laura Mills

Meanwhile John stood, motioning Melissa to follow his lead. They trailed away, spotting two huge rocks to sit upon at the edge of the stream. As they sat across from each other, John opened his journal so they could carry on with business.

Melissa observed John scrolling through his notes and took the opportunity to linger over his features. He was a handsome man, she couldn't deny that, but he was a handsome man with a title, money and a charismatic personality, every feature needed to attract any number of women he preferred. Melissa imagined there were many and most, she presumed, were beautiful. She found herself attracted to him as well, to everything but his title.

Being born and raised in the country had influenced her established opinion of wealthy people with titles. They used their title to gain superiority, but in Melissa's mind all men and women were created equal. She made an exception for Lord Blackburn, though. There wasn't any doubt of his passion for the teachings of thoroughbreds.

"Melissa, would Mondays, Wednesdays and Fridays work for you?" John asked, lifting his head to hear a response when instead he found her observing him again. "Melissa, what are you thinking about? Apparently not the schedule."

His last question startled her out of her engrossing thoughts. "I, uh, yes, those days you said will suit me."

He cast an odd expression her way, wondering what she was thinking about. "Do you not remember the days I asked about?"

What were they, oh, what were they? Think, think. "Mondays, Wednesdays and Fridays, I believe." Somewhere in her subconscious echoed the days he'd said.

A witty smile reflected on his face. "That's correct. Now tell me what you were really thinking about?"

My Forbidden Mentor

He shocked her with his innate awareness. The partial truth would be better than a complete lie. "Your passion for thoroughbreds," she revealed.

"Interesting. What made you think of that?"

"I realized how much we're alike regarding horses."

"Well, you're right about that, although, I believe we're alike in more ways than one," he commented, turning his attention back to his journal.

Her head tipped to the side, her mouth bearing a teasing smile. "Oh? Observing my qualities, Lord Blackburn, and comparing them with yours?"

His eyes lifted from the book, his smile mirroring hers. "Observing, yes. It's crucial when working together."

She straightened as his remark had piqued her interest. "So, share with me other ways we are alike."

"Are you sure you want to know?" he asked with an arch in his black brow.

"Of course. Why wouldn't I?"

He debated before deciding whether to bring up a subject he knew he shouldn't. "Let me tell you beforehand Melissa, that I am a very honest person and I don't sugarcoat anything. Now do you still want to hear my observations?" He felt better giving her a chance to change her mind.

Why does he sound so serious? "Yes. You have me curious, please share with me."

"Well, first of all, we're both determined. We're both driven by the adrenaline of the race. We have a unique fondness for horses, as you pointed out," he began saying and then hesitated, knowing his next words would impact their relationship, but he believed in being straightforward from the beginning. "Second, we're mutually attracted to each other."

"And why wouldn't we be with all that in common?"

"By mutually attracted, I meant, physically." He studied her reaction, her mouth opening and closing without a sound.

Breathless, she couldn't speak because she knew he was right. They did seem to have an inescapable attraction to each other, and it unnerved her at how easily she weakened around him. They stared for moments longer until Melissa got the courage to move. She stood and stepped away. She was stunned after he spoke such blatant words, even though he had warned her of his honesty. Would they be able to work together, she wondered, after what he had just announced? But she couldn't jeopardize her chance because of some initial physical attraction. They would find some way of clearing this up and move on like they devised to do. Finding her voice, she tried moving on, "Please, I'd prefer to discuss the schedule like we had planned."

He wasn't about to let the subject drop without freeing the tension between them. "Not yet." She swung around to face him. "I also believe you're curious about men and women...together, and I have to admit that your curiosity intrigues me." When her eyes widened in disbelief, he concluded, "Melissa, I'm sorry if I've shocked you, but I believe it to be true."

Jolted from her happy mood, she could barely choke out a reply but managed in defense, "Is this the real reason you're participating in our arrangement? To be intimate together?"

Perturbed that she assumed wrong and took his whole statement out of context, he hadn't replied yet when she ventured on.

My Forbidden Mentor

"I would have preferred you told me from the beginning so you wouldn't have wasted so much of your precious time, Lord Blackburn." Frustration poured out of her being while standing a few feet away, and she went from a state of distress to anger. "I for one have other intentions, like our original arrangement, so please tell me now if I am wasting my time?"

He stood also, towering over her small frame with his hands on his hips. "I cannot help but speak the truth no matter what it is. Obviously you can't handle it and that's why you're acting accordingly. And no, lovemaking is not the reason I'm participating in our arrangement. Anything else I can answer for you?"

Oh, how accurate he could be, but continuing their battle of words would get them angry and nowhere with their schedule, so she conceded and asked about the schedule again. "Can we continue with the schedule, then?"

"First let's resolve this matter," he replied in a demanding tone.

She could feel his hold on her full force now. She had to cooperate if they were to work together. Through a tightened jaw, she responded. "Yes, I am attracted to you. Is that what you want to hear?"

"Good enough. Now let's finish the schedule."

His nonchalant attitude annoyed her. Somehow she would find a way to curb his authoritative position. To prove their physical attraction would not stand in the way of progress she made a suggestion with eagerness. "Can we begin today? After all, it is Friday."

Bending over to pick up his journal, he decided after today's frank conversation they both needed a couple of days to recover. "I had planned to start on Monday as I have business to take care of before then," he answered, shifting to stand before her, clutching his book with one hand.

They stood there staring at each other in contemplation. John was wondering if he'd made a mistake taking on this endeavor and Melissa was questioning her judgment in character.

John's doubts lingered as his gaze drifted over the sheer summer dress flowing along the shape of her body. Sunlight spilling through tree branches from above didn't help to conceal a perfect figure of ample proportions, giving the teacher the wrong ideas about his student.

Melissa grew conscious that their relationship of mentor and student could take the wrong course if they exchanged any more ardent looks like the present one. The palms of her hands began sweating, her heartbeat accelerated, and stirring in her belly was a kindling of intoxicating heat. The boldness of his heavy lidded eyes roaming over her body caused these sensations to form. Damn him, she would not be another prey for him to pounce on, their relationship should reflect only business. Gaining control of her senses she stood tall and proceeded to step closer to him. The necessity to put her training into effect took precedence. "It's early yet. Can you spare some time so we can get started at least?"

Her determination matched his, he noted. To be honest he could work with her today, there was plenty of time left, but her nearness was suffocating him. Strange sensations were taking over, making him feel out of control. "I can't," he regretfully told her.

"Other business, I know," she voiced in a selfish manner, assuming the lust he exposed in his eyes a moment ago was a seductive scheme that failed with her but would be successful with one of his paramours. Yes, that had to be why he rejected her suggestion. Wasn't it just like a lord, a philandering horseman, to always have seduction on his mind? Before he could answer, she let her assumptions take over. "I see you have different kinds of business this afternoon and that is why you hesitated in answering." Her eyes were downcast, glancing at her fumbling fingers, and then she raised them back to his steadied gaze. "Presumably a lady suitor awaiting your presence?" she guessed, amazing herself by talking to him in such a manner but she didn't feel he was better than she, regardless of his status.

Surprised by her speculation he wavered, searching for a reasonable excuse, but it wasn't necessary with her accusation. With narrowing eyes, he made himself plain, "First of all, it's none of your concern what kind of plans I have and with whom. Second, I can't work with you today and that's the end of it. We start on Monday. This conversation is over."

Still facing him with a look of astonishment, a finger came up, poking at his chest as she spoke through tense and tightened lips. "Fine then, if that's the way you want it," she told him, feeling angrier than usual and not understanding why.

She turned to leave after her childish remark but John grabbed her arm. No woman was going to get away with talking to him like that. Time for her first lesson. Swinging her around, instead of quarreling with words, his lips found hers. He wanted to shock her, he supposed, but instead shocked himself.

Taken back, Melissa resisted at first with tightened lips, but then gradually gave in as his mouth moved sensually over hers. Softer and warmer than she imagined, her eyes were closing and her lips were softening to his rhythm of movement. His tongue skillfully probed between her easing lips, expanding them so his tongue could fully engage hers with a light sucking motion. Becoming absorbed in his exploration, there was minimal awareness of his hand gripping the back of her head, his fingers tangling in her silky hair, pressuring her mouth harder against his. Without realizing her voluntary response, her lips pressed with greater force against his, her tongue freely venturing. She heard a groan emerge from John which sent her racing thoughts into a dizzying state. Astounded by the distinct feelings of arousal she was experiencing, in an instant her hands nudged against his chest to stop him.

With reluctance he ended the kiss that was meant as a warning, a kiss that had been impulsive, one that had turned into a pleasurable initiation. His lips stayed close to hers. Their foreheads touched as the heaviness of their breathing intermingled. His voice, velvet and husky, spoke against her trembling lips, "Lord, you taste sweet," he whispered. Just as he had suspected she would.

Confused and frustrated, Melissa pushed against his chest, harder this time, causing John to balance himself as she spit back, "Is this one of your spontaneous notions?" And not waiting for an answer, she headed back for the carriage.

John sighed in deep conflict, deciding to wait before returning back to the carriage for his current predicament was quite visibly evident. He sat on the rock again, pondering about the kiss. What had just taken place? That kiss wasn't supposed to happen. Puzzled by his lustful mind and by her method of producing these reckless reactions from him, he was grateful for the next couple of days away from her. At least by Monday things should be back to normal. By then he would have a clear mind and be able to treat their relationship with proper authority. It was just one kiss, after all, and it didn't mean anything.

On the journey back, John and Melissa stayed silent toward each other, letting Miss Beckett do all the talking, which she joyfully did.

Chapter Seven

Monday morning finally arrived and so did Lord Blackburn. Melissa caught a glimpse of him through the barn doorway as she readied her gelding. He looked magnificent atop a thoroughbred, masculine sleekness and naturally at ease. His expression remained neutral. She had expected a scowl of some sort after Friday's incident, but when she led her gelding outside the barn he appeared calm and even gave her a smile as he rode up to her. She returned his smile, feeling relieved from the nervous tension she'd dealt with the past couple of days. Not only was this her first lesson in racing, it was also starting under awkward circumstances all because of that burning kiss.

"Good morning," John said, sliding off his mare.

"Good morning," Melissa replied, wondering what he was searching for amid the saddle on his mare. "What are you looking for?"

"Ah, here it is. I was afraid I had left my timepiece at home." In his hand, lay a miniature clock nestled within a thin rope of gold chain. He turned toward her, showing her the item. "We wouldn't get far without this today. Shall we get started?"

Melissa gazed at the beautiful timepiece and then toward him. He hadn't made any mention of Friday's episode. Did she worry herself to death over the last two days for nothing? She nodded in agreement and watched him while he went over each characteristic of her gelding. "Is everything all right?" she asked.

My Forbidden Mentor

"Everything is fine. I always check over the horses each time before training," he informed her, his hand sweeping along Thunder's long silvery tail.

"That seems like a good practice," she commented.

"It is, and I'll expect you to do the same in time," he replied.

Melissa carefully watched his procedure, studying the motions of his hands as they skimmed along her gelding's form.

"Why don't you go on and warm up Thunder while I put Clara in the corral?" he suggested while he straightened.

She climbed atop her gelding and was situating herself in the saddle when she heard his voice from behind, "Off you go," he said, and she experienced a stinging sensation on the left cheek of her behind.

Melissa expected him to slap Thunder on the rump but didn't expect to be the one receiving the smack of his hand on her own behind. There wasn't any time to make a remark because Thunder jumped forward into a trot. Melissa's mouth hung open, at the same time reaching her hand back to rub her stinging behind. Thankfully father wasn't around to see that, she winced. I suppose I shall have to confront Lord Blackburn about that kiss and how things like that should never happen again.

As Thunder trotted to the outskirts of her family's land Melissa turned to see John's progress and found a giant grin on his face just as he locked the corral gate. Her focus switched to a field of wild flowers she loved so much. Yes, she thought, it's crucial that I deal with this now before he gets any wrong ideas.

As the morning hours flew by John introduced basic instructions that Melissa soared through. The position of her body while riding needed work, but that was to be expected. John had his own inventive ways for effective positioning and Melissa would be the first student he tested them on.

They brought Thunder back to the barn to cool off and retrieved two fresh horses for a short breather ride. They discussed details of different horse breeds, details that would bore the average person but intrigued them.

Carrying on about horses John thought of how nice it was having a conversation with a woman that understood his passion. It was a nice change of pace from the common conversations of the high society females that usually waited around the track. She was different but what completed her unique personality was her natural beauty, and it was her beauty that stimulated his inner struggle to view her only as his student. Being Monday hadn't changed anything, hadn't made him forget that incredible kiss he experienced, the one she had participated in. In fact, it was all he could do not to glare at her mouth in excess. Still he thought he had acted cool and calm about the situation. Of course, the slap on her behind was meant to shake her nervousness, and it had worked.

When they returned Melissa needed to verify their arrangement to make sure they agreed upon the reality of their situation. To have a relationship with a man, even a fleeting one she noted as she glanced at the profile of her mentor, had not been her top priority, and in the case of her mentor it would no doubt be temporary. She couldn't risk the possible pain she would endure if she let their business arrangement turn intimate and personal. No, she would set him straight now.

They rode at a pace of leisure toward the barn when Melissa cleared her throat to inform him, "Lord Blackburn,

My Forbidden Mentor

I think it's necessary for us to both agree upon our training arrangement," she began and broke off as she took another glance toward him, curious of his reaction. When he didn't respond she continued, "That being strictly professional. I feel it's better that way." He had to know what she was referring to. Figuring his impossible attitude had taken over she faced forward to let her words sink in.

He'd heard what she said but he knew differently. She had responded to him when he kissed her and he couldn't ignore that. Perhaps it was for the better, he thought, not to start anything at all, but it wasn't that simple for him. He'd already had a taste of her and he wanted more. Her obvious innocence required more time so he decided to give her that time, the length of time for training, and then there would no longer be the issue of professionalism standing in the way. He would have his choice of women to keep him otherwise occupied during that time if he wished. "That's fine, we're in agreement," he responded and turning toward her he added out of daring interest, "Is there someone else?"

How utterly bold, she thought. That had nothing to do with what she was talking about. Her gaze was direct with his. "Can't you agree without concerning yourself with matters that are none of your business?" she asked, perturbed.

He cast a fixed look in her direction as the idea of another man showing her the art of lovemaking irritated him, which was what propelled him to ask such a question in the first place. Now he had to answer for it but not before she answered him. "Well, is there?"

She decided to indulge him this time, just so they could move on. "No, I do not have a man in my life. Why you persist in this matter with me I'll never know." She shook her head with a roll of her eyes. Returning her gaze upon him, his conquering smile astonished her, so she added, "Lovemaking is not a top priority in my life as it seems to be in yours." Then she turned away from him as they reached the barn. Proud of her final statement, feeling that he had finally gotten her message, she missed the utter look of shock on his face.

The message he received from her spirited words displayed a very innocent nature that needed some coaxing. Now she had challenged him. "Well that's obvious. Perhaps you should try lovemaking sometime, you might like it."

He was blatant in his response as his piercing eyes challenged her. He always brought her down a peg or two but this time she was ready for him. "And I'd have an accommodating teacher, wouldn't I Lord Blackburn?"

They both stopped their horses for they were back at the barn now. Both stayed seated, sitting there with an intense glare between them. After a moment, Melissa pulled her gelding around so she could face John while their horses nudged muzzles.

"I won't argue with that," he told her and without consciousness his eyes trailed along her body.

"Finally, we agree on something," she was saying but abruptly stopped speaking when her eyes found lust in his through and through as they steadied on her face. "Please stop. Why are you staring at me like that?"

He knew the teasing should stop but it couldn't be helped. "I was wondering if you were chilled?" he said as his eyes fell to her bosom.

After following his focus, her immediate response was to cross her arms over her chest and in continued mortification noticed warmth springing into her cheeks. "Perhaps I am," she answered, unable to get a handle on what was taking place, but when she saw a teasing grin

My Forbidden Mentor

form on his arrogant mouth, she claimed enough energy to carry on like nothing unusual had happened. "As long as we're agreeable on our arrangement, I assume we'll resume training on Wednesday?"

John knew that more than likely arousal was more of a reality for her than being cold. She didn't want to admit it, even if the air temperature they basked in was well warm enough. "Yes, on Wednesday. Does that suit you?" he inquired to make sure. She was quite the spitfire today.

She nodded and they went their separate ways.

Later that same afternoon John and Robert were sitting in a local pub completing their schedules of future races and training sessions for the weeks ahead. Robert poured more brandy into their glasses, noticing how unusually quiet John seemed to be. At first Robert decided not to interfere but then John got testy.

Robert watched as John continued scribbling out a schedule, taking frequent sips of brandy in between. Robert couldn't stand it anymore and had to ask, "What's the frustration?"

John picked up his glass and stared into it, then took another swig. Lifting his eyes to Robert he responded with a half-smile. "You noticed, huh?" feeling the comforting smoothness of the familiar liquid sliding down his throat.

Robert inhaled the fumes of his own glass, filling his mouth with the amber liquid as well. "It's hard not to," he answered, adding, "Of late, you're not pleased with the stable boys, the riders, even the horses you've been looking at."

"Yes, I know," he agreed.

"And now the schedule. What's going on?" Robert and John were always direct with each other.

"I'm not sure exactly," John replied. He'd always been an easygoing person. He always remained calm and collected and never got riled enough to attack anyone verbally unless outright provoked, but presently everything irritated him. One could look at him wrong and he'd fire off. Afterwards he'd be sure to apologize but his reactions proved disturbing, especially to himself.

"Is it the young lass you've been training?" Robert questioned, concerned with his partner's state of mind.

"Could be."

"Well you've never taught a woman before, perhaps you're uncomfortable with it."

"It's more than that Robert. She's different. She understands horses, she's determined, and I'm not sure how to deal with her." He took another swig. "She's my student, yet I think about her often in other ways," he explained, feeling ridiculous to admit that he yearned for her.

"Wanting to mix business with pleasure, huh?" Robert inquired and then commented, "I don't blame you John. From what I've seen of her, she's a beautiful young lady."

John answered with a smile.

"It's obvious you must be thinking about her John. I've never seen you turn away so many women in my life," Robert smiled while trying to cheer him up, knowing this had to be a serious issue for John. He'd never seen him in this sort of predicament before.

It was a mystery to John, knowing he could have his choice of women yet he made no effort to pursue his physical needs. "It's driving me mad. I have no desire to be with other women. And Melissa and I get along so well, until..." he stopped talking as he had revealed more than he had wanted.

"Until?" Robert pursued, not letting John off the hook as he'd already said too much.

"Until it involves sex," John finally said and looked around the pub while casually taking another sip of brandy.

"She doesn't find you charming? I find that hard to believe." Robert chuckled, knowing John could charm his way in any situation if need be.

A sly grin cast across John's lips as his gaze steadied back to Robert. "I don't think that's it, but I'm positive she's still a virgin. I'm thinking that's the reason behind her dramatic reactions."

"What have you done, John? Or tried to do?" Robert asked, the anticipation paining him.

"Not much except kissed her once, and the odd thing is I was angry with her when I did it. I wanted to strangle her pretty little neck." Frustration creased his features at the memory.

"Strangling her is not going to get results John." Robert smiled, feeling true compassion for his best friend.

"Well, I've decided to be professional about this and if after her training the attraction remains, well, who knows." Even as he said the words, their meanings weren't solid.

"John, are you brooding because she's a virgin?" Robert asked as his brow arched in curiosity. Robert on occasion had experienced the art of deflowering, but John had not.

"Of course not. After all, I have you to refer to if I have any inquiries," he said with a devious smile.

Robert filled with excitement. "So are you planning on deflowering Miss Howard?"

John's smile changed to a frown. "Robert, her virginity is of no consequence to me and truly I do not plan to be intimate with her." He let out an exasperated breath of air. "I can't be it wouldn't be very professional."

"But you want to. You want to so badly you can taste it, I can tell. And this is the whole reason for your outrageous attitude, isn't it?" Robert beamed proudly when he was confident that he had come up with the conclusion.

"I won't deny wanting her, but it's out of the question. I just have to come to terms with it." A vision of Mr. Howard flashed before him. The awkward request he had of John flooded his mind but John didn't feel anything had changed outside of wanting to bed his daughter because he found her attractive. Certainly his personal feelings toward Melissa hadn't changed, just the physical part, and the physical part he could control.

"Well you need to find some kind of release, old chap. It's not like you to bite everyone's head off."

"Yes, I know, I'm working on it. She caught me off guard, that's all." John seemed satisfied that he had solved his dilemma.

While John took another swig of his drink, Robert leaned forward as if to emphasize his next point. "Who are you fooling, John? That young lady's got a noose around your neck and it's getting tighter every day. I'd like to meet this little tamer."

John about choked on his drink and replied with an arch in his brow above widened eyes. "Noose? Tamer? Robert, I think you've gone mad. Like I said, we get along except for the issue of sex, so if that issue is out of the question there shouldn't be any problems, right?" Robert was right, John realized, he was fooling himself.

Robert reclined in his chair. "Well, my best friend, it looks like you've got everything under control. There's just one more thing?"

"What's that?" John asked, getting frustrated again.

"What about Vanessa? She's not going to be easy to turn away."

"True enough. I'll deal with her when the time comes. She has other suitors to keep her busy," he concluded.

"Not for long. You're her favorite, remember?"

Emptying the remainder of brandy in his mouth, he repeated to Robert, "Like I said, I'll deal with her when the time comes."

"I hear you, but you need to make a decision about this lass you're obsessing over. I don't want to lose my best friend to insanity."

"I know." he said, smiling at his good friend.

"Well, I have a late engagement," he said as he lifted from the chair.

"Rose?"

"Yes, lovely Rose. Until tomorrow then?"

"It will have to be tomorrow evening, I'll be training Miss Howard tomorrow most of the day," John informed him.

"Miss Howard? You're behaving more professional by the moment," Robert said as he strode toward the door chuckling. "Tomorrow night, then."

"Ha, ha," John replied to Robert's bantering. He reached for the almost empty bottle of brandy and poured the remainder into his glass, determined to finish every last drop, and then he ordered another bottle.

John kept wondering why on earth he drank himself into oblivion, and on a weeknight when he knew what his schedule entailed. With one hand on the reins, the other rubbing his face, he tried erasing the stagnant fog that swam around in his head. Topping it off were the daggers piercing his eyes. His hand lifted to his forehead to shield against the bright morning sky. Cursing every movement that made his head pound at what seemed like the bumpiest ride he'd ever had on Clara, he groaned at the invisible hammer hitting his head and began cursing at Clara when she stepped into a pothole. Without delay he apologized to his mare. It wasn't her fault that he'd let himself be an empty well for alcohol last night. His squinted focus spotted a figure standing in the near distance, a golden- haired figure, and the answer became clear, the only thing clear at the moment. She was the culprit. This was her fault.

But when he arrived by her side, still sitting atop Clara, he looked down into her faultless hazel eyes and realized this hangover was his own fault. Being careful not to snap at her he returned her cheerful smile, as best he could, envious of her happy mood.

"Good morning. Isn't it a glorious morning, Lord Blackburn?" she said, eager to get started with her next lesson.

"Glorious? I don't know," he started to say, leaving his sentence unfinished due to the stabbing pain in his head from moving to get off his horse.

He caught sight of Melissa launching toward him. He rested against his mare for support, feeling her warm hand on his arm. His clouded gaze went to her hand and he heard her say, "Are you all right? What's wrong with you?"

He swallowed, mustering up enough control to appear normal. Standing straight, her hand fell away, and for that he was grateful. The warmth from her hand seemed too inviting. He gave her another smile. "I'm fine. I just moved too fast and everything got hazy for a moment," he explained and took out his timepiece from the saddle, taking hold of it in one hand while his other hand came up as a shield once again. "I'm quite fine. Are you ready, then?" he asked, feeling honored that she would worry so much about him.

She studied him some more and without a doubt was not convinced. "Yes, I'm ready, but I don't believe you're all right."

Was he that obvious? "Why not?" he said with a razor edge to his voice, desiring only to be in his cozy bed at the moment and not being asked twenty questions. He'd much rather be sleeping off this horrendous hangover than discussing his pain with her.

"There's no need to get short with me, my lord. I can't help it if you look as bad as you feel."

"Thank you for that," he told her with sarcasm, leading Clara to the corral.

Melissa followed him to the gate. "I didn't mean that literally. All I meant was, well, your eyes for example." With hands on hips, she regarded his movements as he strode past her in slow motion.

He grabbed the reins on her gelding and began leading him out to the fields. "What's wrong with my eyes, Melissa?"

He heard nothing until she fell in step with him on the opposite side of her gelding. "It's apparent you're having trouble seeing this morning. You've been squinting ever since you arrived. What happened to you?"

That was a good question, he thought. The answer always seemed to stem from a particular young lady. "I can see fine, it just hurts to do so this morning. I'll be better tomorrow."

"Do you have some kind of eye illness?" she asked, unaware of how minor his sickness really was.

"No."

A breath of frustration burst out at his short and direct reply. "Why is it always so hard to get a detailed answer from you?" she asked with a rise in her voice.

"Good lord, please keep your voice down," he lashed out, letting the reins drop and stopping to put his fingertips on his temples to apply pressure.

She came around to face him, filled with frantic concern. "John, you're scaring me."

"Well, you remembered my name," he said, a light chuckle escaping his lips, and even that hurt. Both hands came up to shield his eyes that found hers. "Melissa, I have a hangover," he confessed, expecting her to rage at him when all she showed was more concern.

"Hangover? How much did you drink?"

"Enough to regret getting out of bed this morning," he responded in a low pitch.

"Perhaps you should have rested, John. I would have understood."

Her attitude surprised him. Something had put her in a good mood and he wondered what? Here he was blaming her for his rough behavior and she treated him like she cared. Boy, his professionalism was starting off top notch. Wouldn't Robert laugh in his face right about now? He needed to face his demons and make it through the day. "Melissa, I did this to myself. I shall suffer the consequences. Now, did you examine Thunder like I did on Monday?"

Melissa strolled back around the opposite side of Thunder, biding her time in answering him.

His head bent forward, looking around Thunder so he could see her face. "Did you?"

"You said in time I would have to, so no, I have not," she told him.

John straightened. "Come here," he requested while he motioned with the crook of a finger.

They proceeded to go step by step together through the process, and afterward Melissa was glad she had because she learned a lot. There were many details John had pointed out that she wouldn't have thought to look for. His astute knowledge regarding horses clarified that she could learn a lot from him, and because of that, he'd become a very important person in her life.

Chapter Eight

The progress of their sessions claimed to be as successful as the previous. Melissa proved to be the most impassioned student John had ever taught, never failing to amaze him with the speed with which she learned. Beyond question she listened, concentrated, and then carried out the task he'd given her. She'd practice and practice until mastering his instructions. Even the weather cooperated. The skies of passing days were clear and blue, presenting few white puffs of clouds and allowing volumes of sunrays to warm the earth beneath their feet.

The work was strenuous for both though, and the repetition it took to reach perfection was never-ending, still John was right by her side, correcting every mistake along the way as Melissa repeated routines over and over until John was satisfied for the day.

"Tilt your head forward. Tuck your body tighter," John shouted.

She adjusted her weight, tucking her body as he instructed, and it seemed to improve her time. Now it was a matter of concentrating on everything at once.

"Get your behind higher and get your weight in the air. You should know that," he told her, getting used to the snide looks she gave him from time to time.

They ran through the routine once more before Melissa rode in, panting almost as much as her gelding.

"Tired?" John asked, knowing full well she was. She had worked extra hard today and it had been an unusually warm day.

My Forbidden Mentor

She responded with an exhausted, "Yes."

"Why didn't you say so?" he asked, teasing her while she followed him with haggard steps toward the barn.

"I don't suppose you would have let me rest?" she responded, walking alongside him now, giving him a look that said she knew better.

"You're right. You know the routine much too well. I'll have to change it around so I can catch you off guard," he said smiling.

"You would," she said, returning his smile as she opened the barn doors so he could lead her gelding inside.

After brushing Thunder down John suggested they go for a short ride to break from routine. Melissa chuckled at his implication and then agreed. They saddled Clara and Laurel and were off into the fields again.

They always found something to talk about. The majority of the time it was horses but today it was plants and flowers. Melissa stopped when spotting wild berries in the near distance. She jumped off her mare and strolled over to them in delight. Handing the first bunch to John, she picked another for herself. They headed back toward her home eating the sweet berries while continuing their previous conversation.

At a break in their exchange, Melissa noticed John's darkened lips and began giggling. She stuck her tongue out at him to show off the darkened tongue she knew she had. He copied her action. It turned into a game of tease and tag as Melissa reined her mare closer to John and his mare. Reaching over with one hand she jabbed at his arm, her mouth curving into a wide smile of joy. She tried to pull away but John was quick. His hand grabbed her arm to stop her, pulling her close to him again. Her smile waned when she realized he planned an attack of tickling as, unfortunately, she was very ticklish. His hand kept its grip and at the same time his fingers touched the sides of her waist enough to make her squirm and jolt. Her blast of laughter caused him to laugh as well.

"Stop it, John," she said in the middle of a hearty roar.

Of course he didn't. He was having a good time, her protests didn't sound very serious and besides, she had started it. "Why should I stop when it's obvious you're enjoying yourself?"

She jerked back and forth, trying to get away, but she was no match for his strength. "It's not funny anymore," she claimed in a belt of laughter.

"Are you sure? You're still laughing," he said, easing off. His eyes casually drifted down from her face, catching the luscious sway of her bosom, and he realized that if he didn't stop their child's play it would turn into lascivious play for him.

There lay a hint of guilt in his glance toward her eyes, which smiled at him, a charming gaze that gave him a very distinctive look of approval. She was making it extremely difficult to remain professional. Whether her innocence made her unaware or not, her signals were clear: she was thinking about him as much as he was thinking about her.

Why couldn't they have met under different circumstances? Even though he wouldn't change her personality one bit, he would like to change the fact that he was her mentor. His position stood in the way of all they could offer each other personally, intimately. He groaned in silent misery. Tonight he would have those delicious dreams of her again. Only dreams.

My Forbidden Mentor

"I'm laughing because it can't be helped," she said and paused, because all of a sudden his actions ceased. His hand left her side and she noticed his demeanor had changed in an instant. "Thank you," she told him and a wide grin appeared on her face. "Now it's your turn. Are you ticklish?" she inquired.

He would have loved to continue their child's play but it couldn't go on. If she touched him at all right now he would explode. Then she reached over to touch the sides of his ribs. In a gentle motion he grabbed her by the wrist, stopping her. "It won't affect me, so don't even try," he informed her, giving a slight smile.

She couldn't understand his attitude change. One minute they laughed like children, the next he got serious. It seemed all right for him to have fun but not her. "You're not playing fair, John. I almost fell off my horse with laughter and I can't even try to get the same result with you?"

He let go of her wrist. Good lord, she had no clue of the result she already produced in him, but he needed to give her the benefit of the doubt. "I don't tickle easily like you Melissa. You would get frustrated in your attempts."

"Just let me try? Perhaps no one has found that special place yet," she said with honest intentions.

He agreed that her touches would be different, but it wouldn't tickle, it would feel good, too good to have her fingers on his body. "Melissa, no. It's not a good idea," he said.

Bafflement appeared on her face. "Why are you so serious all of a sudden?" she asked.

He reined away, unable to face her inquisitions. He did not answer right away as he wasn't quite sure what to say and so they proceeded to the barn.

She studied his profile, trying to figure out what had gone wrong. "John, what did I do to upset you?"

He looked over at her, purple lips and all. "You didn't do anything, Melissa." He looked away, his teeth grinding together. He should tell her something. On an expelled breath, his focus shifted back to her and he confessed, "It's my own fault for having thoughts I shouldn't."

Her face held an expression of further confusion. "I don't understand."

He gave her a tender grin. "It's not important. I'll race you the rest of the way."

She smiled back and replied with, "You're on."

They hadn't had far to go, but John let her win anyway. Although she kept up, he would have beaten her. He pretended everything was fine again, when deep inside a storm of hellish proportions circulated within him. What was he going to do about Melissa?

The two-day break between their sessions helped his sanity but the tension escalated once more when Monday morning arrived. At least training had gone well as they had both concentrated on getting record speeds. John encouraged and pushed, Melissa accomplished and surpassed.

At the end of the day John and Melissa were in the barn brushing down their horses. As they finished, Melissa asked John about the plans he had for purchasing future thoroughbreds. Melissa listened with intense concentration while leaning against a bale of stacked hay, her fingers holding a single piece of hay between her lips. John continued to talk as he stood across from her, taking off his

My Forbidden Mentor

shirt. Sweat had beaded upon his chest, making his skin glisten. He tossed the shirt on a nearby bale of hay, removing next the leather tie holding his hair together. Bending over at the waist, his hands rested on his strong thighs as he shook debris loose from his long black hair.

Melissa suppressed a groan as she watched his fluid movements. Whipping his hair back his eyes met hers, shimmering gray piercing through her. She couldn't help but stare in unconcealed fascination. "I've never seen you with your hair unbound. You look quite different," she told him, placing the single piece of hay back into her mouth.

"How so?" he asked as he was striding over to her with purpose.

"It's very reckless looking," she purred. Seduction sprang in her eyes while being hypnotized by this tall and dark man stepping toward her. Her words were out before she could retract them. His actions told her he hadn't mistaken her meaning.

"Is that so? Should I act the part?" he asked, positioning his arms around her as his knees were bending in order to lift her. Carrying her up the ladder to the hayloft, her protest didn't put a dent in his progress.

"John, what are you doing? Put me down," she exclaimed, snapping back to reality, unaware of her arms wrapping around his neck for balance.

"I want to show you the view from up here," he said, revealing a devilish grin.

When they reached the top of the loft he set her on her feet, then plopped himself on the dusty wooden floor, leaning his back against a bale of hay. His long legs stretched out wide so she could sit between them. His hand touched the floor, motioning her over. "Come here and sit with me," he said.

Reluctantly she sat between his buckskin thighs with her back facing him.

Leaning forward his mouth whispered in her ear, "You've lost your piece of hay."

Her fingers went to her mouth, realizing how observant he was when she hadn't noticed. She wanted to turn and look at him but the heat from their closeness stalled her actions. As it was the close proximity of how they were sitting seemed a little too comfortable and much too dangerous.

"Now isn't that a spectacular view?" she heard him say, jarring her attention. A long finger pointed toward the window view of lush green rolling hills and flourishing oak and mulberry trees as far as the eye could see.

"Yes it is," she replied as they both stared into the never-ending landscape. Both remained immersed in their own peaceful thoughts until Melissa mentioned her mother. "I often come up here to think. Sometimes when I miss my mother it helps bring back the happy memories. She used to ride all over those hills," she said, her fingers gesturing in the direction she spoke.

"How long has it been since she passed away?" John asked.

There was a moment of hesitation before Melissa responded, as if a few joyous memories had relived themselves in her mind, producing a smile on her lips as a result. "Approximately three years ago," she told him.

"You miss her a great deal, I can tell," John responded and spoke with complete understanding.

His tenderness made her aware of his nearness again. She could feel his warm breath teasing her cheek. "Yes, I do. There's so much more I wanted to tell her and talk to her about," she shared. If her mother were alive she could

My Forbidden Mentor

talk to her about anything, including her handsome mentor, but instead she had to go on instinct. Her mind was telling her it was wrong to be this close to him, but her heart was telling her to open up and take him in, body and soul. Her mind was winning because she knew nothing of his feelings for her.

"I know what you mean," John said as they both kept their watchful gazes toward the wide-open view. "My mother's been gone eighteen years and it still saddens me to think about her not being here any longer."

"What about your father? It must be hard on him as well?" Melissa inquired.

"I suppose," he agreed and then reevaluated his answer. "To be honest, I wouldn't know. I'm not very close to my father," he concluded and his roughened tone didn't go unnoticed.

"Do you have brothers and sisters?"

"No. Do you?" he responded.

"No," she answered. "It seems we have a lot more in common than horses. We both have lost our mothers and we both are only children, although I wouldn't have been an only child if my brother had lived, but because he died at birth I consider myself one," she told him as her fingers tangled within each other.

"Your parents didn't try for more children?" John asked.

"No. I think the death of my brother was too much to bear. After that my mother got involved in women's rights. It took over her life," she told him as a bit of disheartenment sounded in her voice. "She even had meetings at our house. A great number of women would show up and, believe it or not, a few men, mainly husbands that supported their wives, including my father," she explained while her eyes took in the wildflowers dancing in the distance.

"And you were allowed to attend these meetings?" he questioned.

Melissa chuckled softly, "Of course. I am a woman after all," she teased.

His voice turned deep and husky. "Yes, but at the time you would have been a girl," he said, taking a strand of her hair and twirling it in gentle motions. "Could you interpret the full meaning behind the proposed actions?" he asked.

Was he referring to women's rights or something else? Something sinful, something pleasurable? Didn't she wish it were that way? Without realizing her words were testing, she played along with his bantering. "I understood enough, and when the girl became a woman, I understood even more," she said, watching the same wildflowers continuing to wave back and forth.

She missed the wicked grin he now displayed, keeping her face averted from his, but the blush on her cheeks revealed another side, her naive side. Her innocence taunted him, urging him to discover hidden parts of her.

Everything with Melissa seemed to be a first. She loved horses as much as he. She was able to coerce him into any task, whether he approved or not. She made him roar with laughter more often than he remembered in the past. She also created a desire in him so strong the strain of it lingered, lingered and simmered. But their mentor-student relationship froze all intimate actions. Still, could she be the first to make him fall in love? Now why had love involved itself in this picture? It was natural to want to be intimate with a beautiful woman, especially when he'd gone so long without one, and he was spending so much time with Melissa it seemed instinctive to desire her. "Is that so?" he said, leaning closer with his mouth inches away from her ear. "Care to share your knowledge with me?"

Melissa started to shake. She kept telling herself it was the brisk breeze coming in from the open lookout and not from his fingers playing with her hair. "Are we talking about women's rights?" she quietly challenged.

His voice remained deep, possessing a silken tone. "I don't know, are we?"

Her eyes shut to endure the heat from his heavy breathing, which was blistering the side of her face. Her voice came out breathless, "I assumed we were, but you seemed to indicate something else?"

"Did I?" he breathed into her ear.

She turned to look over her shoulder when she realized how close he remained. His fingers let go of her hair to comb through his own loose mane. Melissa's breath caught in her throat. He was concentrating solely on her and it was a look of true interest and something forbidden. His examination included every part of her face and then settling on her trembling lips. It couldn't be helped that her eyes did their own analyzing. He's so handsome, she thought, knowing she was wrong for wanting to feel his mouth on hers. Being together frightened her and tempted her at the same time. Her focus hesitated on his perfect, full lips. Will he kiss me?

But he didn't make a move, and in the next moment their eyes caught and time stood still.

Chapter Nine

A cool breeze whipped across their faces, swirling down over them. Melissa's hands went to her chilled arms, rubbing them briskly in response to the cold that raced over her.

Aware of her motions, John reclined into the bale of hay. "Lean back," he commanded.

She leaned forward to think about it. What would happen if he touched her? Twisting to look at him, his hands were supporting his head, which was tilted against a bale of hay, and his eyes, well, you couldn't ignore his half-closed, glistening eyes. He waited in silence and she faced forward again. Am I reading too much into this? But his lingering stare was different this time, there was genuine hunger in those gray eyes of his. How could she mistake the look in his eyes? Her eyes found his again. "What are we talking about here, John?"

His lips curved into a lazy grin. His hands came free from behind his head, allowing his fingers to motion her toward him. "You're cold. Let me warm you," he suggested.

"Answer me first," she said while running her hands up and down her chilled arms.

"After you come here. You've got goose bumps, for heaven's sake," he responded with an impatient tone.

Her eyes narrowed in response while scooting closer to him. Her back slid into his bare, muscular chest with a snug cozy fit. The heat from his body radiated into hers and still she shook.

"Would you relax?" he told her, taking her hands in his and placing them on his buckskin-covered thighs.

Her fingers dug into the material, her eyes shutting when absorbing the texture. A light gust whipped around her again, filling her nostrils with the scent of his masculine sweat. Initially her body jerked and her eyes flashed open when his hands touched her arms, but then her body eased into the slow motion stroking that he applied to her arms.

"I'm not going to do anything you don't want to do," he said in a quiet voice behind her ear.

She stiffened while his hands completely embodied her arms. Those long fingers of his extended down to reach her clutching hands, then in slowing progress they would trail back up to her shoulders.

This is too much, Melissa thought, watching the sliding motion of his fingers, knowing it would be too easy for him to warm the rest of her body if she let him. "What does that mean exactly?" she asked, wishing he'd give her a straight answer once and for all. As if reading her mind, a dense heat developed against her buttocks. Her naivety wasn't so much not to know that his body was having a reaction to hers. A masculine reaction. She had gotten her answer even if he hadn't verbalized it.

As much as he tried to hold back and not get excited, his body had other ideas. He was sure she could feel him, feel his body responding to hers. His control was getting worse. He hadn't been with a woman since the day he met Melissa, which was hard enough to fathom. He'd had plenty of opportunities but a particular student of his had claimed all of his attention.

His hands trailed over her arms again, feeling her skin, which was smooth like satin. Getting caught up in his adventure, he kept remembering the way she looked into his eye's moments ago, making her signals seem so apparent. He could tell that she wanted him, but her inexperience left it up to him to control their momentum. He'd restrained himself long enough without touching her, and now with just the stroking of her arms, he needed to touch more, if only to bring her pleasure this time. It would be enough to satisfy his initial curiosity.

His fingers lifted strands of hair away from her neck. He leaned forward as his hands were drifting down to the sides of her breasts and touched his lips to the side of her neck. Leaving a soft kiss, he then whispered in her ear, "It means I've been thinking a lot about you, Melissa. In intimate ways," he confided.

His kiss on her neck created a whole new sensation, one that streamed down from where his lips touched to the depths of her nervous stomach. His hands, now cupping her clothed breasts, tempted the next words she spoke. "And I of you," she finally admitted on a shaky breath, feeling bold and unsure at the same time, caught up in disbelief that she had admitted to him the same kind of thoughts he'd had.

A silky sensation coursed through his body when he heard confirmation of their mutual desires. His hands closed over her bosom and squeezed. He heard her moan and watched her eyes close in response. Her fingers dug deeper into his thighs and her head fell back against his shoulder. "I want to feel them naked," he whispered along the arch of her neck.

Her breathing escalated at his request and she couldn't answer. Without any verbal disapproval from her, his fingers began unbuttoning her top. "So many... buttons," he muttered, out of breath.

The rising in her chest increased as buttons came undone. When he started opening her top shivering cool air touched her skin, causing her eyes to open and her hands to clasp over his. "Perhaps we should stop?" she suggested, not wanting to, but was she ready for this? She needed to stop this. She wouldn't be that easy for him.

He'd already had a glimpse and wanted to explore the curves of her figure, so with coaxing words he persuaded, "Relax, trust me." He took a light nip at her earlobe. "I just want to feel you," he said.

While analyzing her reasons to give in or stop, his hands beneath hers began fondling her exposed bosom, sending waves of tingling sensations that spread down to her thighs and making them quiver. That shooting pain of desire from his teasing fingers had made the decision for her. She wanted to sample what he had to offer.

As soon as her hands released their grip, he gained a better grasp and groaned in approval.

Melissa closed her eyes when hearing him groan, losing herself to the warmth of his hands. They began breathing in unison, reaching higher levels of excitement and agony in this unforgettable moment that only they would share.

Even though there were no words spoken, her moans of pleasure directed him to advance, knowing she was drinking in every detail of this experience. His right hand drifted down to place itself between her legs. When he tried cupping the curved shape of her he heard her sigh, which made his caressing fingers grab at the hem of her skirt and bunch it around her waist. He could feel her eyes watching him with curiosity and he saw that her legs were trembling from his exploratory touch. It was then he commanded, "Open for me."

Melissa froze at his request. This is really happening, this is not a dream.

Laura Mills

"I want to pleasure you Melissa," he said with a voice growing hoarse. "Only with my fingers," he reassured her.

She was shaking inside as her mind shouted to stop any proceeding actions for it would just bring an unwanted outcome, but her heart screamed that her attraction to this man, her mentor, went beyond mere interest. She'd become emotionally attracted to this man as well as physically. Enjoying the pleasure he was giving her at the moment made that realization abundantly clear. His seductive ways made it impossible to resist.

Her eyes closed and her body shuddered to every burning sensation he caressed into her. She didn't sound like herself when a deep moan of pleasure escaped her throat. Her body wasn't behaving normally when her fingers ingrained themselves into his thighs. Losing control, her head tipped back against his shoulder with force. His probing fingers were magic.

John comprehended the change in her body. His face brushed through her long golden hair, inhaling its scent while shutting his eyes to take in all the new wonders of her. His mouth found her ear, sending a blaze of heat with the one word he murmured, "Melissa."

Her closed eyes fluttered and her mouth parted at the way he spoke her name. Gasping breaths came faster. Feeling defeated, her hips began to move with his rhythmic strokes. She prayed in silence for John not to stop, never stop this wonderful sensation.

"Yes," John whispered in response. She was sultry and responsive to every movement he evoked.

Melissa submerged, becoming mystified by his touches. He had control over her whole body. Profound pleasure came from everywhere his fingers aroused. What is he doing? I've never felt anything like this. "John?" she started to ask in a moaned tone of bewilderment, but was unable to finish for her body drowned out any more speech ability, sending her into a spiral of floating waves.

"That's it, kiss me," he told her. She started to turn toward him and, sensing her loss of concentration, he lunged forward, taking her mouth with his. Able to stifle both of their groans, he continued to kiss her. He stopped only when she relaxed.

"What just happened?" she asked, fascinated. "I never imagined...I didn't know if I could take much more," she admitted.

His handsome mouth grinned, knowing she could and she would when the time was right. "That's just the beginning, sweetheart."

Although she couldn't deny the pleasure she had just experienced, she'd let it go too far. Now it wouldn't be the same. It couldn't be, not after this, certainly not if they had...joined. This wasn't proper. He was her mentor and she was his student. It should be nothing more than business between them. "Oh dear, this should never happen again," she said aloud, lifting his hands from her waist and leaning forward to button her top.

John slid his knees into a bent position, surrounding her. "What do you mean?" he asked, confused by her sudden change of mood.

She was still fumbling with her buttons when she answered him, "I don't want to go beyond the beginning...because I shouldn't."

His arms lay relaxed over his bent knees. "Aren't you even curious?" he asked, finding it hard to believe she didn't find pleasure a moment ago.

She was tightening the strings on her drawers, in awe at his response, when she replied, "Please don't make me answer that."

John leaned forward having his face parallel with hers. Speaking in a softened tone he asked her, "Melissa, what happened? A minute ago everything was fine."

She stared into his face longer than she should have and then finally responded, "A minute ago I lost myself to a brief moment of passion, but it was wrong."

The tilt of his head caused long strands of hair to fall across his shoulder, unknowing of the temptation it brought about. "Tell me why it's wrong?" he inquired.

He looked so serious but also seductive with his hair unbound, it was all she could do to keep her fingers from drowning in that black satin of his. "Our relationship is strictly business, John. It was a mistake," she told him.

His fingers reached over to place a loose strand of hair behind her ear. "I don't see it as a mistake," he informed her in a tender voice.

He was so calm. How could he be so calm about this? And he needs to stop touching me, she thought as she pushed herself up from the ground to stand. Turning around to face him, she tried to explain, "John, I'm innocent in these matters," she began, trying to keep her fingers from tangling in nervous tension. "Very innocent, which I'm sure you've figured out by now," she said and then hesitated. Although she became uncomfortable with what they were discussing, she was learning to be straight forward with him as he had always been with her. "I'm embarrassed by how I acted with you," she told him on a sigh of relief.

He looked into her eyes laced with confusion while his arms were hugging his knees and his hands were clasped together "Melissa, please don't feel that way. It should be pleasurable. An orgasm is meant to be pleasurable."

Her eyes widened. "An orgasm? It must not be common for women. I've never heard them discuss it," she told him.

He shrugged upon explaining, "Some women don't have them. It depends on how caring a man is toward a woman's pleasures. Even when a man tries, a woman still may not have one," he explained, and then gave her a seductive smile. "You certainly don't have trouble having one," he told her.

Melissa wrapped her arms around her waist, mainly because she was feeling naked standing above him while he sat there gazing at her, but the breeze pouring through the hayloft, stirring up sprigs of hay didn't help either. "Don't tease me John. This is not a laughing matter," she said in all seriousness.

His gaze drifted over the curves of her body before his eyes settled on hers. "I'm not laughing Melissa. I was being serious. It gave me pleasure when you had an orgasm."

"I'm glad you're caring enough to think of my pleasure, but I still think it shouldn't happen again John," she responded and then suddenly sank to her knees, pleading with him, "John, the ways you made me feel...it..." Her eyes briefly shut as she was catching her breath, "It scared me and I felt out of control."

His hands went to her face, cupping her cheeks. "Don't let it scare you Melissa. Please don't let it scare you. Your body was experiencing the pleasures between a man and woman. Why would you deny your body those pleasures?"

His hands were so warm. Her eyes shut once more, knowing she would never feel his hands on her like this again, knowing she could live for his touch for a lifetime if it were possible, but their situation made it impossible. Her eyes opened to find him studying her. "John, don't you understand? You're the first man to touch me that way. I'm very confused by what's going on. All I know is that it's got to stop between us. You and I, we can't go any further touching like that."

The tone of his voice sounded stern, despite the softness of his features. "What's really scaring you Melissa? For a woman as confident and determined as you are...is it because you're a virgin?"

It didn't surprise her that he'd guessed her a virgin. Talking about it in the open surprised her though and if things were different, she wished John to be her first. "It's not about my virginity John," she said as her hands reached up to take his from her face. He grasped her hands in his before she could let go. "It's about my feelings," she told him, focusing on their holding hands.

"Feelings?" John inquired.

Her eyes met his. "It's more than physical with me John. I can't just be intimate with you," she began but was unable to finish due to her father's inquisitive voice. Her father had arrived home earlier than usual.

"Melissa?" her father called from the house again.

Melissa tore away from John and started to shake. "Oh no," she said in a panic.

Feeling a little nervous himself, John stood. "Go to him," he told her but before she got away he grasped her arm to stop her. "This conversation is not over."

"It needs to be John. Let's just forget this ever happened, please?" she begged while trying to break from his grasp.

Even though her words pleaded, her eyes told a different story. In her eyes he saw the truth. "I can't forget. How can you?" he asked, and leaned into her. "I don't have any regrets Melissa I hope you don't," he made clear as he released her arm when he heard her father's voice again.

"Melissa, are you out there?" Mr. Howard hollered.

"Hurry up and go to him. We'll talk later," John said, and began picking out pieces of hay from his hair.

She skimmed down the ladder, asking herself, what have we done?

John hadn't planned on what happened, it just did and he wasn't regretful about it. He watched Melissa dash down the ladder, on the way brushing her skirt straight and checking her top and then smoothing her hair as she walked out to greet her father.

Once John reached the bottom of the ladder he grabbed for his shirt and slipped it on, thankful that he still had his pants on. The palms of his hands skimmed over his thick mane of hair that had turned wild and he tamed it with a leather tie. He was feeling like a young lad again by his having to sneak around. It was almost dreamlike, but the reality of her pushing him away, only made him want her more.

He was saddling his mare when Melissa returned. Her arms were lying against her back and her fingers entwined as she walked up next to him, whispering, "It's safe now. Father just wanted to know how it was going with training and if you'd like to join us for supper."

He smiled as he was tightening the saddle straps, his eyes meeting hers. "Tell your father that training went very well and that includes my personal session with his daughter," he told her as he was looking her over with a wide grin.

His grin faded significantly when her eyes narrowed on him. "John, I was serious about what just happened. How can you treat this so casually?" she asked, and when he gave no reply and just stared at her, Melissa made assumptions of her own. "This is not hard for you, is it? You treat it casually because that's all it is to you. You made me have an orgasm so now you've raised your male pride a notch. Is that how it is?" Her hands went to her hips as if readying for a fight.

His full lips tightened and his eyes narrowed as well. How dare she accuse me of something so ridiculous? He tugged tighter on the saddle straps, giving his mare a short jerk. His eyes pierced into hers. "I'm not going to respond to your outrageous accusations," he told her and began leading Clara through the barn to outside.

Melissa watched the back of his tall form leaving. Her hands fell from her hips, clenching into balled fists at her sides. His walking away perturbed her more than anything. "Answer me John. I want to know the truth." Still there was no response as he continued toward the barn doors. By now she was spitting nails. By ignoring her he had definitely gotten her attention. "I'm thankful we didn't go any further. It would have been the worst mistake of my life," she shouted, practically regretting her words as she spoke them, but they did serve to stop him in his tracks.

In a quiet voice that Melissa couldn't quite hear, John finally spoke. "Shall we find out?" he mumbled, not meaning for her to hear what he'd said, but if she happened to hear it, oh well. She had pushed him to the limit, a limit he didn't like dealing with because he might say some damaging words to her, and that was the reason he had stayed silent, but she had kept up and was forcing him to respond.

Her impatience got the better of her. She knew he had said something but not what. She pushed further, "What was that? I didn't hear you," she inquired and was witness to his state of frustration as his hands were wiping with rough motions over his face followed by an audible sound of irritation. He started turning around to face her when his name was spoken in a heightened tone, loud enough to be heard outside.

"John, why won't you answer me?"

John dropped the reins to his horse and headed toward Melissa with purpose in his stride, ending up inches away from her. "Will you lower your voice? Your father will hear you," he ordered, at the same time motioning with his hand in the direction of her house. "We will talk about this but not right now, not today. Another time when we have privacy."

Her face remained stern, but he was right. Her father couldn't know what had happened. "All right," she answered.

As she agreed his features softened. "Give your father my apologies regarding supper please," he said, staring into her eyes for a minute longer. "I must be off. I'll see you Wednesday," he told her and retrieved Clara before leaving the barn.

Chapter Ten

The very next day Melissa was on her way to John's country manor. She had tossed and turned all night thinking about a resolution and had decided that waiting until Wednesday to talk to him may be too late for what she had planned. The quicker they resolved this issue the better. They had serious training to continue with.

She had been to his place one time and hoped she remembered how to get there. As she came around a group of bushy trees the landscape opened up and in the near distance she saw three groups of stables that could only belong to John. As she reined in her gelding along the stone drive to his manor, the splendid bodies of thoroughbreds parading the corrals distracted her. Her original intentions were forgotten as she admired John's beautiful horses, but by the time she arrived at the front door, anxious anticipation had set in again. What kind of resolution would they come to? Would courage remain with her if she were forced to find another trainer? She slid off her gelding and tied him to a sturdy branch. Taking a deep breath she stepped toward the front door and rang the bell.

"Good day Miss Howard," Charles greeted.

Charles had caught her off guard with his good memory. "Good day Charles. You remember me?"

"Yes my lady," Charles smiled.

"I'm impressed," Melissa commented.

"Come my lady." He gestured with his hand. "How may I help you today? Are you looking for Lord Blackburn?"

My Forbidden Mentor

She admired the entryway while responding to Charles. "Yes, I am here to see John, uh, Lord Blackburn."

Charles smiled at her blunder and then offered, "He's not here at present, but I do expect him shortly. Is he expecting you?"

She tore her focus away from the paintings of horses that graced the entryway walls. "Well no, Charles, he isn't. I don't mind waiting, though."

"Then may I offer you some tea while you wait?"

"Thank you. I would like that."

"Would you care to wait in the sitting room?" he asked, his hand motioning to a room off to the left of the long and wide entryway.

Melissa smiled, stepping toward the sitting room. "That's fine, thank you."

Three quarters of an hour passed by and Melissa turned fidgety. Already being nervous about the conversation she planned to discuss with John, further waiting sorely tested her courage. Charles had walked by once already, giving her an apologetic look. It was obvious that he had expected John by now. It wasn't his fault. Perhaps she could explore the library. She remembered John telling her the library was one of his favorite rooms in his manor, and she loved to read.

She rose from the sable colored couch, set her teacup on a walnut side table, and began her journey to discover the library.

Charles startled her from behind. "Miss Howard, are you looking for something specific?"

Melissa jumped. "Oh, yes. The library. I was searching for the library."

"That would be the double door at the end of the hall." Charles pointed in the direction before being called away by the housekeeper. "Excuse me."

"Thank you," she started to tell him, but he had disappeared.

As her half boots glided along earth colored tiles she continued in the direction of the library, admiring the many gallant paintings of stallions and mares John had. She stopped in front of one in particular of a small boy with black hair sitting atop a solid white Arabian. John, she thought. She continued the few remaining steps to the library.

Her hand went to the doorknob when a distinct sound came from inside the room. She leaned closer, putting her ear to the door before opening it. At first she heard groans and wondered if John had a hangover again. She was about to open the door to lecture him about his drinking when she heard another voice. This one was feminine and she groaned also. Could they both have hangovers? Perhaps, but what was a woman doing alone with him in the library? She knew this to be none of her business. After all, she had pushed John away, stating that they couldn't have that type of relationship. Even so, she continued to torture herself by keeping her ear glued to the door.

"Don't stop love," she heard the feminine voice say.

"Never," she heard the male voice groan out.

Melissa's mouth fell open, shocked by what she was hearing. This man and woman, John and somebody, were apparently doing very private things to one another. Well he didn't wait very long did he? She should have known she was another conquest. Men! Why couldn't they be satisfied with one woman? Why is this bothering me so much? She continued listening, knowing she shouldn't.

My Forbidden Mentor

"That's it love," the female voice cried out. A groaned response sounded in return.

Her hand came off the doorknob. Bursting in wouldn't solve anything and she would come off like a jealous mistress. Instead she headed for the front door, her pace picking up faster and faster. Why did Charles lie about John's whereabouts? Well that should be obvious Melissa of course he's going to obey his lord's wishes. Perhaps Charles himself was unaware? And why should it matter. John didn't expect you, and you had your chance. If you wanted to be with him you had your chance and you didn't take it. Relief spread through her at the same time a stinging of tears formed in her eyes. I don't need this heartache anyway, she thought.

Charles saw a golden streak dart by and wondered what had happened. He set down his polishing rags and went to her. "Miss Howard?" he called out.

John's morning in town had been productive. Encountering numerous business opportunities helped to lift his mood. He intended to spend the rest of the day deciding how to handle Melissa. In blatant denial, she wouldn't acknowledge the pleasure they'd had. Her words spoke of how wrong it was and John would have agreed in the beginning, but the passion they had experienced had been undeniable. He couldn't comprehend how she could forget the experience. He wondered what her secret was for forgetting, he'd like to know, but instead the experience they shared persisted in his mind and wouldn't allow him to ignore the obvious.

Nearing his manor, his mare trailed down the worn, grassy path at a leisurely pace. John hadn't been in a hurry as he had plenty of thinking to do. His relationship with Melissa had turned chaotic. His options were narrowing.

Could he continue to work with her without touching her? Should he forget their arrangement so he could touch her? Was he a complete fool to think this arrangement would work in the first place? There were plenty of risks to be taken involving her.

Answers began surfacing like a bright sun breaking through a mass of clouds. Melissa would rather keep their intended arrangement and forge ahead, not thinking about any consequences whatsoever. Forget any attraction at all between them, as long as she was able to race nothing else mattered.

He was pondering in disappointment when he heard the sound of horse hooves slamming into his cobblestone drive. He was a few hundred yards from his drive when he saw a flash of gold streak by on a horse of gray. Melissa? What did she want? And why is she riding away as if her life depended on it? She looked upset. He had better go after her.

Just reaching the outskirts of his property at full speed, Melissa heard a familiar voice calling her name. At first she ignored it. Why should she bother responding to a libertine lord who had his way with her and every other woman he baited? He might want to apologize but it wouldn't work with her.

Abruptly she felt doomed. She had let their physical attraction advance and it had jeopardized their business relationship, spoiling any chance of success for them. It was especially true for her. Her chance was blown, but she wasn't the only one to blow it. All of a sudden her vision became blurred from an outbreak of tears and again she heard her name being called, louder this time. Out of hurt and disappointment and sheer anger, she shifted to acknowledge him.

My Forbidden Mentor

He was motioning for her to slow down. He seemed urgent, almost frantic for her to stop, but she figured he was using his overpowering sense of self to get his way. When she turned back around she was faced with a dilemma, one that required a decision to be made in a split second.

A thick bush stood straight in front of Melissa and her gelding. She had involuntarily steered Thunder for dead center of the bush. Her pulling efforts to steer clear of disaster met with another challenge, a confrontation with a covey of quail that came fluttering out, trying to escape the massive beast of horseflesh running straight for them. Unexpectedly Thunder reared, causing Melissa to lose her grip on the reins. She tried regaining control when he reared again. Instead of gaining control, she could feel herself lifting from the saddle. Out of desperation she grabbed for his neck when he stood erect one more time. Her ardent grasps resulted in hanging on by his mane. The gelding's head shook violently, his body rearing again as the wings of quail flapped around him. His mane came free from her fingers and she was falling toward the ground. "God help me," she prayed. Her eyes closed, she held her breath and in the next instant her body pounded into the earth.

With eyes squeezed shut, she endured an unforeseen explosion of pain stomped into her body from the gelding's jittery hooves. Sharp reflexive pains shot through her right calf as she lay there stifled without an ounce of energy to move. Keeping her eyes shut as if to withstand another expected jab of agony, seconds went by and nothing more happened. Silence filled the air around her as if all the startled animals involved had disappeared at once. She blamed herself for what had just happened. Thunder would never intentionally hurt her. She had led him into this disaster. She herself hadn't seen it coming but John had, and because of her defensive emotions she ignored his warning.

Her eyes opened after everything had stayed quiet. Subconsciously her hand grabbed at her right calf. A throbbing discomfort stemmed from that part of her leg, keeping her immobile. Glancing around it was apparent that Thunder had vanished. Had he deserted her? Panic set in, seizing any movement in her until she heard the rustling sound of the bushes. John called out to her, sounding as panicked as she was feeling. Two solitary tears streamed down her cheeks in relief that John had found her.

When he saw her lying on the ground in pain it shook him miserably. He rushed to her side, and saw that her hands were cradling her leg, so he squatted down next to her and lifted her hands away so he could see her leg for himself. Pushing her skirt up to expose the wound, he pressed in light motions around the hoof-indented marks left on her swollen calf. She winced as he touched and cried aloud, "John it hurts."

"I know sweetheart," he said, continuing to thoroughly examine her injuries.

Her head lay still on the ground as her eyes watched the caring expression he had while looking over her injury. His endearment made her feel special and for a brief moment she cherished his closeness. He seemed truly concerned despite his previous actions. Another rustling of bushes sounded, veering Melissa's attention.

John and Melissa both looked up toward the nearing noise. Charles rounded the bush on horseback. "Lord Blackburn, Miss Howard, are you in need of assistance?" he asked in a state of alarm.

John stood and Melissa tried sitting up. John caught her motion. "Don't move," he told her, stepping toward Charles. "Yes Charles. I need you to fetch Dr. Bennett please. Tell him it's urgent. I'll bring Miss Howard to the manor myself."

Charles nodded, reining his horse in the direction of the doctor.

"Charles," Melissa shouted to stop him. John looked at her, bewildered. Charles stopped immediately. She turned to John. "John, I think it would be better if I went home."

"But it's closer to my manor. You shouldn't be moving a lot until we know what's wrong," he cautioned, but the pleading within her shimmering eyes made him give in. He gave Charles new instructions. "Charles, have Dr. Bennett go to Miss Howard's home in Scotch Corner. Jess knows the location."

With a nod Charles complied, "Yes my lord. I will locate Jess right away." Charles left in a fit of speed before John could thank him.

John led his mare next to Melissa then went to retrieve her gelding. He'd been a short distance away, feeding on masses of grass. When John brought him alongside his mare Melissa asked in a worried tone, "Is he all right John?"

John rigged up the horses, readying them to go, when he responded, "He seems to be fine. My concern is with you." His brows creased in aggravation. Her concern for others was overwhelming when she remained the worst injured party. "Are you sure you can handle the ride to your cabin?" he asked.

"Yes," she answered, trying to rise on her good leg but failing.

In a flash John advanced toward her. "Damn it all, would you stay still? You could cause further injury to yourself." Her face filled with anguish as her hand went to comfort her swollen calf. John exhaled, frustrated and angry. He cursed himself for lashing out at her like he did. He squatted down next to her again, his tone softening considerably. "Melissa let me help you. I'm almost ready. Give me another moment and I'll take you home."

"I don't need your help or anyone else's," she exploded, knowing how ridiculous she sounded and knowing she wouldn't get anywhere without his help. But she was upset with him, grateful and upset at the same time. Continuing to haunt her was the incident in the library, but not for long as another sharp pain shot through her leg, making her cry out.

Infuriated with her attitude and obstinate disposition, he took matters into his own hands. "You stubborn, obstinate woman," he said aloud, and wrapped his arms around her, arranging her to be carried. Ignoring her protests he strode over to his mare with Melissa gathered in his arms. Coaxing his mare into a laying position, carefully he stepped over the mare and eased down, aiming for the saddle. About half way down he encouraged Clara to stand. After a mild adjustment John began his journey with one arm dedicated to holding Melissa, his other handling the reins of both the mare and the gelding.

They rode in silence except for an occasional sniffle from Melissa. Any jarring movement at all sent a new flare of pain through her injured calf.

"Shh, it's not much further," John would whisper, trying to console her.

My Forbidden Mentor

When they arrived at her home Miss Beckett helped as much as possible but her strength didn't match John's. He took over by carrying Melissa to the couch in the sitting room, figuring the stairs would add further discomfort when she could walk again.

Miss Beckett brought blankets and pillows from Melissa's room, making her as comfortable as possible, and then she retrieved fresh tea and offered John his choice of drink. He chose brandy.

While Melissa rested John stood before the front window, sipping his drink and staring out into nothing. His mind was lost and confused as not knowing the extent of her injury bothered him. Could she ever ride again? And if she couldn't, what a horrible fate to overcome, especially for Melissa. Then there were her outbursts, which he assumed came from the pain she was feeling, but why had she run from his manor? The sound of hooves thudding into the ground interrupted his thoughts. The doctor had arrived.

After careful examination Dr. Bennett looked up into faces of concern. John, Miss Beckett, and Mr. Howard all stood around Melissa, waiting with struggling patience for the doctor's prognosis.

Dr. Bennett lifted to stand, collecting his supplies. "Well Miss Howard, it seems you have a contusion. What this means," he said as he straightened with his supplies in his hand, "is that the strike of your horse's hoof caused deep bruising and tearing to your calf muscle." The doctor caught everyone wincing but his patient. "The swelling and pain are normal, of course, but functionality is sometimes questionable. Initially you will need to stay off it to bring the swelling down, but once most of the pain is gone you can begin stretching it and walking on it again." He kneeled next to her. "Because of the extent of damage done, mainly from the weight of the horse, it may never heal completely, meaning you may be left with a limp." Everyone remained quiet and the doctor sympathized with Melissa. "I'm sorry about that, but the good news is you will be able to walk again, almost normally, depending on how hard you work at it and how cooperative the muscle is."

The idea that she was left with a limp hadn't sunk in yet. Her main concern dealt with her ability to race again. She looked to John then back to Dr. Bennett. "Will I be able to ride again Dr. Bennett?" she asked with shakiness to her voice.

John prayed in silence that the doctor would say yes.

Dr. Bennett smiled to reassure her as best he could. "I can't say for sure. It will depend on how well the muscle heals and how strong it becomes with regular exercise," he told her and rose again. "Rest for now and I'll check on you in one week. Meanwhile I've given your aunt instructions to help you. Take care."

John walked the doctor out to his carriage.

When John returned he saw that Melissa's aunt and father were reassuring her by giving her hope that everything would be all right. John stood in the doorway a moment studying her reaction to them. Detachment is what he saw. He guessed that her thoughts dwelled on the doctor's words. She responded to her family's suggestions but her response was distant.

Mr. Howard noticed John then. "Lord Blackburn I can never thank you enough for the care you've given Melissa."

John stepped forward, stopping next to where Melissa lay on the couch, and faced her father. "I feel thankful I was able to be there for her," he said and glanced in Melissa's direction, unexpectedly receiving a glare of animosity. Was it only yesterday he'd had her moaning with pleasure, he reflected, staring into her eyes of anger?

The sound of liquid pouring returned his attention to her father. Phillip was lifting a glass of scotch to his mouth when John tried focusing on Phillip's words instead of the angered glare he'd gotten.

"The point is, Lord Blackburn, that our little girl here will recuperate and be better than ever thanks to your immediate actions," Phillip boasted.

John smiled and nodded in agreement for Phillip's sake. Something else was going on with his daughter that he didn't seem aware of but John was, and the distinct notion that it had to do with yesterday's turning point in their relationship amid the hayloft seemed reasonable.

Unenlightened by the turbulent emotions floating between his daughter and her hero, Phillip searched for his pipe. Remembering that he'd left it in his bedroom he excused himself. Miss Beckett followed behind him, inquiring about supper.

John believed this would be a perfect time for a confrontation, at least to find out why she had left his manor in such a hurry. Shifting to face her, her neutral expression left him dazed. He couldn't read her at all. He decided to kneel beside her. "Melissa, why did you run away? From my manor, I mean?"

"Why do you care?" She reacted out of hurt. The physical pain she was experiencing didn't compare to the emotional one.

"What kind of question is that?" he questioned because her drastic response staggered him.

She wouldn't look him straight in the eye when she responded again, "Well, I know how busy you can be entertaining."

Even the emphasis on the word *entertaining* puzzled him. Did his touching her upset her that much? "What are you talking about? You're not making sense," he expressed with genuine sincerity. There wasn't any laughter behind his serious eyes.

"It doesn't matter anymore John. Nothing matters anymore."

"I don't want to hear you saying things like that. It's not like you."

Prompt and direct, her eyes found his. "Oh, and you know me so well, don't you?"

For a short time he just stared, trying to make sense of her change in attitude. Her focus hadn't let go of his and she looked like she was about to cry. "Why are you so upset with me? You're so hostile. You weren't this mad yesterday," he said, mystified by her behavior and searching for some suitable explanation

Her eyes blinked and she turned away. "Yesterday, I don't want to talk about yesterday. Yesterday everything was normal."

He wanted to yell out of frustration, but managed to contain himself. Taking a couple of deep breaths he switched the subject back on track. "You still haven't answered my question."

Phillip entered the sitting room heading for his favorite chair. John resigned himself to the fact that his questions would not be answered today. As he started to rise Melissa touched his forearm, thanking him. "I know you've got business to take care of I understand. Again, I'm ever so grateful for your help."

The kindness she showed was her way of getting rid of him. How could he not notice that clue? Her strange behavior had him flustered. A reaction of despair seemed appropriate but this underlying anger she vented was aimed straight at him, extreme anger, and he intended to find out why whether she wanted to tell him or not. He had his ways of finding out, which were maybe different than hers, but he would attain the results he searched for. He made sure there was complete understanding between them when he rose to leave. "Yes, I should be going," he said as his eyes gripped hers, leaving no misunderstanding about his intentions. "I'll be by tomorrow to see how you're doing." The grin he flashed her way ensured that her father was a witness to his intentions.

Melissa smiled long enough to avoid suspicion with her father. "I would appreciate that."

John bid her father a good evening and left.

Chapter Eleven

A few weeks passed and John faithfully stopped by to check on Melissa's progress. To his misfortune, Miss Beckett was around all the time so John couldn't confront Melissa about anything between them personally, but John did notice an improvement in Melissa's attitude toward her leg. Dr. Bennett's encouragement appeared to help, for oftentimes John would find Melissa in the middle of stretching and exercising her leg.

Most of the time John updated her on the present races going on and upcoming, and although she was cordial to John, he couldn't escape the distinct feeling that somehow he had disappointed her, how he wasn't sure, but something had caused relentless friction between them.

John had to be out of town for a couple days as business regarding Chief required that he be there, but after his business trip he'd been anxious to see Melissa again despite the inner battle they seemed to be fighting. In a joyful mood one afternoon, John rode his horse at a galloping pace to reach the Howard's home, not sure why he was in such a hurry to see his student, who hadn't been so eager to see him lately, but he was. He slowed his mare to a trot when trailing down the familiar path to the familiar country home. At first he spotted Mr. Howard feeding the horses. John's gaze continued scanning the surrounding environment but Melissa didn't seem to be anywhere in sight as John pulled his mare to a halt next to the barn. Mr. Howard greeted him while he slid out of the saddle. The men chatted about business and related subjects while Phillip finished the outside chores. John found himself following Mr. Howard into the cabin as they continued their conversation. As John took the seat offered to him he continued wondering where in the world Melissa could be as by now she would have made herself present.

John's curiosity had curtailed long enough for he couldn't concentrate on a word Mr. Howard was saying. When Phillip took a breath John inquired, "Mr. Howard, may I ask where Melissa is?" Sounding somewhat forward, John made sure to add, "I've been wondering about her progress with her leg for training purposes."

Phillip smiled at John's inquiry. It had become obvious that John cared for Melissa as much more than a mere student. "Have a drink John," Phillip asked. The last few weeks spent together took on a personal note for John and Mr. Howard. Mr. Howard called John by his first name now but out of respect for his being Melissa's father, John still addressed him as Mr. Howard or sir.

John readily accepted the glass of brandy Miss Beckett handed him.

"As you know Melissa's progress has improved dramatically in the physical sense, but I've been worried about her mental state. She hasn't been herself of late. Even the healing of her leg hasn't helped her emotional well-being." Phillip downed a large amount of scotch as John waited, listening with engrossed enthusiasm. "So, I decided to send her on a short trip for a few days. Somewhere she's always wanted to visit." Phillip saw surprise grace John's features and knew he would have questions, as he should. If John sincerely cared for his daughter, as Phillip had guessed, then he should be concerned for her whereabouts.

"May I be so bold as to ask where she's gone to?" John asked, trying to sound unaffected by gulping a large amount of brandy.

"Dublin, Ireland," Phillip replied.

Dublin, Ireland! "She has an escort I presume?" Most likely she did and now he wondered whom.

"Yes, of course. I sent Kurt with her, one of my workers. I can trust him." Phillip had to take another swig so as to not give away his devious smile. The look on John's face when Phillip mentioned Kurt was unexpected, quite amusing, actually, even though the intention of sending Kurt had nothing to do with making John jealous but to protect his daughter.

"I see. How did she take to having a chaperone?" John asked.

In the corner of Phillip's eyes lay a twinkle. "You know my daughter well enough by now, John, to know she disliked the idea originally. But, being her father, I had a way of making her understand: either the trip with an escort or no trip at all." Miss Beckett brought Phillip a full pipe. "Thank you," he told her. His attention went back to John. "I would have rather you'd been her escort, but I surely can't expect you to handle such a task when you've got your own business to run."

John needed to appear relaxed. The thought of an eighteen-year-old young man with raging hormones protecting Melissa made him tense. "I wouldn't have minded." That was all he could say while he came to grip with the situation. He hadn't any rights to Melissa, none at all. A deep breath served to calm him enough to be rational. At least she wasn't alone, alone going to a new place, a place she knew nothing about. Oh lord, what am I doing to myself? Phillip's voice strangled further deliberation.

"It's only for a few days. She left this morn and I expect her back early next week," Phillip revealed and then decided to test John's shaky ground. "You know that girl of mine need's stability in her life. She's not getting any younger," he admitted, as if expecting a confession of love for his daughter.

Phillip noticed the way his daughter admired John, pretending he didn't matter while her eyes gave her away. Phillip also observed how much personal time the lord spent with her. Assuming they'd taken a liking to each other beyond their teacher/student arrangement, Phillip wasn't opposed to a marriage between them. With Lord Blackburn there would be financial security, a life surrounded with thoroughbreds, a passion they clearly had in common, and the ability to travel, not to mention making handsome babies together. Assuming they hadn't been intimate, Phillip knew too well of the potent affects a young couple endured during courtship or otherwise always being together a significant amount of time.

John wondered if Mr. Howard had any knowledge of the private liaison he'd had with his daughter in the hayloft and if that was the reason for his implication of marriage, after all, his daughter still remained a virgin.

Just then Mr. Howard lit his pipe full of tobacco. A mischievous smile appeared on his lips as if he knew why John had become quiet. Phillip had surprised him with his observations. Why wouldn't he encourage their relationship? He noticed their mutual attraction even before the training had started. Why not give a little shove, he thought. "John, I know that Melissa is very fond of you. She looks up to you." Phillip took a quick puff on his pipe, as John turned attentive. "She's learned a great deal in the time you've spent with her thus far." John took a sip of his half-emptied glass of brandy as Phillip continued. "I have a favor to ask of you." John's reaction was a lift of one black brow. Phillip took another puff, this time a longer one.

The tension was excruciating for John, expecting Mr. Howard to give him an ultimatum regarding his daughter, but to John's surprise it was completely different. Smoke lazily spiraled above Phillip's head as he went on. In nervous tension John downed the remainder of his drink.

"I've noticed that you have a way with her. She listens to you, so I'm asking if you could keep an eye on her for me when I'm not around." Phillip stopped to puff some more and saw John's expression of confusion.

"What do you mean Mr. Howard?" The empty glass he held started to slip from his sweating hand so he set it on the table.

Phillip needed to explain. "I can see I haven't made any sense. I don't plan on leaving any time soon, my friend, but I can see true friendship between you two, and after I pass away, to know you will look out for her would give me peace of mind. She hasn't many relatives left, especially nearby. It would settle my heart to know she has someone in her life that she can trust and rely on. I trust you, John."

John's features froze. He hadn't given John an ultimatum; he'd requested him to be his daughter's guardian for life. John didn't know how to feel. He never expected that Mr. Howard would want a lifetime commitment without marriage. John had to make sure. "Mr. Howard you're putting a lot of faith in me," he said, leaning forward in the chair. "What I mean to say is, I care a great deal for Melissa, I truly do, but that is a lifetime of responsibility you're asking of me. What if she doesn't approve? You know how stubborn she can be."

Phillip's smile widened, never imagining a lord of his status having to question his own abilities. "Precisely what I meant earlier, John. She will listen to you. She doesn't have to be aware of this particular part of our conversation." He paused to give John a way out. "I understand if you're not

My Forbidden Mentor

able. Please don't feel obligated," Phillip told him, and let John ponder some more, discreetly adding words of confidence. "I do have faith in you, though."

John remained quiet before answering. He hadn't objected, but if Melissa were to marry someone else could he handle it? Could her future husband handle their relationship? Here this kind man, Melissa's father, was asking him to always be there for his daughter no matter what. How could he turn him down? How could he agree, when at present Melissa only talked to him to be courteous? It would prove challenging. John looked into Phillip's eyes, Melissa's eyes, and said, "I will. I will do as you ask."

Phillip rose from his chair to fill John's glass then grabbed the bottle of scotch and filled his own. Lifting his glass in the air, John did the same while Phillip said, "Thank you. I'm forever grateful. Now my worries will be lessened." Both smiled and drank, then spent the remainder of the evening enjoying each other's company. By half past midnight, John climbed atop his mare in unsteadiness. Heading for his manor, he wondered if he should have accepted Mr. Howard's offer to stay the night. Too late now, he thought, he was already half way home.

At the rise of dawn, while heavy clouds still floated low, John was already half way back to the Howards' home. He and Mr. Howard had made plans to go hunting since neither had done so in some time. Hunting wasn't a common outing for John but periodically he engaged in the activity. The way Mr. Howard talked of his experiences, John could learn a lot from him. Melissa wasn't around to spend time with so why not spend time with her father? He could turn out to be the father figure he'd never had.

John arrived at their arranged time. Sliding off Clara, an eerie silence surrounded him. Strangely, the front door was wide open but there wasn't a soul in sight. John strode toward the entry of the cabin. He called out in greeting but no one answered, and then the sound of weeping pierced his ears. Without hesitating he entered the cabin, trying to locate the person in need. He followed the sound to a room toward the back of the house. As he approached the bedroom he found the source.

The door was open and he saw Miss Beckett sitting in a chair next to Mr. Howard's bed. Phillip lay still in his bed, looking peaceful. "No," John mumbled under his breath. He walked over to Miss Beckett, handing her a handkerchief. "Miss Beckett."

Taking the handkerchief from his hand, she looked up through wet lashes. "Oh Lord Blackburn, it's Mr. Howard, he's gone. I came to wake him for breakfast and he didn't answer his door," she paused to gain her composure and John kneeled before her. "So I came in and he was lying in his bed as he is now."

While Miss Beckett was blowing her nose John gazed at Melissa's father, thinking that just last evening he was laughing and talking with him. Just last evening he had made him a promise.

"I shook him and he didn't move. He didn't seem sick at all," she cried.

John rose and as a precautionary measure he took Phillip's pulse and found none. Turning back to Miss Beckett, he quietly agreed. "You're right, he's gone."

Miss Beckett used John's handkerchief to wipe the wetness from her sorrowful eyes. "It's an incredible shock," she said with a cracking voice.

Unbelievable, John thought. "We were going hunting today," he mentioned. His eyes scanned the masculine room he was standing in, taking in Mr. Howard's character.

My Forbidden Mentor

Custom crafted, high dollar oak furniture encircled him, the same as in the sitting room. More amazing designs embedded this light oak as well. Paintings of both his wife, who was quite stunning herself, and of Melissa decorated his walls. His eyes fell back on Mr. Howard, the sunlight now cast across him as the morning clouds began burning off. John reached over to close the dark green drapes near his bed, keeping the morning heat off his peaceful sleeping body. John's hands covered his face, rubbing his features like he was trying to wake from a bad dream.

Miss Beckett began to panic. "Oh, my dear, I've got to get word to Miss Melissa. She's going to be heartbroken. Both of her parents are gone now. Somehow I'll have to get word to her. You know she's in Dublin, Ireland?"

John shifted toward Miss Beckett. "Yes, I know. I'll take care of that. I'll go get her," he told her.

"I've got to make arrangements for his burial." she responded, feeling weak and overwhelmed by everything to be done.

John kneeled down again. "You do that and I'll pay for it. Don't worry about the cost. Get the best of everything," John offered.

"That's very generous of you Lord Blackburn, but it's not expected, and I'm not sure if Miss Melissa will approve," she told him.

His authority won out, as it usually did. "I insist. I'll make Melissa understand." His new friend deserved any comfort John could offer. With everything else going on all at once, the last worry Melissa needed was any financial burden.

"I'll get started then." Even in her distress, Miss Beckett gave John a smile.

"Will you be all right by yourself?" John asked in genuine concern.

Miss Beckett lifted from the chair. "Yes, I have a neighbor friend that can help." She smiled again, feeling blessed to have such a generous person as Lord Blackburn to help with their family.

"All right then, I'll get Melissa." He took her hand and squeezed in reassurance.

Climbing his mare, he rushed home to make preparations to collect Melissa from Dublin.

John was in such a hurry that he hadn't notice the plain black rig parked near the front of his manor. Striding down the entry hall toward the stairway, Charles frantically got his attention. "My lord."

John stopped. "Yes, Charles, what is it?"

"Miss Walker awaits you in your library sir."

Charles looked uneasy. John could only imagine the verbal torture Vanessa had put him through.

Vanessa. He didn't have time to deal with Vanessa. Good lord, how was he going to get rid of her? Undoubtedly she would be expecting to spend time with him to make up for these past weeks. Oddly enough, he hadn't given Vanessa a single thought in the time he hadn't seen her.

"Charles, I'll take care of Miss Walker. Have Simon ready my carriage. I'm taking a short trip." With a half twist he headed for the library.

"Vanessa, how are you?" he asked after closing the library doors behind him, trying not to sound transparent.

My Forbidden Mentor

She turned from her exploration of a wide selection of books. "Hello John. The question is, how are you?" she asked as she pranced toward him, feeling hurt that she hadn't seen him for some time.

Not sure how he was going to handle this, he carried on. "I'm doing well. You didn't tell me how you're doing?" Knowing by now she wasn't falling for his evasiveness, her blue eyes, normally full of lust, were cooling before his eyes.

"You have to ask? I haven't seen you for weeks. This isn't like you, John." Her tone came out perturbed, as he expected.

The time had come to deal with her flat out. "I have to ask, since I haven't seen you." That wasn't flat out, that was digging himself in deeper.

Her finger went to his lips, tracing them. "And why is that?" she purred.

His hand braced over hers, pulling her finger away from his mouth. After letting go of her hand he strode over to the window to look outside. "I've been busy." Especially right now, he wanted to say as he blindly gaped into the spotty clouded landscape.

Her blond brows arched out of keen interest as she walked up behind him and wrapped her arms around his waist. "Too busy for little Vanessa?" she whispered in a flirtatious tone.

It had been a long time since he'd had that kind of pleasure and here was Vanessa, willing and able. They'd had a pleasurable time in the past but now it wasn't Vanessa he hungered for. "Vanessa, I can't." His hand grasped hers to stop her from sliding them downward.

Pulling away from him, she stood facing his back, her hands on her hips. "You can't or you won't?" He looked over his shoulder at her. She received a concentrated stare from him, like he was lost for words. "What has gotten into you? What has changed over these past weeks?" she demanded, confused and hurt.

He faced her now, looking distraught while telling her, "I just can't. I'm tired." He could reveal no more than that. How could he tell her that he desired only one woman and it wasn't her? It was a mystery to him that one woman could consume his sole attention. This was new territory, making it seem even more exasperating that with a chance to find pleasurable release, he didn't take the offer.

Because of his recent behavior Vanessa urged, "You've never been so tired to pass on our lovemaking before. There's someone else, isn't there?" And while waiting for his answer, he didn't respond. "You don't have to say anything John. You've found a new distraction, it has to be that, but with our long history, well, I'm sure it's just a phase you're going through. When you're bored again, you'll come around and I'll be waiting." Her voice that turned to ice camouflaged the pain she was feeling.

John changed his mind and decided to explain to her, try to explain about something he wasn't sure of himself. His mouth opened to speak when her arms slipped around his neck, pulling his face down to hers, her mouth consuming his.

They were interrupted by a knock at the door. Their lips broke apart. "That's something to remember me by," she told him before turning to leave. Opening the library door she brushed by Charles in a rush.

"Yes Charles?" John said, retrieving his breath, thankful for the interruption. The familiarity of Miss Walker was enticing enough to give into, if only temporarily to sate his bountiful appetite.

"Your carriage is ready, sir. May I ask your destination?" Charles, who always saw to every detail, needed to know.

"Of course. I'm off to Dublin. I shall be a day or so." John gathered his bearings, trying to think of everything he needed to take with him.

"Thank you sir. Also, Sir Robert has just arrived. He's in the stables conversing with Simon." A slight crease developed on Charles lips.

"Thank you Charles," he said, remembering to give him a nod of release.

John had his arms full with his coat, gloves and a leather pouch he usually carried along if he planned on staying somewhere over night. Robert knew him too well. "Leaving? I've just arrived," Robert asked, as he entered through the front doorway.

In deep concentration, John responded. "I'm off to Dublin. It's urgent. Are you up for a short trip?" he asked Robert as he whisked by him, placing his belongings in the carriage.

"Of course," Robert replied and was curious about John's previous visitor. "Was that Vanessa leaving?" he asked, following him back outside.

"Yes. She's not in the most cheerful of moods. Charles had perfect timing, I must say." John's grin widened as they both settled inside the carriage. "It's been so long I almost gave in." He chuckled. "I'm so wound up I could have taken her even if she was scratching my eyes out." He hadn't wanted Vanessa, but damn, Melissa had been driving him crazy because of her inexperience. He needed to go slow, painfully slow, with her, more than ever now that she had so many crises thrown at her at once, and the most recent could be the most devastating. It was up to John to soothe her.

"Perhaps you should have, John, release some of the pressure, as they say," Robert commented, as they both got comfortable in the leather seats.

John smiled at Robert's comment, keeping his thoughts private. Along the journey John explained what the urgency was about, how Melissa's father had just passed away and how delicate the situation would be.

Robert knew it was more than that though, and he knew that John would bring her back home offering more than genuine comfort. John had never spent so much of his free time with a woman before. Melissa might be his student and she might have been injured recently, but John had more than the standard agenda on his mind. For a man who usually remained calm, now he seemed uptight and out of control.

Chapter Twelve

They arrived in Dublin in the evening hours. They checked a few of the local lodgings until they found the one where she was staying. Finding her room, John knocked but there was no answer. He waited a few moments and still there was no answer, so he figured she had gone out for supper.

He suggested to Robert that they wait at a local pub to pass the time until she returned. They entered a pub a few buildings down from the hotel, sat at the bar, and ordered drinks.

The increasing laughter and volume of music got John's attention. Turning to look at the commotion he saw a golden haired woman being entertained by a group of dancing Irish men. He couldn't see her face but he could hear her laughing. Her laughter sounded familiar and intoxicating, having a full-bodied ring to it. The only other woman whose laughter intoxicated him like that was...Melissa.

His brows creased with the shifting of his head. Through a fog of smoke filling the room and hordes of dancing male bodies surrounding her, his tall, extraordinary figure lifted to get a better view. His height towered above most average men, so now as he was standing, his viewpoint allowed a clearer look, a much clearer look. The young lady wasn't just an Irish lass enjoying an evening of entertainment but in fact was his charming, not fully recovered student, yes indeed, the same student who had been aloof in his presence of late. Aloof with him, but laughing with these dancing men she didn't even know. She was having a good time and so were the men around her, panting about her like dogs in heat. So she's not as innocent as she appears to be, he convinced himself. His expression turned angry and his breathing turning violent as he watched. Unable to bear anymore he poured the remainder of his drink into his mouth and told Robert through tightened lips, "Let's go. I've seen enough."

Melissa's day had been a long one. Even after traveling the whole day before she hadn't slept a wink thinking about the events of today. She hadn't planned to join in the pub's entertainment this evening but Kurt had talked her into it. She admitted to enjoying herself but the time had come to rest and recharge, for tomorrow was a new adventure. She bid Kurt a good evening and left.

Kurt, bless his soul, agreed to be her chaperone but learned from the beginning that Melissa would not tolerate his constant attendance, so they made a deal. He would know the locations she planned on visiting but would only check on her periodically. They agreed and went their separate ways.

Trailing down a cobblestone walkway she gave thanks to her father again. This trip may have been the diversion she needed. Thoughts of John had trickled into her mind over and over since their intimate encounter. It hadn't helped when he'd come by her home every day to verify her progress, and although she hadn't forgotten his actions in the library, she had to admire his loyalty as a friend. Even before their single intimate act Melissa believed they'd become good friends. She assumed that's why it hurt so much when hearing him with another woman. If they hadn't been intimate, perhaps it wouldn't have bothered her so much.

My Forbidden Mentor

Lost in her thoughts she started to stumble on the uneven cobblestone due to the shuffle in her footing. She managed to regain her balance by putting the majority of her weight on her good leg but before she knew it a gentleman had flown out of a carriage and tried to help her. Leaning against the hotel building she thanked the gentleman for his efforts. "Thank you sir. I can manage now."

"Are you quite sure you're all right?" The gentleman asked.

She seemed more mentally shaken up than anything. "Yes, I'll be fine. I have a room in this hotel. Thank you." She smiled, stepping toward the door of the hotel.

Entering her room she was feeling relieved and lucky to have escaped further injury to her bum leg. She sat on the bed for a moment thinking about the kind gentleman that offered to help her and then lay back, shutting her eyes. Letting out a long awaited breath, she started to relax when a deep, inquiring voice spoke to her in the darkness of her room.

"Did you enjoy yourself tonight?"

Jumping from the sound of his voice, her eyes flew open and she sat up. She couldn't see him but she recognized his husky, powerful voice. She stood, scrambling to light a candle. "Where are you?" she asked with impatience. Once lit, she held the candle in her hand. The glow of the flame flickered brighter, enough so her eyes adjusted to the figure of a man sitting in a chair near the window. The back of his form was shadowed from the darkness of the night but his face was lit by the candlelight and appeared so concentrated she could see the muscles in his jaws tightening. "What are you doing here?" she demanded, her features no longer startled but displeased to be staring into the face of her mentor.

"I'm here to protect my investment," he told her, her continuing anger at him mixing up his reasons for being there.

"Investment?" she asked, not understanding his meaning.

"You're my student. I can't have you getting into trouble," he told her, his face remaining stern and unmoving, although to him the investment included more than being a mere student of his.

"What do you consider getting into trouble and since when is this any concern of yours?" she hissed through tightened lips and a moment of silence stood between them.

Lord, if she only knew how much of a concern she'd become to him. Her own father had made sure of that. "I don't believe you realize how attractive you are. Having all those men lingering around you is dangerous," he spit out, angered by the company she kept tonight and lusting after her himself.

"What?" She wondered what he meant, and then it dawned on her that he must have seen her at the pub, although she didn't remember seeing him there.

Watching the flame flicker against her beautiful face made him want to throw her on the bed and make her his once and for all, but he didn't move, instead telling her, "I saw you, Melissa. I saw you laughing with those men. They were salivating all over you." His jealousy was coming on full force now, making his hands grip the arms of the chair. He never got jealous like this and he wasn't sure how to handle it. His narrowed eyes followed her as she placed the candle on the mirrored dresser.

She stood with one hand on her hip and the other making gestures toward him as her voice sounded strained. "How dare you spy on me and accuse me of philandering with those men. You have no right accusing me of something you know nothing about, especially when you've got your own harem back home," she flung back.

He didn't want to argue about his supposed harem so he ignored her statement. He leaned forward in the chair, anger seeping through his teeth. "I'm telling you what I saw with my own eyes," he told her while his body was teetering on control causing the knuckles of his interlocking fingers to turn white.

Her brows creased with the narrowing of her eyes. "What you saw and what you imagined were two different things John. I didn't want those men," she countered and wouldn't give him the satisfaction of knowing that he was the only man she wanted, even as arrogant and possessive as he was. "They were showing me an Irish dance, if you must know. I've always wanted to learn one," she pointed out. As angry as she was even seeing him through dim candlelight he was extraordinary, despite his angered expression. She cursed him in silence for wanting to feel his lips against hers. Craving his affections but knowing it would complicate matters, she restrained herself.

Lifting from the chair and stepping toward her, he stood facing her with candlelight glowing between them. He didn't speak for a long time, his gray eyes staring with a look of passion. He knew she spoke the truth but his eyes had deceived him. He still saw those men around her, lusting after her, lusting after his woman who remained untouched.

By the look in her eyes he knew she was his for the taking, but he wouldn't, not their first time together, not in his angered state. He had to get her out of there. Damn her for being alone, he thought. She was lucky one of those men didn't force themselves upon her. And where was Kurt? Knowing Melissa, she had probably made a deal with him.

His lips twisted. "Well, I'm glad you learned a new dance, it will give you something to practice...at home," he authorized, picking up her suitcase which he'd taken the liberty to pack earlier. "We're leaving, let's go." Waiting for her, she didn't move but stood her ground.

His commanding image dominated her for a moment but then a stir of anger arose and her power regained. "You can't just waltz in here and expect me to obey your every command." She was livid. For him to assume he could take over and run her life was absurd.

"Watch me," he told her. On instinct his hand tightened on the bag as she lunged forward to grab it but his grip was too strong.

Frustrated, she stood there with hands balled into fists at her sides. She realized now the power she gave him by giving into their stolen moment of pleasure in the barn. Because she had allowed him to touch her, he now took possession of her? That wasn't going to continue, she would set him straight now, before it got out of hand.

The challenge of stubbornness began and could be seen in the narrowness of their eyes. Stuck into a locked gaze that could only be broken by one of the challengers forfeiting, Melissa said with unmoving eyes, "I know why you're acting this way and it will not work."

His velvet brows arched in response, curious as to what she meant. "Acting what way? What are you talking about?" knowing emphatically that his jealousy was no secret, even to himself.

"This possession of yours has got to stop. Just because I let you touch me doesn't give you the right to own me," she whipped out, setting him straight so he wouldn't be left in the dark about her meaning.

His thoughts reflected back to the hayloft, immediately knowing what she referred to. His teeth ground together as air exhaled from his nose. "I am not trying to own you, Melissa, and as far as touching you, you wanted to be touched. Even if your mouth didn't speak the words your body told me as much." His angry mouth curved into a devilish grin. "I didn't have a fight on my hands, now did I?"

Sometimes he's to blunt for his own good, she thought. All her denying couldn't battle the truth he spoke. On purpose she avoided giving a response to his bold words, instead making her conclusion clear. "What happened in the hayloft should never happen again so there is no need to be possessive with me anymore. Are we agreed?"

"Are you asking this of me because you truly didn't like it or because you can't handle how good it feels? And don't say you're scared, either you liked it or you didn't," he questioned as his eyes were daring hers.

She stepped closer to him with only inches to spare between them, her soft lips reddening and firming in annoyance. "What I can't handle is your possessive nature. It's maddening," she voiced in a low and stern tone while keeping her eyes glued to his and not backing away one bit.

Staring into the sparkling hazel depths of her eyes all temptation to conquer her mouth with his flamed before him. Instead he used the last ounce of control he had left and chose to put her in her place once again. "What you call possessive, I call protective. You need my protection, damn it."

Laura Mills

She was impressed with how he could turn situations around. He was downright jealous and he wouldn't admit it. Protective, huh? He was supposed to be her mentor of thoroughbreds, after all, and it appeared he planned on being her mentor in all areas of her life. "Whom are you protecting me from? Yourself?"

That could be the truth, but in John's mind he had made a promise to her father that she was unaware of and that promise included protecting her from reckless situations with other men. As for himself, that became another struggle with a life all its own. "Be reasonable Melissa," he told her as his head shook from aggravation. "I'm finished with this thrashing of words with you."

"You haven't agreed with our situation?" It was for the best, she kept telling herself.

"And I'm not going to," he informed her. It was time they faced the reality of their relationship. She might try to avoid it but he couldn't. He needed to have a calm conversation with her about this and now wasn't the appropriate time. Before their personal talk, she needed to know about her father.

"Why not?" she pushed since he had inflamed her anew.

"Now is not the time. We need to leave now and talk later," he told her as he motioned for the door with her bag in hand.

"I'm leaving in a few days as I planned," she stated, by now tired and flustered at his powerful ways.

"You're leaving now," he commanded as he grabbed her hand and they were out the door.

On their way from the hotel to John's rented carriage John noticed her limping was worse. "Your limp is heavier," he commented.

"What?" She hadn't paid it any attention, but her leg did ache more than normal.

"You've been walking too much too soon on your injured leg."

Instead of responding, knowing he was right, Melissa stayed quiet.

"Where is Kurt?" John inquired.

The anger hadn't left his face. She was about to answer him when stepping out of the carriage was the same gentleman that had offered his assistance earlier. Her eyes widened. A friend of John's, she supposed.

"Melissa, where is Kurt?" Her eyes cut back to John when his tone became demanding.

"Kurt? How did you know about Kurt?" Her dazed mind began clearing. "No, never mind. My father told you, didn't he? You're his new best friend. I suppose he'd tell you anything you wanted to know, particularly about his daughter."

John's glare competed with hers. "Just tell me where he is. We need to take him back with us."

She glanced in the other gentleman's direction before pointing toward the pub. "He's there, in the same pub you saw me in."

John motioned to Robert to get Melissa settled in the carriage. "I'll be right back."

Melissa watched him stride down the cobblestone path, infuriated with him but at the same time relieved because he was here with her.

"Miss Howard." Robert opened the carriage door and guided her in, taking a seat across from her.

He had a nice sounding voice, soft, yet deep like John's. If she hadn't been so enamored of John, his friend would prove quite handsome. He had dark brown waves of hair that reached his shoulders and emerald green eyes that one could fall into. They hadn't time to converse before John and Kurt returned.

Kurt went to sit next to Melissa when John stopped him. "That seat is taken." John caught the roll of Melissa's eyes.

Kurt obliged. John and his friend were too big to mess with so he sat next to Robert in silence. John had mentioned to Kurt about the passing of Mr. Howard. Shocked, he swore not to say a word to Melissa.

Once they were all settled in the carriage it was off to the ship.

On the way John was so entranced by his own thoughts that he'd forgot to introduce his best friend to his favorite, impossible student and he realized it when Robert introduced himself. He felt like a clod but his anger level had reached unknown peaks.

"Hello, Miss Howard. I'm Robert Gibson, John's best friend and partner," Robert offered while extending his hand out to her.

"Nice to finally make your acquaintance, Mr. Gibson."

Her courteous manners were loathsome, smiling in excess, trying to dig at John, he could tell. He watched their hands clasp for a quick shake and then drop.

Robert added, "I would have met you sooner if I'd known you were at John's manor the day of your accident as I was there. I'm sorry about your accident, by the way."

My Forbidden Mentor

John observed Melissa's expression when Robert mentioned the accident. Shock and then remorse flooded over her honeyed features. It seemed odd to John at first, but then remembering an accident like that again could be a reason to react so strongly.

Robert became aware of Melissa's change as well and voiced his regret. "I shouldn't have reminded you. I apologize."

Robert didn't need to apologize. Her changing mood wasn't due to the accident, as horrible as it was. It was Robert's announcement that had her rattled. If Robert was the one in the library and John had been in town, then what a dreadful mistake she'd made. Have I got a limp for life because I assumed wrong? And I've treated John in a horrible way. At that thought she looked over at him. He was staring out the window. She focused back on Robert. Somehow she would talk to Robert alone to confirm her suspicions. "Please Mr. Gibson, I'm quite fine about it. I appreciate the concern, and at last we've finally met." Her eyes took in John's profile. "I've heard a lot about you, good things." That made Robert smile. It added bewilderment for John when his head turned her way at the change of tone in her voice.

They boarded the ship and all retired to their own cabins for the few hours of travel. John arose before dawn. Not able to sleep, his thoughts deliberated on Melissa and what to do about her. Her father's passing created an additional responsibility toward her, a promise, one that he'd made and intended to keep.

The ship took its time reaching the docks. John gripped the wooden railing in anticipation of the incredible deed he still needed to complete. In the near distance he could see his carriage parked next to a giant oak tree, his driver,

Jess, snoozing with reins in hand. There was an additional rig parked next to his. John had made arrangements earlier so he and Melissa would have privacy so he could tell her about the passing of her father. He hadn't been looking forward to this moment and now it was time to face it.

When departing the ship, John looked up into three sets of eyes. Two sets reflected grief and the third set, the important one, looked perplexed.

John nodded to Robert and Kurt, who headed for the opposite carriage. Melissa started to follow them when John stopped her. "Melissa, you and I will take this one."

"All right." She didn't argue but complied and waited for his assistance to enter the carriage. Another idea she had to get used to, at least for now, was that her injured leg wouldn't allow her the task of steps unassisted.

Once she was inside John was right behind her, tapping the roof and signaling Jess to carry on.

Sitting across from her, his mind scrambled on how to begin. This wasn't just anyone he had to inform about a parent's death, it was Melissa. Melissa, whom he'd come to know as a person, a person who'd become a friend, one who'd already lost one parent.

His nervous tension showed because he saw Melissa's stare lingering on his tightened fingers forming into fists on his lap. Damn. It shouldn't be this difficult.

Her eyes found his. "John, why did we have to take separate carriages?" Her fingers gripped the material of her dress at her sides. He was awfully quiet.

Slipping next to her made him feel more at ease. "I need to talk to you about something."

My Forbidden Mentor

With a cross look on her face, she asked, "What is so urgent that I had to end my trip so abruptly?" She thought his jealousy had pushed him to pursue her. When his eyes blinked and turned solemn, a gut feeling told her something was wrong. "What is it John? Is it my father?"

How was he going to tell her? He knew her father meant the world to her, but she had to know. Carefully he took her hand in his and looked directly into her frightened gaze. "Yes, it is," he said with gentleness.

Her eyes searched his, not wanting to believe his words. "What's happened? Is there a doctor with him? Is it serious?" she asked, her voice breaking up. Her senses told her it was worse than she imagined. No, not my father's death.

John took a moment to answer. "No," he said, swallowing hard when seeing her eyes begin to mist. He squeezed her hand in comfort. "He's gone, Melissa."

She held his gaze, wishing, hoping, wanting him to take back the words he'd just spoken, those last critical words that had revealed the unbelievable truth. Why? Her eyes began stinging with new tears as she asked herself the reason why. She looked away, not wanting John to see her falling apart, but her emotions were overflowing, ready to flood at any moment. She kept denying his words, hoping it was a nightmare and soon she'd wake up. Holding herself in check, teetering on the brink, she glanced toward John again. His sympathetic expression hadn't changed. "This isn't happening. It isn't possible. Please tell me this is a cruel joke," Melissa begged out of desperation, hoping he'd have a different answer.

"It's true, sweetheart," he said, trying to stay calm for Melissa's sake. It wasn't easy when his heart was racing a mile a minute. He understood her denial, as denial seemed to be a natural part of the course for losing a loved one.

Her voice crumbled in the dryness of her throat as she tried to ask, "How did he die?"

"I'm not sure, in his sleep, though." John's voice was tender.

Pulling the curtain aside from the dampened window allowed her blurred vision to examine moonlit trees passing by as fast as her scattering thoughts. Without realizing it she squeezed tighter on John's hand as reality surfaced over and over again. "When," she paused to control her tears. "When did he go?"

John's voice was right above a whisper. "Sometime this morning, I think."

"Did you find him?" she asked.

"No, your aunt did. He was still in bed. He never woke up."

"How's auntie?" she asked, concerned for her dear friend.

"She's doing all right. She has a friend with her."

"Good." Continuing to stare into the morning darkness, the back of her free hand covered her mouth to muffle any sobbing sounds.

John watched her. She was trying to be strong but was failing. He could tell by how solid her grip remained on his hand. He was searching for some kind of consolation when he heard her speak again.

"You went there to see my father?"

"Yes I went by yesterday to see how you were fairing and stayed for supper and conversation with your father." He gave her a smile. "I enjoyed his company very much." He stopped to study her features. "We made plans to go hunting this morning. He said he hadn't been in ages. He seemed very happy Melissa."

My Forbidden Mentor

A moment of silence fell between them. She tried thinking happy thoughts. "Yes, you know he encouraged me to take this trip. It was his...idea." Her voice sounded strained. "He always thought of everyone else except himself. I'm thankful to have had a father...so...wonderful." Her lips pressed together but a surge of fresh tears broke through.

Losing the battle of her welled up feelings, she turned to John, looking for comfort. His free hand went to her face, his fingers wiping the wetness from her honeyed cheeks, and still more came. "Oh Melissa, I'm so sorry about your father," he told her.

Her lips pressed together again and her view of John's handsome face blurred even more. "I never expected this, not so soon after my mother." Her eyes searched his in close proximity. She knew he understood and she needed his comfort. "John?" she paused before asking, "Will you hold me?"

Identifying with her pain, he didn't hesitate. "Come here," he told her as his arms opened to her. Her arms went around him in a powerful grip. His hands slid along her back, his face dissolving in her golden strands. He knew she was about to burst. There had to be rage, hurt, and sadness wanting to emerge. "Let it out," he told her. "Come on, Melissa, let it out." He began rocking her in his arms.

Muffled sobs started escaping her mouth. Her saturated cheek lay against his sleek black hair when the words poured out of her. "Oh, father." she wailed. "Father, why did you leave me?" John closed his eyes and tightened his arms around her, empathizing with her pain. "It's not fair, why him, why my father, God? It's too soon," she cried, almost choking on her words.

John held her close while she voiced her sobbing anger. After her cries had quieted, she murmured near his ear, "I'm all alone now."

His deep voice reassured her. "You're not alone. I'm here," he told her. I will always be here, he wanted to tell her. They held each other until her breathing was almost normal. His hands were rubbing her back when she lifted away.

Settling her hands on his shoulders, her red swollen eyes stared into his that expressed compassion. "John, thank you for being here," she said.

He gazed into her beautiful, saddened face, stained from paths of tears, and became aware of a strange sensation that shot straight to his heart, a first of this kind of feeling, and in gathering his bearings he spoke the truth, "I want to be here for you."

A slight smile pierced her lips as she moved away from him and leaned into the soft leather seat. She laid her head on his broad shoulder and grasped for his hand again.

His nose dipped down, touching her shiny head of gold, and he inhaled her flowered scent. His eyes closed and he thought of how increasingly difficult it was becoming not to touch her. Even now, when emotions ran rampant, he wanted to show her he cared, not just tell her, but it was too soon for that. He didn't feel she was ready to handle physical closeness yet.

She fell asleep until they arrived at her house in the late evening. John awakened her. "Melissa, you're home."

Stepping to the front door she froze, unable to go in. John sensed her hesitation. "I'll go in with you," he offered.

Upon entering a gust of tobacco filled her nostrils and the familiar scent unnerved her. She stopped at the doorway of the sitting room. She stared at the couch which had been her temporary bed for almost a month. Tonight she couldn't sleep there, not when there were so many past memories.

My Forbidden Mentor

"Are you going to be all right tonight?" he asked as concern crossed over his features.

Her eyes downcast as she peered at her folded hands and then lifted back to his as she made a request, "John, I'd rather sleep in my own bed tonight. Could you help me?"

"Of course. I'll just grab your blankets and pillows," he told her and went to fetch the items she needed. When he returned to her side he sensed there was more she wanted to ask.

She was seeking the appropriate words for another request when she noticed how much he was concentrating on her. "John, I don't want to be alone tonight. Will you stay?" she asked but paused because of the startled look on his face and then changed her mind. "I understand if..." She was stopped short.

"Of course," he answered without thinking twice. She had taken him by surprise but he couldn't refuse her request. It was obvious she needed additional comforting. "I need to tell my driver to go on and bring back my mare tomorrow."

"Oh dear. I had forgotten about that," she said sounding apologetic.

He handed her the blankets and pillows. "Don't worry yourself. Wait for me and I'll carry you up." Even as he said it, he knew she hadn't any choice but to wait.

"Okay," she faintly replied. She found it easy to obey him for she was numb and needed guidance.

Turning on his heel, in no time he was out the door.

Melissa stepped over to the bottom of the stairway, waiting for John's return, when Miss Beckett hurled down the stairs toward her.

"Oh come here, love." Her arms opened to Melissa. They embraced each other before Miss Beckett lifted away to hold Melissa at arm's length. "Has Lord Blackburn left already?" she asked.

"No he'll be back," she said before explaining, "Auntie, I've asked Lord Blackburn to stay here tonight. I wanted you to be aware." She waited, nervous of her reaction.

Her startled features became soft again. "I understand, my love. I'm grateful for everything he's done," she said and smiled, giving Melissa a quick peck on her cheek. "I'll see you in the morning then. We have a long day ahead of us. Good night."

John watched his driver leave before stepping back inside the house. He had already been strained about the closeness with Melissa and now she had begged him to stay with her all night. Well, in any case, he was sure he'd be sleeping on the couch after she fell asleep, or at worst on her bedroom floor so she'd have him near. What was there to worry about?

New tears spilled down Melissa's cheeks while awaiting John's return. Piled on top of the most draining day of her life she couldn't even climb the blasted stairs to her bedroom. It didn't mean forever, but that didn't mean now either, when her whole life was falling apart. Her hand covered her mouth to stifle any crying sounds she made.

Just then the front door swung open and John entered. When he came up next to her he could tell that she'd been crying again, but he didn't say anything. If she needed to cry then let her. "Ready?" he asked, his legs bending to prepare for her weight.

"Yes," she replied, tugging her blankets and pillows into a ball.

My Forbidden Mentor

While he carried her so easily up the stairway, Melissa imagined she was dreaming. Instead of carrying her out of necessity, he carried her like they were lovers searching for her bedroom. She'd almost forgotten how good he smelled, how warm his body felt next to hers. When they reached the top of the stairs Melissa tucked her face into his neck, continuing to believe it was a dream.

Reality brought her back when he asked, "Which way?"

Her dizzying head straightened. "Left," she told him.

He set her down at the doorway of her bedroom. Needing to bring her traveling bags up was the perfect excuse to leave so she could undress for bed. "I'll be right back. I need to get your bags."

"All right." She almost looked disappointed that he was leaving again but then she gave him a small, sweet smile that he hadn't seen in some time.

Melissa was lying in her bed with a long nightdress covering her body by the time she heard a soft knock at the door. "Come in," she called out.

John walked in with her baggage, set it on the floor and then shut the door as he stepped over to her. He sat on the edge of the bed while she lay on her side toward the middle, facing him. A lavender coverlet covered every part of her except her hands, which were tucked beneath her cheek. John's finger went to her temple, pushing a strand of loose hair away when he asked, "How are you feeling?"

Her focus was intense on his relaxed hand, which rested on his thigh. "Okay," she replied, sounding distant.

He could tell she needed more rest. His fingers brought the edge of the coverlet around her, securing her shoulders even more. "Do you want to talk?" he asked.

She shook her head.

"Where would you like me to sleep then?" he asked, feeling a bit uneasy that she might have an inappropriate answer.

Her eyes shifted to his. She didn't have to think about it but her concern lie with his reaction. Would he think her too forward? "In bed...with me," she replied. As she had expected, his expression changed. "I hope it's not asking too much," she said and her eyes cast downward. "It's just...it helps when you hold me."

Her sad eyes were precious when they found his again. In his wildest dreams he hadn't expected this. He thought about turning down her request because he wasn't sure how much constraint he had left. She had asked him to hold her. How much closer could they get without the inevitable happening? Of course, the inevitable was entirely controlled by him.

He understood the death of a parent quite well. Melissa shouldn't have to go through those lost feelings by herself. It would please him to give her comfort, and that was all it would be tonight. His selfish needs could wait. Right now she was fragile, like a small child needing his arms to embrace her. "It's not too much to ask," he said, giving her a warm smile. Then the plump little figure of her aunt came to mind. "Melissa, what about your aunt?" he asked with growing concern.

Her sleepy eyes found his. "I've already spoken to her. She's aware."

He studied her dreary features, deciding not to push the issue. "If you're sure?" he questioned to verify.

"Yes," she answered with certainty.

Rising from the bed, he began undoing the buttons on his shirt. After slipping off his shirt and tossing it onto a chair he bent down to take off his boots. He stood straight again, pulling the tie from his hair, letting the black silkiness flow freely across his back. Leaving his trousers on, he tugged the blankets down and slid in next to her.

She hoped she hadn't made a mistake being this close to John, but she knew John had respect for her and would know what she was going through, which was why she needed him now. He could understand her and reassure her, reassure her that the numbness and emptiness would disappear, that life does go on. Her father had told her that when her mother had passed away, but now she needed John to tell her. He'd made it through his mother's death. She needed his strength to make it through her father's.

She observed him with intent as he lay on his side, facing her, leaning his weight on one elbow, his palm supporting his head. She watched his black hair fall loosely around his shoulders, then captured his gray eyes piercing through her, his mouth sending her a smile from heaven. She voiced her thoughts aloud before thinking about it. "You're beautiful," she whispered.

His smile faded after she whispered those words. Stunned by her comment, he could see in her eyes that she meant it. Lord she tempted him with her honesty. The willpower it took not to devour her became devastating. Never had he wanted a woman so much. Melissa tested every throbbing nerve in his blazing body. His smile returned as he leaned closer to her. "So are you. Now go to sleep, you need to rest," he told her, his head tilting as his lips placed a quick tender kiss upon hers. "Turn the other way," he said, and with gentle ease motioned her to face away from him.

His chest fit perfectly against her back. His mouth was content swimming in her golden streams of hair while his arm wrapped around her waist and pulled her snug against him. Her arm slid over his and eventually they fell asleep that way. Once in awhile periodic sounds of crying woke John during the night. Hearing her sobs, he would draw her body tighter against his own, soothing and coaxing her back to sleep.

John woke up early. He didn't want to let go of Melissa, didn't want to leave her warm concealed body, but he decided he'd better in order to fetch her some breakfast. It was the perfect excuse, leaving him without an option to take advantage of the situation, which would be the last thing she needed to deal with on the day of her father's funeral. With quiet movements he slipped out of the bed, got dressed, and headed downstairs to the kitchen.

Miss Beckett was bringing breakfast to the table when she just about ran into John through the doorway. "Oh, I didn't see you coming Lord Blackburn," she gasped.

"It was entirely my fault. I was in a hurry," he smiled.

"That hungry, huh?" she said, teasing him.

"I could smell your cooking through the house and my appetite became ravenous." His words were complimentary.

"Thank you Lord Blackburn. I've cooked for many years, I would hope it's edible by now," she laughed. "Here, sit and eat. I hope you like crepes, ham, and porridge?"

"Indeed I do." His mouth began watering when she placed the heaping mound of food before him.

"I hope you slept comfortably," she commented with a distinctive gleam in her eye.

John glanced up between bites of food and responded; "Yes," he acknowledged, choosing not to let his previous night's resting place be challenged, and he changed the subject. "How are the funeral arrangements coming along?"

Miss Beckett sat across the dining table from him, noted his reaction and realized the subject of his sleeping arrangements was not up for discussion. "Everything is set. The funeral will take place this afternoon. There will be a few neighbors and friends attending, and Mr. Howard's workers, of course. Thankfully everyone has offered to bring food and, oh dear, I hope I haven't forgotten anything."

"It doesn't sound like it," he commented, now realizing how hungry he'd been.

A distant stare displayed on Miss Beckett's features. "You know we just went through this three years ago. It's not fair to Miss Melissa, simply not fair."

John stopped eating to ask about further arrangements. "What will happen to the carpentry business?"

Miss Beckett gave him a slight smile. "I'm not sure. That will be up to Miss Melissa. She owns it now, you know."

John continued to finish his breakfast.

Miss Beckett watched him devour his food and offered him more. "A might hungry, Lord Blackburn? There's more if you'd like some."

He returned a grateful smile. "Thank you but I've had plenty. It was delicious, by the way."

"You're welcome."

A brief period of silence intervened.

John dabbed his mouth with an available linen cloth. "How are you doing?" he asked, knowing she had had to make all the preparations for the burial.

"I'm doing all right. I'm more concerned with Miss Melissa." Her eyes began to water.

"Yes, I know."

There was another moment of silence.

Miss Beckett backed away from the dining table, lifting to take their empty plates to the kitchen. On her way back, she had a full plate of food for Melissa.

John could see that she was upset and offered to take on the task at hand. He rose with a scrape of his chair to catch Miss Beckett before she started up the stairway. "Let me take it up to her, Miss Beckett. I'll make sure she eats."

Miss Beckett was glad that he was there in their time of need. Although she knew that she and Miss Melissa could take care of themselves, it was comforting to have a man around to take charge in these troubled times. "Thank you Lord Blackburn. I might lie down on the couch for a bit."

"You do that. You need to rest after all the work you've done." John took the plate from Miss Beckett and headed up the stairway.

Making his way to Melissa's room, he stood inside the doorway watching her sleep. She was laying in the fetal position, facing the wall, her long golden hair floating onto his pillow. An image appeared in his mind that they were husband and wife. He'd never had extended thoughts like that before. He'd seen plenty of women lying in bed, but the concept of being his wife never entered his mind before now. He set the plate of food on the nightstand, shaking off his unusual thought. Kneeling on the bed, he reached over to wake her. "Melissa," he spoke, "Melissa, wake up. You need to eat."

She groaned at him, not moving.

My Forbidden Mentor

He called her name again, "Melissa," using more insistence.

Pulling the blankets over her head, she muffled, "I'm not hungry."

"Oh no you don't," he told her as he tore the blankets back down.

"John," she replied in a perturbed tone, trying to pull the covers back up.

He wouldn't let her have them. She was being stubborn so he decided to try another tactic that was sure to get her attention. Slipping back into bed, lying next to her as he had before, his arm went around her waist, pulling her snug against him. She didn't seem to mind until his hand reached down to lift her nightdress up around her waist.

The cool air drifting along her legs stirred her further, but the warm hand gliding across her bare buttock drove her full awake. "John, what are you doing?" she exclaimed, flipping over toward him, in innocence pulling her dress back down. He lay on his side, leaning his weight onto his elbow, smiling at her.

"What was that all about?" she hissed at him.

"I was trying to wake you. It seems I've succeeded." His grin was devilish this morning.

"Yes, well, I'm up now," she told him, not sure what else to say. Having never woken up with a man in her bed, a most handsome man at that, she wasn't quite sure how to act.

Watching her trying to cover herself, her actions proved again how innocent she really was, and he treasured that. She teased him without any notion of doing so. "You need to eat," he told her, sitting up to get the plate of food.

"I'm not hungry John," she said, wondering if he had heard her the first time.

"At least try a crepe. They're strawberry. I know you like strawberries. I've already had some. They're delicious," he informed her as he cut a piece to feed to her. She sat up, staring at him with her arms crossed and lips pouting.

"You need to be strong today. Come on," he said, placing the fork near her mouth. She opened her mouth and took the food. He continued to feed her, although all she ate was the crepe. When he was satisfied at how much she'd eaten he tried his best to convince her to sleep more, but he didn't push today and she got her way. He left the room so she could dress, then came back to carry her down the stairs, telling her he'd be outside tending the horses.

She followed him to involve herself with the horses as it helped take her mind off her father. When the undesired time arrived they stood under an apple tree on their property where her mother was already buried. Her father was to be buried next to her mother. Melissa looked around at so many familiar faces and was thankful for their caring presence. John stood by her side the whole time, holding her hand as she had requested. Her focus swung to her auntie, who held onto her opposite hand, her sweet auntie who was about the only family she had left.

After the funeral services John remained behind. Sitting on the porch swing, they had trailed off talking about her father. Melissa admired her mentor's profile while asking him about his mother. "John, how did your mother pass on?"

He was quiet for a long time, staring ahead at nothing, his expression becoming sullen. "I can't talk about it right now," he told her.

My Forbidden Mentor

"I was just wondering," she persisted, but was cut off.

"Anything but my mother Melissa," he requested.

A longer period of time passed before they spoke again. Melissa wasn't sure how to end her curiosity. "She was obviously special to you. I presume her to be a fascinating woman."

Shifting his focus her way, his voice released unwanted anger. "She was very special to me, and I don't care to talk about her right now!" He didn't want to be angry with her, especially today, but he couldn't talk about his mother. It was too painful and the memories were too fresh from today's event. Standing, hoping to escape her questions about his mother, he trailed away from the swing to lean against a thick post on the wooden porch. His arms crossed over his broad chest and he stared out among the lush green landscape of hills.

Feeling bad that she had upset him, an equal part of her grew angry that he didn't share his experience with her. She went ahead and apologized but had decided they needed a break from each other. "I'm sorry if I've upset you. I won't ask about her again." At least for a while, she thought. Coming to care too much about this remarkable man, she wanted to know everything about him.

"Thank you," he said, hoping he didn't bruise her feelings too much, but he had never talked about his mother and he wanted it to stay that way. That was a profound wound he didn't want to open up again.

Feeling put off by his sudden mood change, she needed time to think. As she glared into his back she said, "John, I appreciate everything you've done for me these last couple of days but I'd like to be alone now. Auntie is here so there's no need to worry about me."

His head turned in her direction. His features were distant and he was not surprised by her request. "How much time do you need?" he asked, growing accustomed to seeing her often and not wanting it to change.

"I'm not sure," she told him, not knowing how much time she needed alone.

His arms unfolded and, taking two strides in her direction, he kneeled before her. His fingertips lifted her chin and his lips grazed over hers. His kiss increased in intensity, exploring her mouth as if to memorize every detail, but he could feel the tension in her kiss. When his lips left hers, his eyes opened, reflecting sadness that tore at her heart.

"I understand," he responded, and then rose to walk over to the barn to get his mare.

What am I to do about him? Melissa wondered as her eyes followed his spectacular physique. I'm so confused. Why am I letting myself have feelings for this precarious man? She started to shake, a delayed reaction to his thorough kiss.

He was already atop Clara when he stopped in front of her. "I'm only waiting a week. After that I want to see you," he plainly stated, and with that he heeled Clara and headed for the trees, leaving her no time to respond.

She couldn't believe the audacity of him to order her around like he owned her. She needed to think, darn him. She needed time alone with Robert to find out the truth. John had done so much for her and she hated treating him so brutally, but he made it easier when he refused to tell her about his mother. She had thought they were close enough to at least confide in the death of their parents. She hadn't realized until the moment of his outburst how close he had been to his mother and how painful her death must have been for him. She longed to relieve some of his burden as he had done for her in regards to her father.

Nevertheless, she took this time alone to devise a plan to meet with Robert.

Chapter Thirteen

Without John around to carry her up and down the stairway Melissa maintained her sleeping arrangement on the couch. Tossing and turning on the narrow cushions of the couch, her mind was scrambling with ways to contact Robert so she could discover the truth about the day of the accident. Unfortunately she hadn't a clue as to Robert's schedule, and she didn't dare ask John.

Her thoughts wandered to her father, her caring father who'd left this world too soon. Tears and reminiscent memories flowed through her once again. Wrapping her arms around herself, images of John came to mind. She missed him. Clutching tighter on the blankets, the warmth of her body couldn't compare to John's enveloping embrace the night before. She craved his sympathy and maybe more than that. One night, just one night he stayed with her, and she longed for his comfort. She knew if he'd been there again, wrapped around her, she'd fall asleep without a thought, so she drifted from her thoughts and dreamed, dreamed of a dark and handsome man and his body of warmth. By the early morning hours Melissa conceded to much needed rest as her body eventually gave in to her exhausted mind and weakened leg.

A knock at the front door startled her awake. Drowsy-eyed and wondering why her aunt hadn't answered the door, she threw the blankets off and hobbled to the door and as she reached for the doorknob she remembered that her aunt had errands in town this morning.

To her relieved surprise it was Robert standing before her, holding a package of some kind and wearing a generous smile on his handsome face as he greeted her with concerned enthusiasm. "Miss Howard, how are you fairing this morning?"

"Better, thank you," she said, standing in the open doorway when a light breeze blew across her form causing her hands to rub along her naked arms.

"Oh, forgive me, I've awakened you," Robert said as he gave her an apologetic expression.

Waking her wasn't her concern at the moment since she'd just realized her fingers brushed along naked skin, her own exposed skin, while standing in the doorway of her home before John's partner and even worse, his best friend.

Robert acted oblivious to knowing where her thoughts had traveled but the sudden change in her sleepy look prompted him to question her. "Are you all right, Miss Howard? You look distraught?"

She replaced the shock on her face with a kind smile. "Melissa, please." In a flash she turned away from him and crossed her arms over her chest to conceal any exposure of her body through her nightgown. She invited him in while she hobbled back to the couch. "Please, come in," she told him as she retrieved her wrap from the couch. As she closed the wrap around her body she gestured for Robert to sit down. "Have a seat," she offered.

"Thank you," he said, sitting in the wingback chair across from her. His hand loosened its grip on the package he carried, reminding him of its purpose. "By the way, this is for you," he told her as he handed it over to her. "It's cakes and muffins and such. My friend Rose made them." Robert watched her unwrap the folded linen and saw her eyes widen in delight when observing the array of treats.

"They look scrumptious. Please thank her for me," she told him as she kept her eyes on the single cake she brought to her mouth.

"Rose is quite the baker. I have to limit myself of her treats or I will ruin my perfect physique," he chuckled. Melissa didn't respond verbally but nodded with a mouth full of cake.

His laughter declined when he spoke again, "My condolences regarding your father."

She had just swallowed the last bit of cake as her eyes took in his pleasant features. "Thank you, Robert, if I may call you by your first name?"

"Of course. I see us as friends. You are a part of our team, are you not?"

Licking the remaining crumbs from her lips, she responded, "Well, yes. I mean, I started out that way. I'm not sure now that my leg is ruined." She looked away from his concentrated stare. She was using her leg as an excuse when she shouldn't have. By now the doctor had approved of her riding again as long as she kept up the strengthening of her leg. Could the real reason for her statement be because of the intimacy she had engaged in with her mentor? Could she continue to work with him under the circumstances?

Robert appeared baffled. "I thought with exercise your leg would be fine, regarding riding, at least?"

Does he know what happened between John and I, she wondered. "To be honest Robert, it's confidence that concerns me. My leg may be dead weight. I'm not sure how John feels about that, if he still has confidence in me, that is?"

"Why don't you ask him?" he suggested.

There was hesitation, then the truth. "Because I'm afraid to hear the answer," she confided.

"I think you should ask anyway. You can't deny he cares about your welfare?"

"No, not at all. He's been here practically every day." That was until she had asked him to leave because of his reluctance to indulge her about his mother.

"Well then, the next time you see him, ask him. Then your confidence will be restored."

Melissa's brow lifted in curiosity. "So then, you're sure that he hasn't given up on our arrangement?" she asked.

"Has he given any reason to show different?" Robert countered.

"No. No, he hasn't," she rushed out.

"I'm curious about something, Melissa. Forgive me if this isn't the proper time, but it's been bothering me since we met in Dublin." He had attained her full attention. "When I mentioned being at John's manor the day of your accident, I noticed you tensed immediately. Did my being there have anything to do with your accident?" he questioned.

"Why would you think that?" Melissa asked him as her body tensed.

"I'm not sure, but for you to run off before John arrived, I thought perhaps someone or something had upset you." Robert looked worried, like he was accusing himself.

"Yes, I was upset. But your being there did not cause my accident Robert." This was her moment to discover the truth and learn how wrong she'd been. "I have an inquiry of my own. Around noontime on that same day, were you in John's library?" She saw his brows crease at the question.

His features softened when he recalled that not only had he been in John's library at the time specified but what he'd been doing in there. A blush of color heated his face. "Yes. Yes I was," he admitted, leaning forward and without further explanation, snatched a tempting cake.

Melissa hadn't noticed the cake he took because the truth had been verified. Just to make sure she asked another crucial question. "Robert, did you have a lady friend with you?"

She must have heard us, he thought. He had sincerely hoped his cheeks weren't turning red but was doubtful because he could feel his cheeks warming as he answered her, "Yes, it was Rose. How did you know?"

It was Robert and Rose, not John and another conquest. She sighed as she responded, "I was bored waiting for John so I thought I'd look over the collection of books he'd talked about. When I got to the library door I heard voices, a man and a woman's."

In abrupt realization it dawned on Robert the scene that must have taken place before Melissa. It would be hard on any woman to hear what Melissa had heard, but knowing Melissa and John's intimate history he couldn't blame her for escaping like she had. His hands covered his face, no longer from embarrassment but from the fact that everything had turned upside down. His fingers combed through his thick hair. It all made sense now. "You thought that I was John?"

He'd figured it out on his own. That was good because it would humiliate her to explain every detail. "Yes."

"And that he was with a woman?"

She delayed in answering, even though the answer became apparent. "Yes," she acknowledged.

My Forbidden Mentor

"Well, everything is clear now," Robert replied in good spirits.

"What do you mean?" Melissa questioned.

"Well John, Charles and I have been beating our heads against the wall trying to figure out why you took off the way you did. It will be a relief for all when I tell them the reason," he explained.

"Robert, no," she responded sharply, causing Robert to look alarmed. "Please don't tell John or Charles for that matter. He may mention it to John," she pleaded.

"What do you mean, lass? John needs to know. He's mentioned you've been upset with him and he doesn't know why. I presume it's because of what you thought to be true. It will relieve him to know the explanation."

"He cannot," she begged.

Now he understood her harsh reaction. She was humiliated. "He needs to know something Melissa. You had reason initially to be upset but John is unaware of your reasons," he attempted to convince her.

"You're absolutely right, Robert, but I feel ashamed as it is," she agreed although her eyes remain full of worry.

"You'd go on letting him think otherwise?" Robert asked, trying to see her point of view but knew it was unfair by not explaining to John.

"No. I don't know," she said on a defeated breath.

"His reaction may surprise you. You need to tell him," he ordered as he pointed a finger in her direction. "In fact, you two need to sit down and have a long talk about everything. Clear the air, as they say," he recommended since he knew both sides of the story.

Melissa grew wary of his solution. "You know more than you're letting on, don't you?"

He gave a handsome, devilish grin. "Not every detail, Melissa. But I am John's best friend."

He didn't have to say any more as she guessed the extent of Robert's knowledge. Robert knowing about the intimacies between she and John didn't bother her as much as she thought it would. Robert seemed caring and concerned about his two friends. She supposed he was right when he suggested she and John talk. She owed John at least that much, and more, to make up for her unreasonable behavior. She gave Robert a sincere smile. "I think that's exactly what John and I need to do. The next time I see him we shall talk," she told him and since John had said he'd see her in a week that gave her enough time to prepare an appropriate apology.

"Good. It eases my mind that you two will work this out," he told her as he returned her smile.

While Robert rambled on about the progress he'd had with his students and how it hadn't matched the progress she and John had made, Melissa drifted into ways of telling John about the misunderstanding she'd had, concluding that there wasn't any way around the truth. He needed to know and a week's time remained for her to prepare.

The front door burst open and Miss Beckett trailed in with supplies piled high in her arms. Robert rose from the chair to help her.

Melissa hadn't thought of her auntie's reaction finding her alone with an unknown man. Her aunt smiled when Robert lightened her load but she remained distressed. "What is it Auntie?"

My Forbidden Mentor

Miss Beckett set the rest of the items on the hardwood floor. "My aunt has taken ill," she said in disbelief. "I received a message while in town. I'm afraid I must go to her."

As if there couldn't be any more bad news. "Which aunt?" Melissa inquired, knowing what a large family Miss Beckett had.

"Theresa." She stepped over to Melissa and sat next to her. "Oh love, will you be all right by yourself?"

She covered her aunt's hand with her own. "Yes, but I'll go with you if you like?"

Miss Beckett shook her head, squeezing Melissa's fingers. "No, that's not necessary, love. You need to get better. I've already made arrangements to travel with cousin Harriet."

"Good. It comforts me to know you're not going alone. Is there anything I can do?"

"Just get better. I feel guilty leaving you like this and so soon after," Miss Beckett swallowed to contain her tears. Emotions had run high all week with the passing of Melissa's father and now with her aunt. It seemed unbelievable to deal with so much tragedy in one week's time.

Melissa used the edge of her wrap to dry the tears forming in her aunt's eyes. "Auntie, please. Don't feel guilty. I know how close you are to your aunt Theresa."

Robert kindly interrupted. "Pardon me. If it will make you both feel better I'll send John out to check on Melissa. He lives close by and I'm sure he wouldn't mind."

Miss Beckett shifted toward Robert, her eyes narrowing. "May I ask who this young man is?"

"Oh, forgive me, Auntie. This is Robert Gibson, Lord Blackburn's partner and friend." Melissa informed her.

"Well," she spoke with creased brows, a look of interrogation taking place. Then her face softened and a teasing smile curled on her lips. "I think you have a superb idea there, Mr. Gibson." A hand shot out to his. "I'm Miss Beckett."

"Miss Beckett," Robert said as he bowed, "Allow me to escort you to town. I was just leaving myself." He turned in Melissa's direction. "I will send John out at once."

"So soon? That isn't necessary." A week, I need a week, Melissa cried in silence.

Miss Beckett cut in. "Oh that's a marvelous idea, love, that way I won't have to worry about you." She sent Robert another smile. "I better get packed." She scooted away, climbing the stairs to retrieve her things.

Melissa stood, astounded, as Robert made further suggestions. "Melissa, you're putting it off. Unfortunately for your aunt she has an ill family member. Fortunately for you and John, now you'll have time to talk."

She witnessed Robert's wicked, matchmaking grin. "Robert Gibson, you'll pay for this!"

He didn't respond right away to her playful threat. He wanted her to ponder on it awhile, think about the right thing to do. He was about to reply when Miss Beckett came down the stairs lugging a couple of bags.

She entered the doorway of the sitting room, dropped her bags, and went over to Melissa to hug her goodbye. She lifted away and made a request. "Knowing that Lord Blackburn will be caring for you, would you mind if I take a week's time to be gone?"

My Forbidden Mentor

Initially Melissa did not want to agree, but for her auntie's sake she did. "Of course. Take all the time you need. I'll be fine."

"Bless you, love. One week's time should be enough." Miss Beckett started looking around the room as if taking inventory. "Oh, I've prepared some food. You should be all right."

After placing a kiss on her cheek Melissa chuckled at her auntie's mothering ways. "I'll be fine. Now get going so you're not late."

Miss Beckett smiled. "All right, love. Be good." She went to lift her bags but Robert took them from her and carried them to his carriage. Miss Beckett started to follow Robert when she remembered something. "Oh, Melissa love, there's some soup on the stove ready to eat."

"Goodbye, auntie. I love you."

She watched her aunt's stout little body turn and leave. Leaning over she grabbed another cake, biting into it as she heard the carriage leaving. Her throat tightened when trying to gulp down the delicious treat as anxious feelings started dominating her body. Being alone hadn't distressed her as much as the thought of John stopping by. Together they would be alone.

The plan was to talk. She would even make him supper and surprise him, then they could talk some more and he would be on his way. She rose off the couch and decided to heat up the soup that was already prepared. She had a clumsy shift in her step when trailing to the kitchen. John had been right. She had pushed her leg too far too soon. As long as she took it easy she could rest again. All she needed to do was warm up the soup.

Not only was there hot soup simmering on the stove, the cabin itself had been whipped into shape. Blankets were folded and placed in a neat pile. Supplies left by her aunt were picked up and put away. The dining table held two candles casting a glow of light across their best dishware. There was a cup of tea for her and a glass of brandy for him, and with everything else shimmering, Melissa had chosen to wear one of her mother's evening dresses. Her parents' room being downstairs invited the perfect opportunity. She selected a longtime favorite, a satin evening dress the shade of blushing carnations adorning a trim of snowy white ruffles. Putting it on, Melissa transformed into an ambience of femininity laced with elegance.

John finished settling his mare in the Howard's barn. Sliding his leather pouch over his shoulder he strode to the front door. He started to knock and then thought it would be less hassle if he just let himself in. Melissa would be expecting him.

Upon entering her home an appetizing aroma filled his nostrils. He strolled to the doorway of the sitting room and when he didn't see her, he continued to the kitchen. On his way a glint of burning light caught his attention. He stopped to observe the dining table. His mouth curved upward. What kind of plans had she for them? This was unexpected.

Approaching the kitchen doorway he had to suppress a groan that threatened to make his presence known. There she stood, wearing a light cherry colored dress that cascaded around her like she was an angel as she stirred whatever it was that she was cooking. Her hair lay loose down her back, sparkling like solid gold. He ached because

My Forbidden Mentor

he was already aware of how soft it was, remembering how it had slipped through his fingers as he was caressing it.

A familiar presence taunted her. She breathed in a whiff of a familiar scent, a masculine, forested scent that made her body flush. He was here, she sensed it, and she found she'd been correct after turning her focus onto the most handsome man she'd ever known. Oh dear, she wished he'd stop looking at her like that. The gaze he gave could make her forget about supper, forget about the talk, forget everything except him and diving into his luscious world.

His eyes lit up as his mouth gave her a grin that sent a spark of heat to the feminine core of her being. Her body had recalled his touch and all it required was that look he presented.

"I see you're making supper for us?" he asked out of hope, enjoying her cheerful disposition. Earlier when Robert had approached him about Melissa, telling him how she'd be alone for a week, he hadn't hesitated. His doubts were dealing with her sour temper, especially when he'd let her know he'd be staying with her until her aunt returned.

Her smile held promise of a generous mood. "Yes, for us. It isn't anything fancy, I have to warn you." She scooped a spoonful. "Come taste it for me."

He wasn't about to let the opportunity of closeness go by. Stepping in her direction, he stopped before her and opened his mouth. She lifted on her good leg to feed him.

On purpose he sipped in slow deliberation from the spoon. His lips were wet and his tongue licked at the wetness. He watched her dip the spoon in nervous anticipation back into the soup. "Tastes good," he told her, reminiscing about the time they had spent in the barn almost a month ago.

His motions were personal. How could they not be, licking his mouth the way he had? "You like it then?" She wouldn't look at him as she asked. Her hand on the wooden spoon kept stirring the well-stirred soup.

He slid the strap of his pouch off his shoulder, holding it gathered in his hand. "Yes, very much," he told her as his stare lingered a second longer before he shifted to walk out of the kitchen.

Noticing his movements and now glancing at the back of his form, the leather pouch stood out. As he went to turn the corner of the kitchen doorway she inquired. "John?"

His stride halted. "Yes?" he responded, turning toward her.

"What is the pouch for?" she asked, pointing at it.

He was about to diffuse her joyous mood. "It holds my belongings."

"Pardon me?" It sounded like he planned on staying awhile.

"You heard me," he told her in defense.

Her mouth fell open. Setting the spoon down, she hobbled over to him with her arms crossed over her chest. "Let me clarify the plan for you, then. You were to check on me periodically, perhaps come by once a day and make sure I'm still alive," she informed him and couldn't help the sarcasm.

He stepped back into the kitchen, coming closer to her, and threw an all-knowing smile her way. "The plans have changed. I have free time so I'm staying here twenty-four hours a day, every day, until your aunt returns." She was about to speak when he cut her off. "That way I can be sure you'll stay alive." He didn't wait for her response. He thought he'd made himself quite clear.

My Forbidden Mentor

After he left, she stomped her foot into the hardwood floor. Frustration commanded her to do so. Not a moment later she was sorry she gave in to that frustration for it was her bad leg that did the stomping. The first half of a painful yell emerged before her hand could cover her mouth in time. She counted to five, knowing John would be there before reaching six.

Sure enough. "What happened?" he asked, his eyes widened in alarm.

She tried her hardest, with gritted teeth, not to reach for her leg with him standing there. She couldn't answer him right away because of the pain shooting through her calf.

He stepped closer. "What happened?" This time his eyes showed concern and his tone lowered a notch.

"I stmpd th grnd wth my bad lg," she muffled through slender fingers, her eyes watering from the pain she withheld.

"I'm sorry, I didn't get that." he moved his ear toward her mouth, using his hand to fan behind it.

Her eyes molded to his profile. Even that part of him was stunning. Her hand ripped away from her mouth and she spoke into his ear. "I said, I stomped the ground with my bad leg."

His face turned into hers. "Because you were upset with me, right?" he said and his deep, calculating voice consumed her, being that close.

"Yes," she hissed back. Unaware of his intentions her body was swept up and she was carried to a chair at the dining table.

John arranged another chair adjacent to hers so she could elevate her sore leg. She started to protest when he said he would serve supper. Ignoring her, he proceeded.

With soup, bread and drinks before them, John couldn't help but comment. "Damn, you're stubborn," he said, giving a shake of his head.

She leaned across the table toward him. "Yes I'm stubborn. I have to be to deal with your overbearing ways."

"I think you've twisted things a bit here, sweetheart. Maybe your stubbornness brings out my overbearing nature," he responded and began eating, essentially ending that part of their conversation.

They were quiet during supper but both ate and drank with renewed enthusiasm. When John began clearing the table Melissa figured this was as good a time as any to confess. It took three attempts before words could come out of her mouth.

By the time she found the courage to talk to him he'd sat down and was sipping his drink. Good, she thought, his glass is half empty. He'll be more relaxed now. "John, I have a confession to make."

His eyes lifted from his motion of swirling the amber liquid around to find her focus on him serious. "Yes."

It was easier talking to him when he wasn't watching her with in-depth concentration. How to begin? "On the day of the accident involving my leg, I never told you the reason," she cleared her throat and tried again. "The reason I ran away from your manor as I did." He continued to listen while his eyes were peering into hers. "I had been waiting for your return when I decided to venture to your library." He didn't move a muscle. "When I approached the closed doors of the library I heard voices from inside." A hand came up to shield her eyes from his with her fingers rubbing into her forehead. "A man and a woman's voice," she mumbled and waited, hoping he'd already figured out what she was trying to tell him.

My Forbidden Mentor

"So?" he said shrugging his shoulders and thinking nothing of it.

She hadn't given enough detail. "Well, they were talking, or more like groaning, to each other."

"What?" He thought it over and then started to chuckle. "You must have heard Robert and Rose. They're the only two I would ever allow that kind of freedom in my home."

He still hadn't caught on. "I realize that now, John, but at the time..." She didn't need to finish when his eyes grew bold and the peek of a grin stole across his mouth.

"Are you telling me that you thought it was me in the library with another woman?" he asked.

He almost sounded excited by her mistake. "All I heard was groaning. I couldn't tell otherwise. I was at your manor," she cried, set back that he could be so indifferent to the situation.

In a matter of seconds he apologized. "Forgive me. I didn't mean to upset you. Again," he added. Her jealousy flattered him. So, she did have a stronger attraction than close friendship toward him. Yes, very flattering indeed. He pondered instead of giving further response and hadn't noticed his preoccupation until his gleaming eyes found her observing him with dismay.

Her eyes narrowed on him. Why couldn't they agree on something? "I knew you would react differently than I expected. I'm trying to apologize for my behavior of late, but you cause me to be so annoyed I can't think straight."

His tone softened with sincerity. "Melissa, thank you for telling me the truth," he said and her response was to roll her eyes at him. "I mean it."

Lifting her achy leg from the extra chair she steadied both feet and stood. Looking at him now her anger began diffusing and all of a sudden those nervous, odd sensations came back. Her body grew warmer as he perused her at a leisurely pace through black velvet lashes.

Being alone with him made it very tempting to give in to the desires he fired in her. Nakedness came to mind under his scrutinizing eyes that feasted on her. Feeling uncomfortable, she couldn't take his seductive glare any longer. "Can't you say something and stop staring at me like you're going to eat me alive?" she said, standing straight and proud.

As if reading her mind, he was presumptuous, tilting his head to the side. "Is that an offer?" his silky voice asked without shame.

At his words her glance fell to his fingers holding the glass, remembering the way they'd brought pleasure to her body, causing her to flush and heed a familiar sensitivity she got only around John. The need to gain control came on like a rampage. Their situation needed resolution now that the truth had been revealed regarding the accident. "What about the agreement you put off in Dublin?" she asked, ignoring his implied question.

The stare of his eyes reflected into hers, not with anger but with careful consideration. An extended moment passed before he replied, "I'm tired of making agreements with you. They don't work between us. It's time to face reality Melissa and forget about damned agreements," he told her in an aggravated tone because he was starting to care too much for this independent young lass, and worse, his lust for her was reaching arresting proportions. To him they were meant to be lovers. It was time, way past time, to discover each other intimately.

Then again, he decided, maybe they should talk about their conversation in Dublin. Perhaps this time she would admit her true feelings about when he had touched her. He straightened his head. "Agreements aside, let's talk about Dublin. Why don't you start by answering the question I asked you?"

With eyes averted and uneasiness casting across her features, Melissa responded, "Which question was that?"

His full lips curved into a delicious grin above the rim of his glass of brandy. Playing ignorant wouldn't work with him. "Whether or not you enjoyed my fingers touching your beautiful body," he reminded her and adored her reaction of enlarged eyes and opened mouth of innocence she displayed so often. Was it always innocent, he wondered?

She cursed him mentally for his directness. "Why do you have to say it like that?" she asked in a harsh whisper while her darting eyes lifted to his. "You could refresh my memory by mentioning the hayloft and I would know immediately to what you refer."

He leaned back in his chair. "Melissa, it's just you and I here, sweet. I thought I would give you a detailed description to refresh your memory."

Her lips tightened. "I don't need a detailed description. I remember it well."

A brow perched. "You do? You say that like you were disgusted by it."

She failed to comment as her eyes drifted down to her fidgeting fingers. How was she supposed to answer him without thoroughly shaming herself? As she contemplated, he spoke, the pressure to reply lay heavy upon her. Her eyes lifted, finding his gaze eager and requesting.

"Well?" he continued to pursue.

"I wasn't disgusted. It was surprising, that's all." She had to say something but could almost bet he wouldn't be satisfied with what she'd said. He had this way about him, she was learning, that could persist without him saying a word. Feeling vulnerable and drained from emotional uproar she gave in, hoping her admittance would settle matters right here and now. "Oh, all right. It was incredible. It's all I've thought about. That's why I needed to get away from here, from you. I need to think, John." With emotions strung high her true feelings emerged, not meaning to. "I'm afraid," came out in a shaky tremor.

"Afraid of what?" he asked, sitting up.

"Losing my freedom. Losing my independence. You," she told him as she gestured a shaky hand toward him.

"Is this independent streak an inheritance from your mother?" he asked.

"Yes, I suppose," she agreed and continued on by giving details. "And I have all the advantages. I'm not married, no children, no responsibilities holding me back right now."

He nodded in response to the reasons she gave. "Well that explains a lot," he commented, wondering what her reply would be to his next question. "Where do I fit in your future?"

How to answer him? Should he hear the absolute truth? "Because of our working relationship, I feel we have become close friends. I cherish that. Besides training, I'd enjoy spending time with you occasionally. You know, the races perhaps?" Her explanation seemed vague but the rules she set for their business relationship had demanded she not give in. She had broken her rule once with him already and now she must abide with strict effort.

"I can't handle occasionally," he told her, raking a hand over his pulled back hair. His eyes peered back to her. "It's obvious to me that our relationship has gone beyond mentor and student, beyond just friends. Would you agree?" he asked, knowing she couldn't deny it.

My Forbidden Mentor

To deny him the obvious truth would be pointless. Of course she agreed. Friends don't kiss and touch the way they had that cool afternoon sitting high in the barn, sheltered by bales of hay. Yes, there were more than friendship feelings going on between them. She had tried to stop them, she really did, even after he'd touched her, but it hadn't worked. He was all she thought about and now, well, now if she admitted this to him, what action would proceed?

Her dress swayed with her graceful movements of staggered pacing before the dining table. Unaware of the bold gestures her body presented to him, she answered truthfully. "Yes, I would."

Chapter Fourteen

As she stood opposite him, he rose from the chair, taking his glass with him. Melissa, feeling uneasy, watched him maneuver toward her. She desperately wanted a sip of his brandy to ease her nerves. When he stood very close to her, without thinking about it, she took the glass from his hand, her fingers brushing his, and sipped a decent amount of the intoxicating liquid. Her eyes closed at the smooth burning in her throat.

Her movements caused a stirring in his body. They had finally agreed on something about their relationship, it was time to satisfy their raging passions.

Handing him the glass, her eyes traveled the length of his body while he drank, beginning with his silken black hair, down to his broad chest covered in crisp white linen, and stopping at the waistband of his trousers. Slowly, she raised her eyes to meet his seductive ones.

He set his drink on the table. A lone finger went to her face, tracing along her golden hairline. "What shall we do about it?" he asked, watching her eyes steadily focus on him and having her sole attention made him want her even more.

"I'm not sure," she responded through trembling lips.

Slipping his fingers through her soft, flowing hair, his head bent so he could kiss her. Their eyes transfixed with their lips a breath apart. When their mouths finally met, their eyes closed and they moved in a gentle rhythm against each other. Both were forgetting the anger that had transpired between them, both were intent on fulfilling the longing to kiss each other again. Waiting any longer was a true test of their sanity and exploration of mouths was a priority at the moment. Temporarily satisfied, John left her mouth to breathe kisses along the line of her jaw and then down her neck, murmuring into her ear, "I believe you want me as much as I want you," he told her while his hands took hers and placed them on his hips.

His heated sensations continued down her neck. Her eyes remained closed as she replied, "I believe you're right." Lost in his kisses and the passion rising in her, for a time she was open to him, giving him unrestricted rein to kiss her anywhere he wanted. Anticipation seized her, making her fingers grip into the sides of his waist before sensually crushing into his body. Strong hands traveled down to her lower back, pressing her even more into his body. His actions unleashed waves of desire. She became eager for his touch, and it set off an alarm from the conscious side of her mind, reminding her of their status. Her will to fight the warning lessened. She had to use every ounce of strength left to tell him, "But I can't."

Surprised by her sudden change of mind, he placed a gentle kiss on her reddened lips and inquired out of breath, "Why not?"

Her opening eyes lingered with his. "Because it goes against everything," she started to say and then went mute. She didn't want to stop, but determination had her hanging on by a thread.

"It goes against what?" he asked as his voice turned rough. He couldn't stand it any longer, this battle she insisted on fighting within herself. "Our wanting each other? What is so bad about that? Tell me, Melissa."

Tears began forming in her eyes.

His tone softened. "Please, don't cry. I'm not trying to upset you," he told her and took a deep, steadying breath. "Don't you know that in the beginning I felt the same way about us, the need to keep us professional?" He laid his forehead against hers. "I've tried, Melissa, I've really tried, but I want you so much."

His staggered puffs of breath heated the shiver of her lips. "John, please don't," she pleaded and shut her eyes as she was enduring the honesty of his words.

He lifted away so he could see her face. "Why do you say that when you don't mean it?" he implored.

Her moistened eyes opened, followed by quivering lips. "You're making this hard for me," she whispered.

"Do you want me?" It was a direct question, requesting a direct answer.

Why am I denying myself? She wondered as her eyes searched the simmering gray pools of his. "Yes," she replied in a mesmerized tone. John kissed her in response. When his lips came off of hers, she answered again, "Yes, I do." He kissed her again, this time with possession.

He spoke against their mingled lips, "Then take me." In an instant her body grew tense.

"John, I, I don't know how," she said, feeling her cheeks flush and become warm, while her limbs stiffened and strained.

Simultaneously, his lips curved into a smile against her mouth. "Then let me take you first so you can learn," he said with breathless urgency.

He'd never been this shaky with a woman, feeling like he'd never made love before. When their lips met again both were ravenous and consuming. "Let's go to your bedroom," John rasped. His potent suggestion had her following his

My Forbidden Mentor

lead. Picking up a candle from the table he took her hand in his and they stepped over to the bottom of the stairs. Handing her the candle, he lifted her in his arms and carried her up.

This time it wasn't a dream. This time he was carrying her to the bedroom to make love. She was about to make love for the first time. The willpower needed to stop what was about to happen, disappeared. She wanted this experience.

Upon entering her room he set her down, taking the candle from her and placing it atop a tall dresser. Melissa stepped toward the bed and waited for him. Unfamiliar with what was about to take place, she relied solely on his guidance.

After closing the door he stepped over to the bed and sat on the edge, motioning her over to him. She stood between his thighs that were opened wide, waiting and wondering. A silent moment fell between them as mutual desire flared in the mirroring of their eyes. In growing anticipation John's fingers found the beginning of the many laces trailing along her backside. The pace of loosening them grew feverish when inch by glorious inch each layer of clothing that peeled away exposed skin made of tawny satin.

Melissa tried sweeping aside her tumbling clothing but the effort backfired when a snowy ruffle caught around the heel of her boot. Reaching out for the closest proximity to balance on landed her hands upon John's shoulders. When she dared to straighten and settled her eyes on his, she found a heavy lidded gaze that rested not on her face, but on her bare breasts.

He leaned forward, touching her with his mouth, and her back arched in sheer abandonment. She heard him groan as delicious sensations took over. Melissa embraced his dark silky head within her arms, and through a spinning haze she realized that this was something she had craved, John's body loving hers.

She was so lost in these new sensations that she hadn't registered the two warm hands clutching and squeezing her behind before being lifted and placed on the bed.

After taking off her boots and stockings, John stood above her and gave a seductive smile while unbuttoning his shirt. "You're more beautiful than I imagined Melissa," he told her and his confession made her eyes close and her breath shift.

Full of bolstering need, taking time to undress became an undesired chore for John. In reaction, the sleeves of his shirt practically ripped off his arms. His boots were tossed, sliding and speeding, across the hardwood floor, and his fingers tugged and jerked at the leather tie confining his hair, finally managing to set it free. All that remained were his trousers, which he chose to take off with careful consideration so as not to frighten her the first time seeing a naked male body. "What are you thinking about?" he asked, standing still before her once again.

Her eyes opened. She seemed oblivious to the commotion of his shedding of clothes. "The feel of your hair through my fingers," she said, gaping at his broad chest laced with wisps of black hairs.

Pushing his trousers off, he climbed onto the bed next to her. Lying on his side, a warm hand glided along her outstretched body from her bosom to her thighs, followed by his mouth trailing kisses along the same path. "Are you frightened of the pain?"

Caring and considerate, he'd be a gentle lover as his compassion confirmed. Her eyes glossed over and she smiled at him. "A little," she whispered.

"I'll be gentle," he whispered back.

He rose to kneel before her. Lifting her knees, he shifted them into a bent position, and then slid his palms down her inner thighs to part them wider. Before settling his body onto hers, his gaze concentrated on her trusting features. Her eyes staring into his gave him the approval he wanted to see. He lowered himself above her, resting his weight on his elbows before noticing her distress. "What is it, sweetheart?"

Melissa debated on whether or not to mention her concerns. Her virginity being no secret gave obvious meaning to an expected, non-existent performance, but Melissa wanted to satisfy him and make their experience worth it for him, the same as he was doing for her. The debating came to an end when he noticed her anguished features. "I want to be pleasing for you," she confessed.

Her admission surprised him. He'd already anticipated her to be anxious, this being her first time, but not worrying about pleasuring him. Didn't she know that just seeing her naked body of lush curves pleased him beyond any dream he'd imagined? Making love to her had crossed his mind about a trillion times but even so, her concern touched him. "You are pleasing me," he told her, watching the blush on her cheeks darken and her eyes close. His hands sank into her golden strands, cradling her head. "Melissa," he said in a comforting tone as her eyes opened. "Being here with you, together like this, is enough. We can wait if you're not ready." Although he meant his words, he prayed he wouldn't have to wait.

"I'm ready, John," she announced with renewed confidence, trailing a finger from his forehead down a subtle path along the bridge of his nose and then over his full, soft lips.

His mouth opened, capturing her finger between his teeth, and their eyes met. Her finger slipped out of his mouth and he kissed her in slow degrees, as if to savor each taste.

"I want you, Melissa. I've wanted you for a long time," he told her.

The need to connect with him on every level came on like a raging force. The fear of being her first time was fading. Her body twisted against his challenging his restraint.

"Patience sweetheart. Have you forgotten you're still a virgin?" he murmured, reminding her the first time was going to be different even though he agreed with her impatience.

"You need to relax," he advised and waited for her body to ease its anticipation. Cradling her head once again he braced himself for entry. His eyes closed as he took in the sensations. Feeling a stabbing of fingernails brace the skin of his shoulders, his eyes opened to witness a bewildered expression.

Without saying a word, John chose to act instead of explain. He pushed forward, applying a surefire thrust that pierced her maidenhead. Simultaneously he heard a muffled cry escape her. He looked down into hazel eyes opened wide and sweet lips pressing together to force away any more sound. He stayed still. His eyes shut as his lips brushed over her chin. "Are you all right?" he asked against her cheek. Feeling her nod, his mouth drifted to her ear. "It won't hurt like that again, I promise." He tried to be soothing, knowing that she was hiding the full extent of the pain she was feeling.

She began to calm from her startled state. The sharper pain than she anticipated was beginning to lessen. As the initial pain faded, she was able to comprehend how substantially his body filled hers. Naturally her body

My Forbidden Mentor

accepted his, amazing her at how easily a man and woman could adjust to each other so intimately. The sensations of pain that were fading away were being replaced by a wanton urge. Releasing her gripped fingers from the muscles of his shoulders, they slid down his smooth back to firm buttocks, motioning him to proceed. "Please go on," she told him in staggered breaths, wanting to feel the pleasure awaiting her.

Their gaze upon each other intensified as their breaths mingled and he began moving inside her. Her imaginations of how this would feel didn't compare at all to having him flesh to flesh. His caressing manhood created the beginnings of an insatiable appetite. A craving she hadn't known existed until her forbidden mentor had made it possible.

"Better?" he asked as his momentum sped up, sensing her enjoyment.

"Yes," she answered as her eyes were filling with passion and her hips were rising to meet his. Instinctually moving with him now, together their rhythmic moves were gradually climbing to a state of pounding fury.

John groaned, kissed her, and murmured, "Oh Melissa, I knew it would be good, but my God."

They intuitively formed together like mating parts, and being the only virgin he'd ever made love to, he had expected a different reaction. A shy, follow his lead reaction, but as soon as the pain disappeared for her, she responded without any apprehension.

Becoming one with Melissa stirred his soul, and that stirring escalated when Melissa's golden head began tossing back and forth across the pillow as she called out to him.

"Oh, John!" she released in a throaty wail.

He pulled her against him as close as she could get, and reached his climax split seconds after her.

They lay together, John still on top, their sweating bodies still connected, both trying to regain their natural breathing. Raising his head from the pillow, his lips went to her neck, planting tender kisses that tasted of her fragrant aroma. Her lips also touched his neck, leaving trails of feathery kisses amongst the beaded sweat sticking to his skin. "That was wonderful," she said near his ear.

"You're wonderful," he told her as their lips found each other again.

While savoring their kisses, Melissa thought she had indeed gone to heaven. He had opened a whole new world for her and she wasn't planning on leaving any time soon. Just then his lips parted from hers, and pulling away from her, he left the bed and went to the washbasin. After cleansing himself, he came back and cleansed her as well.

Admiring his sensitive actions, she asked, "Have you ever bedded a virgin before?"

He was taken aback by her question and while finishing up, he answered, "No."

"Then how do you know what to do?" she asked.

He knew what she was referring to, the gentleness, the knowing how painful it could be. He answered as he rinsed the cloth. "Robert's had the experience once or twice. He's shared his wisdom with me."

"Do you two discuss your conquests?" she asked out of interest as she was hoisting herself up on her side and holding her head in the palm of her hand.

"Sometimes," he told her, wanting to be honest with her, although he didn't view her that way.

My Forbidden Mentor

Her curiosity tempted her to pry further. "Do you compare?" she asked and was interrupted.

"I don't think of you as a conquest," he told her in a stern tone as he lay on the bed on his side next to her.

Her hand skimmed over his arm and then her eyes found his. "What am I to you, then?"

His hand caught hers and clasped them together. "Someone I truly care for," he revealed, knowing she was beyond any experience he'd ever had. Making love to her only enhanced his unusual feelings.

"Do you plan on making love to me often?" she asked.

"I'd like to," he answered.

Raising their joined hands, she placed a kiss on his palm. "I'm not opposed," she said with a smile.

He smiled back, giving her hand a squeeze. "Have I got a little wanton on my hands?"

Her smile widened and her eyes sparkled through dark golden lashes. "Are you complaining?"

He responded to her wittiness. "Not at all."

She reclined into him. "After all, you created her," she purred, the sparkle in her eyes glowing dark and passionate. "I want you again, John."

"Mm. The feeling is mutual," John groaned.

They made love again, exploring each other with earthly passion until falling asleep.

Chapter Fifteen

Melissa awoke stretching from a glorious night of lovemaking. Looking over at the sleeping lord, her movements didn't seem to disturb him until she attempted to lift his arm from her waist.

"Where are you going?" he asked in muffled drowsiness, his arm returning possessively around her waist. He lay on his stomach, his head turned away from her.

"I've got to get up, I'm famished," she told him as he stayed silent. Figuring he had fallen back asleep since he hadn't responded, she lifted his arm again.

His head swung in her direction, with his eyes still closed and his mouth grinning. "I imagine we worked off supper, huh?"

Melissa rose from the bed, smiling inside, while leaning over and asking, "Yes, are you hungry?"

His eyes opened halfway, finding that her sweet face was close enough for him to kiss. "Yes, for you," he replied as his hand was reaching for her bosom.

She teased him by backing away so he couldn't touch her. She was getting impatient. "John, a serious answer, please?" By now her stomach was ordering her to the kitchen.

"Is food my only choice?" he asked, prolonging their discussion, finding their easy back and forth banter an accepted comfort.

"Why are you answering a question with a question?" she inquired as she came close to him again. "And, yes, at this moment, food is your only choice." This time her arms crossed over her bosom.

Not to be detoured, he lifted onto one elbow. His hand cupped her cheek and he pulled her closer to him. Sleepy-eyed, he kissed her, feeling refreshed and alive. Whatever spell she had cast on him, he couldn't get enough and he didn't want it to end. Last night had changed something for him. The lovemaking was different, explosive, even doubling in degree of passion the second time, leaving him more confused than ever. These mixed-up feelings alarmed him, yet as alarming as they were he yearned for more.

Her arms unfolded and her hands went to the bed for balance. She was delirious, no longer denying her true feelings for this handsome lord. She was beyond mere curiosity and making love with him had confirmed that.

His lips left hers. "Good morning."

"Good morning," she replied, breathless.

His finger tapped the tip of her nose. "And yes, I'm famished." The same finger went to her lips, tracing them. "May I have you for dessert?" he asked, his husky voice getting permission.

Dizzy from their kissing, she began falling into a downward spiral toward his web of intrigue. His kiss had brought back too many wonderful memories from the night before, allowing her to barely decipher his question. "Yes, you may, but only if you're good and eat all your breakfast." She smiled in reaction to his happy features, giddy like a little boy.

"Hurry back," he whispered, his twinkling gray eyes following her naked body as she straightened and stepped over to the closet to retrieve her robe. Disappointed when she slipped the robe around herself, covering the source of his private inspection, her slight limp caught his attention instead when she stepped back toward him. It hit him then that she planned on fetching their breakfast, which meant taking the stairs. She gave him a smile as she unlocked the door and turned the knob. "Wait a moment," he said.

Startled, she stopped to face him. "Yes?"

He shoved the blankets off himself and was swinging his legs over the edge of the bed. "Where do you think you're going?" he asked as he was reaching down to grab for his trousers.

Her brows creased in confusion while her cheeks colored at the sight of seeing him nude in the daylight. "To get...breakfast," she replied, not too steady and trying not to be obvious about her gawking.

"I don't think so," he said shoving one leg into his trousers, unconsciously aiming his focus toward her legs.

She caught his glare, which explained his sudden actions of panic. Her face softened, aware of how distressing her condition was for him, but today she was like a new woman ready for a new challenge and trying the stairs was a perfect way to start. She stopped him before he went further. "John?"

He had his second leg through and was about to stand to finish putting on his trousers when the sound of her voice made him look up.

Her sedate expression had his complete attention. "I want to try this. I think it's time."

His velvet lashes blinked once as if determining if her choice was rational. "Are you sure?" he asked, aware it was to be her decision.

"Yes," she answered in undeniable confidence.

"Perhaps I should go with you, just to make sure." He felt helpless when he should feel happy about her determination. He rose from the bed.

"John, I'll call for you if I have trouble," she told him as the beam in her eyes was imploring him to be agreeable.

When she walked out he was left standing in the middle of her sun- brightened bedroom with his trousers pulled up to his hips, buttons undone. He sat back down, eyeing the door, desperate to watch her progress. He hadn't heard her calling him yet, which was a good sign. He stretched out his legs crossing them at the ankles, and he folded his arms across his bare chest with his eyes fastened to the door.

By now five minutes had passed, at least by his calculations. Not able to stand the waiting he rose from the bed once again and stepped to the door. Cracking the door open, his immediate view was empty as she wasn't anywhere in sight. The door flew open and his body leaned through the doorway, his head swinging from one side of the short hallway to the other. He stepped further out toward the stairs. Standing at the top looking down, sounds of rustling from the kitchen got his attention.

In an instant he returned to the bedroom. His trousers slipped off and his naked body slipped back into bed. After waiting another five minutes he sat up, placing his head against the oak headboard and taking the time to straighten the lavender blankets that were covering his hips. The door burst open and John jumped at the sound. He had been so involved in his thoughts of their previous night together that he hadn't heard her footsteps before the door opened. She wore a gratifying smile though, and her victory was contagious making him grin in return. He could let go of his short-lived worries regarding the stairs since she had made it. "All went well, I see?"

Sliding on the bed next to him with a full plate gracing her lap, she boastfully responded, "Yes."

"Well, I'm proud of you. I knew you could handle it." His grin proved flattering and his words of praise meant a great deal. Robert had been right about John's confidence in her. It hadn't waned. But what had happened to the apprehension he had expressed before her victory lap? "Thank you, John." I'll bet he checked on me. "I hope I didn't worry you?"

He chuckled, the gleam in his eyes not as bright. "No, of course not. I told you I knew you could handle it, and see, you proved me right." Even his fabricated smile had a melting effect. "Now, what did you bring us?"

He obviously didn't want to carry on. Laughing to herself, she let the subject drop. "Berries and various breads. I know you like berries but I'm not sure about bread?"

"Certain kinds are alright. What do you have?" he asked.

She unfolded the linen cloth covering their food. "A variety of sweet breads, actually."

Opening his mouth, she brought the bread to his lips. He moved forward and took a bite. After swallowing, he gave her his opinion. "Not bad, but I prefer the berries," he told her as he took the remaining piece of bread from her and finished it off.

They fed each other berries and bread while talking of past events they'd shared, making each other laugh recalling ridiculous mistakes and stunts they had pulled on each other. Comparing the extent of such ludicrous behavior, both agreed that Melissa topped them both with the story she had concocted for her father, but the mere mentioning of her father brought them to silence. Their smiles diminished and Melissa's head hung low, studying the berries that remained.

My Forbidden Mentor

John watched her reaction, seeing and feeling her pain all over again. His fingertips went beneath her chin and lifted it up. Glassy eyes captured his. "Are you alright?" he asked so quietly that she almost didn't hear him. Their happy reminiscing had brought unguarded pain at the same time. She nodded while giving him the best smile she could manage. His smile in return relayed that he understood.

Worn down by the fight to stay strong, fresh tears began rolling down her cheeks. Melissa turned her watery gaze away from John. "I'm sorry," she said, apologizing for her lack of control.

"Why are you sorry?" he asked.

She swallowed hard at the memory of her father as his death began dominating all of her thoughts now, all of her thoughts except the acknowledgment of John's understanding of the situation. She hadn't expected his constant consolation, but then she hadn't anticipated this wave of grief to cascade upon her, especially when she was experiencing happiness for the first time in a long time. Her gaze shifted back toward his, which penetrated her very soul. "I'm sorry for falling apart on you like this."

John's gaze never wavered. His hand came up to embrace the back of her head, guiding her to rest upon his chest. A dam broke loose within her. Her hands gripped the sides of his waist as her whole body jerked with an overflow of emotions. She clutched at his upper body as if she would fall from the earth.

John could feel hot streams of wetness flow down his chest, receding toward his belly. Wanting to relieve her grief, he offered reassurance. "Don't be sorry for grieving, Melissa. You've been through a lot more than you know. You're allowed to let go every now and then," he told her and then paused when he could feel her shudder against him. "I don't mind you falling apart as long as you put yourself back together again." That got a light chuckle out of her.

She lifted her head, revealing red and swollen eyes that bore into his. "How would I get through this without you?"

His opposite hand brushed away the damp strands of her hair, which clung to her face. "You would find a way, although I'm glad to be here for you." The realization that his words were sincere, that he really meant them, sent a jolt of reality through his concerned mind. This was where he wanted to be, with her, whether consoling her, riding horses, sleeping, making love, it didn't matter, just to be in her presence was enough.

A smile appeared within her puffy features. "Thank you."

His fingers stopped their caressing motion to obtain a berry to feed to her. "You're welcome." Her mouth opened and she devoured the plump blackberry. "Now, I'd like to go to my place today and check on Chief," he said while popping a berry into his mouth. "It will give you an opportunity to see how training stables are run, which in training you will have to learn anyhow." His gaze shifted from the plate of berries to witness a maneuver that made his groin ache.

Melissa was licking at the fruit juices dripping down her fingers. "That sounds fine to me," she replied, her tongue stopping mid-motion when her eyes caught his in a seductive stare. Suddenly the air around them turned smoldering.

John reached over and placed another blackberry in her mouth. His voice was soft yet husky. "I'm ready for dessert now," he announced with renewed vigor.

"A sudden burst of energy?" she asked in teasing manner.

My Forbidden Mentor

He reached down to untie her robe. "It's your fault. You wanted to feed me."

When John awoke he wasn't sure how much time had passed. His head lifted as he looked toward the window, mentally trying to determine the time of day by where the sun was sitting. Well it wasn't early, he gathered. His hair tousled and his body cramped from their cradled position, he started to pull away from her when she groaned.

"No."

He bent close to her ear and murmured, "Sweetheart, we need to get moving."

She responded in a languid tone. "Not yet. Want to sleep more."

He slid out of the bed and reached back over the bed to drag her over to him, lifting her into a sitting position. "Time to get up," he insisted. He was learning her ways and how to deal with them.

Propped up on the edge of the bed Melissa was wide-awake now, glaring at John in frustration, ignoring her state of complete nakedness. She hadn't wanted to get up, wanting to forever keep him in her bed. She watched him get dressed, unaware, her lips curled into a pout as the last button of his trousers closed.

Glancing up to catch her frowning face, he read her mind. "Later," he told her. Her hunger was something he could get used to, but they had work to do today so her impetuous appetite would have to wait. When she hadn't moved an inch, John realized he had a struggle on his hands. "Do I have to dress you as well?" he inquired.

Without her help, John managed to produce her clothing, dress her and dress himself in record time. Although he would much rather undress her than dress her he rather enjoyed the unique experience, purposely revealing only frustration for her benefit. He left to saddle Clara while Melissa finished with her shoes.

She was in love with a lord, she thought, a handsome, tender, sometimes difficult lord. Was he capable of returning her love? Could he give up other women? Somehow she would have to find out.

Finishing with her boots, she heard his footsteps approaching. When the door opened, she quickly uttered, "I'm ready." She could tell she'd already pushed her limit by letting him dress her this morning.

To her relief he gave her a smile. "Good," he said, swooping her into his arms to be carried down the stairs. He propped her up on top of his mare and slid up behind her.

Chapter Sixteen

A short time later his large manor came into view, with three enormous stable houses and beautiful thoroughbreds prancing about. Their racing bodies were in superb condition, their muscles lithe and sleek with every springing step.

John slid off Clara then helped Melissa down. One of his stable hands came over to take care of Clara for him. "Thank you Todd. Have Simon ready Chief for me, will you?" John directed as Todd nodded in agreement. After Todd took Clara John shifted back to Melissa. Anxious to gather necessary belongings and be back into Melissa's warm bed, he led her to the front door. "Would you like to come in with me or see the horses? I noticed you studying them on our way in."

A smile appeared at his observance. "Well, if you don't mind, I have been eager to see your horses up close. May I?"

His smile mirrored hers. "You don't have to ask, sweetheart, and I don't mind at all. It shouldn't take me long." He leaned over and planted a gentle kiss upon her lips. "Simon should be in there. You'll know him when you see him, he's the one giving orders. He'll help you with any inquiries you have until I return."

"All right," she said and turned toward the stables.

John followed her movements before pivoting toward the front door. He missed the inconspicuous, unmarked carriage parked behind a shading limb of trees that graced the side of his manor.

Laura Mills

Once inside Charles got his attention. "Good day my lord."

John headed for the stairwell, saying in passing, "Good day Charles. It is a marvelous day in fact, is it not?" Sensing something was wrong, he inquired just as Charles was about to speak again. "Is there something else, Charles?" His gleeful pace stalled halfway up the stairs.

Charles winced before responding. "Yes my lord," he said, stepping next to the railing of the stairwell. "There is a female visitor here to see you and she's been here quite some time. Her visit was unannounced. I tried to tell her you weren't available but..."

He never finished, for John just wanted to know who it was. "Who is it, Charles?" John's brows were creasing in frustration because he wasn't in a generous mood when it came to any delays that could thwart the plans he'd already made with Melissa.

"Yes sir. It is Baroness Lindsey Pope." Charles shot a brief glance toward the closed doors of the sitting room, adding in a whisper, "Ghastly chit if I may say so my lord."

John chuckled at Charles attempt at humor. "You may say so, Charles, and may I say that I agree with you one hundred percent." John spun down the stairs to take care of the disturbing annoyance once and for all. "I'm freeing you from her company Charles. You may go."

John heard a sigh of relief and chuckled some more.

Sitting in a wingback chair, sipping a cup of tea, was a young lady sporting auburn hair and green eyes, someone he'd had a one-night fling with some months ago, which had been enough for him. She'd begun stalking him after that, becoming overly possessive. Finally he'd had to put her in her place by reminding her she had a husband who

My Forbidden Mentor

might be interested in her extracurricular activities. Since then she'd left him alone until now.

Looking up as he entered, she stood and pranced over to him. "Lord Blackburn, how nice to see you. I've been waiting some time. I assume you've just arrived." Seduction was written all over her entrapping features.

He grinned at her attempts to wile him. She was playing a dangerous game with a non-existing player. "So proper, Lindsey. What brings you out to the country?" he asked, even though he already knew.

Her hands reached for the collar of his shirt. "It's been awhile darling. I thought you might be lonely." Her voice dropped an octave. "Lonely for my company. I sure am for yours. Remember how much fun we had?"

His hands caught hers before they could get a grip on his collar, a reaction that temporarily stunned her. Lindsey Pope was used to getting her way and this time she wasn't.

John's annoyance shifted to mild rage. Her persistence on a matter that had been resolved months ago astounded him. "I'm not interested Lindsey. You should have gotten the message the last time we conversed," he told her, making his point clear once again. He didn't need this now. She was wasting his precious time.

Stepping over to the large framed window of the sitting room, looking out into green lush landscape, her eyes scanned along its entirety. Numerous corrals dominated her view and past them a particular female caught her eye. The young lady seemed to be very enthusiastic about John's horses along with Robert.

Yes, Robert, another conquest if he'd be willing. Her green eyes full of spite left Robert to focus on the young lady accompanying him. "Who's the young lady chatting with Robert?"

John strode over to the window, seeing Melissa and Robert. "She's a student of our company." There was a sternness to his voice, revealing his rising anger.

Her smile turned devious. "Your student, huh? What are you teaching her?"

"None of your business Lindsey," he spoke through tightened lips and clenched teeth.

"She's certainly attractive."

John was beyond the point of caring. She was taking up too much of his time. His eyes narrowed when he turned to face her. "It's time for you to leave Lindsey. I'm not able to service you anymore, you need to go elsewhere."

His mind was made up she thought as she walked back over to the couch, picked up her purse and headed for the door. She gave it one last effort. "If you ever change your mind, I'm available," She informed him while disappearing through the doorway.

Relieved that she was gone he headed for his bedchamber to finally change his clothing and gather necessary items.

But as John's mind was preoccupied with his own ideas, Lindsey took full advantage of the possibilities presented to her, namely intimidating his female student. What in the world was he teaching her anyway besides the pleasures of his bed.

She approached Robert and Melissa before taking her leave. With a toss of an auburn ringlet and a smile bearing an undermining recourse, Lindsey played her part well. "Hello, Robert. It's been a while."

Robert knew what John had gone through with this wench, and if he'd been alone he wouldn't have had a second thought about being rude to her, but for Melissa's sake he behaved. "Hello Lindsey."

My Forbidden Mentor

Assuming she'd have to introduce herself since Robert hadn't done the liberties, she faced Melissa with her hand outstretched. "Hello, I'm Baroness Lindsey Pope."

Melissa smiled but was overcome with a sensation that this woman had a deceitful nature. "Hello, I'm Melissa Howard." She shook Lindsey's hand, catching a distinct beam in her eyes.

"Pleased to meet you, Miss Howard. John tells me you're a student of his company?" Lindsey asked, waiting to see what kind of reaction she would stir.

Melissa wasn't aware that John freely mentioned she was his student to anybody but as he had to be the only one to tell her she went along with Lindsey's inquiry. "Yes I am. He's a very thorough teacher. I'll be forever grateful for his knowledge," she stated, hoping her words revealed a double meaning like this libertine woman wanted to believe.

Lindsey retaliated by giving her a sneering smile. "Yes, I'd have to agree with thorough."

Annoyed, Melissa tried tuning out this obstacle of a woman by letting her attention wander to a nearby mare.

Lindsey caught her drift and shifted her gaze to Robert. "It's certainly nice to see you again, Robert. If you ever get lonely for company I'm available," she offered.

Appalled, Robert couldn't believe the gall of this woman. His reply was direct and plain. "No thank you Lindsey, I'm already taken, remember?"

Well her progress surely lacked today. Three evading attitudes in a row wasn't terribly flattering. Her eyes flashed toward Robert and then to Melissa. "It was a pleasure meeting you, Miss Howard. Good luck," she remarked, spun toward her carriage and was off.

Melissa watched as she left, still annoyed by her tactics, telling herself not to give in to this proposed jealousy. And what did she mean by good luck?

Robert noticed Melissa's apprehension. "She's not worth it Melissa."

Melissa's attentions turned to Robert. "I had only heard about women like her. I see now they exist," she stated as if ridding the taste of disgust from her mouth.

Agreeing with her, Robert confided, "Yes, they do."

"Please excuse me Robert but I'd like to finish looking at John's horses now," she said and with a smile proceeded to the stables, on the way trying to clear her thoughts regarding Lindsey Pope and John.

Robert responded with a faint, "Sure," as his focus lingered on her departing form. He had to get a hold of John.

"Robert, how are you this fine day?" John asked upon finding his friend standing at the front entrance.

"I'm fine," Robert replied.

They walked together to the stables when Robert stopped halfway.

"What is it Robert, you look serious?" John inquired, realizing Robert's quietness was not without a reason.

"Can you spare a few moments?" he said, his arm's crossing over his broad chest.

In unison, John's arms crossed as well. "Of course. What is it?"

"It's about, Melissa." Robert was at odds about approaching John in such a manner regarding a woman, but Melissa wasn't ordinary and John had never been this serious before. Even if John was denying it, Robert saw the visible truth. John was falling in love. "I like her a lot, John."

"I like her a lot too." John's brows creased in bewilderment. "What is this leading to Robert?"

"You seem quite serious about her," he said before giving a straightforward opinion. "Look, John, if you're serious like I think you are, you might want to advise her about previous women you've been with." Robert's hand gestured in the direction that Lindsey's carriage had left. "That wench, Lindsey, didn't help matters. She even propositioned me in front of Melissa." Robert watched John shake his head in dismay as he added, "Melissa handled herself well but I could tell she had some doubts about your relationship."

John sighed while sweeping a hand through his unbound hair. "The dame's gone mad," he muttered.

Robert responded out of concern. "Whether Melissa is long term or not John, she definitely doesn't deserve that kind of harsh treatment." Even as he finished Robert noticed the intent expression on John's face, an almost painful demonstration of the confused emotions he was dealing with. Robert smiled to ease the tension.

"I know," John mumbled. Everything seemed to be happening so fast. He would speak with Melissa but in the meantime he'd relish their private moments. There would be plenty of time to inform her about obnoxious types of women.

With the seriousness his best friend displayed Robert sensed progress in John and Melissa's relationship, otherwise John would have reached a decision by now. Maybe yesterday's talk went better than expected Robert concluded and decided to him question further. "Did you two have a talk yesterday?"

John looked directly at Robert curious by what he meant. "Sort of. Why?"

Robert's smile broadened. So she had taken his advice. "I just figured that since you two were alone you'd been able to sort things out."

"Are you talking about the misunderstanding Melissa had about me the day of her accident?" John asked.

"Yes, precisely. I knew you two could work it out," Robert replied, revealing the most mischievous grin.

John immediately became aware of Robert's devious plan. "One moment. How did you know before me?" John inquired in defense.

"John, ease off man. You're forgetting my visit with Melissa a couple of days ago. We compared stories and I advised her to tell you what happened. She was quite humiliated about it. I hope you didn't make it harder for her?" John didn't reply but Robert guessed by the guilty look on his face that he most certainly had. "You did more than work it out, didn't you?" By now Robert saw John as clear as a blue sky without clouds.

A slight grin appeared on John's lips. "Let me just say that everything is going quite well right now."

"Was going well, John. I really think a little subtle consolation is needed." John kept grinning while Robert voiced his thoughts aloud. "At least you two haven't," Robert stopped when he realized what John had meant by his words. "You've bedded her, haven't you?"

John bent forward so his eyes could stare into the toes of his black riding boots.

My Forbidden Mentor

Robert wasn't surprised and took the opportunity to harass him. "What happened to being professional?" Robert readily reminded John.

John's head lifted. His stance appeared triumphant as he returned his gaze toward Robert. There was no reason to feel guilty about this he told himself no matter how protective Robert was being in regards to Melissa or harassing toward him. "You know how long I've wanted her, how long I've waited. Anyway, it just happened," he ended on a sigh and added in order to ease Robert's protective mind, "And it wasn't against her will, it was mutual."

Robert's brows arched at John's statement, coming back with his opinion of the situation. "Well you've just verified my hunch. You're hooked."

"What? I'm not hooked." John's grin began fading.

Robert spoke as if John hadn't responded. "Well it's about time. You are getting on in age." Robert's hand patted John's shoulder as if soothing him.

"Damn it all, I'm not hooked." John's narrowing eyes didn't seem to bother Robert one bit.

Robert carried on like he was having a conversation with himself. "No wonder she had a glow about her this morning, at least until Lindsey showed up." He looked straight into John's face as if studying him. "As a matter of fact, you have that same glow."

John rolled his eyes, a habit he was picking up from Melissa.

"You're glowing, John. Beaming from a mile away."

"Sod off," John said over his shoulder.

"Are those wedding bells I hear in the distance?"

Robert had caught up to him by now. In a lowered voice before approaching the doorway John commented, "You're insane Robert."

Their laughing ceased after they entered the stables. Melissa had shifted in their direction when hearing them approach. When John first appeared Melissa was caught by his attractiveness. He always seemed to amaze her with his striking good looks.

Their eyes met and their smiles collided. John strode over toward her, leaning along the metal gates when she commented. "You have beautiful horses John."

"Thank you," he told her, trying to concentrate on Melissa's fascination instead of Robert's warning. "Have you seen Chief yet?"

"No I haven't. I was so enthralled with your horses I forgot to track down Simon." In actuality, though the horses had claimed her attention, her primary focus had been that lecherous woman and her disturbing comments. She tried to appear serene when inside brewed anger, jealousy and sadness.

John took Melissa's hand in his and led her down another path in the stables. "Over here," he said.

Robert followed behind, watching them with approval.

When they arrived at Chief's stall Melissa gasped. Close up Chief was the most stunning stallion she'd ever seen. His coat glistened in its rich array of chestnut coloring. His demeanor was proud, demonstrated by the powerful swish of his tail. He neighed merrily when John approached him. "Let's get you out of there boy," John said to Chief as he unlatched the metal gate to release his prospective champion. Chief continued to neigh, his head bouncing with excitement as he followed John's lead.

My Forbidden Mentor

Melissa stood before Chief, commenting and stroking his neck with enthusiasm, "John he's so handsome. Hello Chief. I finally get to meet you," she said, chuckling after his nose playfully nudged at her cheek, then in her hair.

John took note of her ease with horses, determining she was a natural. "He likes you Melissa. He's not that way with everyone," he told her with a soft smile.

She turned toward John and responded, "Really? He's wonderful." She smiled toward Chief while stroking his head, adding, "He and Laurel would have had a beautiful baby together, wouldn't you have, Chief? It's too bad thoroughbred rules are so strict," she went on, enlightened by John about how critical the process of breeding was for thoroughbreds, but John no longer listened to Melissa beyond the mention of a baby.

All of a sudden John's equilibrium came off balance. The keyword, baby, hit him like a ton of bricks, thinking that he must be losing his mind because he hadn't made sure to use protection during lovemaking, something he was always adamant about. What was I thinking? His brain rattled. That's the problem, I wasn't thinking, he answered himself. The truth was that any thoughts beyond the moment hadn't crossed his mind, at all.

As his gaze skimmed over Melissa's figure he couldn't help but think that she could be pregnant right now. The thought of Melissa pregnant with his child held appeal but it would be unfair to put her in a position of being pregnant and unmarried. Was he ready for that kind of commitment? Their relationship was already unusual in itself. What was he going to do? Was he ready for marriage? He was so busy cursing himself he barely heard Melissa's compliment.

"John you've raised a perfect stallion for racing. Not that you don't have others, but I like him a lot. He's got a fine temperament," she told him as her mood was lifting considerably. When a period of time passed and he hadn't responded, Melissa spoke to get his attention. "John, where are you? Didn't you hear what I said?"

His thoughts that were dwelling on the chance of her being with child had preoccupied him and although he had heard her, his mind was still debating on how to resolve their current situation. He figured until deciding about marriage they would use protection and somehow he would have to explain that to her. After making a resolution, he returned a reply. "Yes. I thought you would especially like him. Chief is my pride and joy."

Melissa stared at John, concerned about his sudden change in behavior. It didn't make sense. Something recent dominated his thoughts. Lindsey Pope maybe? She didn't want to jump to conclusions again and be wrong. "Are you all right?" she asked instead.

His fingers filtered through her shining hair, pulling her head forward so he could place a kiss on her forehead. "Yes. My thoughts drifted. Forgive me?" While assuring her, his attention shifted above Melissa's head toward Robert, who tormented John with the devious grin he possessed.

Melissa, reassured, focused on Chief again. She excused herself, stepping away from John when Simon approached to ready Chief. She trailed off with Simon, asking questions that he happily answered.

John looked back to Robert and caught him almost laughing aloud until he quieted him with a penetrating glare.

Robert stepped over to John's side, asking out of desperate interest, "What were you thinking about?"

John responded, "I had a realization, that's all." Watching Robert's reaction, he saw the humor in it. If their roles had been reversed, Robert would have received the same treatment.

Robert persisted. "It took that long to sink in that you're hooked?"

John wasn't sure he wanted anyone aware of the chance that Melissa could be pregnant. First of all it would prove how irresponsible he'd been, which meant dealing with Robert's chastising. Second, there was still a chance it wasn't true. Damn it all, why didn't I pull out, he questioned. Because it was the last thing on your mind, you bloody idiot. Lord, he was answering himself again, but his thoughts served to remind him to gather necessary means for future protection. I'm literally going crazy, crazy with Melissa. He needed to give Robert a reply that would be sufficient. "Maybe it did finally sink in and maybe I am hooked," John answered with a grin as his eyes were scanning for Melissa's whereabouts. He spotted her and Simon preparing Chief at the opposite end of the pathway from where he and Robert stood.

Robert grinned in response to John's admittance, which coincided with his constant need to observe her every move. He was more than hooked, he was caught and reeled in by Miss Melissa. "Have you talked to Ainsworth yet about Melissa racing at Catterick?"

"No. The injury to her leg has delayed training and I want to be extra careful in approaching Ainsworth. You know what a stickler he can be," John said as he looked her way again and found her gazing at him in a provocative manner. He gave her a delicious smile and his eyelids became heavy when he returned an examination of sexual intent. With reluctance she turned back to Simon, who was explaining something to her. John switched back to Robert, who didn't say a word but sent a knowing look. "As I was saying," John continued, clearing his throat. "I want to be sure she's ready before I make my intentions known to Ainsworth, and I fear it won't be long. Just this morning she took the stairs herself."

"Well good for her. She's not one to give up, don't we know that by now," Robert chuckled and then added, "Of course I agree with your reasons for waiting to approach Ainsworth. At least Paul will be agreeable."

"No matter. We won't have to deal with them for a time." Both of John's hands slid through his long hair.

"You're quite right, but once we get Ainsworth's approval our chance of getting into other tracks may bend easier," Robert suggested, crossing his arms over his chest.

"True, but if all else fails, before it's revealed I want her to race at Catterick. I'm part-owner, after all. My weight should carry," John replied, already feeling the pressure of her gender in regards to racing, but he had expected this and reminded himself he'd be up for the challenge. Ironically, he was treating the situation as if she had an exclusive right to race because she had proved to be a damn good rider to him. Why should her being a female matter? He was sounding like her now. He looked once again in her direction.

"It will John, it will, and I'll back you, but because we involved ourselves with a more elite track which prides itself on rules and regulations, it's going to be tough," Robert reminded him.

"Yes, well, where there's a will, there's a way," John told Robert, distracted by the tempting female they were referencing.

"I agree," Robert said, shaking his head at John and his infatuation with Melissa.

My Forbidden Mentor

"Do me a favor and tell Melissa I'll be right back. I need to finish up with packing," he asked as he was walking away.

"Of course," Robert verified.

Melissa returned back to where Robert stood. Simon had finished with Chief and left to return to other work he had. "Where's John?" she asked, leaning against a gated stall.

Robert leaned against the stall as well. "He had to finish packing. He should return shortly."

She shifted her body to face him. "I suppose you know John and I talked?"

Robert faced her. "Yes. I asked John and he told me so. I'm glad you did because it seems to have worked out."

Melissa's eyes downcast and her cheeks were blushing as she was thinking about how well it did turn out. Robert had to know and was being a gentleman for her benefit. Nevertheless, she appreciated it. "Yes. I'm grateful for your persistence Robert. I can see why John has you for a friend."

"Thank you, but it goes both ways, and of course I think of you as my friend as well."

Melissa eyes lifted to find a pair of emerald green eyes staring at her with admiration. Indeed, and what a handsome friend he was. Rose was a very lucky lady. "Robert, I was wondering how long you and John have known each other?"

"Almost eighteen years."

"Where did you meet?" she asked.

"We met in Catterick village. We had to be around twelve or thirteen. My father was an avid horse trainer and of course I was dragged along when he worked. That way he could keep an eye on his boy," he chuckled. "Needless to say, there weren't many boys my age around there, none I took a liking to anyway. Then one day John came walking through the front gates. I spotted him instantly. Even then he stood tall and was so sure of himself." He laughed again as he was recalling the moment.

Melissa laughed with him. "Really?"

"Oh yes. Anyway, I went up to him, introduced myself, and told him my father was a trainer there. We just took to each other. We had a lot in common and still do," he told her. He remembered his father's easy nature, treating John like his own son until his passing about ten years ago. He smiled again at the happy memories. "My father sort of took John in. He doesn't get along with his own father. He's really more like a brother to me, especially since he practically lived with us for five years."

Melissa appreciated what he had told her as it enlightened her to the little boys they once were. "I got that impression about John and his father but he hasn't talked about it. Where's your father now?"

"He died about ten years ago."

"I'm sorry, Robert, I didn't realize."

"It's all right. I know you've had your own losses to deal with so you understand." He smiled in reassurance and his hand went to cover hers that lay atop the gate between them.

"Are we ready, then?" A deep, familiar voice interrupted their like-minded sentiments.

John strode toward them. His inspection of their engrossed conversation became envious when he witnessed his best friend's hand touching Melissa's. He couldn't deny wondering what they were talking about and how personal it was. By the way Robert had touched her it seemed very personal. He tried to keep his gaze from lingering on their hands that were now separating, but he couldn't help himself and directed a glare toward Robert that sent a warning of possession.

Melissa seemed unaware as she took John's hand in hers. "Hello. Yes, I'm ready."

John gave her a warm smile. "Great, let's go." He started to turn with Melissa when Robert got his attention.

"John, might I have a word with you?" It came out in a demanding tone, letting John know it was crucial they talk right now.

John asked Melissa to take Chief to the front of the manor to be loaded with supplies. He didn't want to alarm her of a possible storm that may erupt between him and Robert. After she obliged, he swung back toward Robert.

Both men watched Melissa take Chief by the reins and lead him out of the stables then they switched back to face each other.

"Yes?" John asked with impatience.

"What were you thinking a moment ago?" Robert had a pretty good idea but he wanted John to be aware of how ridiculous his assumptions had been.

"What were you doing a moment ago?" John slammed the words back into his face.

"You can't possibly think I was coming on to Melissa?" Robert retorted. John was in worse shape than he figured if he'd gotten jealous of his best friend. Robert admitted to being admirably attracted to Melissa but that was as far as it went. Never in their lifetime had they taken advantage of each other when it came to women. That was a promise they had made to each other long ago and Robert wasn't about to destroy their friendship over a woman. Melissa was special indeed, especially to John, and Robert couldn't have been happier for him, which was why anger surfaced immediately when John had gotten an attitude with him.

John's arms crossed over his broad chest in firm determination. The narrowing of his brewing eyes coincided with his clenched jaw. "What was I supposed to think?"

Robert almost laughed. "John, you've lost it. Yes I was touching her, only her hand, I might add, but instead of finding out the true reason why you insisted on jumping to conclusions." By the time he finished, he was almost shouting.

John's stance hadn't changed. "Give me the true reason why it was necessary to touch what is mine?" His voice rose in volume as well.

Robert studied John in amazement. "My God, John, I thought you were possessive of your thoroughbreds." John didn't reply, just stared. Robert decided to tell him exactly how it was regarding this insane situation. "You know, it really riles me that you don't trust me, your best friend. I would never, ever come on to your territory. You've got bloody balls to believe this about me after everything we've been through."

His words must have made an impression for John's eyes closed and his stance relaxed. Robert could see that he was feeling bad about losing control. Damn, what would have happened if Robert hadn't been his best friend and confidant? John's eyes softened as they opened. "John, Melissa and I were sharing a sympathetic moment toward our fathers that have passed on. She asked me about my father and when she found out he'd passed away she felt bad, that was all. I was only consoling her. You've lost a parent, you should understand that."

"Oh, lord." John shook his head, disgusted with himself. "Forgive me, Robert. I was out of line. This girl is," John inhaled a deep breath. "She's driving me mad."

"I can see that," Robert commented.

"I'm not sure how to handle this," John confided, sounding lost.

"I'd say go with it and see where it takes you. The craziness can't last forever," Robert suggested.

"Lord, I hope not, or you may be visiting me in an insane asylum," John said on a chuckle.

Robert reacted with a friendly smile. "Not to worry, old chap. We've already concluded you're hooked, which explains a lot."

"Yeah," John agreed.

"John, you will have to contend with other men where Melissa is concerned, you might as well adjust to that fact. Why don't you marry her? Being your wife could make a difference." Robert stopped speaking when he heard footsteps nearing. He and John both looked toward the sound approaching them.

John knew instinctively it was Melissa by the staggered pace. "It's Melissa," he whispered. They both played innocent now that they'd resolved John's impossible attitude.

Melissa had heard their voices rising from outside. Although she couldn't make out their words with any clarity, it had sounded serious. Maybe talking business had riled some emotions but she didn't like the sound of it. As soon as Chief was ready and packed it was the perfect excuse to relieve her curiosity. By the time she reached them, they appeared happy and content, both smiling at her profusely. Her gaze switched between the silent men and then she fixed her gaze on John. "Please excuse the interruption but Chief is ready now."

"Good. Robert and I are finished here," he said as he and Robert nodded to each other while John took Melissa's hand and led her to the manor.

On the way Melissa couldn't help herself. "John, were you and Robert arguing?"

"No. Why would you say that?"

"Well I could hear your voices out here."

"We were having a discussion and it got a little heated, that's all. Everything is solved now."

"Good, because I'd hate to see you two not getting along. It wouldn't be good for business or your personal well-being."

"You're absolutely right, but Robert and I always manage to solve our problems when they happen." He pointed toward the entrance, "Watch your step," he said, feeling relieved to be let out of that discussion with her.

Chapter Seventeen

John led her through the massive doorway of his home, showing her the sitting room first. Its masculine décor included an enormous fireplace and fine suede colored leather furniture. One large wall was graced with an elegant painting of a black stallion. They continued down the familiar entry way covered in thoroughbred paintings, disappearing briefly into the dining and kitchen areas until finally reaching the library at the end of the hallway. There they admired John's many books for a few moments before John took her upstairs.

Occupying the second level were seven decorated chambers, each with their own color schemes, but basically earth tones. They came upon an eighth chamber set apart from the rest. John told her it occupied most of the backside of the manor. This chamber did not at all compare to the other seven. This one was lavish, plush with a cobalt blue color that covered almost every inch of the room. Except for a dresser, captain's chest and bed frame, all made of walnut, the rich blue color dominated. As she explored every personal facet about him John's aroma filled the air around her, making it all the easier to drown in the sea of color of his chamber. It was by far the most elegant bedchamber she'd ever seen.

Her eyes stopped on the bed. How could she have missed his bed? It didn't lack for size, being twice the size of hers. She stepped next to the enormous bed, dying to touch the lush blue velvet spread adorning it. Her fingers brushed across the softness and her eyes closed to take in the feel of it more soundly. When she opened her eyes she gazed into the wide-open bed, drifting into its deep blue ocean effect, dreaming of lying upon it and floating away in its waves.

"Do you have a fondness for velvet?" John asked as he stood next to her.

Her eyes found his and her lips curled into a smile. "Yes, it's so soft. It's the softest texture I've ever felt."

John grinned, admiring her innocent nature and realizing she hadn't had luxuries all her life like he had. "Yes, but it's not the softest texture I've ever felt." A hand went to cover hers as it caressed the spread and his other hand went to cup her cheek, his fingertips tracing down her neck and along her collarbone. Trailing further down he took her clothed breast in the palm of his hand, showing her the softness he referred to.

Melissa's eyes began to close when she remembered the chamber door was still open. What if someone were to walk by, she thought, and her eyes flew back open. "John, the door is open."

His grin turned wicked as he glanced over his shoulder toward the door. "So it is," he whispered back.

"John," she said in a pleading tone. She left him to stand there while she went to explore a copper tub she'd spotted. It was tucked away in a private corner of the room and as she approached the tub she realized it seated two. She looked beyond the inviting tub to the window next to it, discovering the magnificent view you would have while bathing. It must be glorious at nighttime when the stars were out.

She didn't hear him come up behind her but she could feel him and smelled his masculine scent as he neared. She backed away from the tub and turned to face a very large walk-in dressing room.

My Forbidden Mentor

"I've never seen such a spectacular looking room before John. It's heavenly," she told him as she ventured into the closet and using her fingertips, skimmed along his varied wardrobe.

Had she known how convenient she'd made it for him to take advantage of her she never would have entered his dressing room, and had John been better prepared regarding contraceptives, he would have taken the opportunity, but nevertheless he followed her in the room. "I like it. It's very accommodating," he said in a silky tone, watching her back stiffen as he trapped her in a corner.

She swung around to face him, aware now how tempting she had made it for him for they were far from any open doors at present. Her arms folded over her breasts. "Now I know why you picked out this dress. It's obvious blue is your favorite color," she said, trying to say anything to distract him.

"Very perceptive. But I have another favorite color I've discovered recently," he said, his fingers reaching into her loose strands of hair.

His mouth was so close to hers she couldn't breathe. Damn it, John, this isn't the time or place, she voiced in silence. That door was still open to his chamber and anyone, the maid, Charles, anyone could walk in at any time. Having discovered that she wasn't the quietest person when it came to lovemaking, she doubted they would go unheard. She played along anyhow, ignoring her inner thoughts. "Really? What color is that?" she inquired, smiling in a way that would not give away her thoughts.

"Gold," he told her, his devilish grin coming closer to conquer her smile.

"John," she warned.

Laura Mills

He groaned out his intent. "One kiss, sweet." His lips touched hers. "Just one?" he asked this time.

She was breathless. "Let's wait, John. I want to wait until we get home." Where we can be free and as loud as we wish, she wanted to say.

His lips touched hers anyway, lingering in a closed mouth kiss. When they lifted, he warned her, "Melissa, when you look at me like you did in the stables, undressing me with your eyes, well, it gets me excited and I can't help but want you at that very moment. Do you understand?"

"Does that mean I can't look at you that way?"

"No, it means that if you do, you had better be prepared for an instant reaction from me. It flatters me when you look at me that way but sweetheart, it makes me want to touch you and feel you and do very private things to you." He decided to curb his language for her naivety. He realized her misinterpretation wasn't deliberate but he had to make her aware of the power she held.

"I see," she said, using his usual response.

He backed off, taking her hand and leading her out of the dressing room. They stood before the copper tub. "We'll wait until we get home, all right?" he smiled as he told her, feeling grateful they were out of that dark cozy corner. The two reasons he had to stop his advancement barely held him contained but he would not go against her wishes and he would not take another chance of getting her pregnant.

"Yes, thank you," she replied, still in awe of his luxurious room. As she turned to step toward the main chamber door she saw a painting of a woman, a very beautiful woman, she hadn't noticed before. Stepping by his washbasin, she studied the painting hanging on a secluded wall. Its size monopolized the wall it hung on. She let go of John's hand and stepped closer to the painting.

My Forbidden Mentor

She had to be one of the most beautiful women she'd ever seen and one couldn't ignore the intrigue of her presence. John's mother. It had to be, for she had dark brown, almost black, hair and gray eyes, just like John's.

John came up behind her, wrapping his arms around her waist, and gazed at the painting as well. "Your mother?" she asked.

"Yes."

"She's stunning, John." She looked over her shoulder at him. "Will you ever tell me about her? I'm curious." He wasn't smiling anymore as his expression had turned melancholy.

He stood there holding her and remained quiet for a long time. She faced the painting again, thinking she had pushed him too far with his mother again.

"What would you like to know?" he finally said.

"What was she like, her personality?" she asked, still surprised that he was willing to tell her.

His comfort level had grown with Melissa and he decided it wouldn't hurt to tell her about his beloved mother. "She was a very vibrant woman, always active helping less fortunate people, especially women, but she always arranged a certain amount of time every day to spend with me." Thinking back on those precious times brought a smile to his face. "Very adventurous. We were always involved in all kinds of activities." His eyes closed recalling the activities they endeavored.

"We'd go fishing for hours and talk about anything. She taught me how to swim. She was an excellent swimmer. We'd go riding and when a clearing appeared, we'd race." A light chuckled sounded from him. His eyes opened.

"Although she won most of the time, she'd let me win once in a while. I didn't realize it at the time. We were very close."

Melissa turned to look at him. Gazing into Melissa's tender expression he remembered something his mother had told him before passing away. She advised him to marry for love. Truly love each other and be kind to one another. Have trust. At the time, being only twelve years old, it hadn't meant too much, but he hadn't thought about it again until this moment, until Melissa beheld him with that enamored look of hers. He continued, "Everyone liked her, something my father couldn't handle." His jawed tensed after mentioning his father.

A vast display of emotions graced his features and Melissa desperately wanted to know about her death but thought the timing would be wrong to ask. He'd opened up today, which was progress, so instead she smiled and replied, "She sounds wonderful, John." Not expecting the moment to arouse such strong emotions she froze in her speech, unable to carry on a conversation as the situation seemed fragile. She shifted back to the painting of the woman whose son still mourned her.

John stared into Melissa's profile. Talking of his mother, delicate emotions surfaced, straining to be freed. A sense of safety filled his senses when he searched her soft features. She made him feel he could talk to her about anything, just like his mother had, but his mother was gone and Melissa was here now. Trust, have trust, his mother had told him. He did trust Melissa, which was why he had an overwhelming urge to release some past pain and humiliation.

"Right before my mother died my parents fought a lot, and I witnessed it unfortunately." He took a deep breath before going on. "Their fights were over my father's jealousy of my mother. He stopped taking her to the balls she so enjoyed

My Forbidden Mentor

as he couldn't handle any men around her at all." He stopped, temporarily relating to his father's wariness. Melissa didn't move, keeping her gaze directed toward the woman he was revealing. "Eventually she never went anywhere and began drinking. Meanwhile, my father was out with other women."

John stopped. Melissa could hear the shakiness in his voice. She remained unmoving except for placing her hands over his across her belly, gripping them with an understanding that she knew this wasn't easy for him.

"One night mother was considerably drunk and upset with my father as he'd been out with another woman again and she couldn't take it anymore. She'd waited for him at the top of the stairs when he came staggering up the stairs drunk." His eyes closed and then opened as he went on. "I was down the hallway, looking out my chamber door at them. They were arguing." His eyes squeezed shut once more, remembering the loud, screaming voices of his parents. "It was horrible," John whispered, replaying the memory. "He began slapping her around and saying mean things to her. I was trying to get the courage to stop him but when I finally did, I didn't get there in time. He'd hit her hard, so hard that she fell down the stairs."

Melissa heard the panic in his voice turn to anger. "We both ran down the stairs to catch her but she reached the bottom before we got to her." He paused. "She wasn't dead then but she did have internal injuries and the doctor wasn't hopeful. She only lived three days longer. I wasn't allowed to see her on the last day. No one saw her. My father wouldn't allow it. I've never forgiven him for what he did, I can't." A feeling of relief washed over him and his voice dropped an octave. "And I've never forgiven myself. I should have helped her sooner," he said in a saddened tone.

Tears filled Melissa's eyes. She blinked and single streams ran down her cheeks. When she turned to face him her compassion showed. She couldn't decide whether to say something or simply hold him. Her arms went around him, holding him with a death grip. "You can't blame yourself John," she whispered into his ear.

He saw how emotional she was about his past and it made his heart ache even more. "Perhaps," he whispered back, holding her just as tight.

"I know it wasn't easy telling me. Thank you." She had never been as close to anyone as she was to John at this moment.

All packed and loaded atop Chief, John and Melissa made their way to her cabin. Evening was approaching when they arrived, and while John unloaded Chief, Melissa prepared a bath for herself.

John took his time brushing down Chief while Melissa bathed. He used the extra time to decide how to approach the subject of birth control with her. Obviously she hadn't thought about it herself or she would have said something, and their first time together had been so intense, so ravenous, neither had thought about anything but pent-up desires that had reached their limit.

He figured their chances were slim that she'd conceived, but nevertheless he knew it was his responsibility to make sure as he was the experienced one here. Already they had made love three unprotected times, three times which raised that slim chance that they had produced a child. His focusing gaze found his leather pouch lying on top of a bale of hay. He glared at the pouch while he was finishing the brushing of Chief as the pouch contained enough sponges to last a month. He then wondered, How do I approach her with this? How will she react?

When he found her lying on the bed she looked refreshed and sated from her bath.

A thrill of exhilaration seized Melissa as John stood above her, watching her with those eyes of his. She followed his movements as he sat on the edge of the bed, lifting his leather pouch to his lap. She observed him fumbling with the opening of his bag and saw him pulling out a small sponge. She raised her gaze and searched his face.

His eyes found hers as he sensed her bewilderment.

"What is that for?" she asked, shifting her eyes to the sponge which lay in his hand and then back to his gaze.

"It's a device," he answered, then gave a more accurate description, "A contraceptive device."

She rose onto her elbows and examined the sponge. "Really?" she replied, taking it out of his hand and viewing it at closer range. "What is its accuracy?" she inquired, as if it were an everyday question.

John carefully monitored his words. If he gave her curious mind any reason at all to question him further than he intended the delicate situation could turn fierce. He wasn't about to speak of his past experiences with her. "I'm not sure of the exact percentage, but it's fairly high in preventing pregnancy." There, that sounded safe enough.

"Well." She thought about it some more, handing him the sponge. "I trust your judgment, John."

"You'll wear it then?" He had to verify she was agreeable.

"Of course. But there is one condition," she said with a surfacing smile.

"Yes?" John waited with bated breath.

"You will help me with it every time." Her smile turned into a full-fledged grin.

"Of course," he said. Holding the sponge in one hand and his pouch in the other he rose from the bed. Stepping over to her dressing table he found a small porcelain dish and dropped the sponge into it. He opened the pouch, retrieved two more sponges and placed them in the dish as well. Melissa watched with earnest, interested in the process. Next he pulled out three separate strings and tied their ends to each sponge. Then, to her amazement, he pulled out a bottle of brandy, at least she assumed it was brandy because that was what he drank, and saw him pour just enough of it into each sponge to dampen it. He placed the cork back on the bottle of amber liquor and began unbuttoning his shirt while the sponges soaked.

"John?" Melissa asked, having that inquisitive tone in her voice.

"Yes?" he acknowledged while tossing his shirt across a chair near the door and proceeding to the buttons of his trousers.

Melissa sank back into the bed. "What about the other times?"

John's nonchalant attitude took over. "I wouldn't worry about that. What's important is we're taking precautions now." John tried to slide out of that one as smoothly as he was sliding out of his trousers.

She turned away from him, her eyes staring into the ceiling of wooden beams. "But there is a slight possibility I could be pregnant, right?"

She turned away from him, her eyes staring into the ceiling of wooden beams. "But there is a slight possibility I could be pregnant, right?"

She was full of questions he didn't want to answer. After all, she would know the possibilities just as much as he, but feeling guilt ridden since he should have known better and taken care of matters on their first encounter, he would answer her.

Discarding his boots and trousers, he picked up the dish holding the sponges and brought it over to the nightstand. He sat on the edge of the bed and then obliged her with an answer to her satisfaction. "I'm going to be honest and say that yes, there is a slight, very slight, chance you're pregnant. I wouldn't worry about it. I'm not. And from now on, with the use of these," he reached over, took a sponge in his fingers and squeezed it to rid the excess liquor from it. "We won't have to wonder about it any longer."

Her eyes met his. "I trust you, John."

He gave her a smile. "Good."

Chapter Eighteen

John and Melissa started their week together in adventurous bliss. It was a week to explore their innermost thoughts and feelings about life in general. They took long walks in the afternoons, holding hands as they journeyed through trails of shading oak trees and thick green grass. They searched for creatures of nature to investigate, Melissa's favorite pastime.

By the middle of the week they had ventured further out, and around noon one day they were sitting on a high ridge of dewy grass, eating berries and speaking of their childhoods. They discovered that although they were raised in different environments, their heartfelt admiration for horses had led them to common ground and had led them to each other, and that was all that mattered as they chased each other down the ridge like children, like two children reliving their childhood but together this time.

Although Melissa suffered a disadvantage because of her injured leg, John had difficulty keeping up with her as she twirled and dodged his pursuing maneuvers. When he would catch up to her she tried to trip him, and as he gave in he took her down with him. They rolled together in the moist green grass, laughing and holding onto each other until the bottom of the hill smoothed into flat ground.

Coming to a halt, John landed on top of Melissa, his grin wavering as his eyes lingered into her happy, smiling face. His gaze traveled down to her elevating bosom, recovering her breath from their child's play. To John, she could have been catching her breath from a passionate interlude, in that moment it was the same and as real to him and his features turned serious.

Melissa's smile diminished when looking up into gray eyes that held her speechless. Of their own accord her fingers swept through his long hair, which hung loose around his shoulders. Her eyes found his again and an apprehensive shiver ran through her as she examined his contemplating expression.

These past days spent with Melissa had caught up with John. He realized that watching her now. The bond between them was growing stronger every day, more so than he had ever imagined. He'd never been this close to a woman before, reveling in the comfort she offered. Never had he shared every aspect of his life to this extreme, but with Melissa it came naturally. The only person who had even come close was his mother, but that was when he was a mere lad. Now he was a man, a man whose desire for this woman lying beneath him went beyond any imaginations he had of what a woman could bring to his life.

John's hand went to Melissa's face, his fingers caressing along her hairline. His true feelings wanted to be expressed but he couldn't manage a word. Instead, his head lowered and his mouth kissed hers. It was a deep, thorough kiss, trying to show her his feelings. Is this love? The realization scared him to death. Loving someone this much created feelings he'd been numb to for quite some time, for the only other person he had loved without restraint had been taken away from him. His kiss turned persistent, devouring Melissa's mouth, ensuring she was real and wasn't going to disappear.

John's kisses had always been delicious and consuming but now they were demanding, requiring her to continue at a maddening pace. What had gotten into him? She could hardly breathe.

Sensing her struggle beneath his conquering mouth, he released her. "Lord I want you," he breathed along her cheek. His fingers located the buttons of her top and began undoing them.

His insistence produced a flare of heated excitement. Oh yes, she wanted him too, and she didn't care that they were out in the open. In fact, it felt right to be free out here with all of nature, relishing in nature's sweet pleasures of human intimacy.

Melissa lay floating on a heavenly cloud.

John collapsed on top of her and she embraced him once again, not minding his extended weight at all. To have him this close was all that mattered. They seemed to be merging on all levels of this extraordinary relationship they had, although she wished it to be more permanent. John hadn't confessed to loving her, but then neither had she. In her heart she knew she loved him, and the more her love grew, the more frightening it became because she wasn't sure of his feelings. To be willing to spend this much time with her he had to care. This wouldn't be a game to him, would it? He wasn't having his way with her until he became bored, was he? She had to mean more to him than that.

As if he could see in her mind the million unanswered, insecure questions, John expressed his feelings in perfect timing. "You're special to me, you know that don't you?" he murmured in her ear before raising his head.

She gazed up into his handsome face that stole her heart, reaching with one hand to lace through a long strand of his hair, which lay across his forehead. "I hope so," she said, as her insecurities were overpowering her confidence.

John stared into her hazel eyes that sparkled like glitter under the noonday sun, trying to find in those eyes her true feelings for him. Did she truly love him or was she just infatuated? "Well believe it, it's true," he told her before rolling his weight off of her, and he proceeded to slide his trousers back up.

Melissa didn't know how to respond. As she and John put her clothing back together she wanted to ask more questions but decided to leave things the way they were. After all, she didn't want to scare him off. If she revealed that she loved him it might do that. Maybe she was special to him but maybe that didn't mean love.

They both stood. John took Melissa's hand in his and they walked back to her cabin with questions unanswered.

They carried on with their routine for the remainder of the week, waking every morning entangled in the lovemaking motions that began and ended each of their days. After a light breakfast, usually muffins and berries, they tended to necessary chores, primarily regarding the horses. Feeding, grooming, exercising and cleaning their stalls all took place before Melissa's training sessions.

When Saturday morning arrived, they lay intertwined beneath the lavender coverlet, treasuring the morning hours that remained. By tomorrow Miss Beckett would return.

Both tried not to linger on their necessary separation, discussing instead their chances of entering Melissa into racecourses. Catterick seemed like the logical choice, but before they could begin Lord Ainsworth would take some convincing. John was sure of it. Out of all four partners, Lord Ainsworth was always contradictory to any new idea or event. He was a conservative to the extreme. A decision was made that Melissa and John would confront him this very day.

After settling that issue Melissa stretched to lay straddled over the top of John, her golden head resting upon his shoulder. Her fingers were swirling through the wisps of black hairs on his chest when he commented, "Sweetheart I could always whisk you away at nightfall when your aunt thinks you are asleep." One hand rubbed along her naked backside and his other hand pushed strands of hair away from her face. "You could stay with me at my home during the night hours."

She tipped her head up to see if he was serious or just being lighthearted. Gratefully, he looked serious. "You would continue to see me in this manner?" she asked, almost reluctant to hear his response.

His lazy gray eyes glistened while he searched each feature of her face. "Yes, I would. I don't want to lose you, Melissa."

She smiled at his ridiculous assumption. "Lose me? John, why would you think that? I enjoy being with you." She lifted and moved closer, her face close enough for her lips to almost touch his. "I don't want to be away from you. Why would you think that?"

"It's more involved than that." John was about to continue when the sound of horse hooves approaching outside could be heard. Both startled, they scrambled out of bed to glimpse out the window. Whoever it was had just ruined John's moment of courage he was daring to take. He was about to tell Melissa how deep his feelings were becoming, but for fear of Miss Beckett returning early, they both stood naked before the bedroom window, looking down to see who had arrived.

Both were relieved when it turned out to be Robert. Their serious talk would have to be postponed. John bent down to retrieve his trousers while he spoke to Melissa, who was also getting dressed. "We'll finish this conversation later," he told her, swiftly slipping his shirt on and giving her a quick kiss as he strode out the bedroom door.

Melissa hadn't realized how important she'd become to him. Standing before her closet in her undergarments, she searched for a dress to wear as she pondered his recent mood. What was he about to tell me? She slipped a summer dress over her body and reached for her brush.

She would learn the truth the next time they talked. She laced up her favorite cream colored half boots which went well with the simple muslin dress she wore.

She was just about to step onto the hardwood floor from the bottom of the stairway when John strode up to her in a quickened pace. As he neared she watched his eyes examine her attire. She also noticed Robert disappear into the sitting room, mouthing hello on his way. She watched John take her hand in his and lead her back up the stairs to her bedroom.

She swung around to confront him as he was shutting the door. Confused by his recent actions and thinking it may be another tragedy of some sort she inquired, "What's the matter?" She observed him changing into clean clothes while she waited for his reply.

"You need to change as well Melissa," he told her in response, slipping a fresh silk shirt into the waistband of clean trousers. Searching for a pair of silk stockings, his focus was concentrated and ignorant to the shock Melissa demonstrated. He slipped on the stockings he'd found and reached for his boots.

Stunned, Melissa didn't understand his change in attitude. "I'm already dressed, John," she informed him with a crease beginning in her brows as she watched him tug on each boot.

He looked up and over her form again. "You're not going to the track in that dress."

"What!" She was about to explode. If he didn't like the dress, why not say so.

He leaned over, grabbed her brush and started taming his wild hair. "That dress is far too revealing to wear to the track. It needs to be changed." He didn't wait for her response as he set the brush back on the dressing table and stepped over to the closet, sorting through her dresses for an appropriate one.

She stepped over to him and stood behind him with her hands on her hips. She couldn't believe his actions. He was actually picking out a different dress for her. "It wasn't too revealing for you the day we had lunch and toasted champagne to our partnership."

"That was different," he said in response while continuing to sift through her dresses.

"How?" she asked with arms crossing over her chest and a boot tapping against the hardwood floor.

He didn't bother to answer. He finally pulled out a dress, an older style, hunter green-colored dress with a high collar, fabric that covered the entire bosom area, long sleeves, and a million buttons made from material as thick as molasses. "Here, this one will do," he told her as he spun to find her standing right behind him.

Her gaze dropped to the boots she wore. Her eyes lifted again. "It won't match my boots, and besides, it's too hot to wear in this weather, John."

John didn't care what excuses she had. There was no way she would go out in public in that dress again. The first time he'd seen her wear it, the dress had posed a great deal of carnal ideas in his own mind. He didn't want to imagine

My Forbidden Mentor

the ideas other men would have regarding his woman. "Melissa, I like the dress, but so will every other man at the track. You're not wearing it."

"It's the perfect dress, John. It's lightweight and sheer, made just for this kind of weather. Let the other men look. They're not going to touch." Had she been aware how her words would affect John she probably wouldn't have said them, but instead her innocence made her unaware.

John's narrowed gray eyes darkened, his voice unaccountably stern. "Exactly, it's sheer. That's my point, Melissa. It's sheer enough that if other men are looking, they can see the outline of your beautiful breasts that are for my eyes only." He stood still with the green dress draped over one arm, his opposite hand clenched into a fist at his side. "And you're right, they're not going to touch. They're not even going to look." His blood pumped faster as the volume of his voice got louder.

Melissa saw how angry he'd become but still thought he was overreacting. "John the dress you're holding will reveal more of an outline of my breast than this one will. It's tighter across." She indicated on herself to prove her point.

He calmed himself with a deep breath, knowing that in the end when they walked into that track, she would be wearing hunter green and not translucent cream. "Melissa, this dress will not reveal the tips of your breasts so readily." When her eyes got big, he turned her away from him and guided her toward the sunlit glare casting on the window. Standing behind her he patiently waited for her to take notice. "As you can see this one does." There wasn't any need to point out the obvious to her.

He was right. As she gazed at her own reflection she realized he had reason to be upset. She never imagined how sheer it really was until she stood in broad sunlight. She inched closer to the window and sure enough, it was almost as if she wore nothing at all. Her fancy, silk chemise beneath didn't help to conceal anything.

She turned back to him, snatched the heavy dress from his arm, laid it on the bed and began undressing. Her look of defeat confirmed that she agreed with his reasoning, even if forced to do so.

"Thank you," he said, and then proceeded to leave the bedroom so she could change in peace. It wouldn't be fair to gloat about getting his way. That she was changing her clothing without further deliberation confirmed progress regarding her stubborn nature.

Chapter Nineteen

The track was swarmed with multitudes of people. Luckily John and Robert, being part owners, had their own private viewing box. After they arrived Robert went his separate way to conduct business. By the time John and Melissa reached their destination they had stopped and conversed with a great number of John's associates. Seeing him at his own track, in his own element, Melissa knew she'd picked the perfect team partner. Intelligent, talented, fascinated with horses in general, John proved to be the ideal partner for her, in more ways than one, she sighed.

Staring into his profile as he gave his opinion to an interested patron, his handsome features could not be dismissed. By far he easily attracted any status of the female gender and suddenly they seemed to appear in droves. Scanning the crowd of women settling around their viewing box, Melissa's thoughts ran astray.

When she should be concentrating on her presentation to Lord Ainsworth, instead she was wondering if any of these women floating by them were past lovers of John's. That thought led to how many lovers he'd had. The glares and whispers of these women promoted her insecurities, making her clasped hands perspire and tighten their grip. Any one of these women could have been a past lover.

She sat when John did, her fingers sliding below the edge of the collar of her dress, her neck feeling constricted from the hot and binding material. Carefully she stretched the collar so she was able to breathe again. Her confidence was plummeting and her imaginations were turning frantic while women pointed and whispered.

Her attention swayed when John asked how she was doing. She replied with a quick, unsuspecting smile and told him she was fine. Before he could comment another person greeted him, raving about Chief's progress. Usually confident, Melissa was surprised to find how much she was struggling with this situation.

She tore her view from the glaring women and shifted toward John. He didn't seem bothered one bit by the situation, as if it were a common occurrence. She glanced at the track where preparations were taking place to begin the races. Did John pick and choose among these women when he finished his day? Is that why they waited around?

"Melissa?" John called out to her.

"Yes," she responded in irritation, not meaning to but her thoughts had led her there.

"Are you all right?" he asked.

She made a quick glance toward the women close by. "I'm sorry. I'm nervous about Lord Ainsworth and it's quite hot out here," she told him, fanning herself with one of her hands.

John's mouth curved into a half grin. Her glance a moment ago had revealed the reason for her irritation. The women. They were indeed a nuisance to both John and Robert, but their husbands and or male friends were supporters of Robert and John's endeavors regarding the track so they were tolerated. It seemed Melissa would have to learn to tolerate them as well. "Ignore them," he advised her.

Melissa looked straight at John. "What? How? They're, they're," She hesitated for lack of a ladylike remark.

My Forbidden Mentor

John chuckled, which drew the stares of some ladies close by. "Go ahead and say it. Talk to me in your language, sweet, you will not offend me."

He saw her continuing to struggle so he leaned forward, putting his ear near her mouth. "Whisper it to me."

"They're the most bloody, vile creatures I've ever seen and their actions disturb me."

This time he laughed out loud. Melissa tried hushing him but without success. He shifted to whisper in her ear away from ogling inspections. "I agree with you, sweet, so ignore them," he told her and gave her a love bite on her earlobe. Her shoulder shrugged at the ticklish sensation. "Think about what I'm going to do to you when we get home, what I'm going to do in bed under the covers, like this morning." He placed a soft kiss upon her cheek before pulling away.

Melissa fidgeted in her seat. Darn him. Her body responded to his words as if he was actually performing the actions he described, but then again, it did take her mind off those bloody vile creatures.

In a matter of minutes Melissa's newfound peace was destroyed. John had departed in search of Lord Ainsworth and when he left most of the women left as well, all except one, who it seemed had only recently appeared.

Attractive in her own way, the young lady kept checking her surroundings as though she was either looking for someone or making sure she wouldn't be seen. Melissa focused her attention toward the track, ignoring the blond miss as John suggested.

She liked her life now. Despite losing both parents she was happy. The new companion in her life made moving ahead worthwhile. Would they marry? She had dreams of it happening and she truly believed her father would have approved.

"Pardon me, are you with Lord Blackburn?" The young lady asked, making Melissa jump.

Melissa looked over the blond, petite woman who dressed in rich clothing. She was very exotic looking with her unusual shade of platinum hair, and the blue of her eyes could cut daggers they seemed so cold. She stood out from the rest of the women and now had Melissa curious as to whom she was. "Yes, may I ask why?"

The young lady stood along the outer edge of the viewing box, boasting a spiteful gleam in those icy blue eyes of hers. "I know John personally. I'm Vanessa Walker," Vanessa relayed, taking note of Melissa's questioning image. "Oh, so sorry to have startled you by using his first name, but you see John and I are good friends," Vanessa told her as she poked and prodded.

Holding her tongue, Melissa wasn't sure of what being a good friend of John's involved with this forward stranger. "Lord Blackburn should return shortly if you wish to speak to him."

Quite pretty for a country girl Vanessa thought, making her own evaluation, but what does John see in her? She smiled despite the venom wanting to burst out. "Actually I do, but I also wanted to meet the mysterious woman who's been occupying so much of his time. And you are?" Vanessa asked, pleased with herself for the way she'd shaken the country lass.

Vanessa had come to confront John about his absence of late and other important matters, hoping she'd find him at the track. Her luck stayed with her when she spotted John in his private viewing box, only to feel dire disappointment when she saw a young lady seated next to him. John never had ladies in the box with him and he never showed open interest as he'd done today. Vanessa didn't lose hope as she stepped closer to John until she saw him lean over and

My Forbidden Mentor

nuzzle the lass's ear, then laugh and act playful with her. Fury lit inside Vanessa like never before.

She wanted to kill the wicked woman that had stolen John away from her but instead ordered herself to be patient. Nothing like a slow painful death, Vanessa sneered. Yes, that was the least this country lass could endure.

"Melissa Howard," Melissa revealed, keeping her answers short and to the point. After all, she hadn't any clue what this woman meant to John.

Vanessa's smile turned vicious. "You see, Miss Howard, I used to be the one entertaining John not long ago. I know how impatient he can be so I'm not surprised that he's found a new diversion, but being his favorite I know he'll return to me. John and I have a history."

Melissa was taken aback but she had to believe that John was true to her. Trying not to believe this gossipy woman, Melissa asked while keeping control of her anger, "What is the purpose of this conversation, Miss Walker?"

Still smiling, Vanessa spoke with a warning tone. "It's a friendly warning, Miss Howard. I hope you don't think you're something special to the handsome lord. Believe me, he can be deceiving. His lovemaking is extraordinary and he's full of charm," Vanessa paused, watching Melissa's jaw tighten. Her plan was working. "I know. I've known him long enough to see how he operates. He is insistent on you wearing sponges, is he not?" Melissa's reaction was what she expected. "Even so, Miss Howard, I understand your attraction to him. I feel the same way. I put up with his philandering because I treasure our friendship, among other things." While Vanessa finished her damaging speech she watched and waited.

Melissa was infuriated. "How can you say such disturbing things to me? Whether this is true or not Miss Walker, I don't care to hear about it."

"Oh, it's true Miss Howard. Why don't you ask John if he knows me and how well? He won't lie to you. He's the most honest person I've ever met."

Indeed, she was right about him being honest. "Regardless of your past history with John, Miss Walker, I think your intentions are cruel to tell me about it in this manner."

Vanessa leaned into Melissa, putting pressure on full force. "His life is his thoroughbreds, Miss Howard. You'll never compete with them, much less the other women in his life. I'm afraid you're just a temporary plaything to fill his lonely hours away from his horses."

Melissa didn't say another word. Self-doubt was creeping in, changing her state of anger into fear, fear that this woman could be telling the truth, fear that if she'd known John longer herself maybe, just maybe, she'd be accurate about his pursuits, but she didn't want to show Vanessa that she'd gotten to her. What little pride she had left she used to make it through the unbelievable conversation she was having with a lover of John's. "Miss Walker, I wish to be left alone with my thoughts. You've been a wonderful insight."

Vanessa relished in seeing that she'd said enough to give this country tart some words to think about, and hopefully she'd back away from John, so she granted her wish and bid her goodbyes with some parting words. "Good day Miss Howard. It was nice meeting you, and if you ever need to talk, I live in the town of Richmond." Her smile became more devious. "You never know, perhaps the three of us can participate in a private, uh, meeting of our own and all become good friends. I'm willing to share if you are?" she extended, feeling satisfied that her visit had proved successful she left.

Melissa was so stunned that she sat there frozen, amazed at the type of women John kept company with, but this one had made some valid points. Why was this happening? The questions were coming back again. Am I just a plaything on the side? Will he tire of me? What exactly do I mean to him? Does he love me, because he hasn't said so yet? And the sponges? Vanessa had hit that one on the mark. Her glorified daydreams were shattering from the words of a jealous lover. How do I deal with this now? Do I confront him?

In the next moment she was looking for John among the crowd, her worried eyes scanning over and over through the mass of people until she found him. His height made it easier to spot him. He was striding in her direction and he seemed to be on his way back when a familiar platinum-headed female appeared before him. Vanessa, Melissa thought, grinding her teeth. She continued to watch them, curious as to how John would react to her.

They both stopped, facing each other. Melissa could see the front of John from her view. He had a faint smile on his face when Vanessa began talking to him. Then the smile disappeared and a stern, serious look took its place. What was she telling him? Melissa leaned forward in her seat as if trying to hear their conversation but they were more than a hundred yards away, making it impossible.

Suddenly, John took Vanessa by the arm and escorted her in the opposite direction toward the front gates. Melissa stood to get a better view. Her curiosity led her out of the viewing box and through the crowd, following them.

What had Vanessa told him? Melissa wondered as she shoved her way through the massive crowd. Pacing on the tips of her toes hadn't given much of an advantage.

Periodically John's dark head would appear in the distance and still bobbing beside him was a platinum blond one. Melissa's brow creased with tension, her breathing came faster, and her heart pounded in anticipation of the results she might find.

Am I just jealous and acting like an outraged lover or is there a reasonable concern here since it was her vicious new acquaintance he was leading out the front gates? Melissa slowed her pace so she wouldn't be seen. John still had quite a tight grip on Vanessa's arm as he led her to his carriage. Why the privacy of his carriage? Melissa closed in on them, just slipping out of the front gates herself.

Melissa bounced from carriage to carriage until she reached John's but by now they were inside. She noticed the curtains closing for privacy. Her heart thudded in her chest, her limbs shook, and her mind was racing with irrational thoughts. He couldn't possibly be making love to her in his present state. At about that time, with Melissa concealed behind the carriage next to John's, her eyes attached to the closed curtain, John's carriage began to rock back and forth.

Melissa's eyes grew wide, her mouth frowning as she clung between hurt and anger, but as the carriage continued rocking, her anger escalated, subduing her hurt feelings. Tired of being stepped on and made a fool of she marched over to John's carriage and was about to open the latched door and say a few choice words when John's words stopped her.

"Vanessa! Get off of me. Stay on that side of the carriage and tell me what's so damned important that you had to drag me away from the races?"

She could tell John was holding his temper in check. The carriage stopped rocking and relief came to Melissa in a heartbeat. John's words consoled her, easing her tension, until Vanessa spoke.

"All right. I'm pregnant, John, and I need your help."

Melissa gasped for her next breath. It was worse than she had thought. Just then Melissa noticed spectators watching her as she stood before the door of John's carriage, obviously eavesdropping. Melissa calmed herself enough to change her position so there wouldn't be any questions about her intentions. As she strolled to the opposite side of the carriage anger struck once again for she was eager to hear John's response.

By the time she had made her way to the opposite side Vanessa was speaking again.

"Besides that John, I need to count on you. You've helped me before, why won't you help me now?"

Melissa moved closer.

"This is different Vanessa. You're pregnant." There was a slight pause and Melissa bit into her lip, awaiting his next words. "When you say, "count on me", what exactly do you mean by that anyway?" John sounded irritated, like Vanessa was wasting his time.

There was silence for a brief moment. Melissa strained to hear, not wanting to cause suspicion. She readied herself to move but not before she heard Vanessa's reply.

"I'd like for us to be married. It's the least we can do for this child."

"What? Married! The least we can do? Vanessa, have you gone mad? "We" aren't going to do anything about this, you are. I am not taking responsibility for something that was completely your slip up."

No, Melissa cried in silence as she turned from the carriage. Seeing a big oak tree nearby, she slowly strolled over to it, beyond caring what onlookers thought as she eased her shocked body down along the trunk of the tree. Leaning her head and back against its solid form, her bottom nestled in warm green grass below, she drew her knees up and wrapped her arms around them. Her eyes shut and she thought of nothing but the horror of her day.

It was quite some time before the carriage door opened. Melissa heard the sound of a hinge creak and opened her eyes to see Vanessa stepping out of John's carriage. She didn't look very happy as she slammed the carriage door shut and stormed off into the distance. Melissa didn't want to feel sorry for her but John's refusal to accept his responsibility left a tinge of sorrow in her case as that meant if she ever got pregnant by John he would shun her also. It was obvious he didn't want children in his life, or at least the responsibility of them. How many did he have? Maybe Vanessa was telling the truth about John's philandering ways. Maybe I am just another convenient distraction.

Moments later John stepped out of his carriage. He looked around, his features strained, his hair disheveled. Melissa sat still against the tree which stood directly across from the back of John's carriage about fifty feet or so. She hadn't expected him to go to the back of his carriage but for some reason he did.

She remained still as he sat on the rim of the carriage, taking the leather thong out of his hair. His black tresses flowed around his broad shoulders just like Melissa preferred it. He was beautiful, beautiful but troubled, and he looked truly upset at the moment. She watched him in admiration despite her previous dismay with him. His head fell into his hands, which rubbed across his face. He hadn't noticed her yet as his palms came up to smooth his hair

My Forbidden Mentor

back, eyes closed, and he did so without effort. As he regained his composure he retied the leather thong around his long hair before opening his eyes and staring right into Melissa's teary-eyed gaze.

Oh lord, he groaned in silence. What had she heard, what was she believing? Vanessa had shocked him with her ridiculous marriage proposal, which he had no intention of carrying out. He would never marry a woman he didn't love. Now, as he stared into Melissa's sad eyes, he knew there would be extensive explaining to do and he cursed Vanessa for putting him in this position.

He stood, his eyes never leaving hers as he stepped over to her. He held out his hand, motioning her to take it. "Come, we need to talk," he said.

Melissa remained seated, hesitant, her eyes downcast, torn between wanting to trust him and not, and feeling foolish for her innocent behavior toward their relationship. When her eyes lifted back to his the motion left streams of tears running down her cheeks.

John's eyes shut when he saw her tears. Taking a deep, calming breath, his eyes opened and his hand reached down for hers again. "Give me your hand," he implored.

His insistent tenderness encouraged her to take his hand. Instead of going to his carriage, though, he took Melissa for a short walk away from the track, away from everything. They stopped at a nearby cliff that overlooked a valley of bright green land and emerald topped trees. A wide ribbon of water flowed down the middle of the scattered trees and green earth, sparkling as the sun cast its rays upon it. The branches on the trees in the valley stirred but a moment later cast a light breeze to cool her face and dry her tearstained cheeks.

She let go of John's hand to wipe her face. John continued to gaze out over the wide, expansive view, considering how to initiate this necessary yet awkward conversation.

John shifted to see Melissa staring out into the distance. The bitterness, the hurt, the anger showed through her rigid features. Unaware of what she'd heard, it seemed she'd heard enough to cause her pain. John leaned toward her and took her hands in his. "Melissa," he said gently.

Melissa gazed at their clasped hands, afraid to look into his eyes. What was there to explain? She'd heard enough to know what the situation entailed.

John squeezed her hands, trying to gain her attention. "Melissa, look at me."

"I can't," she said in a whisper. She swallowed hard and thought about leaving his grasp and running back toward the track.

John let go of one of her hands, his fingertips lifting her chin from beneath until she had no choice but to look at him. "Let me explain what happened, please."

She was weak from crying but she held onto the anger as best she could so no more tears would escape. Her lips stiffened and her eyes narrowed as she gave him a chance to explain, against her better judgment. "All right."

"I'm not sure what you heard but I think there's been a great misunderstanding here." He watched closely for her reaction but so far it hadn't swayed. "The lady in my carriage was Vanessa Walker."

Melissa interrupted him, revealing that in fact she knew who Vanessa Walker was. "I know who Vanessa Walker is, John. I met her not moments before you two discussed your personal matters in your carriage." She pulled her

My Forbidden Mentor

remaining hand out of his and stepped away from him, walking along the cliff's edge. The mere mentioning of the dreadful woman stirred anger in her once again.

John was surprised by that piece of news for Vanessa hadn't said a word to him of meeting Melissa, but then why would she? She had more pressing matters concerning John. John sighed and strode to catch up to Melissa. He came up behind her as she faced the open land, standing on the cliff's edge. Afraid to touch her, he kept his distance but kept it close. "I hadn't realized you had already met her. She didn't mention it."

Melissa's head shook while her arms folded across her chest. Of course, why would she? Vanessa was a cruel, vile creature, she reminded herself. Melissa was about to comment when heated arms wrapped around her waist from behind, followed by the warmth of John's cheek caressing hers. Her eyes closed in reaction to his closeness. His comfort made it so much harder to deal rationally with this difficult situation.

"Melissa," he murmured. "Will you not listen to me first before you pass judgment?" He took her silence as understanding. "Yes, I have a past with Vanessa Walker and yes, we were lovers, but it's been over between us for months now." There was a pause before he added, "Before I met you." While John carefully contemplated his next words, Melissa spoke up with controlled force.

"I believe you John," she said quietly enough, but her forgiving tone didn't last. The anger of betrayal surfaced, leaving John without any option but to endure her hailstorm of words, "And I also believe I'm your present conquest." She turned in his grasp to face him, her features stirring between hurt and fury. "Shall I speed up the process of our affair and perform as your whore right here in the open?" Her fingers reached for the button on his trousers.

This was not his Melissa. "Stop it," he said. He grabbed both her wrists and held them until her movements ceased.

Tears spilled down her cheeks when she realized what a fool she'd just made of herself. She'd lost control and something wicked had taken over, causing her inappropriate actions, but the pain still lingered and the tears wouldn't stop. John let go of her of wrists and cupped her wet cheeks with his hands. Melissa, too ashamed to look him in the eye, dipped her head into his chest, her hands clasping at his coat lapels. She could feel his hands smooth down her back, gentle and caressing. Between a sob and a swallow, Melissa unknowingly muffled a confession against his chest. "Why did I have to fall in love with you?"

John went still. Her admission halted his caressing hands and caught his breath. His hands slid to her arms, pushing her out at arms length. "What did you say?" His eyes searched hers, praying he'd heard her right.

It took Melissa a moment to recall what she had said as her emotions were so tangled, but his reaction brought her words back with clarity. *What have I done? Now he knows how you feel, you fool.* With her pride hanging on by a thread, Melissa held on to what little self-esteem that remained. She let go of his lapels and backed away from him. Her embarrassment and humiliation compelled her eyes to shift away from the intensity of his stare. "I said...I'm in love with you," she admitted in a frightened whisper, gazing over the grassy cliff that they stood upon. In his state of silence, her eyes stole a glance in his direction. His gaze of astonishment left an unreadable expression. Was he happy? Was he angry? The pressure was unbearable. She whirled out of his reach and headed toward the track, tears blurring the path ahead.

"Melissa," John called out to her. "Melissa, please wait," he called again, almost tripping over his own legs until gaining lengthy strides and catching up to her. One last long step and he had her twisted to face him. "Melissa, I didn't realize how serious you were about me." John lingered on her admission. He had suspected she had strong feelings about him, but in fact the truth revealed she was in love with him. His own feelings had been guarded but relief pooled inside him now knowing that his feelings were reciprocated. This was a foreign situation to him, putting into words what he was feeling, and his desire to explain, to make her understand the truth about his conversation with Vanessa, left his mind scrambling. Any words at all seemed to choke in his throat.

His eyes searched hers for another instant, and with John's delayed response Melissa came to the conclusion that he was trying to figure out a way to gently let her down and ease her pain by telling her she was special to him, but that was as far as his feelings went.

Well, why not just admit out loud that she'd been taken, that way they wouldn't have to protect each other from more pain. Get it out in the open and confess to what an absolute idiot she had made of herself. "I'm in love with you John, and I feel like a fool, a complete fool," she added and jerked herself from his gripping hands, continuing her quickened pace toward the track.

The word fool struck John like a knife. What ideas had Vanessa given her? He spun in her direction. "Because of Vanessa's lies you feel like a fool?" John wailed at her backside. "You've got to learn to ignore her. Know that I'm with you and that is where I want to be."

His suggestion only fueled her fire for he still hadn't admitted his feelings for her, hadn't mentioned any words of love, especially after her recent confession. Vanessa's damaging words of John's philandering ways swirled around her head, blinding her to anything John had to say, and the fact that Vanessa was pregnant and he wouldn't help her revealed more of his character than she had imagined. Why hadn't she seen this before? Was she so blinded by John's charm and charisma? Melissa didn't slow down in her stride but continued on, not knowing if he followed or not. In fact, she had stopped listening to him when he had suggested that she ignore Vanessa. She had just confessed her feelings unwillingly, leaving her raw and open, and he couldn't respond. And why couldn't he respond? Probably because he doesn't feel the same way, you fool.

Well that was fine with her. From now on she would no longer be seen as the foolish country girl obsessed with the pretentious Lord Blackburn. From now on she would be her old, independent self. She'd make her career top priority and men dead last.

John wasn't used to chasing after women, but the further Melissa trailed away from him the stronger the sensation of loss surrounded him. She was a distant figure now, almost invisible in that damned green dress that blended so well into the background. Except for her golden halo of hair he could barely make her out. John sighed as he strode at a normal pace back to his carriage. How were they going to get along tonight if they couldn't even talk to each other? He couldn't imagine going through the night without touching her or at least holding her.

Approaching his carriage, John found Melissa leaning against the door with her arms crossed over her chest, staring into the distant activity involving the track. He stopped next to her, not saying a word. He didn't know what to say. What would make a difference? She had stopped listening to him once he was honest about his relationship with Vanessa. He sighed while leaning against the carriage next to her.

"Can you take me home, please?" she asked in a strained whisper.

John's stare lingered on the back of her golden head. "Of course," he answered, pushing away from the carriage to open the door for her.

Melissa moved forward while John opened the door, then stepped in and settled on the soft leather seat. It took great effort to even look at John when he informed her that he needed to locate his driver. She gave a short nod of acknowledgment and waited for the door to shut before pulling aside a sliver of the closed curtain. Her eyes watched his tall presence trail away.

Torn, completely torn over this man who had become first her mentor, then her close friend, and finally her lover. His world had become hers. How would she make it without him?

By now John had blended into the crowd and Melissa had lost sight of him, she hadn't lost sight of her feelings. She let the curtain fall back into its closed position. Her head hung low, her watery eyes intent on her twisting fingers, deep in thoughts of struggling, turbulent emotions.

For most of the ride to Melissa's home they were silent. They sat across from each other, Melissa staring out the window, absently watching the passing scenery, while John sat gazing at Melissa's profile through glistening hooded eyes.

This should be a glorious moment, John thought, but instead she had turned against him. The moment had turned disastrous because she wouldn't let him explain. Should he have lied instead of being honest about his relationship with Vanessa, for it seemed to have coincided with the corrupt words that were fed to her?

There was no telling what Vanessa had told her, and of course whatever parts of the conversation Melissa had heard from the carriage must have been the damaging parts. John let out a breath of exhaustion as his hand swept over his tied-back hair.

His sigh caught Melissa's attention and she turned to look at him. His eyes were closed and his hands were folded across his lap. She noticed the frustration in his face, his brows creasing in pressure, the skin on his forehead crinkling, and his lips, usually soft and full, were strained and thinning. She hadn't wanted to be in a dilemma with John, but even when she had slipped and announced her love for him hadn't seemed to help matters, what choice did she have? Over and over her mind tried summoning a quick resolution, only leaving her with one solution she didn't want to face. "John, I think...I think we should part for a while." Her emotions were crashing high and low as she waited on bated breath for his reaction. She was clearing her throat when his eyes opened.

John's expression spoke volumes. He looked surprised, angry, and upset all at once, and it hurt to tell him what she did but she couldn't continue their relationship without more commitment, she'd decided. Sitting across from him, she tried to conceal her shaking body while waiting for his response, hoping he'd confess his undying love for her and they could return to their fairytale romance.

John had expected her to be angry but not to the extent of parting. Anger arose in him. Instead of solving their

My Forbidden Mentor

problems now, she had chosen to ignore their importance and opted to escape. "So that's it?" He swallowed hard. "Everything between us means nothing to you? Nothing at all?"

Melissa started to shake internally at his inquisition. "That's not true, John. This is not easy for me. I need to gather my bearings regarding our relationship, that's all."

John switched his gaze to look out the window. "You're running away from us." Keeping his anger under control, he returned his gaze upon her. "A few words from that harlot and you're off running."

His contained temper reflected onto Melissa, making her reply appear storm-driven. "I'm running?" Her chuckle sounded devilish. "What about you? You're a fine example."

"And what do you mean by that?" he asked.

"If you're that oblivious there isn't a need for me to explain."

He leaned forward. "I'm not running from us, Melissa. I'm trying to figure out what has you so angry besides Vanessa's lies."

"Are you telling me that she lied about being pregnant?" she asked with an arched brow.

He settled back into his seat. "No, she probably is due to her recklessness."

"Then why would she lie about anything else?"

"Depending on what she's told you, I'm sure her insecurities made her fabrications seem real."

"Whether she lied or not John, I'm not feeling very secure myself." She turned to look out the window.

"Well if you're determined to believe the words of a jealous harlot, then I can't help your insecurities."

She turned back to him with widened eyes. "You just live life to the fullest and forget about consequences don't you?"

He didn't respond right away for she seemed to blame him for Vanessa's dilemma. "You only live once, Melissa. Yes, I want to experience many things in my lifetime, as you should want to as well, and I'm sure you're aware there are risks to be taken at some points to achieve your goals, so when there are consequences, you weigh them carefully and deal with the choices you make."

"Just like Vanessa has to deal with getting pregnant?" she replied.

"Precisely."

Crazy for feeling sorry for Vanessa, Melissa became well aware that even women like Vanessa made mistakes, proving once again that a woman's status in life didn't matter. A woman's position was always to stand below a man. A woman's mistakes compared to a man's were magnified over and over again.

But in Melissa's mind John had been cast in a different mold from other men, believing women should be given more rights, making him seem unusual and understanding, at least until this present situation involving Vanessa came about. How could he cast her aside while she carried his child? This thought only clarified Melissa's reasoning for parting with John. There could not be physical contact between them for risk of a child now that his true colors were showing. Why wouldn't John acknowledge his responsibilities? John's voice broke through her silent questions.

"Melissa, I need you to tell me what you heard. What's causing your exaggerated reactions?"

Melissa stayed quiet.

"Talk to me."

"I need time to decide about us, John."

"Why? Everything was going so well between us. What did Vanessa tell you? I'm curious because apparently you believe her over me." John's frustration level gradually climbed higher.

"That's only part of it, John. Your reaction to her situation is disturbing."

His brows arched in disbelief. "Disturbing? What do you want me to do, marry her because she's pregnant?"

"Of course I don't, but what about the child?" Melissa cried.

His features turned grim. "The child is not my concern. I will not marry a woman I do not love."

"And if a woman you loved was carrying your child, would it then be a concern?"

He looked at her in amazement. "What has gotten into you? Why are you so defensive on Vanessa's behalf?" He couldn't believe he was still fighting this battle with her. "I think you can answer that question without my help."

She gave him a matter of fact, look. "You're right, John. This bantering is getting us nowhere."

John could tell she had resorted to silence. He let a few more moments pass before stating the obvious. "So now it's silence for the remainder of our trip home after you've conveniently avoided answering my questions."

She didn't answer but continued peering out the window, biting her tongue and swallowing the lump in her throat while staring into nothing. He wasn't trying to understand her side at all.

As soon as the carriage stopped in front of her house Melissa fled the confining quarters she shared in silent scrutiny with John. John followed her, striding scant paces behind. Once inside Melissa headed for the stairway. As she began taking steps John stalled at the bottom of the stairway, insisting that they talk. "Melissa, we need to resolve this now."

Melissa paused in her footsteps, shifting halfway to look down at him. "John, please understand," she began saying in a shredded voice, only to be deserted as she started to explain. Ironically it wasn't anger that had risen this time, it was hurt. She held her tears in check as she continued making her way to the top of the stairs, shaking her head in dismay.

John realized that his driver hadn't received instructions to stay and with that in mind he strode outside, telling Jess to wait and that he may be awhile. By now the predicament of their relationship was wearing on him. They needed to get past the chaos created today. If only she'd let him explain. Extreme frustration claimed him as he stormed back inside, slamming the front door shut.

Melissa jumped when she reached the top of the stairs. The slamming of the door meant he was back and not at all happy. As she approached her bedroom door she heard John's pounding footsteps advancing at high speed. She took in a deep breath and entered her bedroom.

Within seconds he stood behind her. Feeling uneasy, she left his close proximity, stepping toward a chair before the window, gripping her fingers around the top edge of it.

John settled his weight against the wall adjacent to the door, his arms crossed over his chest and his legs crossed at the ankles. He kept his distance, well aware that her present maneuver meant just that. He stayed in that position, waiting and watching, watching the evening sun disappearing before her, taking with it the glow that it cast around her.

John reached for a candle on top of the dresser and lit it. After some moments the room had brightened again and John resumed his previous position. The tension between them remained thick, like a morning fog lying heavy at their feet.

When Melissa dared to glance at John by looking over her shoulder, what she witnessed was disillusionment. His handsome face was distorted; his brows crunched together, nostrils flaring and his mouth tight. Her eyes downcast. If she never saw in his face what she'd just seen it would be too soon for her. He was disappointed with her, but she was disappointed in him as well. Did he think she wanted it this way? Her eyes lifted when he finally spoke.

"What do you want from me, Melissa?" he asked.

He sounded calm and controlled, which with John could mean worse consequences. "Just give me time, John." Her eyes tried to stay steady with his, but after her response the gray storm that lay hidden in shimmering depths forged ahead.

"Time? Time for what? Meanwhile, what am I supposed to do while you're taking time?" His anger was laced with sarcasm.

It was as if her request hadn't mattered. Why ask if he found it unacceptable? She faced him head on. Flustered, the words just came out. "I don't care at this moment what you do."

The elevation in her voice surprised him but it also served to escalate his own state of fury. "Is that so? What did you mean, then, when you said you were in love with me? Now suddenly you don't care? Were they just words for you, Melissa or did you really mean them?"

Now she shook. Her whole day had been full of distress and John seemed determined to keep it that way. "How dare you think I would lie about something as important as that?" she paused, catching her breath. Her heart was pounding fast and hard and she willed herself to be calm. "Why would you think that at all?" she exclaimed.

His arms and ankles unfolded and he stepped toward her, his eyes glaring into hers. "Because you're not intent on clearing the air between us here and now. You want to linger on whatever falsehoods you've heard until you're exhausted thinking about them."

She took a step forward as well and lifted her chin. "I know what I heard John, and I also know that at least part of what I heard was not false."

Their eyes battled in concentration, both thinking the other absurd for their beliefs. Amazingly John conceded this time, putting his hands in the air. "All right. Take all the time you need. I've got other business that requires my attention." He located his leather pouch and started gathering his clothing.

Good, Melissa thought. I've finally managed to make him leave so I can have some peace, and since he was leaving she didn't hold back an unnecessary remark. "Yes, I'm sure your business here was beginning to bore you."

He stopped in the middle of picking a shirt up off the floor and he eyed the remaining sponges sprawled on top of her dressing table. Her view followed his and then their eyes collided. "I'll leave those," his eyes motioned to the sponges,

"So when your need arises, you will have them. I've got plenty more at home." Their eyes stayed steady long enough for John to see the sting he had caused.

He went about filling his pouch with his belongings while Melissa continued to stare at him, enduring the pain meant to sting. She had never realized how brutal he could be when pushed over the edge, and she had done just that, but still his reference was painfully evident. "Bastard," she cried, turning away from him to sit in the chair facing the window, the same chair they had sat in earlier that same morning in a naked lover's embrace to watch the first morning light appear.

He deserved that comment, he knew he did, and saying what he had hadn't relieved the anger stirring inside him. Finished packing, he stared at her for a long unspoken moment, as if taking in all her beautiful features and memorizing them. Even so the level of his anger had risen to surmountable proportions as he comprehended he wasn't getting his way this time. She didn't want to talk right now. He had to accept that and move on, which led to another verbal attack. "Well, you've been a wonderful pleasure Miss Howard, thank you for your hospitality." Shamefully he said the words, thinking that if she wanted to believe a harlot's word over his, he would treat her that way.

Her whole body stiffened. John reached for the doorknob, slamming the door behind him as he left. In shock, her face paled. In slow motion she turned to find an empty room, her focus staying on the door until she heard his last footsteps at the bottom of the stairs. The urge to run after him grew immense, but the disbelief of his hurtful words stopped her. Water filled her eyes, spilling tears down her cheeks. She stood to look out the window to catch one last glimpse of John but it had darkened considerably by that time and only a flash of black metal in the distance remained visible.

It was too late, he'd already left. Sobs started to sound from her dry throat. She turned to step toward her bed, stumbling in the process, weeping louder and cursing her bad leg. Upset that her happy life had been destroyed. No mother to talk to, no father to share with, not even her auntie to listen, and now she'd lost a companion to love. She was alone, completely alone, she thought as she climbed into her bed and curled into a ball.

Entering the gates of his grounds, John thought about his last words to Melissa. He'd regretted them as soon as he had spoken them but he was lost and confused as to how to deal with her. He had to believe she still cared. Why wouldn't she talk to him, tell him what she'd heard so he could explain the truth of it?

As Simon approached his coach John slipped out and asked him to send a stable hand over to the Howard's place to watch over until morning. Still wanting to protect her, it eased his conscious having one of his men there.

Walking into his unfamiliar chamber he dropped his pouch on the carpet, set his long hair free, stripped off his shirt, then landed on his bed from emotional exhaustion and fell asleep half-clothed.

Chapter Twenty

John was awakened by a knock at the door. Lying on his stomach, he raised his head. "Yes," was all he could manage. Recognizing his laundress, he told her to come in. While she gathered his dirty clothing he lifted from the bed and sat on the edge. Rubbing his face, he used his fingers to comb through his flowing hair, noticing his head throbbed as if he had a hangover. Knowing he hadn't had any liquor last night he figured it must be from the emotional chaos he was experiencing, which reminded him of his first priority for the day, that being confronting Miss Vanessa Walker for intervening in his personal business.

Getting up to refresh himself, his laundress asked about a particular piece of clothing. "Milord, do wish this washed as well?"

She held a lady's chemise in her hand. He must have gathered Melissa's undergarment by mistake. "Wait on that, please," he answered, cupping the cool water from the basin and splashing the chilled liquid against his sleepy face, wanting to believe that last night was just a bad dream but knowing it wasn't since he'd woken in his own bed. He continued applying the cool water over his long hair to smooth it down.

His laundress stood before the door upon exiting. "Good day then, milord."

Grabbing a white towel from the cobalt rack, he patted dry his awakening face while striding to the door. His hand reached for the doorknob and, leaning his head out the doorway, he called for Charles.

Making split-second time up the stairway Charles appeared. "Yes, my lord?"

"I need you to have Simon ready my carriage. I'm off to town. I'm not sure how long I'll be gone," he requested.

"Of course, my lord."

He arrived at Vanessa's flat by noon. She wasn't home so John waited in his carriage. While waiting, Melissa's words played over and over in his mind. I'm in love with you she'd said.

Then his eyes spotted Vanessa coming around a corner and he sat up. Approaching the stairway, John sprung up behind her, grabbing her arm. "We need to talk," he insisted.

She was surprised to see him so soon, which pleased her, but her arm was hurting from his tightened grasp. "Of course, John," she said as she fiddled with her keys, sensing something wasn't right for he was never physically abusive. After she opened the door he stormed in before her. Shutting the door behind her, she could tell this wasn't a friendly visit. Her eyes were narrowed as she watched his form spin around to face her, but she smiled anyway and offered, "Would you like something to drink?" Her blue eyes were fixed on his disturbed features.

He stood glaring before he finally answered, "No." Not wasting any time, he went right to the point. "What were you thinking yesterday?" he asked, appalled by her unnecessary actions of confronting Melissa.

Well, her little talk did get him to her flat, she thought to herself, and obviously it had caused some kind of chaos between the lord and the little country girl. Responding with half-truths she replied, "I thought we had already concluded you're not going to help me?" Her blues eyes turned deep and seductive.

His gray eyes met hers, applying just enough chill to take the seduction out of hers. "I'm not talking about the discussion between you and I. I'm talking about the discussion you had with Melissa." His tone became elevated. "The one you failed to mention to me."

So the country lass had told him about that, had she? "I wanted to meet the mysterious woman you've kept all to yourself," she replied, inching her way around the subject.

John knew there was more to it so he pushed. "And?"

Taking her time while slipping off her coat, she sat in a velvet-covered Morris chair and arranged her legs to pursue his attention elsewhere. "I was curious about such a woman who could hold your interest so long, that's all," she said, hoping that would satisfy him and lure him to her bed once again.

He didn't fall for the bait and instead faced her with his arms crossed and his brows creasing in frustration. "You wanted to cause trouble and that's the bottom line, isn't it?"

"John, I miss you and I wanted to find out about my competition," she rushed out, pausing to switch her crossed legs. "I thought she could relate to our similarities since we have the same lover."

Her statement sounded unrehearsed and pitiful, which led him to wonder again about her state of motherhood? "Vanessa, are you truly pregnant?"

The shock appearing on her features seemed real enough. "John I didn't lie to you. My menses have ceased for two months now."

He concentrated for a moment on her genuine expression. "Then why won't you tell me who the father is? You asked me to marry you for the child's sake but won't indulge me about the father?"

She sighed, having to repeat herself to be clear. "John, we already argued about this yesterday. You know the child isn't yours so why worry about it."

"Because when you asked me to marry you, you involved me. What I want to know is why?" His glare stayed heavy upon her, watching her every reaction.

A forced smiled curved on her lips. "I explained yesterday my relationship with the father was brief, he is unlike you, whom I thought to be my friend and not just a lover, someone who would help me. I see now I was mistaken."

His glare continued, stirring hotter and hotter by the minute. "And what about your conversation with Melissa? What point were you trying to prove?"

Vanessa hesitated, knowing her response would upset him even more but also understanding that he wouldn't let up about the conversation with the country lass. Nevertheless, she could handle a little explosion from him since she'd already taken care to plant a very important seed. "That I am involved in your life and she doesn't have you all to herself."

Anger compounded in John as Vanessa sat there basking in sheer delight at her successful undertaking. He'd never experienced this side of her personality and it was riveting. "I never thought you would do this to me. I thought we had an understanding. You've got plenty of male suitors to choose from, why hassle me?" he snarled. He did not want to hear her lying reply but it was necessary to set her straight.

She straightened in the chair and sounded hurt when she spoke. "I told you, I miss you, and it was the only way I could get your attention. I can't help it if you're the best

My Forbidden Mentor

lover I know and I desire you from time to time." She had revealed more than she had wanted to. He had pulled it out of her, and she realized then that this endeavor she relished in might have been a mistake.

John's silent thoughts took over. She really believes she has the power to accomplish her selfish desires. Well the truth had finally come out; the way to get my attention was by ruining my life. Rage was spitting through his clenched teeth when he told her, "Well I don't miss you, Vanessa." His eyes were turning a deep gray as they prodded into her. "I can't believe the audacity of you to choose such measures. You have ruined my life. We are no longer lovers," he stated, and the effect was like a slap in the face.

She was in shock. "You don't mean that John, say you don't mean that," she pleaded with him, not wanting to believe what she'd heard. How could this be happening? She hadn't planned on such a violent reaction from him. She stood then, pleading.

Had he finally gotten through to her he wondered as his arms came unfolded. "I do mean it, and don't go near Melissa again or you'll be dealing with me on a more radical level." His deep voice warned her as he strode to the door and left.

After the door shut, Vanessa flung a shoe at the door in anger. "Bastard!" she yelled out. Her plan had backfired. It was evident he had feelings for the country tart and now she'd lost him as her lover, but she wasn't one to give up so easily. This will be temporary, she convinced herself.

Back in his carriage John actually chuckled amongst the rage steaming through him. For the second time in twenty-four hours he'd been called a bastard. Catchy phrase, he thought to himself, almost fitting since his father didn't act like a father at all.

Disheartened, he thought of Melissa. He would give her a while to calm down and then he would go see her and talk to her again. What kind of hell had Vanessa created between them? It can't be over, he convinced himself. She's in love with me after all, bastard that I am.

By noon, the low clouds began dissipating and the bright sun peeked through, streaming brilliantly onto Melissa's, sleeping features. Awakened in annoyance by the brightness, Melissa turned her face away from the glare with her eyes closed and reached a hand over to grasp onto a warm body lying next to her, John's body, only John wasn't there. Her eyes flew open to verify as her hand patted the cold empty space beside her.

Comprehension sunk in that the nightmare had been real. Still she sat up and her gaze swung toward the spot on the hardwood floor where John kept his pouch. No pouch. As her head began to hang low she noticed she still wore her dress from the day before. Thankful for the warmth it had provided through the night, she decided to change into a comfortable nightdress, as she had no plans of leaving her bed this day.

Her horses. For the past week if she'd slept late John would get up and tend to the horses, but John wasn't here to do it this time. She dragged her lifeless body out of bed and made her way down to the barn. After the necessary chores were done, Melissa climbed back up the stairs to her room.

As she undressed, leaving her chemise on, she thought about the last time she had worn any clothing at all to bed. It had been well over a week as she'd had John to warm her up. Fighting back tears, her saddened eyes scanned her room once more. Many memories had been created in this room in one week's time, especially making love for the first time with a man, her mentor and friend whom she loved. She'd learned a lot about her own desires that she hadn't known existed, but in that discovery she'd been labeled a harlot. A knot of pain flared in her belly, a reminiscent reaction to John's last words. Her blurred focus trailed to the dressing table, spotting the memorable sponges. Oh dear, auntie is due to return today. Her mind searched for the perfect hiding place, a place where her aunt wouldn't find them.

Just then she heard horse hooves pounding the ground, the sound nearing as the horses slowed to a halt. Where to put them? her mind screamed as she sprang in that direction, gathering every sponge and string atop her dressing table. She twisted and turned with her hands full. The front door opened and closed and Miss Beckett called out to her. Think, think. Her eyes landed on the bed. Underneath, her auntie would never check underneath the bed. She tried lifting the bed with her shoulder and full hands. She heard footsteps coming up the stairs. Emptying her hands, she lifted a corner of mattress and shoved sponges and strings underneath. The mattress fell and Melissa jumped into bed, pretending to be asleep.

A knock came at the door before the door opened. "Melissa, love, are you awake?" Miss Beckett stopped in her tracks when she saw Melissa still in bed sound asleep. She decided to unpack and try again later. Melissa apparently needed the rest.

As the door shut Melissa hugged herself tight, resolving herself to the fact that indeed her past may be just that, that maybe her future involved a new beginning. Did that beginning mean without John, without the man she'd fallen in love with?

Melissa awakened the next morning to find an unopened message on her nightstand. She sat up and opened it. The message was from her cousins in Leicester. The letter explained their situation. Her cousin George needed to travel to conjure up more business and his wife had just borne a new baby. It was a request for Melissa to help Cecilia with their three children until he returned. George could possibly be away for an extended time of three weeks. She had helped out once before and got along famously with Cecilia.

Although Melissa was intrigued by the invitation, disappointment seized her. Deep down it was John she had wanted to hear from, John and a confession of his undying love for her and that he couldn't stand being away from her any longer, but that was a fantasy and the reality was that her cousins needed her now.

Miss Beckett sent her off with best wishes. The night before Melissa had explained about the message from her cousins, agreeing she needed the diversion. Not a word had been mentioned about Lord Blackburn, which led Miss Beckett to believe Melissa's sadness had something to do with her mentor.

Miss Beckett took it upon herself to contact Lord Blackburn. In fact, right after leaving Melissa, she searched for him in town without any luck. Her last resort was his manor.

Miss Beckett stood before the enormous double door entry of John's manor. Her eyes trailed over the beauty of its design while knocking on it. To live in such luxury would be heaven she thought as her gaze extended to the windows above, but to clean this many windows, she counted as

My Forbidden Mentor

many as twelve just on the front side of the manor, now that would be tortuous.

"Yes." A deep, smooth voice startled her, gaining her attention.

Her breath paused for a moment when her eyes met with a tall figure of a man with dark hair accompanied by possessive gray streaks and eyes that flashed serene confidence in their light brown depths. Oh dear, what's come over me? she thought. The instant attraction to the man standing before her came as unexpected. Never had she been so lost for words.

Miss Beckett got a hold of herself. "Hello, I wish to speak with Lord Blackburn."

"And whom may I say is calling?" The man answered most professionally.

Oh dear, she'd forgotten her name, literally. In fact, when she finally remembered it, she astonished herself by using her first name. "Darion," she said in a breathy tone. She hadn't used her first name in so long she was surprised that she remembered it. "I mean, Miss Beckett."

Charles studied her with amusement. She'd managed to produce a hint of a smile from him. Clearly she was shaken for some reason or another. Upon further examination Darion, or rather Miss Beckett, proved to be quite attractive.

On his way out to the stables, John appeared behind Charles, breaking the moment between the two. "Who is it Charles?" John inquired, his eyes shifting between the speechless pair. His brows piqued with interest. Since Charles had stalled in his manners, John took over. "Miss Beckett, welcome." John took her hand in his and led her inside. He turned to a mute Charles. "Charles, perhaps you could acquire some tea for us?"

Laura Mills

Charles blinked back into position. "Yes my lord," he answered and left to prepare their tea.

John led Miss Beckett into the sitting room, where they sat across from each other. As John settled into a comfortable position he commented, "Charles was quite taken with you Miss Beckett. I've never seen him act that way before."

Miss Beckett flushed, almost too embarrassed to look John in the face, but she was a proud woman and didn't feel shame over her attraction to his service man. "Well, Lord Blackburn, perhaps I should come back at another time. Apparently you were on your way out."

"Only to the stables. It can wait. What brings you here?" John asked.

Miss Beckett smiled. "Very well. It's regarding Miss Melissa, Lord Blackburn."

John's features grew alarmed. "Melissa? Is she all right?"

Miss Beckett noticed his immediate concern. "Physically yes, but it's her mental state that has me worried."

John stayed silent as Miss Beckett's presence became clear.

"By your reaction you must know something I don't. I had a hunch something was wrong between you two." Miss Beckett's curiosity had peaked.

John's eyes returned to focus on her. "Yes, well, we've had some misunderstandings of late."

"Regarding training?" Miss Beckett asked, searching.

"No. Actually training is going fine. Was going fine." John retracted.

"I don't understand?" Miss Beckett implored.

My Forbidden Mentor

John paused in his thoughts while Charles entered the sitting room with a cup of tea for Miss Beckett. Handing her the cup, Charles mouth curved upward, displaying quite a handsome smile.

John watched him with encouraging interest. He'd never seen Charles so enamored before, and with Miss Beckett responding like she was a young lass in her first courtship, it was quite amusing. John smiled to himself, enjoying the pleasant distraction. It served to give him time to decide how much truth to reveal to Miss Beckett, as he knew that she had Melissa's best interests at heart.

Miss Beckett smiled toward Charles, thanking him, and then heat surfaced to her cheeks. Oh my, she thought, sipping on her tea, not caring at the moment how hot it was. She shook her head as if it would shake away the sensations. Her gaze followed Charles as he left.

Embarrassed or not, Miss Beckett continued her inquiry. "Lord Blackburn, as you've probably guessed I'm a very straightforward person. I can tell we're alike that way. Please be honest with me about what is going on, no matter what it entails."

John had decided not to give details about the intimacy he and Melissa had shared, but how would he explain everything else without that knowledge? "I took Melissa to the track on Saturday. While there she was confronted by an old acquaintance of mine. I had been in search of Lord Ainsworth to arrange a meeting with him when apparently this old acquaintance of mine assumed Melissa to be my paramour and in jealousy must have said some pretty vicious words to her."

John carefully monitored Miss Beckett's reaction, going on instinct as to how much detail to give. She remained neutral, listening with eager involvement. "I was unaware this had taken place until later that day. Melissa hadn't said a word until I pushed her to tell me what was wrong as I could tell by her mood something had changed. All she told me was that a woman I knew said some things about me, things that obviously made Melissa have second thoughts about me because she wouldn't give me a chance to explain myself."

Before John went on Miss Beckett wanted him to be aware of her ideas regarding the matter. "Lord Blackburn, without causing Melissa any humiliation, I must say in my own opinion that the lass is in love with you. Whether you want to hear that or not, I believe it's true, and that could account for her drastic reaction."

He couldn't hide his feelings nor could he pretend to be indifferent toward Melissa, no matter if he was upset with her or not. "You know Melissa very well Miss Beckett, for that same day at the track she revealed that she was in love with me."

"And how did you respond?"

"I didn't respond right away and I think that scared her, but I hadn't expected such a confession."

"Oh dear. Well that explains her emotional turmoil."

"I had planned on coming to see her and talking to her. When we last spoke it wasn't on the best of terms, so I've waited to give her time." Time, John thought to himself, that blasted word haunted him.

Miss Beckett studied him a moment. "Without seeming bold, Lord Blackburn, what are your feelings for Melissa? I realize you are her mentor and I know that you two have become close, but I also realize you may have a previous agenda, one planned before meeting Melissa."

How had he guessed this was coming? John cleared his throat. "By previous agenda do you mean a planned marriage, Miss Beckett?"

"Well one would only assume, because of your position. I just hope the situation with Melissa has not been taken advantage of."

"I see. I know that normally someone in my position usually has their life planned out for them, but it's not that way with me, Miss Beckett. I live my own life the way I want to. I make a substantial living besides what my father has granted me. I live off my own earnings and therefore I make my own decisions." He paused for a breath and a chance to retrieve some brandy. Normally he didn't drink so early in the day but Miss Beckett's interrogation required it.

"Forgive me Lord Blackburn. My way of thinking is commonplace, you understand." Her eyes followed him to the bar.

John's eyes lifted to look in her direction while pouring a small amount of cognac into a glass. "I understand Miss Beckett. I just wanted to clarify my position and also tell you that at present I haven't any plans for marriage."

"Do you have any plans for Melissa except being her mentor?" she asked, observing John while he sat across from her once again.

John took a generous swallow of liquid before answering. Was she implying what he thought she was? "Miss Beckett I'll give you the straight answer you want. I would love to be more than a mentor to Melissa but she won't have me."

"Well Lord Blackburn, considering recent events I don't blame her." She paused, in conflict about asking him a very critical question, one that involved a very important person in her life, as she had to know. "Do you love her?"

John stood, chugging the remaining liquid down in one gulp. He then stepped over to a draped window, slipping his hand in between so he could peer out and see his horses. A slice of guilt pierced him thinking about how close he and Melissa had already been, unbeknownst to her aunt. Miss Beckett stayed quiet, waiting with patience for his response. John turned back toward her and she shifted to find him over her shoulder. "I've never been in love before Miss Beckett. I don't know what it feels like. All I know is that what I feel for Melissa is more than I've ever felt for any woman I've known. If that kind of exclusive feeling is called love, then I would have to say yes."

Inside Miss Beckett was shouting with joy but on the outside her expression couldn't have been more surprised. Here she had two people who had recently become aware that they loved each other and at the moment they could not have been further apart, not just emotionally but physically and graphically as well. "Lord Blackburn, you just admitted to being in love with Melissa but said you're not ready to marry? Wouldn't you want to marry the woman you love?"

"To be honest Miss Beckett, I hadn't thought that far ahead, and at present Melissa and I are not speaking."

"Because of the old acquaintance?" she sighed.

"Frankly, yes," John confirmed.

Miss Beckett stood and stepped over to John. "Lord Blackburn, I really didn't come here to cause turmoil, there's enough of that going on without my help, but I'd like to offer some advice regarding my darling lass. She's stubborn, willful and you have to keep ahead of her. She's smart and oh so very independent, just like her mother." Miss Beckett let out a sigh of frustration. "But I believe if you make her listen to reason, well she won't dismiss you that easily if she has feelings for you. Believe that."

My Forbidden Mentor

"She requested the need for time, Miss Beckett. I have to respect that, even if I don't agree with it." His tone sounded regretful.

Miss Beckett made her way back to the couch in extended concentration and lifted the cup of tea to her lips before replying. "Well I can tell you she'll be taking at least three weeks to think about it," she offered before sipping more tea. Her remark had John sitting once again.

"Why three weeks?" he asked, bewildered.

Miss Beckett set her cup down. "She's left, Lord Blackburn. Left Richmond."

"For where?" he inquired, his brows creasing.

"Unfortunately I have to respect Melissa's wishes for privacy. You understand," she voiced with regret.

He covered up his disappointment. "Yes, of course. I've got a meet coming up anyhow. I will be quite busy during that time."

"Speaking of your schedule, Lord Blackburn, I will take my leave now. I realize you're a busy man." She lifted from the couch just as Charles peeked in to offer more refreshments.

"More tea, Miss Beckett?"

She gave him a wide smile. "No, no thank you, sir."

Charles flashed a quick smile and bowed before making his exit.

Her cheeks flushed again when she shifted toward John. "Thank you for your time, Lord Blackburn. Regardless of what happens I hope you and I can remain friends?"

"Yes, I would like that," he told her as he walked her to the front door.

As they stood in the doorway Miss Beckett made one last suggestion. "Don't give up on her. I can't blame you for your frustration as I know how she can be, but if she feels time is necessary, then that's for the best." She smiled for John. "You'll see. In three weeks, when everything is clear, you two will be on good terms again."

John reached over and placed a kiss upon her pale cheek. "Take care, Miss Beckett. If you require anything, anything at all, just call on me."

Miss Beckett turned tender, sweeping her fingertips across John's cheek. "How did Melissa get so lucky?" and with that she left.

John watched her leave, realizing what a lucky person Melissa was to have a grand lady like Miss Beckett in her life to guide her, also realizing how deep a conversation he'd just had with Miss Beckett and what he'd not only revealed to her but to himself as well. He was in love, in love with the most obstinate, foolhardy, loveliest creature he'd ever known. Listen to reason, huh? He shut the door behind him as he trailed off toward the stables. Three weeks. That should give him plenty of time to prepare for the next meet.

Chapter Twenty-One

Sheffield

Melissa's ride to her cousin George and Cecilia's seemed long. The more she tried thinking of what a great time she was going to have, the more John bombarded her thoughts. Although she hated to admit it, she missed him something fierce. She reminisced about the laughter they'd shared, his melting smile and his glittering eyes that shined and touched her body with their intensity. Closing her eyes as the memories continued, his soft mouth came to mind. Warm and sensual, it always applied heat wherever it touched.

After turning a corner on the path of the dirt road a small white house appeared in the near distance. Melissa, distracted by her reminiscing thoughts, was startled by the voice of a small boy, making her realize that the carriage had actually stopped.

"Lissa, Lissa," Samuel cried. She was his favorite cousin and he always enjoyed their play times together. He was almost five and still preferred to call her Lissa, an easier alternative than her full name. She didn't mind because it was his unique nickname for her.

As she stepped out of the carriage Samuel jumped up and down before her, happy as he could be. Melissa bent down to pick him up. "Come here you big boy." Balancing him on her hip, she turned to retrieve her luggage, but Cecilia came rushing up behind her, reaching to take the luggage. "Let me get that, love."

Melissa put Samuel down and took the luggage from Cecilia. "Thank you Cecilia, but you're the one who should be taking it easy. Didn't you just have a baby not three weeks ago?" she commented as they walked along the cobblestone path to the quaint little house.

"Well if you didn't have my children barraging you the whole time," Cecilia stated while opening the door for her.

Melissa set her bags down and Kirsten, Cecilia's middle child, instantly had her arms wrapped around Melissa's leg. "I really don't mind Cecilia. I love children," she said with a sincere smile, looking down upon a little blond head.

Cecilia went on to get her newborn, excited for Melissa to see her. "And they love you," she said while taking the baby out of a wooden crib. "You're going to make a great mother when you have children Melissa. I can tell," she told her while handing her the baby to hold.

Melissa melted when seeing the newborn, her tiny fingers grasping at Melissa's finger. "Perhaps one day in the future," she commented while having the briefest thought she was holding a baby that she and John had conceived. "But for now I'll enjoy being a favorite cousin," she added, making gestures toward the infant.

"This is Catherine," Cecilia announced, watching Melissa and the children together. She noticed that Melissa wasn't her usual bouncy self and made a mental note to inquire about it later when they had more privacy.

George came home just in time for supper and afterward they all visited. When mentioning Melissa's father they all reminisced about their joyous memories of him. Later that evening, while George and Cecilia put the children to bed together, Melissa sat next to the raging fire pondering more about her father, that she had missed him more than she had realized.

She stared into the dancing flames, asking her father for help on resolving her feelings for John and wondering if John could be trusted. When she replayed John's last words to her only pain, deep, cutting pain, resulted from the memory. This constant turmoil was eating at her insides and it began showing more prominently outward. I need to move on, concentrate on my own dreams, Melissa kept telling herself, when Cecilia appeared.

Cecilia stepped over to the fireplace and sat next to Melissa, interrupting her deliberation. "May I ask of your thoughts?"

Melissa turned in Cecilia's direction. "Nothing really. Nothing to worry about," she said, giving her a faint smile in return.

Cecilia knew better and offered support. "Melissa you're not yourself, I can tell. I'm a great listener," she told her, disliking the unhappiness she saw in her eyes.

Melissa was desperate to talk to someone. Perhaps it would be a relief to let out some of the anguish and internal pressure that had built. Cecilia was kind enough and she trusted her. "I met a man a couple of months ago. An extraordinary man," she was saying while recalling their initial meeting, which seemed so long ago now, and then the words started pouring out without warning. "I'm in love with him Cecilia, and I don't know what to do about it." Her hazel stare turned watery.

Cecilia could see real pain in those eyes, real conflict, and her heart went out to her. "Oh Melissa, does he know how you feel?" she asked, taking her hand in her own to comfort her.

Melissa held the tears back when she answered, "Yes." She glanced back into the crackling hot flames, mesmerized.

Cecilia was curious about this man who had such a hold on Melissa's heart. "Does he love you?" she inquired, asking the one question that caused the most pain.

Melissa answered in a whisper. "I don't think so. I don't know," she said, turning back to Cecilia.

Cecilia remembered the first time she was in love, which was with George, and revealed her own observations. "Melissa how do you know for sure that he doesn't? Men seem to have a hard time with words, I think. They feel more comfortable showing you how they feel. George didn't tell me he loved me right away. Of course I felt better when he did, but men are different at expressing themselves, even with children. They show affection in different ways but it still makes them lovable." Hoping to ease her wondering, Cecilia spoke from her own experience.

Cecilia was making sense but there was more involved between her and John. "Well that helps to understand more but I have an additional problem."

"What's that?"

"A past lover of John's confronted me and said some disturbing things about him, but she left me wondering if they were true. To make matters worse, I found out this same lover is carrying John's child." Her eyes were glassy when they focused on Cecilia's reaction. "As if that weren't bad enough, he won't acknowledge the child. He won't marry her because he doesn't love her, but my concern is for the child."

"Did he tell you this?" Cecilia asked.

"That he wouldn't marry her, yes," Melissa answered.

"Because he doesn't love her?"

"Yes."

"Did he verify the child was his?" Cecilia was making her own determinations.

"Not in so many words, but she asked him to marry her for the child's sake."

"She sounds bold. How does he treat you?"

"He always treats me well." Until he called me a harlot and left me, Melissa thought to herself, and the sobs began. "How could I let myself fall in love with him Cecilia?"

Cecilia reached over with a supportive embrace. "How could you not? He's special to you for a reason, Melissa, I truly believe that." Cecilia stroked the golden head that lay on her shoulder. "Melissa, from my own experiences I've come to rely on someone's actions more than their words. Observe his actions, the words will come later. It's your decision, love, but if he cares as much for you, don't give up yet." She'd never seen Melissa this dependent for affection, but after losing both parents the energy it must take to remain strong had probably caught up to her. Cecilia imagined that being in love and apart only intensified her feelings. "This will work out, I promise you."

For the next hour Melissa and Cecilia stayed huddled together before the dying fire, content to reminisce about their past visits and the fun they'd had. Cecilia, two years older than Melissa, seemed more like a sister than a cousin by marriage. Over the course of the next two weeks the closeness they had developed made them feel more like sisters than ever before.

During her stay Melissa thought a lot about what Cecilia had said that first night. She had become an incredible comfort. Getting her unbiased opinion had helped to clear Melissa's head and finally make some rational decisions. Cecilia and the children were the perfect distraction and they kept her busy the whole time of her visit. Actually feeling relaxed for once since parting from John, she almost hated leaving but knew it was inevitable and knew she would eventually be faced with John sometime in the near future. Until then she would pamper herself, maybe stop and tour desirable towns on the way home.

Cousin George arrived a week early. Luck was upon him for he'd found substantial work to hold his family throughout the wintertime. In the midst of celebrating George's good luck Melissa mentioned seeing some sights on the way back home, deciding upon the upcoming races being held in Sheffield. Cecilia suggested she leave early and take her time since Cecilia knew Melissa's situation and knew she could benefit from some time spent alone.

Melissa finally agreed but decided to stay a couple more days so George and Cecilia could have some time alone. Surprisingly over those last couple of days, Melissa woke up feeling under the weather, accompanied with light nausea. Although she hadn't gotten sick Cecilia made her rest the last day, becoming suspicious of her symptoms, and more questions surfaced in regards to the young man Melissa loved.

Sitting in a chair next to the bed where Melissa lay resting, Cecilia asked while cooling her forehead with a damp cloth, "Are you feeling better?"

It was mid afternoon and Melissa was feeling substantially better than she had earlier that morning. The sickness had subsided but she remained awfully tired. "Yes, thank you," she said in response to her concerned question.

Cecilia debated on how to approach her next inquiry as it involved a very personal matter, but she proceeded out of

My Forbidden Mentor

concern for her cousin. "Forgive me for being so forward, but have you and this young man of yours been intimate?"

Melissa's surprise was evident, and before she answered Cecilia was eager to explain, remedying the awkwardness. "I only ask because your symptoms are very much like being pregnant."

With that said Melissa's face paled as she knew of anyone Cecilia would know, but still there was the high possibility she wasn't as they had taken precautions. "Yes we have been intimate, but we used protection, Cecilia. Please mention this to no one." In telling her, Melissa's thoughts raced back to their first encounter, and even the second and third, which were all without protection. It couldn't be true. It was only those few isolated times. A dreadful thought entered her mind: if it were true now was not the right time, not when the father was no longer around or would even care. If she was pregnant and John found out he would be out of her life for good and she would have to raise their child alone. But who was to say she was even with child. She probably had a touch of some flu, or at least that was what she wanted to believe. The thought of never seeing John again was devastating.

Cecilia defined what the beginning signs were but Melissa was so adamant it couldn't be that Cecilia let it drop. By the next day Melissa was feeling like herself again. Feeling better helped to ease her mind, answering those dreadful questions with confidence. There were no more questions, only long goodbyes as Melissa prepared to leave.

Richmond

The haze of smoke filling the air of Sally's place smelled of cigars and heavy liquor. The cloud of fumes carefully hid

Rose from general view as she stood behind the wooden staircase that towered toward the back of the pub. She'd been minding her own business when she had overheard a conversation between Sally, the owner and Vanessa, the troublemaker.

Aware of what had taken place between Vanessa and John, Rose carefully listened with precise curiosity.

"What is it, honey?" Sally asked.

"I need a small favor," Vanessa had responded. "Have you come across any male virgins of late?"

"Well, they're so rare, I'd definitely remember if I had. For whom?" Sally had asked.

"For me, actually. I need a challenge. Do you know of one?" Vanessa sounded desperate.

There was a motionless pause before Sally responded. Rose couldn't believe the conversation they were having and how odd it seemed that Vanessa would make such a request. Rose thought it was reason enough to be suspicious.

"This doesn't seem like you, Vanessa," Sally commented, then paused, before saying, "Give me a moment to inquire. I'll be right back."

Rose eased back into the darkness of the stairway when Sally breezed by her. Several minutes passed before Sally returned.

"Darling, it's your lucky night. The young gentleman I was thinking of is here tonight. He's at the card table," Sally told Vanessa and then added, "He's quite handsome for a young lad."

"Thank you Sally. You've done me a grand favor," Vanessa replied and came into Rose's view.

My Forbidden Mentor

"You're welcome, Vanessa." Sally reached Vanessa's side, pointing out the lad. "Over there."

"What's his name?" Vanessa inquired.

"Jack. Jack McGuire," Sally revealed. "Be gentle, darling."

"Gentle, of course." Vanessa's response seemed preoccupied.

As both ladies drifted apart Rose captured a bird's eye view, maneuvering behind the staircase, her gaze intent on Vanessa's direction. She witnessed Vanessa approaching a card table with one vacant seat. Vanessa smiled with glory when taking that seat, which happened to be across from the lad Sally had pointed out.

Why a virgin, Vanessa? What could you possibly want with a virgin? Rose deliberated to herself, fishing for clues. A strange sensation came over her that made her believe Vanessa was planning some kind of mischief. With what she had learned from Robert about John and his situation, it gave her all the more reason to believe it.

Should she keep her eye on Vanessa and the lad? She couldn't possibly watch them day and night. With her shift being over, she decided to hunt down Robert and get his opinion about the whole idea. She whirled down the dimly lit hall to her room and readied herself to go.

John had spent two weeks preparing Chief and his stable hands for the trip to Sheffield. With a couple of days for traveling and a couple more days at the track, his trip to Sheffield was calculated for up to a week, which was perfect timing to be back home and hopefully graced with Melissa's presence, but he would think about that in a week. Right now he needed to contact Robert as he planned to leave in the morning.

John stepped into Sally's place hoping to find Robert when instead he found his father. His body stiffened upon seeing his drunk and disorderly father seated at the bar carousing with a young lady. He tried passing by unnoticed but there was no escaping him. Even in his drunken state he recognized his only son.

"John," his father called out, turning on the stool and almost falling off, but his lady friend helped steady him. John stopped and in reluctance turned toward him. It was better to acknowledge him than pretend otherwise as he could get loud and extremely obnoxious when ignored. "Come here and visit your old father, son. I haven't seen you in a while."

John could smell his liquored breath from where he stood. John didn't even break a smile for him and he planned to make this visit as short as possible. "How are you father?" His stomach turned as the young lady twirled his father's peppered hair between her fingers. He still carried on as he always had, more so since the death of his mother, except the women were getting younger. This one in particular didn't look a day over twenty-one, the same age as Melissa, he thought.

John experienced a rise of nausea as the young lady winked his way, making her flirtations brazen. It was quite clear the lady was signaling an evening with both the father and the son. John steadied his eyes on his father and kept them there.

"I'm perfectly fine, son. I heard you've got yourself a young lass you're keeping all to yourself?"

Keeping his patience under control, he answered calmly, "I am well, father, and frankly my personal life is none of your business." Even though John sounded cool toward his

My Forbidden Mentor

father, he had every right to be. Anyone who didn't know their situation would have thought John cruel with his words but they were acceptable considering their wretched past.

Swallowing a single shot of cognac in one gulp, his father slammed the glass down on the bar and replied, "That's my boy, always showing profound love for his father," he said as his voice was rising in volume the longer he spoke. John saw it coming and so did Sally.

"Don't start," John told him under vast restraint.

Albert started to lunge forward at John but stumbled in the process, and as the dutiful son, John caught him before he reached the wooden floor.

Sally stood behind John, asking him, "John, would you mind depositing him outside? I can't afford another of his disturbances."

He returned a faint smile as he lifted his father up and over his broad shoulder. "Of course," he answered. Humiliated once again, he found his father's carriage and dumped him inside on the cushioned seat and was about to turn away when he heard his father mumbling a slurred reference.

"So son, are you gonna share this lass like you did the other one?" Albert stretched his limbs to sit in a normal position, glaring at John with dire intent.

Confusion ran through John's agitated mind. He hadn't a clue what his father was talking about. He never recalled sharing anyone with him. "What are you talking about?" John asked as he stepped closer to his father.

Albert chuckled. "It appears I finally have my son's attention." Albert paused to hiccup. "She came willingly to me John, I didn't force her."

John's brows creased with added tension. "Who came to you?"

Albert was enjoying the bewildered look on his son's face. Perhaps for once he held John's attention long enough to continue a normal conversation. "Damned if I can remember her name, but you can't mistake that platinum blonde hair of hers."

John could feel the color drain from his face. Although he hadn't any deep-rooted feelings for Vanessa, the thought of her with his father bothered him. "Vanessa?" he asked to verify.

"That's her name. How could I forget the name belonging to that body?" Albert sighed.

By now John was devastated. As he glared at his father in his drunken state, he wondered if he spoke the truth or if he was testing his resistance. "So you're saying that you and Vanessa slept together?"

Albert's smile broadened. "We did more than sleep together, son. She's quite a fine piece,"

John covered his ears with his hands. "All right, all right, I don't want to hear anymore. I don't need a detailed description."

His father chuckled some more, catching the attention of his lady friend, and John stepped aside to let her by.

John re-entered the saloon, stumbling into Sally. "Oh, pardon me Sally." John's mind was so preoccupied that he hadn't paid attention to where he was going.

"It's quite all right, John. You can run into me anytime," Sally said, sending a teasing smile that John knew was only to taunt.

John smiled back but his eyes searched the perimeters of the bar, finding no sight of Robert.

"Are you looking for your handsome partner?" Sally asked.

"Yes," John answered.

"Well Rose left to find him, so I imagine he's not here."

"How long ago?"

"I'd say a couple of hours ago."

"Thank you, Sally."

"Anytime, handsome." Sally watched John as he strode toward the door, admiring him and all of his masculine features, and thought someday he'll make a lucky young lady very happy.

John figured Robert would be back home by now after Rose had found him and they would want their privacy, so he decided to catch him in the morning on his way out. At present, he had another mission to carry out before his departure.

John arrived at Vanessa's doorstep twenty minutes after leaving Sally's place and he was about to knock when he heard laughter. Apparently Vanessa had company tonight. Well, she would have to put the brakes on because he had more important matters to discuss with her.

His knuckles rapped on the wooden door with force. A long moment passed before the door cracked open. Vanessa's smile faded when staring into John's features.

"Entertaining?" John asked, not holding back one ounce of sarcasm.

lover I know and I desire you from time to time." She had revealed more than she had wanted to. He had pulled it out of her, and she realized then that this endeavor she relished in might have been a mistake.

John's silent thoughts took over. She really believes she has the power to accomplish her selfish desires. Well the truth had finally come out; the way to get my attention was by ruining my life. Rage was spitting through his clenched teeth when he told her, "Well I don't miss you, Vanessa." His eyes were turning a deep gray as they prodded into her. "I can't believe the audacity of you to choose such measures. You have ruined my life. We are no longer lovers," he stated, and the effect was like a slap in the face.

She was in shock. "You don't mean that John, say you don't mean that," she pleaded with him, not wanting to believe what she'd heard. How could this be happening? She hadn't planned on such a violent reaction from him. She stood then, pleading.

Had he finally gotten through to her he wondered as his arms came unfolded. "I do mean it, and don't go near Melissa again or you'll be dealing with me on a more radical level." His deep voice warned her as he strode to the door and left.

After the door shut, Vanessa flung a shoe at the door in anger. "Bastard!" she yelled out. Her plan had backfired. It was evident he had feelings for the country tart and now she'd lost him as her lover, but she wasn't one to give up so easily. This will be temporary, she convinced herself.

Back in his carriage John actually chuckled amongst the rage steaming through him. For the second time in twenty-four hours he'd been called a bastard. Catchy phrase, he thought to himself, almost fitting since his father didn't act like a father at all.

me to marry you for the child's sake but won't indulge me about the father?"

She sighed, having to repeat herself to be clear. "John, we already argued about this yesterday. You know the child isn't yours so why worry about it."

"Because when you asked me to marry you, you involved me. What I want to know is why?" His glare stayed heavy upon her, watching her every reaction.

A forced smiled curved on her lips. "I explained yesterday my relationship with the father was brief, he is unlike you, whom I thought to be my friend and not just a lover, someone who would help me. I see now I was mistaken."

His glare continued, stirring hotter and hotter by the minute. "And what about your conversation with Melissa? What point were you trying to prove?"

Vanessa hesitated, knowing her response would upset him even more but also understanding that he wouldn't let up about the conversation with the country lass. Nevertheless, she could handle a little explosion from him since she'd already taken care to plant a very important seed. "That I am involved in your life and she doesn't have you all to herself."

Anger compounded in John as Vanessa sat there basking in sheer delight at her successful undertaking. He'd never experienced this side of her personality and it was riveting. "I never thought you would do this to me. I thought we had an understanding. You've got plenty of male suitors to choose from, why hassle me?" he snarled. He did not want to hear her lying reply but it was necessary to set her straight.

She straightened in the chair and sounded hurt when she spoke. "I told you, I miss you, and it was the only way I could get your attention. I can't help it if you're the best

The door opened a little wider. "Why? Jealous?" Vanessa responded.

John chuckled. "Hardly."

His remark caused a frown to appear on her vain expression. "Why are you here then? Are you in need of some comforting?"

"No. I'm in need of some answers, Vanessa." John didn't dally.

"Answers? Regarding what?" She looked confused.

"You and my father, to be specific," John shot out.

At once Vanessa peeked over her shoulder at the company awaiting her, her company who was highly excited in his virginal state. "Who is it, love?" John heard from the background.

"Someone I know," she called back. "I'll be right back," Vanessa assured him, closing her red silk robe tighter around herself. She slipped out of the door and shut it behind her. "What...what are you referring to, John?"

"So it's true?" John said with a smirk, catching her at her game. He had her interest peaked enough to want privacy for their conversation.

"I haven't any idea what you're talking about." Her face stayed solemn.

"Don't you? Playing ignorant with me Vanessa is not going to work. I can tell by your reaction it's true."

"What is true, John?" Vanessa spoke in frustration as she folded her arms across her chest.

"You, sleeping with my father." John leaned forward to emphasize his point.

My Forbidden Mentor

"Did he tell you this himself?" There lay shakiness in her voice.

John knew then that he had her trapped. "Does it matter? Are you that desperate?"

"You're talking about your father here."

"Yes, I am. You act as if you didn't already know about my father's character. What possessed you to bed him, Vanessa? If you're looking for security you won't find it with him. He has different women weekly."

Her silence of hesitation led to an interesting testimony. "I didn't sleep with him for that reason. You know me I like to have a good time. Your father was available at the time."

"And what time was that?" John inquired.

"None of your business, John." Vanessa answered with a tip of her chin.

"How many times have you slept together?" John wanted accurate information.

Vanessa gasped at his personal inquiry. "That is definitely none of your business. I don't ask you how many times you and that country tart fornicated."

His teeth ground together in reaction to her unnecessary remark. "Leave Melissa out of this. This is different, it involves my father."

"He's a man and I'm a woman, it's natural to be attracted to each other. Besides, you should thank me for the discovery of a very promising future for yourself. Your father is a very virile man for his age, John. His stamina may pass onto you."

John shook his head in disbelief. "I don't want to hear about that. I want to know if you're still having relations with him?"

Vanessa was feeling back in control now that John seemed stumped. "Well it was fun while it lasted, but no, I am not. As you predicted he has moved on, but then so have I."

John took a deep calming breath before continuing. "So, you balled my father because he has stamina? Did you catch wind of his vigor from one of his whores?"

"Why do you care who I've balled, John? You've never shown this much concern before."

He leaned into her again. "Because, I don't believe you were with my father just for fun, no matter how virile he is. No, you've got another agenda in mind, Vanessa, and I mean to find out what it is. You can't fool me with this facade you're putting on."

She hadn't convinced him. He was too smart for his own good. She backed away from him. "Believe what you want," she said while turning to approach the door.

John grabbed her arm with force, stalling her movements. "I want the truth and I want it now," he said, his voice low and deep.

"John, you're hurting me," she cried, trying to break free of his grasp.

"Perhaps you need a little pain in your life, Vanessa. You seem to dish it out so well. The truth." His eyes were fierce, sparkling like lightening, his voice like thunder.

"Why have you turned so cruel toward me?" Vanessa cried out of desperation.

"You have to ask? Stop avoiding the issue and give me answers," he demanded. He couldn't trust her after her devious actions a couple of weeks ago.

My Forbidden Mentor

Vanessa turned vicious, losing control. "You're reacting so violently because of that tart. If it weren't for her you'd still be my lover and it would be you in my apartment right now, lying naked in my bed, instead of him."

"Stop calling her that. You and I were finished well before Melissa entered the picture," he clarified.

"Hah, you not only protect her, you defend her no matter how wrong she is. She stole you from me!"

"What?" John asked, completely puzzled.

"Yes, she's stolen you, but there's a part of you she doesn't have." Out of an urgent need to remain in control, Vanessa exposed some truth she would soon have to rectify.

Was she truly insane? "What on earth are you talking about?"

Vanessa deliberately placed a hand on her stomach, rubbing in an answering motion with a wicked smile.

John glanced toward Vanessa's stomach and let go of her arm. "That child is not mine. Whether you verify or not, I know for a fact it isn't mine, Vanessa."

"Yes, John, you're right about that. Because of you and your stronghold on contraceptive measures, unfortunately, it is not yours."

"Will you stop speaking in riddles?"

The wicked grin came back. "Well, John, if I couldn't have your baby, I wanted to have the closest possible to it." She paused as if giving him a chance to guess. "I'd say your father is pretty close, wouldn't you?"

The color faded from John's face once again and his jaw dropped. "You must be jesting? At least I pray you are." Now he knew for sure she was insane.

"No, John. I'm very serious." She wasn't smiling anymore.

"Good God, Vanessa. He can't be a father again, he's old enough to be a grandfather," John exclaimed in horror.

"Obviously his seed doesn't know any better. I'm carrying your father's child, John. In a half years' time you will have a half brother or sister."

John stood there, flabbergasted. "What has happened to you?"

"You happened to me, John. I want to be a constant in your life," Vanessa told him, her tone softening.

John had a need for air. "So you purposely bedded my father to get with child?"

"Yes." Her reply was as direct as the glare of her icy blue eyes.

"And he doesn't know anything about this, does he? No, he wouldn't stand for it if he did, especially if he knew the reason why you were doing it."

"He will find out soon enough." Vanessa pretended to be preoccupied, like she was bored all of a sudden. "Very soon I will be increasing and it will be noticeable. I've waited to ensure he will believe me. The timing will be accurate."

"What's going on in that insane mind of yours Vanessa?"

She chuckled at his astonished behavior. "Becoming your stepmother, John. Won't that be something?"

His anger returned full force. "Oh no, you won't. I admit my father was asinine enough to bed you, but he doesn't deserve to be a part of your manipulative games Vanessa."

She hid the fear he aroused in her. "Good luck trying to stop me John. I have my ways, you know, and we both

My Forbidden Mentor

know that you and your father are not on the best of terms."

He got in her face to make himself understood. "You will not get away with this. Plan on being a single mother, unless you can persuade one of your other lovers to take pity on you," and he turned and walked away.

"I will be your stepmother before this baby is born," Vanessa called out after him. "And work my way back into your bed, Lord Blackburn. Count on it," she whispered to herself.

Robert rolled off of Rose, exhausted. She cuddled next to him and his arm went to her back, sliding down her side, pulling her secure against him. They had been visiting for a couple of hours now and their excess energy was spent for the time being. They were in Robert's bed. He'd visit her at Sally's but only to talk. When they made love, it was always at his house. He had accepted her lifestyle for the time being, but every day it ate at him.

Her plan to save enough money on her own by selling her body seemed preposterous to him.

She had started her career before meeting him. In the beginning, when she had stood up to him, proud and determined, he had given in and accepted her temporary money making strategy, but as their relationship blossomed and his feelings for her grew, he sensed in himself an ultimatum about to be disbursed. His love for her had kept his sanity but her obstinate pride at times drove him mad.

Tonight he could tell there was something bothering her, as she seemed tense. "What is it, love? Is there something you want to tell me?"

Rose had been contemplating telling Robert her concerns regarding Vanessa. She didn't want to be premature about her suspicions, as she needed valid proof. "I wanted to be sure first, but I think Vanessa's up to something," she revealed.

Robert wondered what could be going on for Rose to notice, but with Vanessa, anything was possible. "What do you mean?" he asked.

He listened to her interpretation from beginning to end of the conversation she'd overheard between Vanessa and Sally and how she had a feeling John was connected somehow. Vanessa's recent activities of late served her suspicions.

Robert thought it was better to be cautious than not since he knew even more than Rose did at this point. Earlier, before Rose had awakened this morning, John had summoned Robert from his warm bed to discuss the private issue of Vanessa and John's father.

Robert's reaction was as shocked as John's. Sworn to secrecy, he couldn't tell Rose about it just yet, but this new, interesting information was a call to be on guard. How much more could Vanessa be up to? It wasn't worth ignoring.

Robert had gotten the "virgin's" name from Rose and proceeded to plan the rest of the day investigating. Before leaving for Sheffield he wanted to be prepared whether or not Rose's assumptions were feasible and then he would get John's opinion about the whole scenario, but at the moment Rose, lying next to him in her natural state of beauty, was too appealing to resist. They made love one more time before preparing to go their separate ways.

Chapter Twenty-Two

Sheffield

Melissa's stage arrived late the next morning. Her driver this time was younger and much more attractive than the first driver, but that still didn't excuse his being late. "Did you get lost?" Melissa asked, unaware her tone was so impertinent.

Jack responded with the appropriate courtesy, wondering how difficult this trip would be. When he was initially approached by Vanessa to escort Miss Howard home he'd been reluctant. He thought that surely Vanessa worried too much about her childhood friend, but Vanessa had successfully imposed a frantic concern for her friend Melissa's welfare, emphatically expressing Miss Howard's need for an escort to ward off the stalking Lord Blackburn.

Jack's vibrant blue eyes sharpened as they assessed Miss Howard's piqued features. "This is a new route for me, Miss Howard. My apologies," Jack told her while stepping down from the stage. Standing before her, he introduced himself before gathering her luggage. "Jack McGuire at your service." His hand came out to shake hers.

His kindness changed her mood. Perhaps she may have been a little extreme, always expecting everyone to be as precise about time as she. Her moods did seem radical of late. Still, she blamed the extremity on a certain male lover of hers. Lifting her hand to meet Jack's, her usual smile appeared. "Forgive me, Mr. McGuire. You're here now and that's all that matters. Please, I hate formalities, call me

Melissa," she offered, taking her hand back from his light grip.

His lips curved into a gracious grin as his hands clutched her luggage. "All right and Jack will be fine with me." Jack continued loading the stage while Melissa said goodbye one more time.

She hugged both children with intensity, knowing it would be a while until she saw them again, and then carefully embraced Cecilia with her new baby cradled in her arms. Cecilia mentioned a final time, "Please write me and let me know how you're doing. All right?" Both smiled and Melissa agreed.

"Yes, I will. Thank you for everything." Melissa hugged her one more time. Leaving a dainty kiss upon the newborn's delicate forehead, she boarded the stage. She had said her goodbyes to George last night as he always rose before dawn for work, and George had thanked her, feeling indebted for her help. Melissa waved goodbye as the carriage left down the path toward home.

Arriving in Sheffield, they searched for a hotel in town, and conveniently they found one near the track. After acquiring two rooms, Melissa informed Jack that she was retiring for the night. For someone who usually had an extended amount of energy, all Melissa could think about was sleeping. She changed for bed, then climbed in and settled herself beneath linen bedding that warmed her. The idea of being pregnant surfaced again and dwelled with unanswered questions. If I am with child, should I tell John about it? Would he care? How would he react? Would he think I was trying to trap him?

The agonizing fact that her menses was running late hadn't offered any comfort. She'd been late before when her

My Forbidden Mentor

mother had passed away, and by hanging onto that assumption, she could deny what seemed so plain and clear. She was about to become a mother and John, a father.

She lay upon the soft packed mattress, her head sinking into a feathered pillow, her eyes shutting, taking in the physical sensations of rest. She had missed solitary time for herself. Relaxed now, she half inclined to clutch the heavy covers at her feet and pulled them over her tired body. Turning on her side, feeling snug under the weighted coverlet, her eyes closed once more. As her body drifted into a restful state, thoughts of John came into her mind, imagining him holding her as he did when her father had passed away and remembering the tenderness and comfort he gave. Her wandering thoughts raced to the future and she wondered what he was doing at this moment.

While Melissa pondered about John, John pondered about Melissa as he sat in a local pub only a few buildings down from her hotel. Sipping brandy and never escaping the abundance of female attention, he'd lost count of the many propositions he'd been offered tonight. The muscles in his cheeks ached from smiling so much. The perfect gentlemen he was, behaving cordially to the desiring women. Their painted faces showed disappointment when he declined, but they held no interest for him.

The only offer he had even considered accepting was from one of his past favorites who happened to be conveniently married, Lady Ginger, a tall, full-figured woman from London. Married to some boring workaholic, she took leisurely times of pleasure for herself, although they were few and far between. Always a satisfying lover, she still paled in comparison to the intensity Melissa enticed in him. When she approached him tonight, asking him to escort her to the ball in town, his response was out of courtesy, telling her he'd think about it and let her know the following day. Just three months ago hesitation wouldn't have entered his entangled mind, but that was before meeting a country lass named Melissa Howard.

He poured more of the amber liquid from the bottle into his glass. Staring into the liquid swirling from the motion of his hand, he wanted his business in Sheffield to be over soon. He needed to be back home for Melissa's arrival.

Vanessa had managed to supremely tangle up his life. Now he needed to protect his father, a task he never thought he would encounter.

Taking in the fumes of brandy, his hand raised the glass to his lips, swallowing the welcomed flavor. Lifting from the barstool, he clutched the bottle of remaining brandy. Slipping it beneath his wool coat to an inside pocket he strode from the bar to outside, walking the brisk distance to his hotel room.

Melissa woke feeling fresh and revived until a slight wave of nausea hit as she arose from the bed. Ignoring her stomach for the moment she dressed in a hurry, leaving the room in order to find food. She ran into Jack on the stairway, grateful to see him carrying a tray full of appetizing food.

He smiled when looking up to avoid bumping into her. "I thought you might be hungry," he told her, not realizing how hungry.

His timing was perfect, she thought, and she let him know how thankful she was. "You're a lifesaver, Jack. I'm famished. I'm so hungry I feel sick," she explained, striding alongside him to her room.

My Forbidden Mentor

Jack watched in disbelief as Melissa gobbled down the varieties of subsistence. He couldn't help wondering how a young lady so thin and lithe could eat so much.

Arriving early at the racetrack, Melissa snatched a choice seat, high enough to see most of the action and near enough to the finish line. Although it was closer to the entrance gate than she preferred, she wasn't about to complain.

Jack accompanied her, having nothing better to do. It was his duty, after all, to keep an eye on Melissa at Vanessa's request, though Melissa was unaware.

Jack offered to fetch her something to drink and Melissa was obliging. She watched Jack trail away, appreciative of his generosity. As he disappeared into a group of people, Melissa scanned the filling stands. Her view of blending heads of people seemed infinite until a tall, handsome figure caught her attention.

He stood just inside the entrance, standing well above the men around him. His inherent profile was unmistakable. It couldn't be, she thought. Her heart started to pound fast and hard and her throat went dry. It had been almost a full month since seeing him last and she couldn't tear her eyes away. Out of all the racecourses in England why did he have to be at this one? She had figured her chances were high of not seeing him here, but then this was his business.

Still handsome, she observed, and still breathtaking. Then a tall pretty woman approached him, her hand grasping his shoulder. She whispered something in his ear and he smiled while she talked to him. Melissa's heart began shredding. Her belly started to ache from the sinking sensation forming there and from seeing a woman standing so close to him, making him smile like that. It confirmed his libertine ways. Still charming, her silent thoughts were clarifying. The more shattering the view, the less she could ignore him.

Then it happened. As John tilted his head near the woman's ear his eyes scanned the perimeter of people awaiting the beginning of the race. Once again he looked back toward his acquaintance but within seconds his bold gaze captured Melissa's. His mouth stopped moving, his expression stunned and possibly pleased at the same time, confirming he'd seen her.

Melissa quickly averted her gaze, shifting in her seat to look in the opposite direction. Wrapping her arms across her hurting stomach she prayed he wouldn't come to see her, but his focused gray eyes told her differently.

John had seen her and she couldn't hide from him. He would notice her in a crowd of even the most beautiful women of England. He was well aware by her astounded expression of her accusing thoughts of him. John excused himself from Ginger's company, giving her his final answer regarding the ball. A friend of Ginger's steered her attention away as John glided through the crowd of spectators to reach Melissa. He thought about the last time they had conversed, not exactly on the best of terms. He'd been angry with her but over time his anger had dispersed by her absence. He wondered if she was still angry as he closed in on her.

Arriving at the row she sat in, John took an additional three to four strides to reach her. The wooden bench was empty on both sides of her and her position hadn't changed. Taking the liberty to sit next to her he angled forward, his face almost drowning in her hair. His hand took hold of her arm in a lightened grasp. "Melissa."

Her whole body shivered when he touched her and spoke her name. Feeling shaky, her clasped arms gripped tighter to stop her trembling body when she turned toward him. He was so close, so near that he could probably hear the thudding of her heart. Her eyes focused on her folded arms before lifting to his. "Hello John."

Her eyes searched his features. She longed to forget the turmoil between them and start over again. Only good memories were surfacing as she gazed into the familiar face of the man she used to know so well. She wanted his strong arms around her again, wanted him to sweep her away into their very own private, blissful world. She yearned for the attentions of her long lost protector.

His first glimpse into her misty eyes caused a shudder of sensations to flow through his body. Recognizing the immense affect she had on him, he swallowed once to withstand the powerful surges. When she spoke his daze was interrupted, though he continued to study her reactions as he responded. "How are you? I didn't expect to see you here," he said in that incredibly deep voice of his.

She wanted to tell him "that's obvious", but instead took a more amiable approach. With a glance toward the woman who had whispered sweet nothings in his ear she replied, "Since I had to travel through Sheffield anyway, I couldn't resist," she said, giving him her normal endearing smile. "Are you here on business?" she asked, knowing more than likely that he was.

She surprised him with her response, but he knew her well enough by now despite the tone of her cream-filled voice and her confirming glance toward Ginger. "Yes, of course. It's rare that I travel just for the fun of it." His hand left her arm, clasping together with his opposite hand upon his lap.

Melissa reclined into the back of her seat, switching her crossed legs. "Yes, I know." Her hands clasped together as well. "John, you really should take a holiday. You work too much." She sounded serious and then she realized that she sounded like a wife.

Her relaxed attitude astonished him, which induced his next reply, "My work is pleasurable to me, you know that." Their eyes engaged in brief contemplation. "If you were to join me for a holiday, I'd take one." Apprehension was not apparent in his tone. He was serious as well, damn serious as his lustful eyes displayed smoldering desire that spoke of reestablishment.

Melissa's breath caught in her throat, wondering how to answer him. His gaze on her was very unnerving and was not helping her at all. Their focus was intent on each other, proving that the passion between them still existed.

Melissa forgot all about Jack until a movement coming toward her got her attention. Carrying two cups of tea, Jack's features turned curious. The knot in her stomach returned, concerned with John's possessive reaction. She'd dealt with his jealousy far too much not to think about it.

John saw Melissa's expression change and turned to look right up at Jack. John obliged, thinking the young gentleman had a seat further down. "Do you need to get by lad?" he asked as he slid his booted feet underneath the bench.

Jack smiled while responding, "Thank you," taking the three steps needed to sit on the other side of Melissa.

John took note of the young lad's boldness as he sat next to Melissa and a defensive glare appeared across his face. John was about to say a few select words when Melissa spoke up.

Being literally in the middle of what could become a disastrous confrontation she spoke the truth, trying to play peacemaker. "John, he's with me," she said, giving him a stern look that told him to ease off.

My Forbidden Mentor

Jack, unaware of John's temper regarding Melissa, nonchalantly handed Melissa her tea. "It's hot, be careful," he warned before his blue eyes caught John's stormy glare.

Melissa turned toward Jack to thank him but out of the corner of her eye she saw John's hands balling into fists. Her free hand reached over to his and placed a warning grip upon them, at the same time saying, "Thank you for the tea, Jack."

Her warm hand on his served to calm him, but he wanted answers involving Jack. "What do you mean he's with you?" His tone was low but demanding. This Jack character was a little too close for comfort.

Melissa released a harsh breath before answering, her tranquil demeanor fading from John's insistence. "Please don't take that tone with me and let me explain."

She was the only one besides Robert who could command his attention, the only woman in his life, other than his mother, who held any control over him.

She lifted her hand from his, placing it around the cup of tea. "Jack is my driver, nothing more," she said in plain terms, and after taking a sip of tea she offered some to John.

His eyes were narrowed as Jack's presence perturbed him. "No, thank you," he said. He leaned forward, his face only inches from hers, his tone hushed but direct so only she could hear his deducting words. "He's staying awfully close to you to be only a driver. I believe he has other intentions in mind."

Melissa leaned forward as well, closing the inches between them. "And your lady friend down there didn't have any intentions about you?" Her eyes narrowed as well, her voice speaking in the same whispered tone.

"I turned her down, damn it, like every other bloody female that's come along since I've met you."

At a loss for words, his honest reply certainly gave her comfort. He'd just admitted to being celibate while they were apart and she couldn't respond, but when she did respond it was to clarify her own position. "And you don't think I would turn down Jack if he made a move which, by the way, he hasn't?"

John continued with the same whispered tone and penetrating eyes. "If he hasn't there's a reason why. You're too beautiful for any red blooded man not to notice."

The heated discussion between them brought about unresolved feelings for Melissa that lay fresh and harbored. "Do you really think of me as a whore?"

Now it was John's turn to be shocked. His eyes widened then narrowed again. "What? Of course not."

"From the last conversation we had."

"I didn't mean it," he said in an instant. He wouldn't have her believing his blistering words from that night of confusion.

"Well I didn't know that. All this time I've been under that assumption."

"I was upset and it's something I'll always regret." John looked away as if to endure his painful words once again.

All this time she had taken his hurtful words and pounded them into herself, playing them over and over in her mind until she wanted to scream. Having it out in the open lifted a weight from her shoulders, but the pain he had inflicted had scarred her. She studied his distressed profile and spoke of her true feelings. "You hurt me, John. The implications that you made were hurtful."

My Forbidden Mentor

"I know," he said in a soft whisper. When he turned to look at her misery shown in his eyes. "I need to talk to you." His gaze flicked toward Jack. "Alone. We need to talk, Melissa."

Melissa hesitated as the surprise of seeing him hadn't worn off yet. "I'm not sure, John." She wondered if it would be beneficial, but then she had promised herself while staying at her cousins that when she saw him again she would give him a chance to explain.

John had found her again and he wasn't about to lose her this time, even if it meant competing with Jack, the driver. "Melissa, what can I do to convince you? I want to explain what happened." It was an admirable request.

Her eyes lifted at the sincerity in his voice. If he knew that his innocent boy look could make her lose all restraint he'd stay young looking all the time. Even through the pain and hurt of their situation she wanted to resolve matters with him and much more. He had exposed her to a world unknown, a world she wanted to share with him, together, and have his strength and guidance through the learning of it all, but when the pain had interfered it had ripped her apart, leaving her alone to face this bright new world.

She had exposed herself to him, telling him of her feelings, unfortunately in anger and not in delight like she had dreamt of doing, but even so he knew she was in love with him and he hadn't returned a reply in kind, not any sort of reply at all. She truly wanted to believe John.

In that moment she decided to find out his feelings somehow, someway. She needed to know because it would affect her future and she couldn't stand not knowing anymore. "All right, John, we'll talk."

On the inside John was ecstatic, but on the outside only a smile of gratitude showed. He believed this was his chance to start over with her, to make everything right between them again. He wouldn't lose her this time, although this time there would be a history of intimacy, an intimacy he longed to resume. "Thank you."

She sensed him watching her while she sipped her tea. She met his analyzing eyes and with a shaky hand offered him some tea again. "John, would you like some?"

"Actually I would." He took the cup from her and instead of sipping it he drank it down in one gulp.

Melissa stared at him in disbelief and watched his calculating motions as he leaned across her to introduce himself to Jack. "Jack, I'm Lord Blackburn. Nice to make your acquaintance."

Forgetting the introductions had embarrassed Melissa. "Jack, please forgive me," she told him.

"You're forgiven," Jack responded like a true gentleman, which ate at John even more.

Jack was surprised and amazed at John's transformation. Melissa must have a knack for calming him. He couldn't hear their whispered words but he'd heard enough beforehand to know what their conversation had entailed. It was obvious that the lord was protective of Melissa. Jack's confidence had risen when a hint of jealousy was detected, and although Jack was dreaming of only one woman at the moment, there was an acknowledgment of Melissa's beauty, which reminded him that he needed to send Vanessa a note about their traveling progress. Jack pulled his hand out to address John. "Likewise Lord Blackburn."

After shaking hands John held the teacup toward Jack, saying, "Jack, would you mind? Melissa desires more tea." John was serious, and while Melissa's mouth about fell to her lap, Jack was contemplating.

My Forbidden Mentor

He was sent on this journey to protect Melissa from the boastful lord. He figured she was safe enough because she seemed to handle Lord Blackburn quite well and didn't act afraid of him, and with so many people around he decided she'd be safe for a time, so he smiled, taking the cup from the lord along with his own and replied, "Of course, Lord Blackburn. And would you like some as well?"

"No, that's not necessary," John responded.

After Jack strode away John turned to Melissa, his smile diminishing when seeing her expression. "What?"

"Was that necessary?"

"You were out of tea," he commented, trying to look innocent.

"That was rude, John. It was intentional and I've never seen you guzzle down tea so fast in my life. As I recall you're not a big fan of tea anyway, unless it's laced with brandy."

She knew him too well. When they had spent their private week together he'd had one cup of tea with her. About half way through he'd apologized while adding a sufficient amount of brandy. Giving her a grin sure to get forgiveness, he spoke truthfully. "I couldn't help myself. He irritates me."

"He's not my servant, he's my driver," Melissa told him, then figured if it had bothered Jack that much he would have said something.

Their attentions turned to the racetrack, John pointing out certain thoroughbreds and their individual history. Jack returned, settled in his seat, and was handing Melissa her tea when John leaned over and said, "Thank you, Jack."

Jack was surprised and nodded in appreciation.

Melissa flashed John a secret, thankful smile.

John's attention redirected toward the track when he heard the announcement of his previous champion "Monarch". "There he is Melissa," he said. Adrenaline pumped through him when watching his horses race, and from the start to the end he cheered them on with pride.

Watching John now, Melissa knew without a doubt that whether they stayed only friends or resumed as lovers, somehow, someway, she needed John in her life. She joined John in cheering Monarch on and even Jack got caught up in John's enthusiasm. For the better part of the day all concentration was focused on the races. John's horses won six out of ten races.

Chapter Twenty-Three

As they were leaving they continued chatting about the races. True horse fanatics, Jack thought. Ah, but they seemed like more, much more than that. Vanessa had warned him about Lord Blackburn but Jack hadn't gotten any sign of trouble yet. He would keep his eye on the lord and continue to protect his lover's friend.

"John, is Chief here?" Melissa asked, admiring John's towering physique through a side-glance.

"Yes, he'll be racing tomorrow." John continued to stride forward, unaware of her lingering observation.

"Did you bring James with you?" she asked out of designing curiosity.

John hadn't caught on to her calculated drift. "Yes, who else?" He shifted and saw her eyes flare before him. "Please don't look at me like that. You know I'm not prepared for that." Why did he pretend there was less meaning in her tone when he knew her better than that?

"Wouldn't it be a perfect place to test the waters?"

He knew what the gleam in her eyes meant. John pulled Melissa aside to jar her attention and then shifted, aiming his attention toward Jack. "Jack, will you give us a moment?" John stared him down, daring him to refuse.

"Of course, Lord Blackburn," Jack obliged, trailing off.

What was she thinking? He switched back to her. She was about to expose the plans they had taken such care to guard. He leaned into her. "Have you lost your mind? Pay attention to how freely you speak when around others. Just as well, we are not prepared." He spoke in a low, harsh tone. "You and I need to be on better terms for this to work."

Her head tipped to one side, giving him a direct look. "Is that an excuse, John? You've had reservations from the beginning about me riding for you, haven't you?"

He gazed down into her inquiring eyes, crossing his arms over his chest to keep from touching her like he wanted to. "I have complete faith in your riding abilities. If I had reservations before I certainly don't have them now, but it's not your riding skills I'm hesitant about. It's you and I and having trust."

"Are you saying you don't trust me? In what way?" He needed to explain that one.

"That's not it, Melissa. There's a barrier between us and I don't like it." He stopped to look around, ensuring that they remained somewhat alone. "When you're out there on top of Chief riding like the wind, I want you to be full of confidence. I want you to believe in yourself and the mount you're riding. I want you to believe the only outcome for you is to win. Visualize it and make it happen." His eyes grew large with expression and the tone of his voice elevated with excitement as he explained.

"I'm confident when I ride, John."

"You won't be one hundred percent if you and I are at a standstill. I know, Melissa." He searched her eyes with his, wondering if he should share with her anything of what he'd been going through. Beautiful hazel eyes shimmered back at him, reflecting complete interest in what he was about to say. "Do you know how these past weeks have been for me? Excruciating hell, that's how, because no

My Forbidden Mentor

matter how hard I try to put you out of my mind, no matter how involved I get myself with my thoroughbreds, lingering in the back of my mind is you." He watched her. She stared back at him, unwavering in deep concentration. "And when you're atop Chief, a champion horse belonging to your long lost lover, how can you help but not be distracted?"

She thought about it, her eyes mesmerized by his and the words he'd just spoken. "You're right."

"Melissa, I want to see you ride Chief through that finish line, believe me, I do. But you and I need to resolve this horrible mess that an insane woman has created between us. I want to kill her for what she has done to us." He was steadily watching her reaction. "I'm glad you've agreed to listen to me because I want everything out in the open between us. I'm going to tell you the truth, Melissa. It will be up to you to decide whether to believe it. I hope by now you've known me long enough to know that I'm as honest a man as they come. I will not lie to you," he told her as he displayed genuine sincerity.

She smiled before responding. She missed him, everything about him. "I know you won't John and I'm anxious to hear the truth."

He returned her smile with his own melting one. "Thank you." As abruptly his smile began to diminish while seeing the natural blush in her cheeks paling before his eyes, and her smile turned into a frown. "Melissa, are you feeling well?" he asked, worried.

She hadn't wanted him to witness her anguish. She had tried really hard to hide her state but her stomach wouldn't cooperate. The rolling motion in her belly began once again as she tried to respond. Her hand clutched at her upset stomach without her realizing it until she saw John's eyes focus on that spot. She tried diverting his attention. "I've become famished all of a sudden." A pasted-on smile would have to do the trick. "I just need to eat something."

"Has it been awhile since you've eaten? You seem like you're in pain?"

The concern in his eyes placed guilt upon her for she wasn't being completely honest with him. The more time passed the worse she was feeling, which only confirmed that she and John had created a child. Again memories of his reaction to Vanessa and their child plundered in, reminding her to investigate the truth first before making her situation known to him. "I'm, yes, apparently so. At least that's what my body would have me believe."

John thought her last statement odd but brushed it aside when all of a sudden Melissa began stumbling like she was dizzy. He helped her to the nearest bench and she sat. "Are you sure you're all right?" When she didn't answer he became firm. "Melissa, what is wrong?"

Oh dear, this was first time she'd become dizzy like that. She needed something to settle her stomach and fast. "Food. I just need something to eat, John, then it will be better." When he didn't look convinced, she pressed on. "It must be my emotional state at seeing you again. It hasn't been easy for me." At least that wasn't far from the truth.

"I understand. Stay right here and I will get you something to eat." After she nodded in approval John left in a swift motion to get some food.

After she ate she seemed to feel better and John verified that she could go on. On the way they said their goodbyes to acquaintances that had stopped to converse with them before heading to John's carriage. Jack was enjoying himself until John announced that he was not needed for the remainder of the evening. "Jack I'll take Melissa back to

My Forbidden Mentor

her room tonight. We're going to spend some time together, so if you'll kindly excuse us." John turned to open the carriage door for Melissa.

Jack asked Melissa to verify. "Melissa, do you need my assistance this evening?"

John became annoyed once again but let Melissa answer for herself, telling his driver his plans for their destination.

Melissa assured Jack that John was accurate. "No Jack, I'll be fine. Lord Blackburn is a very close friend of mine. He'll see that I return to the hotel safely." Her hand went to his arm, reassuring him. "Do something for yourself. Surely there's some activity you'd enjoy doing."

He was keenly aware of John's continued glare out of the corner of his eye so he conceded. "Yes, I'll go catch a card game. I'll see you in the morning then." Flaunting an infinite smile, he left.

They stopped by a nearby pond surrounded by shade trees. They stayed in the carriage for privacy while Jess, John's driver, sat by the pond reading a book.

For a flare of a second while sitting across from John, Melissa watched him and thought about the chance that she was carrying his child. It would be a handsome child she imagined, looking over the potential father while he took off his coat and loosened the collar of his shirt. John caught her gaze and returned a look of significance.

She didn't say a word but just watched and waited. This was the moment of truth. John cleared his throat, keeping his gaze steady. "First, I want to apologize on Vanessa's behalf for her obscenely rude behavior toward you."

"John, you don't need..."

John interrupted her. "Melissa, please. I understand, but I feel it's necessary. Please let me finish."

She nodded in agreement.

He took a calming breath. "I never did find out what she had said to you but regardless, her actions were uncalled for. I remember telling you that she was a past lover of mine." He stopped to find that her reaction hadn't changed. "I had not seen her for quite some time and the last couple of times I had, her behavior seemed suspicious. I thought by not associating with her anymore that my problem would be solved," he chuckled. "How wrong I was," he said with a shake of his head. "It started with confronting you that day and then trying to trap me." His features turned solemn. "As you know I will not marry a woman I do not love, and I certainly do not love Vanessa."

Yes, John, but do you love me? Melissa cried in silence.

"I thought about your reactions later and realized that marrying Vanessa hadn't bothered you so much as the mention of the child had. I can only imagine that at the time you assumed the child to be mine." He saw in her eyes that his assumption had been confirmed. "It's not," he clarified.

The child is not his? "You're sure?" she asked, because that would explain his reaction toward the child.

"One hundred percent. Vanessa will attest to that." Softness claimed his stressful features. "I never, ever went without protection with her, or for that matter, with any other woman except you."

"Only me?" Melissa asked, dumbfounded.

"Yes." His hand posed the familiar gliding motion across the top of his velvety black head, smoothing stray hairs. "I have to admit it's the last thing on my mind when I make

My Forbidden Mentor

love to you." John's hand dropped to his side by sheer determination as the urge to touch her became immense.

Those honeyed cheeks of hers reddened. He hadn't witnessed her shyness since before their first intimate encounter.

"I understand the distraction," she said, quite aware her cheeks showed color if the heat burning them was any indication.

"Yes but that doesn't excuse my behavior." He grinned before becoming serious again. "To finish my explanation, I couldn't figure out why Vanessa had asked me to marry her. I didn't know if you knew that, but she did." Melissa nodded in conformation that she did. "Well I tried to find out the reason why but she wouldn't tell me, at least not until a couple of nights ago when I confronted her about it again."

"Who is the father then?" Melissa inquired, more anxious to hear about that than Vanessa's marriage proposal.

"I'm quite embarrassed to say, but I'm also so angry with Vanessa that if I didn't have some kind of human decency I would kill her. That's between you and me."

"Of course." Melissa didn't want to seem impatient, which was not an easy task for her. "But who is the father, John?"

"This also remains between you and me."

"Of course."

"It's my father, Melissa."

"What? I could have sworn you just said your father?"

"That's what I said. There's something evil about Vanessa, for she planned the whole thing."

"You're jesting." Melissa gasped in horrid realization.

"No, I wish I were, and now I must figure out a way to save my heartless father from scandal and financial ruin when she tries to trap him into marriage."

"What she's done to us is bad enough, but your father?"

"It's retaliation against me," he said. Their gazes held, allowing John to witness the astonishment that he himself must have shown in front of Vanessa. "Do you believe me, then?"

"As farfetched as her actions are, yes, I believe you, and I want to apologize for my behavior. I wasn't myself. I didn't let you explain and I feel awful about that." When she saw John start to shake his head, a short burst of anger toward Vanessa burst free. "She shouldn't be putting you or your family through this, John. She's vicious and deceitful and..."

His hand came up to halt her. "Or you. I see now how it would look to you. I'm so sorry Melissa for this whole misunderstanding that has kept us apart."

"I believe you," she reassured because he looked so hurt.

"Forgive me, Melissa, for saying those things I didn't mean. I felt so lost, so confused by your reactions that I lashed out."

She wanted to grab him from across the carriage and hold him tight, wanted to comfort him and let him know that she still cared, still wanted him, and still loved him. "John, now that I've listened to the truth I understand. We were victims of a manipulative plan to destroy us, but we're stronger than that. We're a team and being involved in racing horses we have a strong connection to each other."

John concentrated on what she didn't say, disappointed that she didn't finish speaking the truth. Because the moment was tender, any more pressure on her might backfire, which was obvious when she changed her tactic, so he kept his feelings to himself, letting her decide when the time was right.

Melissa held out her hand to shake. "Friends still?"

He hesitated, realizing how right he'd been in assuming that she needed more time. Reluctantly he took her hand in his and shook it. He smiled, knowing they were more than friends and how ridiculous it seemed to agree to just that. "Friends still," he said squeezing her hand, adding, "Although, I desire more."

The nervous glance of their eyes held. "One step at a time, John," she told him, thinking, you have to love me, John. You've got to tell me so first. I can't be hurt again, especially by you.

At least she hadn't rejected the idea. "Good. Now, about this Jack character."

"John, I explained earlier, he's my driver."

"Melissa I want you to think about moving out of that hotel room. You can stay with me in mine." He didn't trust Jack's intentions.

Melissa liked the idea but it was much too soon. She needed more time. If she stayed with John it would be less than half an hour before he'd have her in bed with him. Not yet, she told herself. "John you're worrying too much. I appreciate the offer but really, I'm only staying one more night and then I'll be on my way home," she informed him, sounding very sure of her plans.

John wanted to kick himself for moving too fast but he needed to get rid of Jack. He would leave when she did and take her home and then Jack could go on his merry way alone. "Perhaps, but if you leave in another day you'll be leaving with Jack. Why don't you stay and I'll take you home? And I think I should stay in your room with you just to make sure Jack stays in line." Pausing, he saw that "I know what you're up to" look on her precious face. "Well, you won't stay in mine." Pausing again, he assured her, "I'll sleep on the floor."

Melissa began laughing, startling John for a second, and then his lips curved into a smile while she spoke with true confidence. "Sleep on the floor?" she said to John with a broadening grin, her brows rising as she proceeded. "John, you wouldn't last half an hour and I'd find you in my bed," she told him, her white teeth glowing.

He responded to her remarks by telling her how it would really be. He inclined forward, "Let's be serious now, sweetheart. Wouldn't it be more like me finding you on the floor next me?" Leaning even closer to her, his face only inches away, he carried on, "Your hands all over my body."

Her face flushed and turned bright red. She interrupted him before he could continue. "Stop it, John. That's enough." Leaning back against the soft leather seat to distance herself, she counteracted his lustful words, "I don't want to hear anymore. You're not fair, talking like that." She caught his satisfied grin before averting her eyes. She wasn't smiling anymore.

He reclined back as well to give her room to breathe for she seemed to be gasping for air. The smile John gave her was out of the satisfaction that he'd affected her and not in a friendship sort of way. "Will you have supper with me?" he asked, hoping to rectify her mood. "I know a nice restaurant we could try?"

A smile crept upon her lips. "I don't give you enough credit, Lord Blackburn. Your approach makes it hard to resist."

"Does that mean yes then?" he asked in that lusty, husky voice of his.

"Yes." How could she refuse?

John was pleased with the results he had attained. Supper was an opportunity to be one step closer to her. Seeing the steaming desire for him in her eyes a moment ago combined with her blushing cheeks was pure torture for him. He became aroused as a result of teasing her when in the process he was being teased as well. Now is not the time he told himself, hoping he would be back to normal before entering the restaurant.

Supper resulted in pleasant conversation and delicious food, although at times the mood was a bit strained due to the history of intimacy between them, and the lack of touching seemed to initiate a battle of inner struggles for both.

Melissa craved his love and affection but swore to herself she would not give in until confirming the reality of his feelings for her.

John wanted to devour her, to imprison her within his embrace to ensure he hadn't lost her, but he kept his distance to avoid scaring her off.

Both were polite and agreeable but beneath their cool and easy exteriors sparks were flaring, their desires for physical contact burning with a heat so hot it left them both flustered.

After supper John walked Melissa to her hotel. On the way Melissa gave infinite details about her visit with her cousins and how much she had enjoyed herself, leaving out any notion at all of her possibly being pregnant.

They weren't far from her hotel so in a short amount of time they were approaching the stairway to her room. Climbing the stairs, her focus moved to his strong, handsome profile, lingering on his lips that she yearned for. He turned to catch her looking at him and she quickly faced forward to avoid his seductive gaze.

Reaching her door, awkwardness set in for both. They stood before each other, not touching but very close. John's gaze shifted downward and he noticed Melissa's intertwined fingers tightening, proving she was just as uneasy. John took the liberty of placing his large hands around her folded ones.

She looked down at their clasped hands. She felt jittery and her body began to tremble. Her gaze was broken when John spoke.

"Melissa, I had a nice time tonight. I'd like to do it again."

After skimming his handsome features her eyes found his, catching in his glistening heated trap. "It was very nice John. I would like to do it again, too," she responded in a sighing plea.

Their eyes steadied as passion was growing anew between them. John directly conveyed what they both wanted. "Melissa, I want to kiss you? May I?"

The heat simmering between their connected hands was only a prelude to the fire beginning to rage within her body. Thirsty to taste his mouth again, she finally replied with quivering lips, "Yes." Yes, she wanted this.

His hands didn't move, only his head lowered so his mouth could kiss hers. Her head lifted to meet him half way. The apprehension of feeling warm, desirable and acquainted lips seemed almost unreal when just a few inches apart. As reality intervened, their lips never met due to an interruption from Jack.

My Forbidden Mentor

"How was supper?" Jack asked.

Melissa witnessed a devious smile upon Jack's face, his eyes appearing glassy. He was drunk. Perfect timing, she thought.

John's chin dropped to his chest, his eyes shut and he began cursing Jack under his breath. Their hands separated as Melissa reached over to steady Jack. John's arms folded across his broad chest as he stood gaping at Jack and Melissa. He was not amused with Jack's performance. In silence he observed them, thinking of appropriate actions to take to make Jack disappear.

"Supper was fine, Jack. I think perhaps you should get some rest," Melissa responded, taking her hands off of his arms once he stood straight again.

Jack's gaze had been unsteady but there was no mistaking John's presence nearby. He remembered John's treatment from earlier that day. Jack's next move was calculating. Placing a hand on Melissa's shoulder, he commented, "Great. I wanted to let you know that I will join you tomorrow and I'm looking forward to it," he told her with a sly smile and a slur to his words. His hand slipped from her shoulder back to his side.

Melissa could only imagine what was going through John's mind about now, but she replied to Jack with courtesy. "That's fine Jack. Good night, then," she said, trying to give him the hint to leave before John exploded.

Jack was tired and drunk anyway and ready for bed. "Good night, Melissa." He turned toward John and bowed, almost falling over. "Milord." He caught his balance and headed unsteadily three doors down to his room. Taking a minute to find the keyhole, he stumbled inside his room, barely managing to close the door after him.

Melissa followed Jack's movements. She could already picture John's expression even before looking at him. Nevertheless, she turned his way. "Don't start John," she said, pointing a finger toward him.

"Start what?" He tried to look innocent but it didn't work. His pause was short as his hand gestured in Jack's direction. "What was that all about?" he inquired, knowing that Jack pushed his buttons on purpose and was taking advantage of Melissa's kindness.

She crossed her arms and tipped her head to one side. "See what I mean?" she paused, gathering her resources to deal with his impossible attitude again. "I'm not a piece of property, John. You don't own me."

He was beginning to loathe her reminders of his not owning her. She was too beautiful for men to ignore and Jack had close proximity to her. John would have to change Jack's position by making it clear that she wasn't available. Only John had the privilege of touching her exquisite curves. He'd already made his stake. His eyes began searching over her body as he resumed his position.

His possessiveness intrigued her and enraged her at the same time. Jack had been every bit a gentleman. Why John was so unruly puzzled her. She could handle Jack. She was in love with this man, who was not so easy to handle, this obstinate man standing before her, looking her over as he had many times in the past. His glare was one that she knew meant he wasn't going to give up without an answer. "I always give in, don't I? Oh, how I hate your persistent ways," she said, shaking her golden head. Moments of silence fell between them and as usual her impatience gave way. "He's bored so I invited him to join me on a tour of the town tomorrow."

Showing temporary satisfaction, John behaved as any jealous lover would. "I see." He hesitated while leaning forward, making his point specifically clear. "He's not to touch you, Melissa. He's not to lay a finger on you again."

Realizing he was referring to Jack's hand on her shoulder, she avoided the flinging of words and only made a comment, unsuspecting of the reaction it would get. "You're unbelievable," and saying so, she turned away from him to obtain her key. As she tried to open the door the key wouldn't cooperate, falling to the floor three times before she could get a steady enough grip on it. She was a wreck, cursing the key aloud. "Darn key." So much for a goodnight kiss, but was she supposed to let him interrogate her all night? She thought not.

John didn't like being ignored or her trying to escape the inevitable. Grabbing her arm before she could open the door, he twisted her to face him then backed her against the wall adjacent to the door. His other hand grabbed her opposite arm, restraining her. Leaning his body into hers, his mouth took over, kissing her hard, devouring her, conquering her once again, ensuring his position, reminding her of the passion between them.

His kiss was like the very first one except this time it was familiar and enticing. It had been so long since she'd had his strong, powerful body against hers. "Mm," she moaned aloud without meaning too.

His lips left hers, only to kiss her along her neck, and then lower.

A single word escaped her. "Please."

"Please stop...or...please go on?" John asked.

"Please...stop," she said.

Obliging her, he lifted his head. "Now we both know that you don't hate all of my persistent ways, do you?" he murmured. "You're mine, Melissa."

Her chest rose higher at his candor and a shiver raced through her body when his hand gently cupped her breast.

His protective motion struck her with such force that her immobile hand poised against the wall fell open, letting the key slip from her trembling hand to land on the carpet at her feet.

"Remember that when you're spending the day with Mr. McGuire," he said. John let her go and bent down to retrieve the key.

He'd caught her off guard with his ravishing display of possession. Thankfully, he had stopped, for she might not have. She shifted to find him watching her. She only smiled as she turned to enter the room.

He thought he'd made a mistake by his actions a moment ago, but he couldn't help himself. Not knowing their future together and the presence of another man in her life, even if he was her driver, posed enough of a threat to make him take action. She didn't fight, she didn't fall apart, and she didn't say anything, until now.

"I'll see you tomorrow, John, if you're free?"

"To say goodbye?" John asked with reservation.

"No. To spend time with you." She needed to clear the air with John. It had to go one way or another and right now it seemed in limbo. She couldn't handle limbo with a man like John.

John couldn't hide the look of shock appearing on his features, yet the shock didn't override his eager mannerism. "Where and when?"

"When are you free?"

"In the afternoon."

"Would you be interested in going to the theater tomorrow night?" She had always wanted go.

Stumped, he didn't reply right away. For all his life a woman had never asked him to the theater, and it sounded like Miss Howard had done just that. "Yes, yes I would," he stumbled out.

Her straightened lips curved into a generous smile. "Fabulous. I've always wanted to go."

He handed her the key. "Does this mean you are extending your trip?"

"Perhaps. I haven't decided yet."

"I see."

They exchanged a lengthy gaze of internal longing. They used to talk about practically everything with each other and would feel comfortable about it, but now, neither could speak a meaningful syllable. Their feelings were closely guarded for pain had stabbed once into their short but illustrious relationship.

"Are you picking me up or am I picking you up?" John offered, unable to withstand the pressure of their quiet stance.

"I only asked for your company John. The rest is up to you."

"What time?"

"How about five o'clock?"

"I'll pick you up at five in front of your hotel then."

"I'm looking forward to it."

"I am as well."

"Until tomorrow?"

"Until tomorrow. Goodnight Melissa."

"Goodnight John."

Upon entering the hotel John went over to a clerk to request bath water. "I need a bath drawn." He thought about his present condition and clarified, "Make it cold."

The clerk made his own suggestion. "There are more pleasant ways of relief, Lord Blackburn." The clerk winked, his eyes shifting to a particular part of the hotel in reference.

John wasn't interested. "Not tonight. Just bring the cold water, please," and with that he headed for his room.

The clerk shrugged his shoulders as John strolled away.

Chapter Twenty-Four

The next morning found Melissa knocking at Jack's door. He hadn't come to her room so she figured he was still asleep, but then she heard his lazy voice, "Melissa?"

"Yes, Jack, it's Melissa."

His voice became louder, seeming to approach the door. "Melissa, forgive me." The door creaked open a few inches. "I can't go with you today. I don't feel well this morning." His eyes were half open, his hair disheveled and his robe hung loosely around him.

Noting his condition, she understood. "I understand Jack. You'd better get some rest then."

His arms crossed over his chest and a slight smile appeared. "You're not upset with me?" he asked, regretting his change of plans but sleep was his only comfort right now.

She returned his smile. "Not at all. Just get better, all right?"

"Thank you, I will."

Melissa left and went about her business.

By afternoon, Robert had arrived in Sheffield. On his way to finding John at the track Robert spotted Melissa walking down a pathway toward the entrance of the hotel. The carriage stopped and he fled from it, dashing to catch up to her. "Melissa," he shouted, waving his hand.

She turned, recognizing the voice before seeing the face that belonged to it. "Robert?" she replied in surprise.

Robert briefly explained the reason he had come to Sheffield, careful not to alarm Melissa. He would explain in more detail when they found John. Nevertheless she needed to be informed of his suspicions regarding Vanessa.

Within twenty minutes of their meeting John appeared and was strolling towards them. His expression of surprise upon seeing Robert changed to dreadful concern after Robert gave a brief overview of his reason for being there.

Robert suggested that they find a private place to talk. Melissa suggested her hotel room but John thought his would be better. "Let's go to mine," he said, attempting to keep plenty of distance between Melissa and Jack McGuire.

"What's wrong with my room? It's right here," Melissa pointed out.

John spoke his mind. "Jack won't be around." His voice was stern and his eyes narrowed when speaking.

Robert was flabbergasted to hear the name mentioned between John and Melissa and immediately inquired, "Jack?"

Oblivious to Robert's state change, John and Melissa carried on with their discussion. "I at least need to change so we're not late for the theater, John," she declared, as she planned to dress very elegantly tonight.

John, who hadn't a clue as to her extensive plans, took the opportunity to keep her away from Jack and ordered, "We'll get your clothing and you can change in my room."

Melissa gave John a familiar look, one he'd grown accustomed to, and was thankful when Robert spoke. They had more important items to discuss than where to get dressed.

My Forbidden Mentor

"Jack who?" Robert inquired, with more insistence. They both switched their view to Robert at the same time.

Melissa answered first. "Jack McGuire, my driver. Do you know him Robert?" she asked. Robert pushed away from the wooden post he'd been leaning on, mumbling to himself.

John and Melissa looked at each other in total confusion at Robert's reaction and watched his expression change from one of awe to satisfying joy.

"Robert, what is going on?" John implored.

"We need to go to John's room and talk, the sooner the better."

John reached inside his pocket and pulled out a key. "Robert, take Melissa to my room, number one ninety-six. I'll fetch her clothes."

Melissa was disappointed. She hadn't wanted John to see the dress she'd picked out. "Why can't I go? You're not certain which dress to get."

John ignored her plea and held out his hand, his fingers motioning for her key. "I won't know which dress because I plan on retrieving all your items." A generous smiled curved upon his lips.

Melissa stalled a mere moment longer, then conceded and handed over her key. "You're going to pay for this John Blackburn."

The stern look on her face didn't faze him and his grin told her so. His confidence soared and he knew that he'd enjoy her paying him back. John proceeded with a cocky grin as he entered the hotel, making his way to her room.

Robert and Melissa strode down the main dirt road to John's hotel. "Robert, how do you know Jack McGuire?"

Robert preferred to wait for John. "I don't really know him Melissa, but let's wait until John comes back and then all of us can discuss it together." When he noticed the worried look on her face, he tried consoling her. "Everything will be fine. Please don't worry. It's just a hunch, and the three of us will get to the bottom of it."

He thought changing the subject would help. While taking her elbow, he helped her onto the wooden planks adjacent to the many shops and pubs. When they neared the entrance to John's hotel, he remarked, "You and John seem to be getting along." His observation wasn't unwarranted. Genuinely pleased for both of them, his instinctual feeling told him that when they cleared up this mess of Vanessa's, John and Melissa would most likely get married.

Melissa threw Robert a sideways glance before responding. "Yes, we are, although I believe there are more issues to resolve between us." Melissa stepped through the glass door Robert held open for her.

As they advanced towards the stairs Robert replied, "Surely they can be worked out."

She debated on speaking frankly with Robert. "Robert, can I confide in you? I don't wish this repeated to John."

Striding down a long corridor of rooms, Robert eyeballed a room number on one of the doors before shifting his focus to Melissa. "Of course you can. What is it?"

Melissa's focus came in direct contact with Robert's green eyes. "John has never told me precisely how he feels about me." She paused, debating on how much to reveal. "I know he cares but I need more." Robert slowed his pace, listening intently. "Perhaps that's asking too much, but that's the way it has to be for me."

Robert's gaze averted temporarily so he wouldn't miss their room. Finding it, they stopped in front of the door. He

My Forbidden Mentor

looked back to Melissa, giving what insight he could. "Melissa, I've known John since we were boys. You know that. I've never seen him act the way he's acting with anyone but you. He's definitely hooked." Robert half turned to unlock the door and pushed it open. Robert gestured for Melissa to enter but before she did her hand went to his arm, gaining his full attention.

"I'm in love with him, Robert. He knows that. But he hasn't told me the same. What do I do?"

Robert felt for the poor lass. John was never good at expressing himself emotionally, but then there had never been a reason to before now. Robert spoke honestly. "Talk to him. Tell him how you feel again, this is new territory for him, and be patient."

Stepping into the room with Robert directly behind her, she thanked him for his generosity. "Thank you Robert for consoling me. I will talk to him." She gave him a smile and turned to walk toward the window, staring into the busy downtown street of Sheffield.

As John picked up the last item he needed to take with him Jack's head suddenly appeared through the open door. Jack's immediate view was John's cheerful face and his expression didn't diminish when he saw Jack. In fact, he beamed even more. Jack spoke first.

"Where's Melissa?" he asked, as a guardian should, curious now that John seemed to be carrying all of her belongings.

Nothing could distract John right now. His beautiful lady was back where she belonged. Nevertheless, John took great joy in telling Jack that Melissa's plans had indeed changed. "Melissa is no longer staying here. She's staying with me," he explained, adding, "In fact, I will be taking her home." John's arms were full, juggling various items of Melissa's while locking the door.

Jack backed away, responding to John at the same time. "I've been scheduled to take her home, Lord Blackburn."

With key in hand, John juggled again while strolling down the hall. "I will pay you extra if that's your concern, so you may leave anytime now." John casually stepped by Jack, striding ahead down the hall.

Jack followed close behind, saying, "I'm not concerned with the money, Lord Blackburn."

John stopped at the top of the stairway, turned toward Jack and asked, "What is your concern, Jack?"

Jack felt dwarfed by John. His towering figure was very intimidating and he was caught off guard by John's abruptness. "Melissa. I feel responsible for her. My passengers are my responsibility until their destination is reached." Jack knew that John probably wouldn't believe his reason but it was the truth for Jack: Vanessa would have his hide if he didn't return with her best friend.

John knew better and thought the time had finally arrived to firmly set Jack in his place. "Jack, I'm responsible for Melissa now. She's with me and always has been. She's no longer in need of your assistance. Now if you'll kindly excuse me." John glided down the stairs with ease. Upon reaching the bottom he looked up to see Jack still standing where he'd left him. By the time John approached the front desk to return the key Jack had turned around and was heading back to his room.

After returning to his own hotel room John carefully laid Melissa's belongings on the bed, then joined Robert and Melissa at a small round table.

Robert proceeded with the information Rose gave him and then added his own insight on the situation. "Because of what's already gone on with Vanessa, I wouldn't put anything past her." He gave Melissa a sympathetic look. "She seems bent on having John for herself, even if he doesn't want her, and as for Jack McGuire, I don't believe it's a mere coincidence that he's here."

John and Melissa both looked to each other, their minds spinning the same weaving pattern of thought. If Jack McGuire was Vanessa's protégé, then the games had only begun.

They all decided to have supper and devise a plan against Jack and Vanessa. So they did just that and afterward, Robert went to his own room and Melissa and John went to theirs.

Melissa began organizing her belongings, which John had casually tossed on the bed.

John came up next to her, settling his shoulder against the bedpost. "Would you like my assistance?"

As her view switched to him her smile was faint. "No, I've got it."

John stood there watching as she laid her clothing across the bed in an organized manner. Observing her, John realized how much he'd missed her company, how much she added to his life. My perfect partner, he thought as he watched her bending over the bed. He loved the way her hair swayed forward with each motion and her hands, so soft, straightened each piece of clothing. There was heavy concentration in her face. Her eyes were focused, accompanied by a tense jaw and lips pressing together. The fact that he missed making love with her only enhanced his feelings. Be patient, he told himself. Right now she seemed so fragile thanks to a woman set out to destroy him. His brows creased as he thought of Vanessa again. He'd finally found a woman he could spend the rest of his life with and his past was determined to haunt him, a past that needed to be extinguished.

Melissa detected John's gaze upon her. Normally she would be self-conscious about it but her revolving mind kept thinking about Vanessa. How incredibly foolish she'd been to believe her over John. John hadn't given her any reason to doubt him, only his past lover had. She'd let Vanessa come between them, She'd let that evil woman have her way by letting her create the friction that continued to exist between her and John.

Enough of this, Melissa told herself, I'm not going to let Vanessa ruin my evening. I'm going to the theater and I'm going to enjoy myself. Following her last thought she looked toward John, whose handsome face made her realize what really mattered. She was going to the theater with the man she loved.

John grinned at Melissa's sudden mood change. He'd been thinking of a way to distract her without throwing her on the bed and having his way but she seemed to have remedied the situation for herself.

"Where can I put my clothing?" she asked in a soft, quiet tone.

He pushed away from the bedpost, gesturing toward the dressing area. "Anywhere you like. There should be room in the closet." He stepped over to the edge of the bed and sat, waiting for her to finish.

After hanging her clothing she let him know her intentions. "I'm getting dressed now so you need to busy yourself." She was not sure what John might pull in his seductive state, but just in case he decided to check her progress, she thought she would make him aware ahead of time that she was on to his desirable nature, but her purpose had the opposite effect. John took note of her tone and lifting from his seated position on the bed he strolled over to the dressing area where she was. Her back faced him as her fingers were struggling to release the tedious hooks along the backside of her day dress. He came up behind her, easily lifting her hands away so he could help her. She jerked so radically that his hands lunged forward, catching her by the waist.

Turning to look over her shoulder she said, "I wasn't aware that you were there." Her face flushed and grew warmer when she realized the reason for feeling the intense heat searing both sides of her waist.

John smiled as his hands came free from her waist once she was steadied and went to her backside to undo the hooks. "You looked like you needed help," he told her as he undid her dress. And my touch, he thought after seeing redness flare in her cheeks.

He started to slide it off her shoulders when she stopped him with her hands. It became obvious that the heat between them had grown scalding. "John, thank you, but we're going to be late for the theater."

In that moment he didn't care about the theater, all he thought about was sliding her clothing off. After the urgent moment passed he gained control. A kiss would have to hold him over. With her hands still braced above his, he leaned forward, placing a warm gentle kiss on her cheek. "You're right," he murmured. Grabbing his clothing, he left the dressing area and dressed as well.

Chapter Twenty-Five

The theater was a success and it turned out to be much more than Melissa had imagined it would be. The story pulled her in and entranced her. Even when saying good night to Robert her mind played over and over the extraordinary evening, an evening topped off with John's private compliment of how beautiful she looked tonight.

John opened their hotel door, letting Melissa in first. As she passed by, a whiff of jasmine drifted over him. He'd smelled her scent all night and it only encouraged the action he longed to take.

Melissa set her purse on the round table before sitting on the edge of the bed to untie her slippers. She watched John approach the table as he placed the key on it. He took his dress coat off, placing it around the back of a chair, his plush waistcoat next and then his silk shirt, slipping it off and draping it over the other clothing. Melissa slid one slipper from her foot and looked up again. He was sitting in the chair now, bending over to take off his boots. His body, which was bare from the waist up, reflected the fine movements of his flexing chest muscles as he slid each boot off.

Sighing internally, her fingers reached for the ties on her second slipper. John stood and began unbuttoning his trousers. Melissa once again observed his motions and her actions ceased. "What are you doing?" she asked in apprehension.

John got as far as halfway down the buttons when he looked up and replied, "I'm getting ready for bed," he said as if nothing unusual was happening.

Melissa averted her view back to the laces she was untying, at the same time commenting, "I hadn't expected you to completely undress."

John grinned as he slipped his trousers the rest of the way down and stepped out of them. He bent over to retrieve them, folded them, and placed them atop his shirt and coat. Untying the ribbon from his hair, his hand glided through his free and loose mane as he walked to the opposite side of the bed. Lifting the bedding, he said plainly, "I always sleep naked. You know that."

Melissa bent down to place her slippers next to the nightstand. As she straightened the bed dipped under John's weight. "I know," she said over her shoulder. "I thought under the circumstances." She trailed off when her heart began beating like a wild hammer. He was close, he was naked, and she was about to get into bed with him.

John lay there with his hands braced behind his head, the ivory linens just covering his pelvic region. His eyes were heavy lidded as they followed the graceful line of her backside. "What circumstances?"

Melissa tried to decide how to approach him about talking. She knew he had only one thought on his mind right now. "Never mind," she said while rising from the bed, thinking of another approach. Trailing by him on her way to the dressing area, she could feel his eyes following her.

While she undressed he made a suggestion. "I really think we ought to stay here for one more day."

Melissa's brow creased with wonder while undoing the last hooks of her dress. "Why is that?" she responded, trying to figure out his plan.

"I believe we've got to have an established plan when dealing with Vanessa. We need to go over all of our options again."

"I'm in agreement. One more day would be sufficient to gather more resources before returning home," she replied while tugging off her petticoat.

John liked the sound of the word "home". She made it sound like their home, together. "Good, then it's settled. At least one more day, right?" John needed to verify that she agreed, but when she reappeared wearing her chemise he became frustrated and disappointment wiped out any evidence of the mischievousness previously displayed on his face. Why on earth was she still dressed?

Stepping back to her side of the bed she answered him. "Right, John. I told you I agreed." Sitting on the edge of the bed again her fingers reached up to expel the pins in her hair.

As John watched golden streams of hair fall strand by strand it took all of his restraint not to get up and take hold of her, pull her on the bed beneath him, and rip off that dreaded chemise covering her body from his view.

Once her hair hung loose and shimmering she slipped underneath the covers and in the process casually snuck a peek of the glorious body she hadn't seen in some time. She began to linger on the expanding ivory linens and then suddenly shifted away to stare at the ceiling. She wouldn't be detoured by her sinful thoughts and trembling body.

Feeling awkward was unnatural where Melissa was concerned, but it was evident that was what she was feeling. "There's a better view down here," he said while his gray eyes blazed into her profile, trying to ease the situation by being humorous.

Her gaze didn't change. "Perhaps," she replied, distant and preoccupied. Not paying attention to her challenging reply, she missed his look of surprise.

My Forbidden Mentor

While Melissa pondered John lifted onto his side and faced her. He didn't notice the linen sliding further down, partially exposing him. "Perhaps?" he questioned, not understanding her timid reactions. His questioning tone caused her head to turn toward him. "Suddenly you're shy around me. Why?" he asked, confused. They had once shared very intimate moments only a man and woman could, and now she was modest.

In a soft, almost whispered tone, she answered, "I'm not shy." She sounded like a lost little girl; her body shook while watching his fingers pull at her chemise.

"Then what's this?" he asked, offended that she would wear her chemise to bed with him. As he let go she responded.

"I always wear this to bed," she told him, mocking his earlier reply. Of course, that was when she slept alone, so undoubtedly she knew what his reply would be.

"You've never worn it with me in the past?"

She couldn't defend herself because he was correct. This whole thing seems so silly, she thought. Finally she worked up the nerve to talk to him when he spoke first.

"It's not as if we haven't seen each other naked before." That prompted her eyes to stay direct with his dark gray ones. Then his voice lowered. "It's not as if we haven't been...together." His look of seduction became unbearable.

She rolled over on her side, her back facing him, not realizing the position she had created could be very compromising.

John released a silent breath. It was beyond doubt that she wanted him, just like he wanted her. He saw it in her eyes but something stood in the way. John scooted close behind her, not quite touching her. His hand went to her arm, lightly stroking it. "What's wrong?" he inquired in a soft, caring voice, not liking the continued friction between them.

Was she being ridiculous? But since he asked it opened the opportunity to discuss matters with him. "We need to talk," she said in a whispered tone.

He didn't think it was the most opportune time to talk but if it would help, why not. "All right, let's talk." As he rested his hand on her forearm her face turned toward him.

"How do you feel about me?" she asked, her eyes gripping his beholding gaze.

John thought it was a loaded question and took some time to reply. While talking was the last thing on his mind, it should have been a priority, he realized. This was his second chance to tell her about his feelings. If only he was better at expressing himself. "Can't you tell?" he asked, clutching her arm in tenderness, hoping it was a sufficient enough start.

It wasn't enough. She was craving the words. "John, I want you to tell me."

He thought back to their week of heavenly solitude, the time when his feelings had changed, becoming profound and everlasting, and the words just came to him. "I know that I want to spend all my time with you. I've never met a woman that intrigues me like you do." He took a deep breath before going on. "It's more than making love with you, Melissa. I want us to do everything together." He noticed her serious, intent features beginning to reflect sparks of happiness, which made it easier for him to continue on, and his eyes stayed steady with hers. "I love you, Melissa." His head lowered, his mouth aiming for hers. "I love you so much," he whispered against her lips before kissing her.

My Forbidden Mentor

He'd taken her breath away.

When his lips lifted from hers she returned her feelings. "I love you, John."

They kissed sensually, his mouth staying on hers while she maneuvered her body. She lay on her back and slid her arms around his neck.

Caught up in the passion of the moment, the thought of being apart from her again accelerated his heightened emotions, and the words were out before he could stop them. "Marry me, Melissa," he said as his lips grazed her arching neck.

Stunned by what she thought she had heard, her first reaction expressed how surprised she was. "What?" she whispered in his ear when her face turned into the silkiness of his black hair.

His head shifted so their eyes would meet, and he asked again. "Will you marry me?" This time it wasn't a slip.

Her lips trembled and her eyes shimmered.

"What's wrong?"

She started laughing, which confused him even more. He was searching her face, bewildered, when she finally replied. "Nothing is wrong. I'm happy, John. These are tears of happiness."

A finger traced the delicate path of her smiling lips. "Does that mean, yes, then?" he asked to verify. He expected surprise, but crying?

With tired, watery eyes she answered, "Yes, Lord Blackburn, I'll marry you." Her hands slid through his long, black hair to cradle the back of his head.

John lay atop her astonished, first at the question he'd asked and then her affirming answer. While looking down at his future wife, he recognized the importance of having a confidant. This was the woman he loved, the woman who would be his companion for life.

"I can't believe it. I'm marrying a lord." John's quizzical features were noticed when her eyes settled on his.

"What do you mean by that?" he asked out of curiosity.

Melissa realized she had never told him of her initial analysis of lords with reputations. "I used to have an opinion about rakes of your nature. I vowed never to marry one if it would ever come about. I could never put up with their stuffiness...and mistresses." His reaction surprised her. She had anticipated anger but instead a slow meaningful grin appeared.

"So what changed your mind?" he implored.

John, she determined, was different from other men. He'd been handed a title but he never used it to gain superiority over others. He may have been popular with the ladies but that was because of his undeniable charm and good looks.

Lady Blackburn. She couldn't believe it, and though her father had been unaware of her personal relationship with John, she hadn't any doubts that he would have approved. She was marrying for love and that was all that mattered. "You, John. You're not at all what I imagined in the ways of being libertine as the gossip says."

His grin continued to grow. My future wife, so confident, he thought. His fingers streamed through her hair as it flowed across the pillow. "Is that so?" he teased.

Her giddiness switched to questioning concern. "Why, John. Do I have a reason to wonder?"

He grinned some more and let her wonder as his fingers pulled at her chemise.

Frustration clashed with ecstasy as he touched her with his mouth. "John," she managed to say before losing her voice.

"Hmm?" His voice vibrated against her breast.

Her hands gripped the back of his head and found enough strength to pull him away. Catching her breath, she inquired again, "Please be honest with me. Do you plan to pursue other women?"

He was going for her other breast when she made herself plain.

"No. Not until you answer me."

His brows arched in surprise. He'd better answer her before she really got violent. "You don't ever have to worry about mistresses. That's not my style. I'm committed to you and you only."

When she showed relief his hand cupped the side of her face. "Thank you for being honest," she said.

"I will always be honest with you. You should know that by now. I was only teasing you," he said with a genuine smile.

"Teasing about that kind of matter frightens me, John. What if you tire of me?"

He shook his head. What was with her moods lately? "Silly girl, I could never tire of you. You're too headstrong to be boring, and I love everything about you, not just your body," he informed her as his fingers slid down her neck and over her full breast. "Although you can't deny the passion we create together when we make love." And make love they did.

Chapter Twenty-Six

The ivory linen drapery brightened from the morning sun, awakening Melissa out of her peaceful slumber. Stirring against John, she raised her head to focus on his tranquil features. She smiled at his sleeping form, so still and unmoving except for the relaxed rising of his taut belly. Quite a different picture from last night, she thought, remembering how they'd stayed up until the early morning hours engaging in endless lovemaking. They had reason to celebrate after all; they were to become man and wife.

Melissa lifted from John, leaving his resting body while she went to relieve herself. Stepping over to the water closet, a significant wave of nausea took over. Her smile turned into a frown and she barely made it inside the closet when the heaving took over.

The horrendous sound of retching woke John. Once he realized the sound came from Melissa, he was out of bed and at the water closet. Upon opening the door, her naked backside stood before him with arms stretched out to the walls on both sides. John's hand touched her shoulder, offering comfort. "Are you all right?" he asked.

Trying to catch her breath, she took advantage of his nearness by reclining into his naked body for steadiness and replied in scattered breaths, "I hope so." While taking comfort in his warm body his strong hand began caressing her shoulder and his powerful arm wrapped around her waist. It was as if he knew another wave of sickness would come about. He held her steady as she flung forward again, her stomach empty but continuing with its heaving motion.

My Forbidden Mentor

She finally lifted her head. For now the sick feeling had passed.

"Better?" John asked as he gathered strands of golden hair that had fallen forward. She nodded in response but had hesitation written in her expression.

"What is it?" he implored.

Then a flush of color appeared on her cheeks. "I have yet to relieve myself."

Comprehension dawned and without delay he prepared her with the necessary means. "Wait here," he told her, coming back so fast she wasn't sure he'd left. He held a clean chamber pot in his hand.

"Thank you," she told him. He waited outside the door to give her privacy, and once she appeared finished, he helped her to the bed.

He tucked in the blankets, and fully covered her, then sat next to her, using a wet cloth to wipe her mouth and cool her forehead. "I'm fine, John, really," she told him, staring into his handsome face. "I need to eat and I'll be better," she suggested. John rose from the bed and began getting dressed. "Where are you off to?" Melissa asked. He hadn't said a word since he'd brought her the chamber pot.

His fingers trailed up the buttons of his shirt. "I'm off to order some food and then I'm going to find a doctor," he said, using his fingers to skim his long hair back before placing a tie around it.

Lifting onto her elbows she pleaded, "A doctor? John, I don't need a doctor. The food always helps."

He came back over to her, staring at her with a look of certainty. "Melissa, I know the food helps, but sweetheart, it isn't normal to feel nausea that strong every time you're hungry, and today you actually got sick. Is this the first time you've thrown up?"

She sank back into the bed, defeated before she could debate. "Yes."

He sat on the bed again, taking her hand in his. "So it's getting worse." Her familiar pout, something he had actually missed, showed itself.

Taking a deep breath, she knew he was right. "I suppose so," she replied. A doctor would confirm if she were pregnant, and most likely she was. There was no more denying it as her menses, as of yet, had failed to start. She didn't need a doctor's confirmation. It was so obvious now. Would John be happy about this?

John was genuinely worried about his future wife. Taking care of her was his responsibility, always had been since his promise to her father. She couldn't have her way this time. A doctor became necessary to ease his mind. He explained as best he could. "Melissa, I'm not giving you a choice about a doctor. I'm concerned for your health. You could have some kind of illness."

As he finished his reasoning a nagging thought flashed through his mind. Her behavior of late seemed nervous and moody, especially around him. His features turned quizzical when staring into her face, now expressing the same nervousness. Connecting her present mood with the actions she had just experienced, his conclusion didn't appear that far-fetched. "Melissa, are you late in starting your monthly cycle?" Her immediate reaction told him everything by her shutting eyes and lips pressing together. He could see the anguish working through her features. "How far is it gone?" he implored, now realizing the role of fatherhood joined his newly adjusted position of becoming a husband.

My Forbidden Mentor

Her eyes opened, expecting to find anger in his piercing eyes but instead she saw binding affection. "Approximately three weeks," she revealed in a quiet tone. Finally she had faced the truth with John and a sense of extreme relief came over her. The tension and pain of her relationship with John, topped with the idea she could be carrying his child, had racked her unbearably these last few weeks.

John hid his distress from her. It seemed all sorts of events were happening at once. Reuniting with Melissa, finding out Vanessa may have more vicious plans, proposing marriage and now a child on the way, all in two days' time. He knew Melissa had been dealing with her own miseries so she didn't need the extra burden of his, but she must have had some idea that she was pregnant. "Why didn't you say anything?" he asked softly.

"I wasn't sure John," she responded guiltily.

"Wasn't sure?"

"Whether I was pregnant or not. I've never been so I don't know the signs." In denial, she had blocked out Cecelia's advising of the signs. "And please don't wonder that it may be yours, if I am, that is."

John began recovering from this unexpected critical bit of news. "Forgive me. It took me by surprise, that's all. A lot of events are happening at once and you being pregnant was the last thing I expected to deal with at this time."

Her emotional state flared again. "John you were the one who introduced me to the pleasures between a man and woman, and you were also the one who didn't think we had anything to worry about. How do you really feel now that it could be a reality?"

His hands flew up in defense, as if to ward off her unpredictable burst of words. "Whoa, sweetheart. I'm just finding out this morning how possible it may be when you've known for some time. Who's facing reality here?"

"John you know we made love a couple of times unprotected." She wasn't ready to take full blame. "How can you pretend you didn't think about it?"

"I figured everything was fine since you didn't say anything," he said in defense.

"When I first noticed strange symptoms you and I were miles apart. I've been going through my own agony, you know." It seemed they were dealing with one complication after another and all at once. "I admit I was in denial, only because you and I weren't getting along, and because I'm not ready for a child."

"If you're pregnant Melissa, the child isn't going to disappear because you're not ready and don't even think about any other options. I won't allow it."

Aghast that he would even think she would resort to such drastic measures, she clearly informed him. "I've never thought of any other options, and I never would." She shifted away from him before asking out of frightened desperation, "Do you still want to marry me?"

"What? Now why would you ask such a question? Of course, I do. Why are you so insecure all of a sudden?"

"I'm scared John. Can't I be scared?"

"Yes, I'm sure it's normal. Now I'm off to get you something to eat and then a doctor." He rose from the bed.

Melissa's hand reached for his arm to stop him. "John, can't we do without the doctor?"

"Why?"

"I'm afraid of doctors. I don't like being sick. Seeing a doctor means you're sick."

He looked down into her innocent, dismayed features, realizing he loved even this part of her personality. "Melissa, if you're pregnant, it's a good sickness. Does that make you feel better about it?"

"No, John. It's easy for you to say when you're not the one who has to go through it."

He rolled his eyes and sat down again. "I told you I'm here for you. Now where's that pouting lip of mine? Come on, show me. I can feel your famous pout coming on. Here, let me help you. There you go, just like that, no, the bottom lip comes out further."

"I don't pout," she said defensively, as her bottom lip extended well past normalcy.

"What do you mean? You're doing it right now. You've pouted for me since the first time we made love."

"And that's what got me into this trouble."

"Making love?" he asked with a light chuckle in his voice.

"Yes."

His head dipped to hers to nuzzle her earlobe and neck. "Yes, but it was fun trouble, sinful, delicious, incredible. There you go," he whispered when he witnessed her mouth beginning to curve into a smile.

"Stop it or you'll make me laugh," she said, squirming away from his ticklish maneuvers.

His head lifted and his smiling eyes were drowning into hers. "That's the point, sweetheart. You're beautiful when you laugh."

"I am?"

"You are to me."

Her eyes lingered on his expression. His handsome face expressed a unique tenderness she'd never seen before. He took the wet cloth from her forehead before sweeping his fingers through her hair and away from her face. His warm lips grazed the bridge of her nose, descending down to her lips applying another light brush of softness. "Even though it's quite likely you're carrying our child, I'm getting a doctor to verify."

"Our child" struck Melissa with intense emotion. Her small hand went to his masculine cheek, smoothing over the earthy texture of his skin. How could she deny the child they had made together? "I agree," she told him, and then added, "John, are you truly happy?"

How could he not be happy with a beautiful woman to be his wife and a child already on the way? Despite a father he didn't associate with and an ex-lover making his life a living hell, everything couldn't be better. "Yes, I'm extremely happy. You're to be my wife and in a short time you're going to make me a father. I couldn't ask for more." His smile shown with radiance and she could see true contentment in his features.

She ate heartily and then got dressed. Afterwards she began periodic bouts of pacing in anticipation of the doctor's visit. Why am I so nervous she wondered, watching from the window as people shuffled through town. Everything was in the open with John now. What was there to be nervous about? A deep voice broke into her thoughts.

"Melissa, relax. He's only going to confirm what we know to be true. There's nothing to be anxious about." When John saw that she was too knotted up to respond he went back to planning his schedule for training and races, marking the first couple of weeks exclusively for Melissa, for he wanted her teachings to be finished while the baby stayed small inside her.

Nothing to be anxious about, she ran over in her mind. What was she afraid of? Birthing? Just then a knock at the door got her attention.

John lifted from the chair, stepping in front of her. "I'll get it. You sit and relax." She sat on the edge of the bed as John answered the door. "Dr. Marlow. Come in." John stood aside, allowing his entrance.

He tipped his top hat in John's direction. "Lord Blackburn, thank you."

While John and Melissa conversed with the doctor, Robert was seated at a café a few buildings down from their hotel waiting for his breakfast. Sipping on tea, he wasn't surprised that he hadn't seen John and Melissa yet. He was sure they were quite comfortable sleeping in this morning. Robert thought about the meeting that was to take place after breakfast. What kind of strategy could they come up with to expose Vanessa? As his eyes skimmed the townspeople through an open window the devil herself appeared before his very eyes. It can't be, he thought, but sure enough there she was, platinum hair, red lips and ice blue eyes, exiting a stage in front of their hotel. Jack must have informed her, and oddly, he didn't see Jack with her. She had entered the same hotel where they were staying. How am I going to warn John and Melissa?

They were in the middle of discussing what to expect of Melissa's confirmed pregnancy when there was a knock at the door. John went to get it. "A message for you, my lord." The messenger nodded then left. John unfolded the note. It was an urgent request from Robert to meet him at the racetrack. Alone. Crucial business arose that needed both their attention. John's gaze went back to the word "alone". He folded the note and placed it among his clothing. The message seemed unusual but it was from Robert and Dr. Marlow was here with Melissa. Perhaps he could convince the good doctor to stay with Melissa while he tended to business.

"What is it?" Melissa asked. It seemed serious from John's concerned expression.

He smiled so she wouldn't worry. "Robert has summoned me. He probably got tired of waiting for us." His hand reached out to take hers.

Eagerly she grabbed his hand and a grin as big as the open country gifted him. "It's just as well, with the news we have for him," she said, and he squeezed her hand in agreement, both almost forgetting the doctor still remained.

"Sweetheart, we'll tell Robert the news later, together. Right now I need to see him alone." His focus switched to the doctor. "Dr. Marlow, I realize we didn't finish, but if you could continue with Melissa I would appreciate it. I shall return shortly." John figured since the doctor hadn't finished it would give him plenty of time to investigate Robert's request and be back before he left.

"That's fine. I've got time, Lord Blackburn." Dr. Marlow informed John.

Something was wrong, she could tell, but she decided to trust John's judgment and stay with the doctor.

John hated excluding Melissa, much less leaving her essentially alone, but Robert had made a point of him coming alone. It didn't make sense and Robert had best have a damn good reason why.

My Forbidden Mentor

It was a strange sensation but as John strode through the hotel lobby a familiar scent caught his attention. It wasn't light and flowery like Melissa's but smelled heavier, French-like. He disregarded the sensation, leaving the hotel and making his way through the crowd toward the track.

While John scanned the racetrack three times over with Robert nowhere to be found, Robert had followed Vanessa discreetly around the hotel, missing John's leaving completely.

Robert was watching every move Vanessa made and so far she had gone back and forth between the lobby and her room, unsatisfied about this and that. When she went to her room for the fifth time Robert decided to wait in the lobby as he had grown tired of striding the stairs after her. Thankfully her room was on the opposite side of the hotel from their rooms. As Robert scanned one side of the lobby he didn't see the server striding at a rushed pace right for him. When he turned around all he saw was a close up of the server's widened eyes and then a tide of milk coming for his face. The server landed on the carpeted floor with the tray next to him, and Robert, who stood above him, held an expression of disbelief as he looked upon his own coat dripping with milk.

John was fuming. Was this some kind of blasted joke Robert was playing? He would definitely pay he thought as he reentered the hotel. The heavy perfumed scent still lingered in the air of the lobby but John dismissed his suspicions again as he approached the stairs, anxious to check on his fragile fiancé. Before he got to the first step though he heard his name being called out by a familiar voice.

"John. Over here." He followed the voice to find Robert's relieved features. Changing his direction, he strode toward

Robert with the full intention and purpose of biting his head off about his harassing maneuver this morning.

"There you are," John said as he was reaching Robert. Robert motioned him over toward a private corner of the lobby, the waiter following him with a towel. John was oblivious of Robert's situation as anger took him over. "What is the meaning behind this?" John asked with the note in hand.

Robert interrupted him. "John, I don't have time for trivial talk."

John became perturbed. After all, it was Robert who had caused the chaos this morning. John watched the waiter with impatience, his angered features clearly expressing his desire for privacy. It wasn't until the poor waiter left that John noticed something had happened to Robert. "What the happened to you?"

"Nice of you to notice," Robert replied, pausing as he looked toward the lobby, watching both stairways. He explained as his concentration stayed on everybody passing through. "That bloody idiot of a waiter ran into me. He didn't pay attention to where he was going."

John began laughing. "I'm sure it wasn't on purpose." His laughter was cut short when he noticed Robert acting intent and focused. "Who are you looking for?"

Robert, frustrated from getting diverted, answered with shortness. "Guess?"

John's bewilderment faded as another whiff of that same familiar perfume drifted by his nostrils. "Vanessa," John said knowingly.

Robert took a moment to reply. He thought he saw a blond head bop by but he was mistaken. "Yes, Vanessa.

My Forbidden Mentor

She's just arrived. I've been keeping an eye on her. Luckily, her room is on the other side of the hotel from ours."

This woman is deadly serious, John thought, which confirmed the urgency of Robert's message. "If this is what your message was about why did you want me to meet you at the track?" John asked out of curiosity.

Robert turned to face John. Robert wished he could have gotten a message off to John but he hadn't dared lose sight of Vanessa. "I didn't send you a message John. I would have but I didn't want to lose her."

Every one of John's nerves flared with new intensity, as Vanessa's plan hit him all at once. If that note was a deterrent and if Robert lost sight of her, like when the waiter bumped into him, oh Lord, Melissa! He hoped the doctor still accompanied her and he prayed to God that Vanessa hadn't gotten to her yet.

John started for the stairway to his room, telling Robert over his shoulder, "I've got to check on Melissa. She could be alone," and he trailed off because he could no longer talk. His mind was rattled with the fear of not knowing how far Vanessa would go, what extreme measures she would pursue in her obsessive, jealous, maddening mind. Robert stayed close behind.

It had been less than five minutes since the doctor had left. Melissa had assured him that she would be fine, not wanting to keep him from his busy schedule, and she figured John would be back soon enough. Turning away from the door, elation consumed her. So many things had been cleared up in the last twenty-four hours and everything was magical. The man she loved also loved her. They were to be married. They were to have a child, a child they had created out of passion and love. Life couldn't be much better.

There was a knock at the door and a charming voice on the other side of the door claimed to be room service.

Melissa's trusting nature was now leading her down a corridor with Vanessa at her left side holding a concealed knife to her ribs. Melissa silently screamed for John while Vanessa told her on the way to the stairs that she planned to take her to her room across the way. Her plans included tying her up and keeping her there until she was ready to dispose of her. She promised Melissa one last time to see John, which would be while he and Vanessa made love in front of her, and then the real torture would begin.

Every time Melissa struggled Vanessa dug in deeper with the blade. When they reached the top of the stairs Melissa knew something had to be done before they got to Vanessa's room. She wasn't about to be hidden away from John so Vanessa could indulge in her warped fantasies.

Approaching the first step, Vanessa insisted, "Now smile pretty Miss Howard, so it seems that we are the closest of friends." When Melissa didn't respond, Vanessa was harsh. "Do it," she told her as she smiled herself, piercing at Melissa's clothing with the sharp tip of the blade to let her know that she was serious.

Melissa's lips curved with slight intent, trying to stay calm enough to perform a beneficial maneuver.

Vanessa leaned into Melissa, smiling sweetly as they approached the third step, and whispered a warning. "Don't try to be courageous Miss Howard or you will regret it. Your lover isn't here to save you." Her laughter dripped with venom. "I've sent him off on an errand, a very urgent errand."

Melissa had had enough and she decided there was still a chance. They were almost halfway down the stairwell when she decided to put a crimp in Vanessa's plans. John may not be here to save her but she would damn well try to save herself and the child she carried. Melissa's strength was returning, her confidence bolstering. Melissa took a chance with a knife at her side but it was a chance she needed to take.

Without warning Melissa turned her body, stretching out her left leg in order to trip Vanessa. She didn't succeed as Vanessa regained her balance by grasping the wooden rail on her left, and it was Melissa who fell in the process, landing on her back and upside down in the middle of the stairway. Her head tipped against the edge of a carpeted step as she struggled with Vanessa, trying to get herself into an upright position, but Vanessa kept pushing at her and she could feel herself slipping downward one step at a time. Reaching for any kind of leverage seemed impossible until Vanessa lifted to better position herself. Melissa pushed and strained for the railing, determined to grasp the wooden spindle at her level. While her arm stretched out Vanessa managed to slice at her forearm, warning her verbally to behave or she'd take more drastic actions. Melissa ignored her, grunting in exertion, and she was able to grab the bottom of the spindle.

John came hurdling up the stairs towards them, taking two steps at a time with Robert right behind him. Vanessa looked up and in desperation tried again to pry Melissa's fingers from the wooden spindle, holding the knife in her other hand at Melissa's throat.

John yelled out, "Vanessa, no! She's pregnant!" he warned, displaying evident fear in his eyes. All he could think about was getting Vanessa away from Melissa.

Laura Mills

The knowledge of Melissa's pregnancy stunned Vanessa beyond belief, and as she turned to face John he closed in on them. Melissa watched the evil pouring out of Vanessa as both of her hands gripped the knife handle, lifting it high above Melissa's head. Vanessa shifted her focus back to Melissa, aiming the blade right for her stomach. Melissa began shaking uncontrollably. I have to save my baby she thought as her right hand joined her left on the spindle and she tried sliding herself out of the way.

But in a flash John had Vanessa pinned down, her arms above her head, and he applied enough pressure on her wrists to release the dreadful knife. "Let go, Vanessa," John demanded. His strength overpowered her, making her hands grow weak and the knife come free. John slid the knife away so she wouldn't be tempted to reach for it, and a glare of disgust filled John's features as Vanessa stared up at him.

"Let me go, you ungrateful bastard," she yelled in his face.

All John saw in her face was pure hatred. She had turned crazy, and her craziness was jeopardizing the lives of his future wife and child. His grip on her arms squeezed harder as his words seared between clenched teeth. "You're insane, Vanessa."

Robert asked Melissa if she was all right and looked over her cut. Seeing it was superficial he took Vanessa out of John's hands. "John let me have her."

John took Melissa in his arms. "It's over sweetheart," he whispered, reassuring her. Then he noticed the slash on her forearm. Seeing the bleeding was light he whipped out a handkerchief from his trouser pocket. Wrapping it around her arm, he kept it snug to slow the bleeding. He lifted Melissa into his arms and she hung onto him for dear life as he strode up the stairs back to their room. Once inside his foot kicked the door shut so he wouldn't disturb

Melissa's position. Sitting on the bed, he held her for a long while.

Curled on his lap, her arms still wound tight around his neck, she buried her face in his shoulder and went from violently shaking to lightly trembling.

In a shaky whisper her feelings flooded and began streaming out. "I almost lost you and our baby." Tears fell from her eyes as she continued on, "I can't live without you John. I almost lost our child. Will you ever forgive me?"

Her words stabbed him like a knife in his belly. Her pain was his pain and he wouldn't have her believing it was her fault. His trembling words reached her ear. "Stop blaming yourself. It wasn't your fault. Don't dwell on what could have happened. You and the baby are safe now." John's lips touched her cheek. He couldn't live without her either.

She kissed along his neck that was saturated from her tears and revealed lingering thoughts of her gratefulness. "If you hadn't come John I don't know what would have happened. I, I just froze when she held the knife." She kissed him again to ensure that he was real, that the nightmare was over, and that she could finally believe they were alive and sound.

John let out an unsteady breath. "I don't want to think about what could have happened. We need to return home and forget about all this madness."

She smiled against his neck. He truly was all she wanted, more than anything. She lifted her golden head away from his shoulder and her weary eyes fastened to his. "As long as I'm with you, I'll go anywhere."

Words couldn't describe his feelings at that moment. His head bent towards hers, his lips reaching for her swollen ones. His mouth experienced the sweetness of her mouth and the salty wetness from her tears. He turned her short intakes of breath into groans and he groaned in unison.

John's hands slid up her back to undo the buttons on her dress and Melissa's hands began shoving John's coat off his shoulders with reckless need. When a knock at the door sounded, they both stopped, their lips parted, and John rested his forehead against hers.

"Should we ignore them?" he asked as his hands were in the process of slipping the sleeves of her dress off her arms.

She smiled while pulling his coat back over his shoulders. "It could be Robert. We shouldn't make him wait," she said, placing a light kiss on his lips.

John wasn't convinced. "What if it isn't Robert?" he asked out of desperation.

"John," Melissa started to say when another knock sounded, and this time a voice spoke.

"Are you two in there? It's Robert." John began buttoning her dress, muttering under his breath, "Damn it all."

"One moment Robert," Melissa told him as she helped John before sliding off his lap and sitting next to him. John lifted from the bed to open the door for Robert. Taking his position upon the bed once again, his glare told Robert the obvious.

Robert sat in a chair across from them. "Have I interrupted something?"

Through frustration John responded before Melissa could. "Yes, you certainly have."

Robert smiled at John's misery. It wasn't as if John hadn't put him in the same position when he'd wanted to talk about Melissa at all hours of the night. He and Rose would be in the throes of lovemaking when John would be insistently knocking at the door. "So sorry," he said, looking in John's direction before switching to Melissa, "but I hear congratulations are in order?"

John and Melissa stared at other in confusion, knowing they hadn't spoken to anyone yet. "How did you find out?" John asked.

Robert's grin widened. "You only shouted it so the whole town heard you John."

That's right, John remembered. He had shouted it aloud, but not in the manner he would have preferred, and by now Melissa remembered the same thing. "Thank you," they said in unison. "You can congratulate us again if you'd like. We're getting married," John informed him.

"Well it's about time. Rose and I were devising a matchmaking plan for the two of you," he told them.

"I'd like to meet Rose," Melissa remarked.

Robert leaned toward Melissa, handing her his handkerchief for her wet face. "And you shall," Robert concurred. Eager to get home, he finished the update on Vanessa. "By the way, Vanessa is being evaluated by the local doctors here. There's no telling where she'll end up, but as long as she's out of our lives I don't care." Robert stood. He still needed to pack so he could leave.

"Hopefully her evaluation will take a lifetime," Melissa replied, taking John's hand in hers and squeezing, and she rose as well as the thought of Vanessa cued her to start packing. The farther away from that woman the better.

As John watched Melissa step over to the dressing area he knew what motivated her actions. His gaze swung back toward Robert.

"Leaving?" Robert inquired.

"Yes immediately," John said with a smile, and rising, he walked Robert to the door, where they said their goodbyes and made plans to meet in Richmond in a couple of days.

Chapter Twenty-Seven

"Has this turned into the battle of wills?" John inquired as he clasped his hands together on top of his lap. His head reclined into the leather seat of his carriage and tipped into a comfortable position so his eager and waiting eyes could watch her.

Melissa brushed the velvet curtain aside, averting her attention away from the handsome, prowling man seated across from her. Since leaving the hotel he'd been tempting her to continue where they'd left off, in the midst of a prelude of lovemaking, blaming Robert for his unreasoned urgency although Robert had unknowingly interrupted.

But Melissa found herself thinking about all the changes that had taken place in the last few days. The shock of Vanessa's maneuver was finally wearing off, letting her mind explore the future, and unfortunately her present mood didn't coincide with John's adventurous one at the moment. Plus it might be sort of fun to put him off for a change and not respond so predictably.

She answered him while her eyes fastened to the passing landscape. "I suppose it has since I need to prove to you that I can control my urges, and it will be you who loses control." Managing a brief glance toward his languid form she saw exactly what she had expected, a lazy smile with equally lazy eyes. Don't fall that easily she warned herself.

John laughed. No, it wouldn't be long. She was as hungry as he was and in a few short hours she'd be melting beneath him, begging him to take her.

Laura Mills

Short Corner

John became quite impressed with the stamina Melissa presented. She hadn't backed down once to all the baiting he had tossed at her.

Once they came to a stop Miss Beckett came flying out of the front door, anxious to greet them. Thunder and Laurel whinnied at their presence. Melissa barely made it out the carriage door when Miss Beckett embraced her. John conversed with his driver, explaining their situation while Melissa and her auntie said their hellos. Miss Beckett was surprised but relieved when she saw Melissa and John together.

Their reunion was pleasant. Miss Beckett had prepared a marvelous array of dishes and she watched the two of them sitting across from her while they all ate and enjoyed their food. Seeing them together gave her the distinct feeling there was something more they had to tell her. "Is there something more you'd care to share?" she asked, watching their matching smiles come to life.

John gave Melissa the honor.

Melissa looked to John for support and he nodded for her to continue. "Yes Auntie, there is more," she started, clearing her throat to go on. "John and I are to be married." One hurdle gone, Melissa thought as Miss Beckett's reaction was what Melissa had expected, ecstatic.

"Oh, that's absolutely wonderful. I'd always hoped," she glanced at both, "Congratulations you two."

Melissa put off the inevitable by commenting, "Yes, I'm very happy, auntie. I believe it was meant to be." She smiled, blushing at the awkwardness, her eyes downcast until John gently nudged her arm with his. Her focus

My Forbidden Mentor

swung to his, perturbed that he was pushing her. It had been exceedingly difficult to get enough courage to announce that she was pregnant. She held the utmost respect for her aunt and to reveal such news before being married would not only be humiliating but meant disapproval from her aunt as it would reveal her promiscuous actions while she'd been away.

"What is it, love?" her auntie implored.

Melissa couldn't tell her now, perhaps she could wait until after they were married. They could marry soon enough to hide the obvious, which wasn't so obvious yet, so she chose to wait, unable to face the disappointment that would be guaranteed from her aunt. "I wanted to ask if you would stand by me?" Melissa waited with the promise that she would accept. Her auntie became so delighted that tears sprang to her eyes.

"Yes, oh, yes love, I'm honored," she happily accepted.

Melissa and her auntie embraced across the large oak table. Melissa didn't dare look toward John, although she had a pretty good idea of the expression on his face right about now.

John sat there astounded as he watched their joyful embrace. What was she thinking? Why didn't she tell her? By now he was fuming. Was she embarrassed about the situation? They loved each other so it shouldn't matter. She may have bypassed her aunt's chastising but it wouldn't slip by with him. He started thinking of a good reason to excuse them both from the table when Melissa spoke first, fabricating a yawn.

"If you two don't mind, I'm going to retire early tonight." Her chair slid back across the hardwood floor, and as she rose her aunt rose as well.

"Of course, love. I'll clean up, then head off to bed myself," and with that, Miss Beckett gathered the empty plates and carried them into the kitchen.

Still avoiding John's knowing glare, Melissa stole more chocolate pudding while her aunt was gone. She turned toward the stairway when a strong hand grabbed her arm before reaching the first step. His tall form stood behind her, his breath warm on her ear. "I thought you ate sufficiently enough for two, why more pudding?" he pointed out, pressing the fact that she hadn't mentioned a word to her aunt about the baby.

Her head half turned to answer him. "I've got a craving for it. Dr. Marlow said I could have cravings."

His pale eyes stared into her profile, so close it burned her, then his mouth came even closer to her ear, whispering his intentions. "Don't pretend to be asleep when I come up. We need to talk. I'm going to assist your aunt right now." He let go of her arm and in a half spin strode toward the kitchen.

Melissa sat on top of her lavender coverlet on the bed wearing only a white linen robe and nothing underneath. Her head rested against the wooden headboard and her legs stretched out with ankles crossed. She thought about the lecture she would have to endure from her future husband while eagerly dipping her fingers into a pile of chocolate pudding. She savored the flavor of the sweet dessert, licking each deliciously coated finger, praying he would be easy on her. She would have to make him understand while at the same time carrying on her "containment" charade. It would not be that easy as she had angered him, and if the only way to calm him was to give in and make love to him, she might have to forfeit this time.

It had been a good half hour since she'd come to her room. Finished with the pudding, she put the plate on the oak nightstand and waited. She jumped when the bedroom door finally opened. John's tall, dark form filled the doorway as he entered. He locked the door behind him and stepped over to a chair, sat down and proceeded to take off his boots.

He was about to unbutton his shirt when Melissa asked, "Do you think it's a good idea for you to sleep here?" Innocence washed over her beautiful face when he looked directly at her.

"I'm not about to sleep on the couch if that's what you're asking." He sounded sure of himself.

He went back to undressing when she replied, "I was only thinking of what impression we would give my aunt."

John stood, beyond caring what excuses Melissa had as he slung his shirt across the back of the chair. "You've already given her a false impression, Melissa. You couldn't tell her about our child." His voice raised in volume to emphasize his point as he continued undressing by expelling his trousers. There was an idle pause between them as he stood naked before her. He was sure of where he was sleeping tonight. Without an ounce of modesty he stepped over to her like a sleek panther, his black mane hanging free and wild, his gray eyes darkening as they narrowed on her. "Why didn't you tell her about the baby?" he inquired, interested to hear her reason.

Melissa slid over to the opposite side of the bed against the wall. The panther had caged her in where he wanted her. Lifting the covers, John climbed in and covered himself. He was propping up his pillow when she responded, "Because it's not the order of things. We should be married first, then I should be pregnant."

His head sank into the feathered pillow, his hands intertwined on top of his mid-section. "Well, we can't undo what is already done. In our case it shouldn't matter," he told her, his expression grim as he turned in her direction.

Melissa looked toward the wooden ceiling, counting the beams as she came up with a plan. Her gaze fell back to John's waiting glare. "I have a resolution that will work. I'm sure you would agree and it would save us the embarrassment of our situation." She spoke with enthusiasm while his features remained unchanged. She wasn't prepared for his brief interruption.

"I am not embarrassed by our situation, and I wasn't aware that you were either," he announced calmly.

Melissa sighed at his misinterpretation. "John, all I meant was that if we were married soon, while I'm not showing, no one except Robert, Rose, you, and I will know that the baby was conceived before we were married."

After she explained, it didn't sound so bad, but it would anger him if she were embarrassed or ashamed of their creation. "So you're not ashamed of the baby?" he asked, disturbed at why she would put off the inevitable.

How could he think she'd be ashamed of their child? It was the standard of society, the forever scorning they would have to endure because of their promiscuous situation. She worried about John's reputation as his prominence in horse racing could label him.

Rising to lean on a bent elbow she pleaded with him. "Please don't ever think I'm ashamed of our baby. That simply isn't true. I'm worried about our reputations with your colleagues and sorts."

He had never cared what society thought before. If people didn't like him, they didn't like him, although that had never been the case since people knew John to be a straightforward, honest person and he'd been accepted as such. "Melissa, I don't care what society thinks, you should know that. I'm surprised you do," he said, taking in her eyes that reflected concern. "If you're concerned about it, you shouldn't be. Other people do things that you probably wouldn't approve of, and do they care what you think? I highly doubt it." His features had softened. He stared another moment into the beautiful face of his fiancé. Observing a dab of chocolate pudding on her chin, he wiped the pudding from her chin and slipped his thumb into his mouth. "What about your aunt? I can't believe you won't tell her. Of anyone you should care about her thoughts." He truly couldn't understand her reasoning regarding her aunt as he believed them to be remarkably close.

"John, I do, of course, I do, but she will be critical of me. She will lecture me and...Why can't we announce our news after we marry? Auntie will be the first person I tell." She begged for his understanding.

A heavy sigh unleashed from him before responding. "If you prefer waiting to tell everyone else I'm agreeable, but I think you should at least tell your aunt."

In her gut she knew he was right, as usual, but since they had some time before the wedding there wasn't any rush to hear her aunt's preaching words.

She had tired of his somber mood and needed to change the atmosphere. Her whole demeanor changed as she rose from her reclining position to straddle his lavender-covered hips. "You're absolutely right. I'll tell her soon," she agreed, her hands reaching to grasp his shoulders.

His strong hands caught hers mid-motion. She gave in too easily. She wanted to move on, obviously having another agenda on her mind, and once they had cleared up the present issue he'd be more than happy to oblige. His fingers slipped through hers, their clasped hands falling to the sides of his hips. "You have one week Melissa Howard, soon to be Melissa Blackburn. You will endure her lecture that you're so obstinately trying to avoid, and then everything will be splendid." His words were softly spoken but stern. Trying to be reasonable with her sometimes wasn't easy. She had a stubborn streak he was all too aware of.

"John, you've never had to experience my aunt when she's flustered. It's not a joy."

Her tone, sounding almost childlike, didn't affect him one bit. "Melissa you've had to endure more harsh circumstances than your aunt's chastising. Tell her and get it over with. You can't change your condition, sweetheart. You have a baby growing inside of you. Our baby. I'm sure once the shock wears off your aunt will be delighted." He watched and waited.

She sensed twin silver flares melting into her even though her own eyes stared absently into his broad chest that lay uncovered. Her focus slowly traveled along the strong muscles of his chest, extending up the length of his tightly corded neck. His pronounced chin came into view and then soft full lips, where her focus lingered. She studied his features before forcing her eyes to meet with his, and she smiled thinking about their future as a family. "She will know within one week. I promise.

He knew with careful deliberation she would agree with him. In his eyes, the matter seemed simple to resolve, but it didn't seem to be for her. If she could be patient and endure her aunt's biting words, the sooner it would be over with and the sooner she could move on. He'd had plenty of practice thanks to his overbearing, drunk of a father. It hadn't mattered what the issue was, his father's anger toward his mother was taken out on him on almost a daily basis after his mother's death. When John could stand no more he'd left and went to stay with Robert and his father.

My Forbidden Mentor

"I'll hold you to that promise, and if you don't tell her, I will tell her myself," he told her.

He meant to keep his promise, she could count on that. Leaning forward, Melissa softened him by placing a surrendering kiss on his lips. "I promise," she whispered as her lips came down on his. The kiss was a soft and tender touching of lips but intent on becoming eager, so Melissa immediately lifted away. You were going to have him beg and plead, remember?

She lifted their entwined hands to place them on the supple rise of her belly, trying to divert his attention away from any sinful thoughts she had provoked.

He became aware of her diversion. Nothing could distract him now. His eyes were glossy, heated, while his clasped hands followed her circular motions over her belly. He became so absorbed in their joint intimacy toward their unborn child that he barely heard the question she asked as his mind was focused on more delicious thoughts. He concentrated on pulling down the blankets, releasing his ardent erection, and penetrating deep inside the hot passage that awaited him. His fingers were beginning to reach for the ties of her robe when he remembered that she had asked him something. His smoky eyes lifted to hers. "What did you ask me?"

Her fingers gripped around his, holding his position at the ties of her robe. "I asked if there was anyone in your family that needed to know about the baby right away?" she asked again, perceptive to his changing mood.

John thought about it. "No, no one I can think of right now." His passionate state had been altered, as just when his thoughts were determined not to be deterred, a mental image of his father intruded. His eyes drifted down to their holding hands.

"John, what about your father?" Melissa inquired, hoping she wouldn't anger John by pushing the issue he seemed to be avoiding.

The heated glaze in his eyes turned cold when they found hers again and his jaw tightened. He hadn't wished to be in this mood, especially with Melissa. "What about him?"

Hearing strain persist in his tone, he obviously held back an explosion that could erupt at any time, and although it seemed dangerous to pursue, Melissa truly believed it needed to be discussed. His father would be their child's grandfather, regardless if he and John were getting along. Wondering if there could be any kind of peace made, she responded with hope. "John I completely understand your hatred toward your father, but he will be our child's grandfather. Can there be any peace at all for the child's sake?" After hearing her curious words the turbulence of his anger came forth like a tidal wave she was willing to ride if she could endure its whipping force.

Peace? Why in the world would she even imagine peace between us, he thought. As far as he was concerned his father would have to earn his way back into his life, much less have any relations with his grandchild. "Melissa I don't believe you have even a minute inkling of the hatred I feel for my father. He is as hard and cold as they come. He will never make a good role model for our child." His distant eyes veered away, knowing he needed to face the fact that one day he and his father would come to heavy blows regarding the same matter he and Melissa were discussing at the present moment. Once his father heard about his marriage he would come storming around, for John hadn't planned on inviting him to their wedding. He wasn't about to be humiliated at his own wedding with the presence of his father escorting his newest whore on his arm.

My Forbidden Mentor

When his focus returned to her softness appeared. "He was never there for me Melissa. What makes you think he'll be there for our child? It's better to leave him out of our lives. So no, there can never be peace between us."

Melissa was taken aback by his harsh words. All she had meant to do was try to make some kind of amends for the child's sake. It quickly became clear to her that after all these years peace between John and his father seemed lost. John's mind had been made up so further deliberating would be a waste of time. Like moving mountains with her bare hands, it would never happen. Assuming this chapter of their lives was closed she concentrated on making peace again with her perturbed future husband. "You're right, my love. I will never bring the subject up again. You know better than anyone how cruel your father can be." She gave him a smile. "I didn't mean to push, except that since my father has passed on your father is the only grandparent that lives," she trailed off, remembering her ever so recent promise of not mentioning his father again, but her feelings had come out of their own free will.

Seeing her eyes glass over was like stabbing a dagger in his gut. Here his father lived and he couldn't stand him, and her father had passed on and was adored and respected. Such was the irony of their situation. John would have gladly traded their fathers' positions. Now he felt that he needed to comfort his future wife for he hadn't fully understood her reasoning to push him about his father until now. "Forgive me, sweetheart." His free hand came up to brush loose golden strands behind her ear. "I didn't mean to seem insensitive toward you. I can't explain in detail the rage my father makes me feel, but I vow to never be the kind of father he was to me. My child will know that I care. I will be there for our child always. I will have to be father and grandfather I suppose."

"You're only one person John. Just be a father. Besides, we will have Robert for an uncle, and hopefully Rose as an aunt, and we can't forget my auntie as a great aunt."

She was a strong person, stronger than he. On the outside he appeared tough and in control, but on the inside turmoil roared. Emotions from childhood were left unresolved and when they festered, they seemed radical. But where Melissa appeared vulnerable on the outside, John knew deep down there was true strength in her, true faith, true love. He admired her spirit. That was one thing he loved most about her. The second, and most delicious, had him stirring once again. "That reminds me, you haven't met Rose yet. You two will get along famously. You're a lot alike, except for the obvious." His first smile in some time was shining through now and he had her playing along with his bantering of words.

"I assume you're referring to her line of work?" Melissa asked.

"Yes."

"Would you object if I decided on that line of work for myself?"

John's head tipped back in laughter, thinking her crazy for even thinking about it. "You won't work as you won't have to now. You will have a husband to take care of you."

He's so sure of himself, she thought. Let's bring him down a notch or two. "Yes, but what if I really wanted to?" she teased as her fingertips glided along the outline of his lips.

His smile started to fade. She's baiting me, he told himself. "Why would you?"

"Well, you specified financially you would take care me, but—" She couldn't finish because he cut into her words so fast she forgot what she was about to say.

My Forbidden Mentor

"No. No is the answer, as if you didn't already know that. Believe me, I will take care of all your needs, especially what you're referring to." His smile had completely vanished now, taking the situation very seriously.

Melissa was enjoying the payback and wasn't about to end it anytime soon. It was time for him to beg and plead.

She placed a light kiss on his tightened lips then straightened in her position astride him. "John, what if you can't keep up with my wanton needs?" Her pretty pout began to set into place.

Immediately he sat up straight. They were face to face with her thighs straddled along his lean hips. If it weren't for the barrier of the blankets she would have yielded by now. His face was so close that the heat from his heavy breaths burned her lips. His eyes captured hers as he spoke in a sultry whisper. "Be my whore, my wife, my innocent lover, and the mother of my children. That's how I want you."

She placed her hands upon his as they rested on her linen-covered thighs, trying to conceal the shivers he just inflicted. Her teasing became relentless, like he had taught her. "In that order?" she asked, the lust in her eyes matched his.

"Whatever order is in need at the time, sweetheart."

"And what need are you finding in me right now?"

His hands left hers as they dipped beneath the opening of her robe. His fingers slid along her smooth thighs, reaching her shapely waist to finally settle against her buttocks.

Scorching heat penetrated her skin where his strong hands were cupping her. She decided now was the time to leave his heated embrace if she wished to contain herself.

Then he returned an answer. "I believe you know what I'm in need of. You have a special talent for sensing my necessities like no one else," he murmured as he squeezed her firm flesh. His eyes closed while his mouth reached for hers, but he never found her lips, instead feeling movement from the mattress underneath him. His hands fell to his lap and his eyes flew open. She stood by the boudoir brushing her hair.

This is insane, she told herself, taking long strokes with the brush. He has me so hot right now I hope I can go through with this. All this to prove a ridiculous point.

"What is this all about? You're acting very peculiar, sweetheart. You know very well that I'm sitting here ready for you, and yet you get up to brush your hair? I don't see the concern with vanity at this moment, when your lovely hair will be disheveled by the time we're through." He settled back down on the mattress and onto his side with his elbow bent and the palm of his hand taking the weight of his head, staring at her, confused by her actions.

Her head shifted to look over her shoulder at him. "Is that so?" she said, continuing to brush. "You didn't specify what you were in need of, so how am I to know how to act accordingly?" She turned away from him because it became unbearable to look his way any longer. He was handsome and chiseled and pure male anatomy, and she would falter if she continued to gaze at him.

He watched her hand gripping the ivory brush, languidly sweeping gold streams of hair, and every shining stroke caressed him even more. "Melissa, you know what I meant by my words. I don't need a whore, I need you." What kind of game is she playing? Then it dawned on him as he remembered their earlier jesting about self-control.

"Well, I'm glad you're honest. I want us to be honest with each other," she replied.

My Forbidden Mentor

It didn't matter, John thought, he was onto her game now. "Melissa." He spoke her name in a sultry, fevered voice, making her shift his way with speedy promptness. Having gained her full attention he took advantage of the situation. "I have something for you, sweet." The brush in her hand dropped to her lap while witnessing his fingers peeling back the lavender coverlet from his hips. John knew he had her by the dreamlike stare she demonstrated. Her eyes were fixed and glowing with rampant need, a familiar glow he was attuned to. "I need you. Do you need me?"

He was sleek, dark, and knew all too well the effect he had on her, the predator enticing his weakening prey. He had her purring and dripping with desire. He knew she was hungry for him and he lay there with the means necessary to satisfy her hunger. She easily set the brush upon the boudoir without looking, her eyes mesmerized, her body rising from the chair as she stepped toward the languid god in heat. Their eyes fastened on one another and there was no doubt she had surrendered. "Yes, I need you." Her tone became charged and silky. She began untying her robe, her eyes never leaving his.

He could not only see the heat in her eyes, he could feel it, and her being hot for him increased his own passionate state. "That's my girl," he said in a somewhat shaky voice.

Her smile showed impish but was betrayed by the innocent blushing of her cheeks. "Yes, I'm yours."

Her words sent tremors down his spine, only to be devastated further when her robe came open. The white robe, framing her womanly figure, contrasted sharply against her golden skin before slipping to the hardwood floor. "Oh Lord, you're beautiful," John told her on an intake of breath. He scooted over to make room on the bed.

His fingers stroked her body. "Oh John, you make me feel good, so good," she moaned when suddenly the sound of coughing startled her.

"Shh," John warned.

Obviously he'd heard it too but chose to ignore her auntie's signal that said she was quite aware of what was going on. Panicking, Melissa's rattled nerves shattered any desires left to be explored. "We better stop," she suggested to John, her body stiffening as she said it.

"Why?" John asked in disappointment, clearly opting to forget about her aunt's interference. "Just be quiet."

"I can't be quiet, you know that," she responded in a harsh whisper as John's lips trailed down her backside.

"Just try," he implored, anxious to relieve the burning, aching needs his manhood had commanded and expected to be filled by this time.

Normally she would have given in to John's enticing ways but this time she couldn't. Concerned with what impression her aunt would have, she stopped herself and him. "No, I think we had better stop."

"Melissa, this isn't fair. I'm ready to burst," he complained.

"I'm sorry, you don't think I'm not in misery?" she said as she flipped onto her back. "Her cough was obviously a warning."

"Melissa, I'm to be your husband. Your aunt is not naïve and I'm sure she's well aware we've already been intimate."

"It's different when she's in the room next door. I don't know what I was thinking," she said, sitting up and shaking her head in disgust.

"You weren't thinking, you were feeling, just as I was. Now come here." He sat up, reaching with his forearm to grasp around her waist when she slipped away from him. "What are you doing?" he asked as she rose from the bed.

"I'm putting on a night dress," she told him, stepping over to her closet.

"A night dress won't stop me, Melissa. You know I prefer you to lie naked with me."

"John, lying naked with you right now is too dangerous."

"Melissa." He said her name with a clear warning attached to it, and exerted a breath of frustration as he lay flat on the bed. He didn't give up but quietly persuaded, "All right, come to bed, naked please, and I won't pursue you."

"Promise?" she asked as she inched her way toward him.

"Promise," he agreed, adding in an aggravated breath, "Even though this is insane."

"John," she exclaimed in warning, hesitating before climbing into the bed.

"You have my word, now come to bed sweet," he promised, sounding disappointed again, but sincere.

"I love you, John," she told him as she snuggled up to him.

"I love you too," he responded, pulling her closer.

Chapter Twenty-Eight

"John's not going to like this," Robert told Rose while guiding her into the carriage. They had just come from Sally's place after having the privilege of a confrontation with Duke Albert. He had questioned them extensively about John's new lady friend.

"What are you going to tell John?" Rose asked.

His hand skimmed through his dark brown hair in a swift motion. While leaning his head into the seat, he released a long held breath. "The truth, I suppose. Warn him, if that will do him any good." His head straightened and turned toward Rose, his emerald eyes searching her light blue ones. "John's handled his father before. It's just that he seems so happy now and I know when his father gets a hold of him, well, the scene probably won't be good. I hope Melissa doesn't have to be subjected to Duke Albert's callus ways. He can be downright cruel, as you've witnessed yourself."

Rose cast Robert a soft smile, her delicate hand smoothing Robert's roughened cheek. "John will protect Melissa, Rob. He won't let his father near her if that's the way it should be."

Robert took Rose's hand in his, caressing it. "You're right." He smiled back and then became serious. The subject he was about to approach with her they had discussed numerous times before. They would always compromise, he more than she, Robert felt, but the time had come when Robert could no longer compromise.

My Forbidden Mentor

He knew he was taking the chance of pushing her too far, but he had to make her understand once and for all how it was for him, how hard it was with their arranged situation. His voice was low and non-threatening. "Rose, I have other concerns besides John and Melissa, and they include us." He saw her face change as it always had before, for she knew instantly what he wanted to talk about.

"Not much longer, Rob. I promise. I'm almost there," she assured him.

But Robert had already pondered over and over the last day or so and had come to a decision he hoped he wouldn't regret. His eyes shut as if to endure her words one more time. "Rose, I know you're true to your word, but we've been together for eight or nine months now." His hand tightened on hers. "What I'm trying to say is..."

Rose could feel the same argument coming about and chose to cut it short for she had a goal to reach and Robert was well aware of it. "Robert, we have been over and over this. I know it's not easy for you, but you've got to believe that my love is all for you, and in a short while I'll be able to show you full-time how much I love you."

Robert stuck by his decision. He'd become tired of the ridiculous situation, and seeing John and Melissa together had encouraged his change of course. "Please let me finish. This isn't easy for me."

Sternness carried from his voice into his features, a look Rose soon realized was different from those during of their previous discussions. "All right," she replied and listened with patience.

Robert cleared his throat and spoke with calm measure. "I love you, Rose. I have never loved anyone as much as I love you. The work you do is extremely trying at times, and I suppose I've come to a point where I can no longer deal with the other men. I've been patient and I've been understanding, but I can't do it anymore." He observed her eyes becoming watery and wanted to kick himself for making her cry, but he had prepared himself that this might happen. "This is hard for me, Rose." He took a long awaited pause, for his next words he had hoped he could have avoided. "But unless you can let go of this lifestyle and be my wife...we need to part ways."

There was the expected silence as the two lovers searched and held each other with their eyes. For a man who never cried, the urge to do so was sorely tempting. He knew it wouldn't be easy and now it was up to Rose to determine their future. Tears started to stream down her cheeks as she pleaded in a last ditch effort to change his mind. "I'm almost there, Rob," she said in a whispered tone, hardly audible, her sobs catching in her throat.

Robert could barely swallow. It tore him up to see the woman he loved in pain, but his pain was just as real so he offered once again a solution to their dilemma. "If you marry me, Rose, you won't have to worry about being almost there. Can't you swallow a little of your pride and let me take care of you?"

Through teary eyes Rose stared at Robert as if he had asked her to give up her most prize possession. Her hard work was about to pay off, but it seemed obvious Robert's patience had worn thin. "I understand. I suppose there's only one solution," Rose replied, a hand violently wiping away the embarrassing tears from her ivory cheeks. Robert watched her as she gathered her belongings in a swift motion.

"What solution is that?" he asked, lost in her abrupt madness.

My Forbidden Mentor

Her face turned away from him, putting an end to searching the handsome features she would never see again. "Turn the carriage around. I want to go home."

Robert's gaze lingered into her mass of copper tresses. Disappointed by the way she had decided to handle their situation, anger began to flare over any other emotions that were surfacing. "Why does it have to be this way, Rose?"

Her response was to remain quiet as sadness filled her breaking heart. Losing Robert in such a quick manner was not what she had bargained for. She wanted to be his wife and have his children in the near future, but the pressure to make a choice was too much too soon, which in turn cast defensive motions against him. "It is my only option. Please turn this carriage around." Turning around to face him she waited for his battling reply. Robert reluctantly motioned for the driver to turn the carriage around and they rode back in silence, both staring out their own windows, immersed in their own thoughts.

As they approached Sally's Place Robert gave her another chance to change her mind. "You have more options than this one and you know it, Rose. Is it wrong for me to want you all for myself?"

Her blue eyes searched his face one last time. The carriage halted and that was her cue to leave. She lifted from the suede seat, opened the door and took a step out. Robert gazed into her backside for as long as she stood there. His hopes lifted when she suddenly swiveled around, baring blue eyes that were sparkling with new tears. "Please remember this, Robert. I love you no matter what happens. I am not trying to intentionally hurt you." She couldn't take any more so she fled.

Robert's first reaction was to chase after her. It killed him to see her in pain. He'd grown tired of sharing her. It was for the best. Perhaps in time things would change, but then, perhaps not. He let her go, and in a sullen tone he told his driver to carry on.

He thought of visiting John. He was the only one who could cheer him up. He was heading in the direction of John's manor when he remembered John had Melissa now and they would be at her house. No doubt they were still there. His course changed toward his own home.

John's luck wasn't any better. He'd gone a whole week now without the pleasures of Melissa's body. He thought her reasoning was ridiculous but he wasn't about to force himself on her. Lying next to her warm body night after night without imposing any touching had become unbearable though, so he had devised a plan which had almost worked. If he couldn't have her at night in bed, he'd thought he would have her in the daylight hours in the barn.

First he had checked Miss Beckett's progress with her cooking, making sure she'd be busy enough not to disturb them. Next, he waited until Melissa was busy with her chores in the barn. Finding her arranging bales of hay, John had strutted in, pleased with himself and presenting a sinful grin that immediately curved into a frown. She was not one to ask for help and as he watched her lift a heavy bale of hay he had become angry. She was pregnant but acting like she wasn't with her physical activity. His pace increased before bending his legs and taking the weight from her, tossing the bale onto the next stack. He had startled her but he didn't care. He turned around to face her. "What are you doing?" he questioned with eyes burning into her and waiting for a reasonable response, even though there wouldn't be one.

It dawned on her why he was so angry, his concern for the baby. She hadn't seen a problem with the activity as she

My Forbidden Mentor

was feeling fine. In fact, of late she was actually feeling great. Her morning nausea was subsiding and her body was beginning to change, adding a healthy glow to her whole being. She'd never been happier except for one thing: being intimate with John. She knew he was probably going crazy. So was she, but unfortunately she couldn't bring herself to make love with her aunt's bedroom next to hers. She couldn't hold in her passion for John and when they had made love before there had always been yelling involved.

How do I get out of this one, she wondered? The innocent routine took over. "I'm stacking hay, John. What does it look like I'm doing?"

His sternness didn't veer. She knew exactly what he meant. Stepping over to her, he lifted her into his arms and set her atop a stack of baled hay. With his hands set firmly into the sides of her waist he began his lecture. "I hope you haven't forgotten that you're carrying our child." He saw her mouth open to voice a reply but continued anyway. "And I hope you remember that you have a strong male body around to help you with these chores." Talking about their child reminded him of her promise to tell her aunt within a week. Had she defaulted, because there hadn't been any word to him about it? "By the way, did you tell your aunt about the baby?"

She realized that she really had forgotten with all the chores she endeavored in the past week. "Not yet, but I will," she rushed out.

"When?"

"Give me one more week."

"Why?"

"It's not that simple for me, John. But I will do it."

Her saddened eyes hit his soft spot. How did she do it, making him give in so easily? "Five days, starting today, and that's it." Although he was cross with her, he had to admit he loved the challenge of her.

Her innocent look remained as she flashed her eyes at him. "Yes, my lord. I will do it. Will there be further punishment?" she teased.

From the tone of her voice, John took this as an open invitation. "That's more like it, and yes, I do believe that further punishment is necessary. I need to remind you of the mistake you made today." His lips curved into a sensual grin.

Melissa returned his grin with her own heavenly smile and his head bent forward so he could kiss her. She met his lips with the same aching need. Punishment forgotten, his fingers gripped her waist tighter while her hands slid into his hair. She groaned as their bodies intertwined. "I like your kind of punishment."

"Then I'll have to punish you more often," he whispered against her mouth. Their lips crushed together, never parting as their need intensified. John wrapped Melissa's legs around his waist and lifted her into his arms to carry her to a secluded spot behind the elevated stacks of hay. Gently, he laid her on a pile of fresh loose hay, and followed her down.

Melissa's hands skimmed along his neck and then pulled at the shirttails tucked in the waistband of his trousers. She started to undo the buttons on his pants when he pushed her hands out of the way.

His mouth came above hers. "They're down far enough," he growled.

"Hurry then," Melissa said, impatient to be with him again.

My Forbidden Mentor

"John, Melissa, are you two in here?"

John couldn't believe his luck. "No, this isn't happening," he breathed along Melissa's cheek, but the familiar voice grew in volume and he knew he couldn't continue. Quickly, he buttoned his trousers closed.

Melissa managed to straighten her clothing before a tall shadowy figure stopped next to the stack of hay, staying out of view.

"Are you two decent now?" he asked, giving them the time they needed. He had heard their heavy breathing and knew inevitably what he had interrupted. No doubt John would remind him of it later, but he wouldn't have stopped them except that he had extremely important issues he needed to discuss.

"Robert, your timing is impeccable. You seem to have a knack for it," John replied, disappointed once again.

Robert's handsome face peeked around the corner of a bale of hay. With a mischievous grin on his face, he said, "Sorry."

"It's all right, Robert. It must be important or you wouldn't have, uh, interrupted us." Disappointment could be heard in her voice as well, but not as raw sounding as John's.

John agreed with Melissa, but he wanted to make his point clear, even to his best friend. "This had better be worth it Robert. I was about to receive a much needed release."

Melissa, shocked by John's blunt words to Robert, leaned forward and punched his arm.

"Ouch. What was that for?" John asked, looking over his shoulder into the angry features of his future wife while his hand began rubbing his sore arm.

"Behave yourself, John. How dare you speak to Robert in that manner?"

"We always tell each other how it is. You had better get used to it."

Melissa's mouth dropped open at the same time Robert turned away with a squint appearing on his face. He knew there was an explosion about to go off. John had pushed her too far this time.

Her eyes shot up to John's when she spoke. "Well Robert, I will agree with John that your timing is impeccable. I think John deserves to wait another week for his *much needed release*." She stormed off toward the house.

Robert apologized again, profusely, upon finding out that John had been patiently waiting a full week to bed his woman. Quickly, he moved on to the reasons why he had come by. First he informed John that Vanessa had miscarried. John was more relieved than anything, even though a tinge of guilt surfaced with the relief for he would never wish anyone to lose a child, but these circumstances were different and it was for the best.

Robert went on to tell John what had transpired between he and Rose, getting John's opinion about the whole ordeal. John had always told Robert he'd been much more patient than he would have been. He wouldn't have tolerated Rose's kind of work that long, but he knew Robert loved Rose like no other so he didn't push his opinion too often. In the end John sympathized with Robert, offering to talk to Rose himself but Robert declined. He prayed Rose would come to her senses on her own and realize exactly what she was giving up.

After their private talk John invited Robert to stay for supper, knowing Miss Beckett would have more than enough food, and Robert accepted.

My Forbidden Mentor

Melissa remained silent the rest of the evening toward John. He knew that eventually she would overcome her anger regarding their little spat. Tonight didn't matter anymore because by now another plan was already forming, and this one would be precise and without fault. There was no way he'd wait one more week to bed her. No way, he'd become desperate.

Chapter Twenty-Nine

The blue velvet blankets were becoming a welcome familiarity as Melissa awoke in John's oversized bed, stretching along the softness of tangled velvet covers and cream satin sheets. Her hand reached for his warm masculine body but instead found a cold empty space. Disappointed, she remembered John would have already left for the day. His business affairs had been put off and he needed to address them.

Leaping out of bed to get dressed her mind scrambled with plans to explore John's household. She could hardly wait. And then there were the stables. Great anticipation filled her senses as she journeyed forward.

By early afternoon Melissa had toured most of the grounds. John's stables impressed her the most. She'd never been around such well cared after horses. He had twenty-two, and she had counted them as she greeted each one. All twenty-two had their own stalls and all twenty-two were exercised every single day. She had to agree that John was top notch when it came to the care of his thoroughbreds. Making her day even more splendid was his household staff, who had been kind and helpful with whatever she needed.

Late afternoon found Melissa in the library. An orange glow casting from the sun's rays filtered through the large windowpane of the library. The glowing light rested on a wall filled with immense selections of history books and horse books. Melissa stood before the lighted wall of books, skimming through the titles to select one. There were so

My Forbidden Mentor

many books that looked interesting that she ended up picking out the first one her fingers landed on. Sitting upon the burgundy velvet couch she started to open the book when her thoughts ran astray.

She remembered how proud she'd felt when she'd finally told her auntie about the child she carried. To her surprise her auntie had hugged her first before imposing her lecturing words, words consisting of how she should have waited to indulge in such intimate activity no matter how inviting her fiancé. Melissa had sat and listened, like John had suggested she do, and afterward it wasn't so bad.

Then her thoughts drifted to John and how one week ago he'd swept her upon his mare and headed for his manor. Her mouth curved into a private smile reminiscing about John's innocent confession their first night at his manor, how he had carefully plotted his plan to be alone with her. The sound of booted footsteps startled her out of her thoughts. Thinking it was John, she laid the book down and rose to greet him, but the man who appeared in the doorway was not John. It was someone she'd never met before.

Being fairly tall, with salt and pepper hair and a mustache to match, he looked vaguely familiar. His eyes were blue, not gray like John's, but he could still pass as a relative. His brazen smile was handsome, consisting of perfect white teeth, and there was a dangerous air about him that struck her as he approached her. He leaned forward to take her hand. "How do you do? I'm Duke Albert," he said with expert finesse.

His presence was as powerful as he made it, so as her shaky hand went to his she returned the introduction. "Hello, I'm Melissa Howard. You must be John's father."

Albert's grin widened before placing a delicate kiss upon her hand. "Yes, I am. Where is that son of mine? I have important business to discuss with him," he declared, his head leaning through the double doorway, motioning for Charles.

While the duke ordered cognac from Charles, Melissa sat on the couch again. All she could think about was when John would return home. He'd know how to handle his father. What if I slip, she thought? What if I give away our marriage plans and the baby?

She tried to remain calm while watching Duke Albert step toward her only to recline in a chair across from her. "John is out on business right now. I expect him home soon."

At her mention of the word "home" she saw Albert's black brow arch in curiosity. "You're living here with John?" he asked, his gaze piercing her while waiting for a reply.

It took her a moment to figure out how to respond and she proceeded with what came to mind. "I...," she stammered, attempting to continue until Albert rudely interrupted.

"Ah, temporarily. You're no more serious than a mistress, then?"

Melissa's jaw fell open at his carefree remark and was about to tell him the truth when he stunned her again.

"Well you must be somewhat serious or John wouldn't keep you here in his home." Albert quickly reassured Melissa regarding her presence. "Your status is fine with me, my dear, for it leaves many options open."

Her mouth came back in position as the muscles tightened along the proud tilt of her jaw. "What do you mean by "many options", Duke Albert?"

Albert chuckled at the humor of the situation. The expression on the young lady's face was uniquely innocent. "Don't be so naive, my dear. I must say, though, John has had many beautiful women in his time, but this time..." He lazily scanned her figure. "I think he's outdone himself. Are you from the country, girl?"

She was beginning to understand John's loathing toward his father. She couldn't imagine growing up with his overbearing, arrogant, self-serving attitude. "Why does it matter where I'm from?"

"You've got fire, girl. I like that. No wonder my son is so enamored with you. What I mean to say is that if you and John ever take separate paths, I could substantially replace him."

Melissa couldn't utter a word and just sat there with a horrified look on her face, not believing the words that had just come out of her future father-in-law's mouth.

Albert planned to continue when John burst through the doorway, heading straight for him.

"That's enough. I want you to leave," he said in a very loud, but controlled voice. John had only heard his father's last remark, but it was enough information for him to guess the nature of the conversation, especially when witnessing the shocked look on Melissa's face. Seeing his father's sly grin angered him even more as he stood before him with his arms folded across his chest. He remained rigid and unfaltering. "Now, before I explode and won't be responsible for my actions."

"You're just going to throw me out without hearing what I have to say?" Albert said.

"I've heard enough of what you have to say and I didn't like it."

"I think you should hear me out before you assume," his father pleaded.

"I am not going to waste my time battling words with you. I asked you to leave." John watched his father rise from the chair to face him.

His voice bellowed. "How can you treat me like scum? Your own father!"

Melissa's hand covered her mouth. John hadn't exaggerated about his father's ruthless ways.

John's narrowed eyes converted to ice and were directed right into the blue storm of his father's. "You're the bastard here, father. You had enough balls to proposition my fiancé." Filled with rage, John didn't flinch at what he'd revealed, and prepared to deal with his father's wrath, waiting for the inevitable explosion.

"Your fiancé? When were you going to share that bit of news with your father? If I had known, I never would have said what I did," Albert responded.

"I never planned on telling you. You've never been a part of my life, why start now?" John explained.

"Come on, John, if you're getting married it means serious business for the family. It means grandchildren."

John turned away, his fingers pushing into his temples. "No way," he spoke through clenched teeth, spinning back toward his father. "No way, you cannot expect me to let you be involved with your grandchildren."

"Why not? They should be a part of my life. I'll be their grandfather, after all." For a moment Duke Albert actually sounded hurt.

Leaning forward into his father's person, his voice lowered an octave. "Listen. In my mind you killed my mother and you destroyed her life. You're not going to destroy mine, which includes your grandchildren." Albert remained silent. Noticeably a tender spot had been opened. It was the first time in a long time John had witnessed a sign of remorse from his father.

Collecting his composure, Albert carried on. "Your mother's death was an accident and you know it. I loved your mother."

From years of hate and not caring for his son's welfare, John ignored the moment of sensitivity his father displayed, knowing it wouldn't last. "She died at your hands." His words were brutal but the pain simmering behind them was real. His father couldn't erase eighteen years of misery in five minutes. Emotions from past memories began surfacing, causing him extreme discomfort. On the verge of a breakdown, John summoned Charles. "Charles."

"You know son, you're not the only one who has suffered. Have some compassion, man."

Charles emerged right away, aware of his lord's situation. "Yes, my lord."

"Would you please escort my father to the door. He's leaving."

"Yes sir," Charles said, motioning for the duke to take his leave as the lord requested.

Albert obliged, gathering his coat and giving Melissa a quick smile. He studied his son with admiration. "You can't ignore me, John." His statement made John look him in the eye.

"Believe me, I'll try," he responded through tightened lips.

An expression of disillusionment graced his father's face as he turned to leave.

"Wait," John said.

Albert became hopeful despite the hostility between them as he longed to make reasonable peace. "Change of heart, son?"

"No. And by the way, father, next time you carouse with a whore, make sure you use protection. You're not always lucky. Now will you please apologize to Melissa?" John wasn't sure why he was compelled to give his father advice, perhaps so John wouldn't be forced to help his father in the future. This time he'd gotten lucky, unfortunately, with the death of an unplanned baby.

Albert's blue eyes bored into his son's angry features, realizing at that moment the extent of his son's loathing toward him, which was beyond what he had imagined. Instead of his usual war of words, he did as John asked, thinking it might make a difference. "I don't know what the devil you're talking about son." His eyes shifted to Melissa when John didn't explain his remark. "I apologize, Miss Howard. I was unaware of your status with my son. I wish to be friends in the future despite my son's animosity."

Melissa had been seated on the couch observing their confrontation. On the edge of her seat, with fists tightening at her sides, she resisted the urge to stand up for John. Even though he had handled himself with grand composure, Melissa wanted to reach out to the little boy behind the angry man. The little boy who'd lost a loving parent only to endure a hateful one. It was a man's body standing now before his father, but a boy's voice that was speaking. Melissa would comfort John in private and let him know how loved he was, but for now she responded dutifully to be rid of the unwanted culprit. "Thank you, Duke Albert."

Albert, satisfied with Melissa's response, spun on his boot heel and informed John in his usual tone of authority, "I'll be waiting for my wedding invitation."

"I'll be in my grave before you get one," John replied.

Albert stopped mid-stride to look over his shoulder at his son. "Can I have another word with you in private, John?"

John had mentioned his father's indiscretion in a moment of frustration, so he guessed correctly what "another word" with him entailed. "Fine. In the sitting room," John motioned, looking back to Melissa, who gave him a silent expression of understanding.

Both gentlemen stepped into the sitting room and John ordered two brandies from Charles. After settling across from each other with drinks in hand, John began, "Father I'm sure you're wondering about my comment. I'll be brief and to the point." John took a long swig from his glass. "You were careless when bedding Vanessa Walker for you made her pregnant."

Albert practically choked on his drink. "I did what?"

"Got her with child, father. Did you not understand that?"

"How are you so sure? She could be making it up."

"No, I believe this time she was telling the truth."

"She's lying. You say I'm careless, that's not true. My women know they need to supply contraceptive devices."

"Well father, perhaps you should start providing your own because Vanessa went without on purpose."

"How do you know all this?" Albert asked.

"She told me herself."

Albert waved him off. "That doesn't mean anything."

"Perhaps not, but I have sources that were able to prove she'd been carrying a child," John said.

Albert was beyond words.

"She miscarried a couple of weeks ago, father. That should bring you relief."

"I see," Albert replied, stunned and without comment.

"So I would suggest you start taking responsibility for your own contraceptives to ensure it won't happen again."

"Wait one moment. I hardly know her. Why would she plan such a thing?"

John knew that once he admitted it was because of him, his father would hold him responsible, regardless of Vanessa's deceit. "In retaliation against me," John honestly admitted.

Albert snorted. "Well then, I say you need to keep your whores in line, son. Your present whore in the library, will she know her place?"

Actions came before words as John bolted out of his chair and lunged for his father. Taking him by his coat lapels with both hands, he lifted his father out of the chair and onto his feet to stand eye to eye with him. Albert's glass slid from his hand and crashed onto the carpet, John's maneuver happened so fast.

Through clenched teeth John responded in a low vicious tone. "You're referring to my future wife. She is above and beyond your status of women. You need to address her as such." John stared daggers into his father's eyes. "She will be Lady Blackburn to you. Is that understood?"

Albert could hardly breathe with the death grip John had around his neck, but even so, his opinion would not go unheard. "Why are you marrying a country lass? She's beautiful, but honestly son, she lacks status. Why would you make her your wife?"

Disgust was John's immediate reaction. "Being obstinate as usual father?" His anger simmered enough to let his hands drop from his father's person. "I'm marrying Melissa because I love her. I don't give a damn about her status. She will become my wife because I intend to marry her." John's arms crossed over his broad chest while his father fell back into the chair, catching his breath. "You see, father, I'm not like you. I'm like mother, which I know infuriates you, always has, and that's why you treat me so badly, isn't it? I remind you so much of mother you can't stand it."

John casually paced before his father. "She had a free spirit, father, until you crushed it. Perhaps you think you've suffered because you have a son that carries that same free spirit. One who lives independently of how others do, who cares less about the status of a person so they can judge if they should associate with them. And even more incredibly, your son takes after his mother in his looks. I can imagine how you've suffered, father."

He stopped pacing to stand before his father. "But did you ever stop and think about how I feel." John paused, waiting for Albert to explode, for John had never taken the opportunity to express himself to his father. When Albert had voiced his crude remark about Melissa it had set John ablaze, and amazingly his father sat there listening. "I've lived more than half my life without a mother. I lost a very special person in my life because of an unnecessary accident that took place. Because her husband drove her into becoming a person she was not." John's voice turned rough and began to break up. "She loved you father. She loved you and you turned against her. You let her die." John's eyes turned to slivers of ice while his father's softened. "I'd like you to leave now. I have nothing further to say."

Albert, who so far had stayed silent, rose from the chair, bent to pick up his empty glass and set it on the table. He turned to look at John, whose back faced him now. John had been absolutely right about everything, and it had taken John telling him to his face to see how bad it had been. He'd never thought to ask John how he felt. He had always figured John could handle himself since he'd always been mature for his age. After his dear Claire had passed on, John had turned to the racetrack instead of his father, while he had turned to more women. It was easier back then to bury his emotions of grief by diverting his attention with young glamorous women. As he had gotten older, the women had gotten younger, but they still didn't erase the memory of his beautiful young wife who died as a result of his superior attitude.

Albert watched John's fingers press into his temples, massaging the pressure away. "Son, I apologize for what I've put you through. Despite everything, I loved your mother. I loved her so much...I drove myself crazy with imagined thoughts. You're right, I killed her, and for that, I'm sorry." Albert didn't wait for a response. Instead he turned and left. His own emotions began surfacing and he needed to be alone.

John glanced over his shoulder. His father was gone. For the first time since his mother's death he could have sworn his father was close to tears. He hadn't expected him to apologize, but a sense of relief had come over John when his father had said he was sorry. In his lifetime he never imagined his father would soften, and to finally tell his father openly, face-to-face how he felt, left a sense of power within him. He had stood up to his father despite any consequences that may have occurred, despite any kind of verbal attack from his father, and to his surprise his father had listened. Listened, instead of giving orders.

He found Melissa, told her about the conversation he'd had with his father, and let her console him. When they retired they talked about their wedding plans then drifted off to sleep in each other's arms, content.

Chapter Thirty

Their wedding day was just two weeks after John's confrontation with his father. John would have liked it sooner but Melissa had wanted more time for preparation, her gown, his suit, guests, food, and all the minimally important items.

When the day finally arrived, the sun peeked through the cloud-covered sky as if appearing to make their day special. John stood by a sparkling stream that ran through his property a hundred yards or so from his "thinking" tree. Robert was by his side, Miss Beckett across from him on the opposite side. It became a contest between Miss Beckett and Robert as to who would comment first on John's restless nature. As John slid his fingers through his loose hair for what seemed like the fiftieth time, he sensed two pairs of eyes focusing on him. "What?" he said to Robert first then swung his gaze to Miss Beckett. "What is it?" he questioned again while his fingers repeated their previous action for the fifty-first time.

Since Miss Beckett still held his attention she took the liberty to speak first. "That," she said, pointing her finger toward his head.

John looked down at the front of his waistcoat and vest, thinking his clothing was the problem. His eyes raised to hers in utter confusion. "That, what?"

Miss Beckett let out an exasperated sigh, motioning him, while telling him, "Bend down here for me." She stood on the tips of her toes to reach his head with her hands and began smoothing his straying hair once he bent to her level.

His constant skimming had made his sleek and flowing hair turn wild and out of control.

"That's better. Now relax and stop that," she said. Miss Beckett did seem to have a parental way about her.

"Thank you," John said. The sound of laughter interrupted his nervous tension. John peered at Robert's smiling face until Miss Beckett made an out of character remark that spun his attention back to her.

"It's not your job to muss up your hair, it's your wife's," she said with a straight face before facing forward to wait for Melissa's arrival.

John swallowed and didn't say another word. He faced forward as well. He hadn't expected a comment like that from Miss Beckett, but then life was full of surprises.

Robert leaned into John and chuckled. "Welcome to the family."

John tried to stay serious but couldn't help the upward curve of his mouth at Robert's reply, although his smile faded when an extraordinary vision appeared before him.

She looked like an angel that had fallen from the heavens, this beautiful woman who was to become his wife. She sat high on top of his number one stallion, Chief, her ivory silk dress draping around the stallion's body. She carried herself proudly and presented the prettiest smile he'd ever seen. This day certainly was full of surprises, because he hadn't a clue she planned to use his horse in the ceremony. Make that a pair of horses, he thought as Clara stepped out before him too. Before climbing atop his mare he took Melissa's hand in his and said aloud for everyone to hear, "You're beautiful."

Her eyes glistened as she gazed down at him. "Thank you," she mouthed.

My Forbidden Mentor

Both horses stayed steady while John and Melissa said their vows. It was quite a reach but they managed to give each other a kiss after being announced husband and wife.

Their guests came over to congratulate them. When Lord Ainsworth gave his congratulations, John had a brilliant, but chancy idea materialize in his ingenious mind.

John's eyes followed Ainsworth as he trailed over to speak with Robert. He leaned toward Melissa, his eyes staying on Ainsworth. "Would you like to race?"

Caught off guard, Melissa kept a plastered smile on her face as she responded. "What?"

"I think the horses were a brilliant idea, sweetheart. Let's race," John said.

"John, that wasn't the purpose of the horses," she explained.

John smiled and turned his attention to the crowd. "Everyone, I have an announcement." Everyone got quiet. "Lady Blackburn and I, I like the sound of that," he said to Melissa's distraught features. "Lady Blackburn and I would like to indulge you in a race." Everyone cheered. "Keep your eye on Ainsworth," he whispered to her as he led them to an imaginary start line.

Melissa found Ainsworth looking enthusiastic and amused. Now she knew what John was up to. Very clever darling, only I'm not prepared, she thought.

"Simon, will you do the honors?" John asked.

Simon called out and they were off. John didn't hold back. He wanted to push her, to give her competition so she would strive to win. He knew by now what got her going and holding back wouldn't do it. She needed a driven, competitive opponent to force her true talent forward. With Chief's power and speed, Melissa would win this race against John, which was just how he wanted it to go for Ainsworth's benefit.

John couldn't help but feel pride and joy when Melissa beat him by a horse's head length. For sure Ainsworth would be impressed, he thought, impressed enough to consider John's proposal that he planned on making at the next business meeting.

There were compliments and praise on Melissa's behalf following the race, and even Ainsworth himself had joked about Melissa racing for their team at Catterick. As tempting as it was to mention it then, John held back, deciding to wait to confront Ainsworth until the next partner's meeting.

The wedding celebration lasted until the wee hours of the morning. John had noticed Melissa weaving as she walked around chatting with the guests, but he hadn't realized how much champagne she'd consumed. He excused himself from Robert's company and approached his wife, interrupting her conversation with his team partner, Paul Ford.

"Hello, love. I've mizzed you," Melissa said, wrapping an arm around John's neck and slurring her words as she spoke.

She tipped an empty glass of champagne toward her mouth and John took the glass away from her.

Looking toward Paul while he arranged Melissa in his arms, he confessed, "She doesn't usually drink. Excuse us Paul, we're going to retire for the evening."

"Of course, John. Congratulations again," Paul smiled, envious of the treasure John had found in his new bride.

Robert joined Paul and both watched John disappear around the top of the stairway with a giddy Melissa in his arms.

Once inside their bedchamber, John undressed Melissa as best he could while her arms and hands playfully fumbled along his body. In a clumsy manner she tried undressing him as well, but she didn't succeed as he lifted her naked body and placed her on the bed.

She wailed in great laughter, feeling numb and silly as John placed her beneath the covers.

John wasn't sure what was so humorous but he gave her a generous smile as she lay inside cream satin sheets, giggling.

Her laughter subsided a moment, long enough to comment, "Come here, lover. Aren't we supposed to consummate our vows?" She brought her arms out of the covers, reaching for him.

He gazed down at his inebriated wife, knowing tonight there would not be any consummation. "Sweetheart," he said, sitting on the edge of the bed next to her.

She rose up, clasping her hands around his neck, pulling his handsome face down to hers. "Why are you still dressed?" she asked, her fingers threading through his long tresses.

"I think we should wait. You've had too much to drink tonight."

Her mouth curved into a sexy grin. "You don't think I can perform drunk?" Her eyelids were getting heavy as she asked the question.

"I think you're getting sleepy and you're not going to last much longer," John told her, noticing the heaviness in her eyes and her hands slipping down to his shoulders in a loosened grip.

"Perhaps," she murmured.

"Goodnight sweetheart," he whispered back, giving her a kiss before rising to undress.

"Night, night," she replied and turned onto her side.

John smiled at her response as he stepped to his side of the bed and removed the remainder of his clothing. He slipped beneath the covers and snuggled up behind her. There would be no lovemaking this night, his wedding night.

When Melissa awakened the next morning she wanted to die. It hurt to open her eyes, it hurt to move them around, so instantly, she shut them. Although closing her eyes helped to relieve the intent eye pain it hadn't helped the pounding in her head. She moaned, promising herself she'd never drink another drop of liquor again in her life.

The sound of the bedchamber door opening made Melissa squint her eyes in order to see who it was. John appeared before her with a tray of liquids. He set the tray on a nearby nightstand and poured a small amount of brandy into a glass.

"Are you quite mad to drink so early in the morning, John?" she asked.

"It's not for me, it's for you," he told her, pushing the glass of amber liquid toward her.

She sat up, backing herself against the walnut headboard. Her nostrils flared as the fumes of alcohol burned and its scent made her stomach want to heave. She turned her head away from the glass. "Get that away from me. I don't want it."

"It will help. Drink a little of this first, then you need to drink a sufficient amount of water to counteract your dehydration," John said, keeping the glass in front of her.

"I can't, the smell of it makes me want to vomit." Her face scrunched as she turned back to him.

"Hold your nose and drink it. Trust me."

Her eyes narrowed, which hurt, while the fingers of one hand pinched her nose shut. She took the glass of liquid and gagged it down.

"Very good." He took the glass from her. "Now stay still for a moment. It will help shortly." He reached over, pouring water into another glass.

"You're up early today," she commented, watching John gather clothing for her to wear.

He chuckled. "It's not as early as you think," he said while spreading her clothes across the bed for her.

Melissa reached over to grab the glass of water. "What time is it?" she asked while taking a sip.

"A quarter to noon. Long past time for you to get dressed so we can venture out."

"Noon? I should say so." She placed the glass of water back on the nightstand and flipped the covers off of her. While reaching over for her clothing, she suddenly realized what he had said. "Venture out?" She started to stand. "What plans have you made?" she asked, standing straight then immediately sitting back down, staying there until the dizziness passed.

"Are you all right?" John asked.

"Yes. I just got up too fast."

"Yes, I know the feeling, and I hope you're up for a little adventure today. I've had this planned for some time."

"Really? I like surprises. Is it a surprise?"

"Sort of. Why don't you get dressed so you can find out?"

On horseback John took Melissa out into the country, where they traveled across miles of vacant green land. Together they hunted for creatures of nature so they could watch them in their natural habitat. They found berry bushes and ate berries while riding through scattered oak and elm trees. They came upon some dense brush and dismounted their horses. John took Melissa's hand in his and led her into the concealing brush. A small pool of water appeared and Melissa sighed in delight. While Melissa admired the private body of water, John admired Melissa with indiscreet ideas.

John stripped off his clothing and coerced her into shedding hers, but getting her into the water presented another challenge. Her arms folded across her naked breasts as she stood on the banks of green grass.

John had already waded in and was waiting in cool water up to his waistline.

She dipped her big toe into the water then backed out. "It's freezing, John."

"Oh Lord, Melissa. Stop being such a coward and jump in here with me."

"I'll watch you swim," she said, quickly spinning around to take a step further up the bank, when two strong hands grasped onto the backs of her thighs.

"Oh no, you don't," he warned.

My Forbidden Mentor

She playfully screamed, her body squirming, her toes digging into the muddy bank, but John's tight grip on her legs was too powerful and the pressure of their back and forth struggle landed them both into sopping soil.

John landed halfway on her backside while the other half of him lay soaking in rich black mud. Unfortunately his poor wife laid face down, plastered from head to toe in the oozing stuff. His extra weight on top hadn't helped, he thought, as he lifted himself off her. "Now you definitely need to get into the water. Come on, we need to clean you up." He smiled. "Then we can consummate our vows, lover," he mocked deliciously into her ear.

They slipped and slid until finally, by grabbing enough bunches of grass, they were able to stand. John and Melissa laughed at how ridiculous they looked. John squatted to pick up his wife and carefully stepped back into the water. He set her before him and she began to shiver. Willingly he took her in his arms, holding her tight against his body so she could warm up.

"Was I so drunk that we didn't even make love last night?" she asked.

"Yes," he said.

"Oh, what a horrible wedding night for you." Her head tipped up and she stared into his face. "You know I hardly ever drink, but last evening the champagne tasted so good and everyone was drinking, even auntie. I couldn't help myself."

"It's all right. After all, you're going to make up for that right now, are you not?" There was a gleam in his eyes.

"I suppose," she said while glancing around. "I'm not sure how John?"

John's gaze traveled between their bodies. "Why don't we rinse first, and then use our imaginations?"

For a whole month after their wedding day their lives were blissful. Even meeting with Lord Ainsworth had been a success. He'd admitted being quite impressed with Melissa's riding on their wedding day, but even so he expressed that in order to comply with social alliance a challenge must be met. Lord Ainsworth would agree to take Melissa on as a rider at Catterick if she petitioned herself. He required five hundred signatures. When that was completed they would meet again to discuss their options. John and Melissa agreed and left the meeting feeling elated.

The next day Melissa began her crusade. Daily she rode through nearby villages, knowing she'd be better received. She'd been successful in the villages but still didn't have near enough signatures.

John persuaded her to go into bigger towns, starting with Richmond, and so the torment began. Not as well received in the beginning, she went half a day without any new signatures. Feeling distressed and defeated she stopped by a market on the outskirts of Richmond to do some shopping.

She had been looking over sculptures of horses when a young lady got her attention.

"Isn't this lovely?" The young lady remarked, holding a black stallion sculpture in her hand.

Melissa smiled at the young lady, who was approximately her age with thick, rich copper hair. "Yes, it is," she replied.

"My fiancé, or rather ex-fiancé, has a real life stallion that looks just like this one." She twisted the sculpture in her hand to see its full depth.

"I'm sorry you are no longer together," Melissa said.

"It couldn't be helped." She looked down at the stack of papers Melissa held. "It looks like you've got a petition there. For what, may I ask?"

"Actually it's a petition for myself. I want to race thoroughbreds at Catterick racetrack and before I can, I need five hundred signatures."

"You race horses? I find that fascinating. I think you're very bold and courageous to do what you're doing. I'll sign." The young woman wasted no time and wrote her name down.

"Thank you. I wish more people had your attitude."

The young lady looked over the signatures. "It looks like you've just started in Richmond."

"Yes, today in fact. The outside villages were very receptive, but I'm finding in town, well, my luck is not with me." Melissa sighed heavily.

"I can help you with this. I know a lot of people in Richmond, very influential people."

"You would help me? I don't know what to say."

"Say yes and I'll do it."

"Yes." Melissa gazed at the young lady in admiration for it seemed generous for a complete stranger to be so eager to help. She glanced at her signature to learn her name. Rose Catley. Rose? Melissa's eyes scanned her red hair before shifting to the stallion sculpture. Robert has a black stallion, Goliath. "Rose? Robert Gibson's Rose?" At

Rose's nod she introduced herself. "I'm Melissa." She held out her hand.

"Melissa? Melissa Howard?" Rose asked.

"Yes, well, I used to be. I'm Melissa Blackburn now," she said.

"You two finally got married. How absolutely wonderful." Rose hugged Melissa in a friendly embrace.

Rose and Melissa spent the remainder of the day getting to know each other. They hit it off marvelously and planned to start the next day ravishing Richmond with Melissa's petition.

Melissa mentioned to John about her day and about meeting Rose. He was glad Melissa had found a friend in Rose as he had known if they ever met they would get along well. When he mentioned their friendship to Robert he seemed genuinely happy for them.

The month of August flowed by and brought new challenges along the way.

It was the middle of September when John arrived home early one afternoon. He'd just gotten settled when the front door bell rang. He remembered Charles had the day off, undoubtedly courting Miss Beckett, so he got up from his chair smiling at that thought as he answered the door.

John signed for a package wrapped like a wedding gift. He carried it to the library and sat down before opening the message that came with it. Casually opening the card, he noticed it had been addressed to Melissa only. He read the note attached and had to read the words twice to make sure he'd read them correctly.

My Forbidden Mentor

Melissa was practically singing as she flew through the front door. She was in a joyous, happy mood because today she and Rose had gotten the most signatures thus far. She spotted John's leather bag on the floor near the stairwell, which meant he was home early. Ecstatic to share her successful day with her husband, she searched and found him in the library. Sitting in his favorite chair, he held a glass of brandy in one hand and an opened card in the other. He hadn't seen her for his head was tipped back against the chair with his eyes closed.

Her smile faded when she noticed an unopened gift lying at his booted feet. Her eyes traveled the length of him to find dark and stormy eyes piercing into her. Something was wrong, terribly wrong, and it had to do with that gift, she gathered.

"What is it, John?" she asked.

"You tell me." His look was dangerous.

"I'm not sure what you're talking about," she responded with bated breath.

John sat up and handed her the card. "This will explain."

Melissa took the card, opened it, and read the message that had put John in this state.

Dearest Melissa,

Here is a belated wedding gift for a very extraordinary lady.

Fondly, Jack.

Her eyes grew large and her heart began to race. She could only imagine the thoughts monopolizing her husband's mind. "I don't know the meaning of this John."

His lips twisted. "Why not open the gift and find out how meaningful it is."

They stared at each other in trembling silence. Melissa shifted her focus to the gift sitting on the carpeted floor. What would she find in there and why was Jack sending her a gift?

She bent down, picking up the small box. She sat on the couch across from John. With the gift set on her lap, she looked up to find intense gray eyes watching her. Normally out of habit they would kiss when greeting each other every day, but John didn't seem like he was in the mood for a kiss and that bothered her. Obviously he had read more into this than there was, although it was quite a bold gesture on Jack's part. What was Jack up to anyway?

Literally frightened of what she might find beneath the beautiful wedding paper, she began gradually undoing the bow. By the time the gift was free and out of its wrappings, Melissa stared down at a blue velvet jewelry box. She didn't dare look at John, who remained quiet. The gift was clearly personal. Slender fingers snatched open the box.

Witnessing her widened eyes, John studied Melissa's reaction. She appeared as surprised as he or was it an act? He'd been correct about Jack's intentions, but what were his wife's?

Melissa's throat tightened. How would she ever explain this extravagance to John? An opaque pearl bracelet gleamed back at her. It was beautiful, something that should have been from John, not a simple driver. But he had also been Vanessa's driver. Could she be behind this facade?

"What is it?" a deep voice inquired.

Melissa turned the box around in his direction. He didn't need to move closer as he could plainly see what the box held within. The bright glow of pearls contrasted richly against the dark blue velvet.

"Very nice," he commented, catching her eyes and holding them with his.

Why did she feel so compelled to explain about something she knew nothing about? "John, I haven't any idea what this means."

"Don't you? It's quite evident that Jack McGuire is enamored with you. The question is, are you of him?"

"What are you implying?" she asked in shock.

"Implying? The proof lies in your hand."

"For Jack, perhaps, not for me," she responded in defense.

He waited, not saying a word.

"I realize it looks a certain way, John, but believe me, I have no part in this." Why was John so angry? Didn't he trust her?

"Did you at one time?"

"You mean was I involved with Jack? Absolutely not. I told you before he was just my driver and that's the truth."

John was silent as he remembered a tidbit of information Robert had indulged regarding Mr. McGuire.

"You don't believe me, do you? You know he was involved with Vanessa. Perhaps she's behind this?"

"What do you plan to do with the gift?" He didn't answer her but proceeded with his own agenda.

"Send it back, of course," she said as though it were an obvious fact.

"With a note, I presume, and what would that note entail, Melissa?"

Oh, he was behaving like a maddened fool. "Why don't you believe me, John?"

"I want to. But I seem to recall Jack having connections at a racetrack in Richmond."

"So?"

"Where are most of your signatures coming from?"

His mind seemed bent on destruction as he twisted every word around. "This is outrageous!"

"Tell me sweetheart, have you seen Jack since Sheffield?" He stayed calm despite her recent outburst.

She had, in fact, in Richmond. How John had guessed that she didn't know since she'd kept it from him with good reason. Of course, now that reason would be exposed. "Yes. I won't lie to you."

"Why haven't you told me about it?"

"Because of the way you're acting now. You're assuming, John. You're wrong." The increased volume of her voice exposed an angry tone not normally heard.

"Did you just say hello, or did you have tea and cakes together?"

"Why are you asking this?"

He leaned forward. "Because, I pegged Jack in Sheffield. I knew then his interest in you went beyond being your driver." John shook his head in frustration and sighed from accumulating fatigue. "I'm a man, Melissa. I know how men operate."

My Forbidden Mentor

"It's not mutual, John," she said, trying to convince him.

"You're letting him get close to you and I don't like it. This gift is an example of how close he's trying to get."

"I was only trying to be nice. I in no way gave him any ideas about intentions other than friendship."

"How can you be a friend with someone who came after you for Vanessa?" he asked.

"He was unaware John, you know that. Besides, he no longer sees her."

"No, now he sees you!" The wave of calm finally crashed.

"You're not being fair about this," she cried.

"You know quite a bit about his personal life, sweetheart. Did you discuss this over tea the one time?" The wave unleashed his sarcastic side.

It was time to set him straight. "John, he's had a hard time. He got caught up in Vanessa's web as well. Yes, I've had tea with him, several times, when in Richmond. And yes, by being my friend he's helped me accumulate an abundance of signatures for my petition, but he's also aware that I am with child, John. That I am carrying my husband's child, my husband, the man I'm in love with." She lifted the box. "This gift, though quite generous I admit, is a gesture of friendship, John. Only friendship."

"Do you plan on staying friends with Jack?" He didn't buy her explanation.

"Why wouldn't I?" she answered guardedly.

"At the risk of your marriage?" John purposely put her to a test.

"Wha...what are you saying?" He was too serious about this mess.

"You know what I'm saying." He gave her a knowing look.

"He's helped me, John," she cried.

"And he'll expect something in return," John concluded.

She didn't respond. Too stunned to reply, she just stared into the angry features of the man she loved.

"Is his kind of friendship worth your marriage?" he inquired again.

A long period of silence fell between them.

The whole situation seemed ludicrous to Melissa. Anger escalated at her husband for not trying to understand the truth of the matter, instead letting his insane jealousy rule. But she still loved him and indeed she would not allow a simple misunderstanding to ruin her union with her husband. "Of course it's not worth my marriage!" she hissed, rising from the couch and tossing the gift toward him. She stormed out of the library and heard a faint "Good" echo from John.

Chapter Thirty-One

The days and nights that followed their disastrous confrontation saw very little communication. Only when necessary did they speak to one another, and even then their replies remained short. Lovemaking became a distant memory as both of them withheld advances toward any sort of intimacy.

Days turned into weeks, with Melissa's anger sustained due to John's unreasonable attitude and his having ideas about her and Jack that simply weren't true.

John dwelled in anger as well. He didn't trust himself not to say something he would regret later, and held it inside, keeping their confrontations to a bare minimum.

Nighttime was the hardest. John had grown used to relying on his wife for comfort, used to having her soft and supple body for warmth, but unfortunately his wife had committed an act that required his forgiveness. Until he could forgive her, he would have to sacrifice their bond of closeness.

By now a couple of months had past and the same routine of courtesy continued to play out. Cordial at breakfast and cordial at supper was the extent of their communication these days.

"Do you have enough porridge?" John asked as his eyes skimmed over the small protruding belly of his wife.

At least he had concern for his child, Melissa thought, he's not totally heartless. "Yes, we're fine thank you." She managed a quick smile.

"Good," John said, giving her a friendly smile that quickly faded.

They proceeded to eat breakfast in silence when the bell sounded at the front door. Charles had barely gotten his greeting out when the sounds of bickering drowned him out. John and Melissa looked at each other in puzzled curiosity.

Charles popped his head inside the dining room. "My Lord?" Charles pleaded in helplessness as the couple entering carried on in high-pitched tones.

"It's all right, Charles," John told him, rising from his chair with Melissa following suit.

John and Melissa both stood in the doorway of the dining room staring down the entryway at Robert and Rose.

Rose perched herself on the tips of her toes to reach Robert's height. "You're arrogant and selfish, Robert Gibson."

"What? Arrogant perhaps but not selfish, Rose. How can you claim I'm selfish after everything I've endured?"

John glanced at Rose, whose face was turning fire red, and then to Robert, who started to cock his head with attitude. John knew then that Robert was bound for the point of no return.

Before Rose could interrupt Robert, John did. "Robert, Rose, enough," he said, stepping toward them.

Rose and Robert both looked in John's direction as if they were surprised that John should be there.

My Forbidden Mentor

"What is going on here?" John inquired. "Rose, you start." John caught Robert's glare of betrayal. "Ladies first, Robert," he said consolingly.

"Well, I was minding my own business, coming to visit my friend Melissa, when Mr. Gibson here accused me of purposely arranging to run into him. The nerve!" Rose was ready to blast off at Robert again when John stopped her.

John held up the palm of his hand. "Rose, it's Robert's turn."

Robert gave Rose a glare of insanity. "It's Mr. Gibson, now, is it?" His focus switched to John. "Well, Miss Catley here acted like she planned on running into me. She was friendly, smiling mischievously, and lord knows what else—"

"You wish. You're reading more into," Rose started.

A loud whistle from John ceased further progression of arguing. Now that he had their complete attention again he looked to Robert. "Robert, Rose has been spending a great deal of time with Melissa. She's been involved with Melissa's petition and they have become close friends." He switched to Rose. "Rose, perhaps Robert misinterpreted your friendly gesture." John grinned. "Perhaps he liked running into you and doesn't want to admit it." Oh, revenge was sweet.

"John," Robert warned, giving John the evil eye for saying more than he should.

Rose glanced at Robert. She had made a decision that morning regarding Robert and was eager to share it with Melissa, which was one reason she had come over so early this morning. Melissa understood Rose's situation with Robert and would help her if she asked. She was taking a chance but she felt it was worth it. Batting her eyelashes, she sounded humble when apologizing. "Forgive me,

Robert. It was not my intention to give you the wrong impression."

Rose had given in and Robert couldn't believe it. She had never backed off before when they had had one of their discussions. It was refreshing but caused him to stagger in response.

"Good. Now that we're being civil again, would you two like breakfast?" John asked, actually proud that he had helped to resolve the battle of wills between his friends, but when he chanced a glance toward his wife his pride was doused with a venomous look. She didn't look happy, not happy at all. He turned his attention back to Rose and Robert, who seemed oblivious to Melissa's glare of disapproval.

They both answered, "Sure," at the same time, smiling awkwardly toward each other. As Robert and Rose headed for the dining table, John stayed behind to confront his wife. He turned to face her. "Have I said something to disturb you?"

Melissa folded her arms across her chest. "No, quite the contrary. You've managed to make peace between them, at least temporarily."

"And why does that bother you?"

"Because you manage to help others with their problems but won't deal with your own."

"I see."

"I'm not sure you do, John," she unleashed, leaving him to stand alone in the entry way as she glided up the stairway to their bedchamber.

John took a moment to gather his bearings before entering the dining room. As much as anger flared in him at that moment, she'd been correct. A couple of months had

My Forbidden Mentor

passed and their future seemed as bleak as ever. In that time he'd yearned for her to trust his judgment of character, namely regarding Jack, but she still defended the scoundrel anytime his name was brought up. So why would he not think otherwise about their situation? After all, hadn't she kept her and Jack's re acquaintance a secret?

As he approached the dining room he heard laughter between Robert and Rose and instantly missed the laughter he use to share with Melissa. Should he give Melissa the benefit of the doubt, forget this one incident with Jack, and move on? He took his seat and joined in the laughter.

Melissa's eyes widened as she sat up on the chaise that graced her bedchamber. Rose had just revealed her plans. "This sudden change of heart took place all because of earlier today?"

Rose sat in a chair across from her. "Of course not, but we had a good conversation at breakfast and it helped to confirm my decision."

Melissa stared into the flames flickering aimlessly within the fireplace. How nice it would be to have a good conversation with her own husband, she thought. Her eyes found her best friend's. "How do you think he will react?"

Rose smiled. "I'm not sure, but I think it will be good." Rose bent forward to emphasize her suggestion. "Perhaps you could have John quiz Robert for me but not be too suspicious about it. It will make what I have to do easier."

Melissa shook her head regretfully. "I can't, Rose. I'm sorry. John and I barely speak as it is, much less if I ask him to spy for me."

Rose turned solemn. "Melissa, you two need to work this out. I can't believe it's gone on this long. You two are married with a child on the way. You two love each other. It's got to work out somehow."

"I just don't know what to do anymore, Rose. We hardly talk without angering each other."

"You're both stubborn is the problem, both of you, and to the point of being ridiculous."

Melissa became defensive. "And you and Robert aren't stubborn?"

"You're right, we are," she chuckled. "Perhaps you could talk to Robert for me and I could talk to John for you."

"Oh, Rose, I don't know." Melissa sighed heavily.

"I was only jesting, Melissa. After all, these are extremely personal issues we're dealing with."

Melissa changed the subject. Her marriage was all she thought about these days and she needed a temporary diversion. Rose's news was exciting enough to capture her attention. "So when is your last day at work?"

Rose smiled. "After today's episode with Robert, it was yesterday."

"Good for you." Melissa leaned forward as well. "And your plan of seduction? When will that take place?"

"When he least expects it."

Melissa was giddy. "I'm so happy for you, Rose. You and Robert will be back together before you know it."

"I hope so."

They chatted on about many things. Rose always knew how to cheer her up.

My Forbidden Mentor

Two weeks later on an early December morning, Melissa sat in her carriage awaiting Rose at Rose's request. They had planned to do some shopping, and then have lunch together. Also, Rose mentioned having some rather exciting news to tell her. Melissa had scarcely seen her for the past two weeks so her plan must have been working.

A knock came upon the carriage door, startling Melissa. Rose didn't usually knock. Melissa leaned over, opening the curtains to find Duke Albert standing at her carriage door. I wonder what he wants?

Actually feeling sorry for the duke, she couldn't turn him away. Ever since he and John had had their in-depth conversation he'd been trying time and time again to contact John, but John had ignored him. Melissa had hoped that John would finally come around. A father and son relationship was an important one but she had little faith that the duke would have success. John not only ignored his father these days, he ignored his wife as well.

The curtain fell back into place as she reached for the latch on the door and opened it.

"Lady Blackburn, I was wondering if I could speak with you a moment?" He gave a handsome smile accompanied with a gracious bow.

"Yes, of course." A few moments wouldn't hurt and she always waited on Rose anyway. If they weren't the best of friends she wouldn't have the tolerance for such tardiness, but as Rose accepted Melissa as she was, Melissa did the same.

Albert sat across from Melissa, still smiling. "Thank you. I'm sure you're aware I've been trying to talk with my son and he's all but ignored me." He chuckled from nervousness. "His behavior doesn't surprise me, nor do I blame him. I want you to understand that."

"John's going through a lot right now. He's been extremely busy with work."

"Lady Blackburn, you don't have to make excuses for your husband. I understand. I suppose I thought by talking to you I could gain some insight into how he's doing right now. I feel like we're starting over with our father and son relationship. Before you know it you'll have," Albert's blue eyes scanned over Melissa's figure and until now hadn't noticed the pouch of her belly, "a child on the way."

"Yes. You will be a grandfather early in the new year." She looked down to her belly and placed her hands over it.

"Congratulations." Albert appeared dumbfounded.

"Thank you," she sighed. The baby seemed to be the only joy in her life of late. "John is doing all right, Duke Albert. He's had a lot on his mind. Just give him time."

Albert sighed. "Yes, time. I've wasted so much time thinking only of myself in the past. I suppose that's why I'm so anxious to earn John's respect." He smiled, glancing toward her stomach. "And I truly would like to be a part of my grandchild's life, even if John won't let me be a part of his."

Melissa listened before commenting. "Duke Albert, without seeming offensive, you have to realize that John has been hurt deeply by his past. I cannot override him in the decision regarding your grandchild."

"I understand."

"Do you really? What I mean is, you have to know that he will not allow you to treat your grandchild the same way he was treated as a child, and I will not allow it either."

My Forbidden Mentor

Albert stayed silent.

"I know I'm being dreadfully honest here but your attitude would have to change, your ways of thinking. Truthfully Duke Albert, I would like for all of us to be a family, a close family that could share holidays together and summer picnics, for you see you will be the only living grandparent our children will have," she explained.

Albert was about to reply when her last words surprised him into silence. This changed everything. "Forgive me. I didn't know your parents had passed on. I see now that you understand more than I thought you did. Thank you for your insight, Lady Blackburn. John's a very lucky man to have you. You have impressed me with your intellect, which of course competes with your beauty."

"Thank you, Duke Albert. I'm glad we had this chat."

"I am glad as well. Good day."

The carriage door flew open. "I'm sorry I'm, oh, Duke Albert," Rose acknowledge, as she slipped in beside Melissa.

Albert stood to take his leave. "Rose, I was just leaving." He turned to Melissa again. "It's been a pleasure," he said, then left the carriage.

Rose sat across from Melissa. "What was that all about?"

Melissa smiled. "I'll tell you later. I want to hear your news that couldn't wait."

A huge grin shown on Rose's face. "Robert and I, he's asked me to marry him again Melissa!"

"What? Oh, Rose that's wonderful." She reached over and they hugged. "I want to hear every last detail."

Rose proceeded to tell Melissa of the events that had occurred over the past two weeks, including the seduction.

She had literally attacked Robert in his carriage not two nights ago.

"And he didn't fight you off?" Melissa asked in a teasing manner.

"I've got skills, darling, that would make you blush. I also have the advantage of knowing what Robert likes," Rose confessed with confidence.

"I wish I had your enthusiasm," Melissa replied.

"That's it, love."

"What are you talking about, Rose?" Melissa asked in wariness.

"Is there anything special that John likes, you know, intimately? Something he couldn't resist?" Rose asked.

Melissa wasn't sure why Rose's boldness surprised her, it shouldn't have. "Well, he likes everything Rose, I suppose, but he's usually the initiator."

"That's it. This will work."

"I'm listening."

"First of all, you need to be the initiator. That will catch him off guard." She saw Melissa shake her head in uncertainty but ignored her anyway. "And I'm going to give you a short lesson in attaining an instant reaction from a man, one I'm positive will make him talk to you." Rose paused a second. "Although, you may have to decipher between the groans."

Melissa looked strangely into her best friend's face.

Rose went on, explaining in detail what she requested Melissa to perform, and she guaranteed her an optimistic outcome.

My Forbidden Mentor

Two more weeks passed before Melissa was brave enough to try Rose's suggestion. It took all of two weeks for Rose to fill Melissa with enough confidence to go through with it. Dressed in a sheer gown, Melissa was full of courage until the moment had finally arrived to get John's attention. He already lay in bed while Melissa paced inside their dressing closet. I can't do this, I'll make a fool of myself she started hammering into her brain. Feeling defeated, her insecurities led to her whipping off the gown and trailing off to bed naked like she always did. That's how John preferred her, only lately she could wear her riding habit to bed and he wouldn't notice.

Sliding beneath the covers on her side of the bed, she lay there staring up at the ceiling. Coward, she called herself. She looked over at John, seeing the familiarity of his back facing her. Her eyes filled with tears as she stared with blurry eyes into the broadness of his upper body. Every night for three months now it had been the same distant motions, both turning away from each other in bed, and this was the hardest part to deal with. In the past, which seemed so far away now, lovemaking had dominated their nights, yet now words were barely spoken, and when they were, they were snapping and out of necessity.

She looked back toward the ceiling. How much worse could it get? And what about their baby? Would having a child make it better or worse? Could she stand to wait another three months to find out?

Melissa reached over to John out of desperation for physical contact, desperate for any contact, for an emotional connection between them had been non-existent.

John could feel the movement of the bed as he lay on his side facing away from his wife. It hadn't been unusual for her to leave their bed in order to escape the resistance between them, but all of a sudden a warm hand glided over the side of his hip and rested on his belly. His breath caught as he wondered what on earth she was trying to accomplish.

"Melissa, don't," John said quietly, hating to tell her that. Even so she kept her hand there.

It had been a long while and he missed her greatly, but their present circumstances kept him from giving into his ardent desires.

Another stab of pain pierced deep inside when he voiced those two disapproving words but she relinquished her pride for all she wanted was her husband. She was beyond proving her innocence of what he believed she was guilty. All she craved now were his affections, his loving touch, and his warm body pressing into hers. She needed to know they could still be together and be one, that they still loved each other despite the pain they were causing one another. Her hand moved lower.

She wasn't making this easy for him. "Melissa, you don't have to do this," he said, unable to conceal his labored breathing.

"I want to," she responded in a shaky whisper.

The bed moved again and her hand disappeared. He stayed still, thinking she had changed her mind and saved him from enduring the torture of blissful pain if she continued. All she did was better position herself for what she was about to do. He rolled onto his back and reached for her hair. He made a fist in it and pulled her head gently toward his face. "You don't need to do this."

Her eyes closed and she didn't say anything, but looked defeated.

John released her hair and sighed heavily. He closed his eyes, but then quickly opened them when a drop of moisture splashed on his belly. Melissa leaned over him, her weight resting on the palm of her hands with eyes shut and tears falling from her golden lashes. John's eyes watered at the sight of her and he shut his eyes once again. They needed to reconcile. He couldn't go on like this and she was obviously miserable.

"John, don't you want me anymore?" he heard her ask before sniffles of weeping began.

He swallowed hard and opened his eyes. He'd never wanted anyone more in his life than his wife. He sat up, wrapped his arms around her, and held her in a tight embrace. "Of course I want you," he rasped into her ear. "Lord, what have I done? To you, to us?" His mouth found hers and urgently they clung together. When their lips parted they continued holding each other.

In the silence of their bonding moment Melissa asked ever so softly against his ear, "Why don't you believe that I love you, John, and have no desire for another man?"

His eyes squeezed tight. He'd hurt her, almost beyond repair, but she needed to trust in his judgment and tell him the complete truth. Hiding the fact that she'd even seen Jack again and didn't say anything infuriated him. Could he have overreacted? Could he finally admit to himself that he was no better than his father, living out of jealous rage, treating his wife like she didn't matter these past months?

His eyes opened and he lean back to look into her worried features. "I do. I do believe you, sweetheart. I just haven't acted like it." He inhaled a deep breath of air. "Forgive me," he said while resting his forehead against hers, not able to look into the hurt he had caused in those saddened eyes. Melissa moved away from him, leaving him to wonder what more had gone wrong. She was distancing herself again.

As she stretched to lie flat on the bed, she consoled the fragile expression on his face. "I have to lay down," she smiled. "The baby is too heavy in that position."

In relief he stretched out alongside her. "Are you chilled?" he asked since they were lying on top of the velvet coverlet.

"No, not at all," she responded.

John lay on his side with his elbow bent and the palm of his hand supporting his head. His fingers touched the golden strand of hair straying along her cheek. He placed the strand carefully behind her ear. "Melissa." The tone of his voice captured her attention. Their eyes caught and managed to hold. "I realize I've been hard to deal with of late. I was enraged that another man could get close to my wife, even under my own roof. It bothered me a great deal, to the point of blaming you for his actions." He paused to scan her body and then his eyes met hers again. "You're my life. Don't you understand that nobody can or ever will take your place? I don't want to lose you, Melissa. I know now for a fact that being married won't stop another man from trying to get close to you. Jack has proven that."

"I hadn't known that by offering friendship to a man it would create other ideas in his head. That was not my intention."

"I know that, and there isn't anything wrong with having gentlemen friends. It's inevitable being in our trade, but with sorts like Jack it's different. Perhaps it started out as friendship but somewhere along the way it changed for him." John's hand went to her belly, smoothing over the roundness. "Sending you that bracelet made his message clear."

"Why did you stay upset so long, John? Why didn't we talk sooner?"

"Because my anger toward Jack wasn't the only reason I was upset." His hand left her belly so his fingers could thread through his long hair. "You lied to me, Melissa. I can't tolerate lying. That bothered me more than what Jack did."

Her breath hitched. "What did I lie about, John? I told you the truth about Jack and me."

"You told me afterward, when it had already come out in the open. By not telling me about seeing him in the beginning, you lied," he explained.

"I didn't tell you because I knew you'd overreact to nothing more than a fleeting friendship," she responded.

"Fleeting?" He chuckled. "Lord Melissa, it sounds like you're describing an affair."

"That didn't come out right. I meant because," she rushed out.

"I know what you meant," he said, interrupting her. "But at the time my mind was insane. I wasn't thinking clearly, so I imagined when you lied to me about running into Jack, perhaps an affair wasn't so farfetched."

She didn't know what to say. She hadn't seen it from his point of view. She should have known better than to lie to the most honest person she knew, but his reaction to the truth was what had scared her in the beginning. "I'm sorry. I didn't mean to give you a reason to think I would be involved with another man."

John smiled. "Inside in my heart I knew you were only friends with Jack, but that doesn't excuse his behavior. You're a married woman. He has no right to come after you so blatantly." He was quiet for a moment. "And it doesn't excuse you for not being straight with me, no matter what my wrath would entail. You'd have survived it, you're tough.

You're a Blackburn now." His hand touched her cheek again. "Please be honest with me from now on. I don't want to go through this again. I love you."

"I will, I promise. I love you too, please believe that," she pleaded.

"I do," he murmured.

She watched as he rested his head on the pillow. His arm came around her shoulders and he pulled her snug against his chest.

At last they were man and wife again, holding each other like they always had. Unexpectedly his warm hand caressed along her belly.

John's hand massaged the firm skin of her belly between them. "I don't recall this being here before?" He grinned.

Melissa returned a smile. "It's been there. It's just gotten bigger."

"How are you feeling these days?" he asked with genuine concern.

His concern touched her. He hadn't asked about the baby in a month or so, and when he had it had sounded like a requirement he made himself do, but this time it sounded heartfelt. "Splendid. The baby has moved, by the way."

His brows arched. "Really? A lot or once in a while?"

"Once in a while."

"Does it hurt?"

"No, not really. It feels different." Having John's interest again gave her comfort but thoughts of further intimacy caused her eyes to cast down before obtaining his attention again. "John?"

My Forbidden Mentor

"Hmm?" he answered idly, his darkening eyes gazing over her naked form.

"Are you tired?"

Her inquiry gained his full attention. "Not at all, why?"

"I was wondering," she trailed off, actually embarrassed to confront her husband with her passionate needs.

"Wondering what?" he prodded, having a good idea of what she wanted by her shy reactions. After all, they hadn't made love in almost three months. When she didn't respond, he let her know that he knew her intentions. "What happened to being bold like you tried to be a few moments ago?"

"Pardon me?"

"You were ready to take what you wanted not long ago," he said.

"You stopped me."

"I did, but that didn't mean that I wouldn't have liked what you had planned on doing." He smiled so wide his eyes gleamed and his teeth shown bright. "I must say you surprised me."

"Well I had to do something to get your attention." Her voice dropped an octave at the same time her eyes cast a rich glow of melting hazel.

"You got it all right." He trailed his hand from her belly up and over her hip to gently squeeze a handful of one buttock. "You still have it," he voiced with a catch in his breath.

His breathy comment stirred her even more. "John, make love to me."

His body rose so he could give her a tender kiss on the lips. "With pleasure," he said and kissed her again. That night changed things for Mr. and Mrs. Blackburn. Their marriage bond strengthened while their love deepened for each other.

Chapter Thirty-Two

Christmas time had arrived. For the Blackburn household it was a joyous holiday. Joined by Robert, Rose, Miss Beckett, and Charles, no less, it was only the six of them and they had the best time together. They enjoyed a feast for Christmas supper. Ellen had outdone herself with the help of Miss Beckett's culinary skills. After supper they all gathered in the sitting room to exchange pleasantries.

Their small celebration lasted until midnight, when one by one each retired to guest rooms. John gathered a sleepy Melissa in his arms and carried her upstairs to their bedchamber. He'd been holding back all night with a surprise for her. Only Robert had been aware of what John had kept hidden.

Now, as Melissa undressed, John was eager to tell her the news. "Melissa?" he said while stripping out of his own clothing. He watched her climb into bed unaware of his excitement. Her eyes were heavy, fighting to stay open. "Sweetheart, I have a surprise for you." He grinned, his hand smoothing her hair away from her face.

His handsome grinning mouth dominated her hazy view, and his deep gentle voice spoke of having something for her? Was the man always in arousal mode? Ever since their reconciliation John couldn't stop touching her. It wasn't that she was complaining but the man did seem insatiable these days. Unfortunately, keeping up with him had become a problem because she'd become so tired lately. Being nearly seven months pregnant, the baby required her to sleep more often.

She smiled to ease the blow. "My love, I desire to accept your surprise," her eyes cast a glimpse toward the lower part of his body, "but I'm so tired right now. Let me rest a few hours first, all right?"

John's grin widened. He truly must have been making up for lost time. "Sweetheart, you're misunderstanding what I mean."

"Hmm?" she responded.

"I have some good news and I wanted to share it with you alone."

"Good news?" That got her eyes opened again.

He studied her, realizing what achieving this goal would mean to her.

"John, if it's good why are you stalling?" He had her curious now.

"I see you haven't conquered the art of patience yet," he commented.

"I never will with all your teasing and taunting," she replied with a pout.

"I have to admit my patience was tried pretty mightily today with this news." His grin turned devilish.

Her pout turned into a frown of utter frustration. "Darn it, John, tell me."

"Ease up on the language, sweet. You need to set an example for our child."

Melissa couldn't stand it. He'd keyed up her interest, causing her to fully awaken as he proceeded to delay. She lifted onto her elbows and planted a hard kiss on his lips. "Did that get your attention?" His eyes widened in surprise. "Now tell me."

"Yes, my lady," he conceded. "Lord Ainsworth has agreed to let you race at Catterick." Melissa's mouth dropped open. "Not only was he impressed with your riding abilities, but you accomplished your side of the bargain sufficiently. You by far surpassed the amount of signatures needed. You're in, sweetheart."

"I can't believe it. We did it. When did you find out?"

"Only yesterday."

"That must have been torture. You know how much I've wanted this, you of anybody." Her words ceased and sadness claimed the sparkle in her eyes.

"What is it?"

"My mother and father. They always encouraged my dreams and they're not here to share it with me."

"Melissa." John paused to remember the time when he had wished his mother had been alive to share in the celebration of his first thoroughbred turning champion. "They would have been proud of you, as am I. You have to believe that they are with you in spirit, that they are aware of your accomplishments."

"Yes, I suppose so," she paused. "I'm so thankful you're here. My life would be lost without you."

"You're a strong, independent woman, Melissa. Your determination alone will get you far, even without my influence." He leaned over and placed a tender caress of his lips upon her forehead. "Come now, this is a reason to celebrate, not sulk." He kissed her soundly on the lips.

During the next couple of months John and Melissa spent a lot of time together. Most of the time they stayed indoors for the air had chilled significantly. They prepared mentally for the upcoming races in June, figuring Melissa could work on her physical conditioning once the baby was born and the weather had warmed.

On the evening of March twelfth, Melissa retired early, saying her back ached and she needed to rest. John became suspicious because the whole day Melissa hadn't been herself. Her energy level had dropped and at times she appeared in pain.

John watched her while she slept, wondering if the baby was coming. He was about to turn and leave when in her sleep Melissa's hands went to her stomach. Her brows creased and her breathing turned shallow. She must be in labor. John paced once, twice, three times the length of their bedchamber. Melissa moaned and John stopped pacing, immediately summoning Charles.

Dr. Bennett arrived a short time later, and Miss Beckett right after him. Dr. Bennett examined Melissa and confirmed that indeed it was time. He shoveled out orders for supplies he needed while preparing himself by thoroughly washing his hands.

John stood in the doorway of their bedchamber, baffled. Everyone was rushing around taking part in the preparation while he stood there helpless, which was how he was feeling, helpless. He tried to see how his wife was holding up but there were so many people around her blocking her from his view.

All at once the doctor ordered everyone out except Miss Beckett. John felt disregarded when his own bedchamber door shut in his face. Overwhelmed by the fact that Melissa was going through this alone he began pacing. He paced for what seemed like hours when he heard Melissa wail. John

My Forbidden Mentor

headed for the door, bursting through it, not caring what the doctor said as he strode with purpose toward the bed.

Miss Beckett was trying to calm Melissa, as was Dr. Bennett, but Melissa fought progress with ear pitching screams. "I want my husband!"

The moment she saw him her arms reached out to him. Miss Beckett rose from the chair so John could sit next to his wife. His heart beat fast and sweat beaded on his brow as her screams had terrified him. He leaned over and embraced her. "Shh, I'm here," he whispered into her ear.

Melissa's arms tightened their grip around his back. Sobbing, she pleaded with him, "Don't leave me. I'm scared, John, I'm so scared."

"I'm not going to leave. I'm staying right here," John told her. Hearing the doctor clearing his throat he looked up in his direction.

"You seem to relax her, so here's what I want you to do, John. Take her hands in yours and let her squeeze," Dr. Bennett suggested, at the same time noticing Melissa's reluctance to let go of John. "Melissa, you need to breathe, dear. John is staying, so take hold of his hands."

Melissa did as the doctor asked but kept her focus constant on her husband. He smiled and soothed and told her he loved her. Miss Beckett stood behind John and watched the miracle happen between these three people. Less than an hour later a fine healthy little girl was born, Anna Clarisse Blackburn.

For the next few days Melissa lay resting in bed, her daughter in a cradle at her side. John would retire early so he could spend time with his family but would also rise early to work. He kept himself busy for Melissa's sake, instinctually knowing she needed time to recuperate.

By week's end John knew Melissa would be getting restless being cooped up in bed so he decided to leave the track early one day. He thought she might enjoy a picnic by the stream behind their manor.

He cracked open their bedchamber door and saw she was awake. As the door opened further he witnessed a sight he'd long dreamt of seeing and it took his breath away.

Melissa was sitting up in bed with their daughter feeding at her breast. Sucking hungrily, the baby fed from her mother so naturally. Melissa watched their daughter as John did. He stepped toward mother and daughter, not rousing them until almost reaching the bed.

Melissa looked up. "You're home early. What a nice surprise."

John cleared his throat. The emotions stirring inside him were surreal as he observed his wife and daughter. "I thought you might like to get some fresh air," he suggested before glancing up to capture Melissa's softhearted expression. The entrancement of watching his daughter had monopolized his attention. "I'm having Ellen prepare some food for a picnic."

Melissa smiled at John's reaction to the baby feeding. "That sounds wonderful. As soon as she's done, we'll go."

John sat on the edge of the bed next to her. "How does it feel?"

Melissa gave him a knowing smile. "Natural. Stimulating in a way," she chuckled. "Not quite as enticing as when you do it," she complimented, making him grin.

"I would hope not, although I am curious about the taste of your milk." His grin broadened, producing a rare dimple.

It didn't take much to catch onto his meaning. "Another time, my love, when we're alone."

"Of course," John gleamed.

That afternoon their picnic proved to be enjoyable. It was only the two of them having private time together, sitting next to a sparkling stream of water, feeding each other and John having his first drink of nature's essence from the bosom of his wife.

A few weeks later, John and Melissa were in the library one evening reading to their daughter when a knock came upon the open door. John looked up and it was Charles. "Yes, Charles?"

"Um, I need to speak with Lady Blackburn, my lord."

Melissa handed the baby to John and rose from the couch. She stepped toward Charles as he led her out of the library. "What is it, Charles?"

She continued following him down the entry hall toward the front door. "Duke Albert, my lady. I'm not sure how to handle this situation."

"I'll handle it, Charles. Thank you." Charles trailed off as Melissa approached her father-in-law.

"Lady Blackburn, you're looking magnificent," he commented while scanning her flat stomach. "I see the baby's been born."

"Yes, about three weeks ago. You have a granddaughter."

"Is there any possibility of seeing her?" He paused. "I guessed the baby would be born by now and that is the purpose of my visit."

"Well, she's in the library with John." She gestured him to proceed down the hall to the library. "I can't promise how it will go, Duke Albert."

"I understand, and I assure you I will be on my best behavior for my granddaughter's sake."

"Very well, this way then." She led him through the open double door of the library. John was standing with his daughter in his arms observing his array of books on the bookshelves. His back faced his wife and father so he hadn't seen them come in. "John, our daughter has a visitor," Melissa informed him.

"Someone must be anxious to see you since their visit was unannounced." He turned with Anna and his smile disappeared when confronting the image of his father standing before him.

"I only came to get a peek at my grandchild, John. Will you allow me at least that?"

John shifted toward Melissa. "Melissa. What is the meaning of this?"

"John, he is her only living grandparent. At least let her meet him."

John studied his wife, knowing deep down she was right. He focused on his father. He seemed to be making a sincere effort, numerous efforts actually. Now, months later, with the addition of his daughter, the importance of family held a stronger meaning for John. He gave in, letting his daughter meet her grandfather. Stepping over to his father, he held his daughter at arm's length so his father could take her from him.

Melissa could feel tears rush to her eyes as she observed the tender moment between father and son, and all because of their precious baby girl who had just entered the world.

My Forbidden Mentor

Duke Albert took his granddaughter with shaky hands. His smile widened as he looked into the tiny features of his granddaughter. "I haven't held a baby in so long," he said in unsteadiness. His eyes lifted to acknowledge John. "Not since I held your father. It was the happiest moment of my life."

Stunned by his father's comment, John turned away before his father could witness any emotional evidence of how his words had affected him.

The duke shifted his gaze back to the baby. "She is lovely. What is her name?"

Melissa watched John tread quietly over to the fireplace to stoke the embers. She reached the duke's side. "Her name is Anna. Anna Clarisse Blackburn."

"You named her after John's mother. How fitting. She will be just as beautiful, I can tell." He gave Melissa a warm smile while mumbling sweet words to the baby.

Melissa turned to come up behind John while Albert coddled his granddaughter. "Are you all right?" she whispered in his ear.

John shifted toward her, his eyes searching her face. "Yes." He looked over his shoulder at his father and daughter, and swallowed while watching them together, imagining his father devoting the same attention when he himself was a baby. His father's words of John's birth being the happiest day of his life had caught him off guard. How could he have known that with the way his father had treated him all these years, especially after his mother's death? Isolated, lonely, and unwanted was what John had felt after his mother's passing. His father hadn't been able to deal with the tragedy himself, so John had been forced to find his own strength within himself to move on and beyond the pain. He'd been numb, retreating from exposing himself to anything meaningful regarding his emotions toward another. Still, John had successfully kept the pain locked up so deep and tight it would have taken a powerful force to free the restraints. And that powerful source, John suddenly realized, had been his wife Melissa.

His father's head lifted suddenly, catching John's scrutinizing glare. He stepped toward John, handing him his daughter. "You've given me a beautiful granddaughter, son. Please consider allowing me visits. I would certainly appreciate the chance to know my granddaughter."

John took his daughter and enfolded her in his arms. Father and son held a glare of compassion between them for a split moment. The baby turned fussy and Melissa reached for her. John watched Melissa leave the room with the baby, leaving John and his father alone.

Albert patiently waited for John's response, feeling hopeful for the opportunity to make things better between them, for the opportunity to gain back the family that he'd lost.

John's gaze was unreadable, his voice unsteady. "I can foresee giving my daughter the opportunity to know her grandfather, but you will have to be there when you're needed." Albert nodded in agreement. "One chance, father, that's all I'm giving you."

"I won't fail, son. This time I won't fail you. It's not only my granddaughter I wish to know better." John stayed quiet so Albert continued, "I'd like to know my son as well. I," Albert faltered on the words he knew John should hear and it suddenly became too much to bear after all these years. He chastised himself for being a coward once again. "Can we be a real family, son?"

John admitted to being curious at what his father had been about to say but decided he'd had enough emotional turmoil for one day. "You've got your chance, father." Although John desired to say more, he held onto the words. Time would tell everything. "I'm exhausted. I'm going to retire now." He turned and left the library, leaving his father alone to ponder in thought.

Albert felt a glimmer of hope. His son had bowed ever so slightly, but that's all it took to give Albert a chance. He headed out of the library and down the entryway to the front door. He glanced toward the stairway as if silently speaking to his son. I'm ready to be a father, John. Just please accept it. He disappeared out the front door.

June eighth Melissa found herself surrounded by family and friends at Catterick racetrack. Sitting astride Chief she was ready to make her mark on history at Catterick, remembering that at one time she wouldn't have given a second thought to the consequences of racing, taking the chance of being caught or even getting hurt. Her life was different now, though. She had a husband, a companion who treated her equally with respect and whose love she cherished and of course their daughter, whom she would give the world if she could.

The love of her life strode toward her as she smiled in nervous anticipation.

"You need to relax," John told her as his hand took a hold of hers, his thumb rubbing across her smooth knuckles.

She squeezed his fingers in the palm of her hand. "I remember the last time you told me that." A lustful smile appeared on her sweet lips, giving away her meaning.

He returned her smile, recalling in detailed memory what she referred to. "Yes, well, this time there will be no pain."

"Can you guarantee that?" she taunted, temporarily forgetting about her nervous tension.

"No, you're going to guarantee it by winning this race like I know you can." His grin was challenging but then his eyes drifted toward her calf. "How's your leg holding up?" he asked, his gray eyes meeting her hazel ones with intense concern.

"Better than I expected. It will be fine," she assured him. Periods of extreme strain would cause her calf to flare up every now and then, the muscle having a sharp temporary pain. As long as she soaked her calf in hot water and let it rest the pain would quickly fade away. She had accepted the condition of her calf as a lifelong ailment, and since she could still walk and could still ride that was all that mattered.

"Good. Remember, you've got the talent and the power to win this race. You're going against professionals. Show them what a woman rider is capable of." He leaned forward, brushing his lips against hers. "Show them what Melissa Blackburn is capable of," he murmured against her mouth and gave her another kiss. "I love you," he said, his eyes fastening to hers as they turned watery.

How did she get so lucky in her life? "I love you, John." She was actually going to race with her husband and her daughter by her side. "Where's Anna?" she asked, searching for her.

John glanced back at Rose, who stepped toward them, handing the baby over to John. John lifted their daughter so her mother could kiss her on the forehead.

"I love you, sweetness," Melissa said, snuggling up to her daughter. A call sounded, signaling the riders to be ready. The race was about to begin.

My Forbidden Mentor

He cradled the baby in the crook of one arm and met Melissa's lingering gaze upon him. Their eyes burned into one another's, expressing in that fraction of a moment all the meaning between them. They had found profound love and respect and the sharing of their imperfect lives. "Thank you," she mouthed to John. She didn't need to explain what she meant for he knew that after all they'd been through together and whatever the future held for them, they would weather through it and make their dreams come true, just as he'd helped her make this dream come true.

John gave her a smile as she motioned Chief toward the starting line. There was a surge of renewed energy flowing through him as he carried his little bundle of joy to his private viewing box. Joining him were Anna's godparents, Robert and Rose, who also idly waited in anxious anticipation for the race to begin.

As the bell rang to start the races John continued to stand. He was so worked up there wasn't any way he could sit down. At once nervousness and exhilaration claimed him and he wasn't sure how to react. All he knew was at this very moment, his best horse and his wife, his wife, could you believe it were racing down Catterick racecourse.

She was going to win. He could feel it in his bones. He cheered enthusiastically for his wife as he held their daughter secure within the curve of his arm.

As Melissa passed by the fifth horse John's tension grew. Silently he was coaching her. Lean forward Melissa, get your body higher and talk to Chief. Chief's powerful flanks reached the sixth contender and passed him with lengthening strides. That's it, sweetheart, that's it.

Behind him John heard Rose and Robert cheering her on as well, not caring how loud they sounded. In fact, as John tuned into the crowd, the entire arena seemed noticeably louder today, and a visible amount of women had attended.

His gaze switched back toward the track. Melissa had just conquered the seventh horse and she and Chief were heading straight for the finish line. John lifted his daughter high in his arms so she could witness her mother accomplish her dream. "Mummy's going to win, Anna," he said in a gleeful whisper against her downy ear. He kissed her puffy cream cheek and then called out to Melissa as she and Chief dashed through the finish line. "You won. She won. My wife won!"

Discover Other Titles by Laura Mills

Find Your Way Back

A Sunflower Harvest

A Brother's Promise

Mail Order Husband

Dear Reader,

I hope you enjoyed reading, "My Forbidden Mentor", as much as I enjoyed writing it.

If you're inclined, could you leave an honest review for this book? As an indie author, I would greatly appreciate it.

All My Best,

Laura Mills

Email: Laura@lauramillsauthor.com

Website:

www.lauramillsauthor.com

Made in the USA
Columbia, SC
14 January 2026